CW00518933

WISHING ON A STAR

A SHOOTING STARS NOVEL

TERRI OSBURN

MACIE RAE PUBLISHING

WISHING ON A STAR

A Shooting Stars Novel

Terri Osburn

All Rights Reserved. No part of this book may be reproduced or transmitted in any form by any means without the written permission of the author, except for the use of brief quotations in a book review.

This is a work of fiction. Names, characters, places, and incidents are products of the author's imagination. Any resemblance to real persons, living or dead, is purely coincidental.

Copyright © 2019 by Terri Osburn

Published by Macie Rae Publishing, Nashville, TN

Cover Design Copyright © 2019 Fantasia Frog Designs

ISBN: 978-0998524603

❀ Created with Vellum

DEDICATION

To Kimberly, for coming through in the clutch

ONE

After five years in Nashville, one lost deal, and one lost duet partner, Jesse Gold's life boiled down to finding a set of dentures.

"Seriously, Silas. This is no time to lose your teeth."

Checking his pockets as if giving himself a pat-down, Jesse Gold's geriatric manager searched for his misplaced mouth-wear and found them tucked in his inside coat pocket. A coat that was likely older than she was. At twenty-eight, Jesse was Silas Fillmore's youngest client by at least three decades.

"I told you I had 'em." He popped them in without bothering to check for lint and Jesse cringed.

"Just don't take them out again before the meeting, okay?"

The manager nodded in agreement as he straightened his crooked tie. "Relax, girlie. This ain't nothing but routine procedure. We'll get this out of the way, and you'll be in the studio in no time."

Since she couldn't enter the studio until they'd found a producer, Jesse had her doubts about the *in no time* part. Two potential producers had passed, stalling the project for a month already. If she didn't hit the studio soon, there was no way Jesse would release her first single *before* her former duet partner launched her own.

From what she'd heard, Taylor Roper, the other half of what was once the Honkytonk Daisies, already had two songs in the can. If she managed to hit country radio first, Jesse's chances of getting an add went from long shot to keep dreaming.

A frustrating state of affairs but normal practice in the world she occupied. Country radio happily played ten male artists an hour, but heaven forbid they play more than one or two women in that same block.

Too anxious to sit still, Jesse retrieved a bottle of water from the mini-fridge beneath the coffee station on the far side of the Shooting Stars Records reception area. Breathing in the aroma of freshly-ground beans, she watched an orange leaf blow past the window and remembered that Honkytonk Daisies had been booked on a fall tour that would have kicked off tomorrow.

One more dream Taylor had selfishly snatched from Jesse's grasp with her abrupt departure from the duo.

This meeting *had* to go well. If someone would just tell her why the other producers passed, Jesse might have a clue what she was doing wrong. Silas claimed that the first had been a scheduling issue, but after the second pass came, her sweet old manager hadn't volunteered any details. Instead, he'd declared that she wouldn't have liked working with that particular producer anyway.

Of course, the only producer with whom she'd actually worked was off cutting an album with Taylor. Jaw tight, she returned to her seat beside Silas and checked the time on her cell. Five more minutes. Dropping the phone and water bottle into her lap, she tightened her ponytail as one knee bounced double-time.

Silas tapped her leg. "Calm down, child. This is the one. I can feel it."

"Do you know who it is?" Jesse asked.

"He's a new producer, but I've heard good things."

Not an encouraging response. "I wish you'd have told me who it is so I could have done some research."

"There was no time, my dear. I only got the name yesterday, and since nothing he's produced is available yet, the name wouldn't have done you any good."

How new were they talking? This album had to be good enough to launch her solo career. That meant working with a producer who had at least a project or two on their resume. Were they going to saddle her with a newbie who couldn't tell the difference between a banjo and a banana?

As Jesse tried not to panic, the glass doors swung open and in walked a ghost from the past. Her heart stopped at the sight of him, and her mouth went dry.

"I told you," Chance Colburn was saying, "Naomi didn't give me any details."

"You're sure Clay wanted *me*?" his cohort asked.

"I don't know any other Ash Shepherds, do you?"

The men continued past the reception desk, oblivious to the pair waiting by the window. She hadn't laid eyes on Ash Shepherd in nearly a decade. Not since the day he'd left her hospital bedside and never returned.

In the five years she'd lived in Nashville, Jesse had miraculously never run into her high school sweetheart. In the beginning, she'd looked for him everywhere. In the corner of every bar, grocery store, and 7-Eleven. When she finally started booking gigs, she'd been certain that he'd come see her, but he never did.

Ash had taught her how to play guitar when they were just kids, and he'd instilled in Jesse the love of music that had driven her to chase this crazy dream in the first place. In essence, this *silly notion*, as her mother called it, was largely his doing.

But they never did cross paths. He didn't call or email, even once the Honkytonk Daisies took off, and she'd been so sure that his voice would be on the other end of every call that came from an unknown number. Despite hating him for abandoning her, her gut reaction whenever something good happened was to share the news with Ash, her brother's closest friend and the boy who'd stolen her heart long before she was old enough to know what that meant.

Eventually, Jesse stopped looking for him. The ache in her chest eased, and she'd vowed not to waste her time longing for someone who'd clearly forgotten she'd ever existed. When Taylor had announced that she was going solo, Jesse had steeled herself in the same way. If someone didn't want her, then she didn't want them. And most of the time, she believed it.

"I can't do this," she muttered.

"What's that, honey?" Silas said, leaning closer. "You need to speak up. That's my bad ear."

Jesse closed her eyes. "Who is the producer we're here to meet?" Maybe this was just a coincidence. Maybe this wasn't what she feared.

"You'll find out soon enough." He patted her arm like a doting grandfather, and she fought the urge to leave while she had the chance. "Don't let the lack of experience worry you," Silas went on. "He's written some of the biggest hit songs of the last few years. You'll be in excellent hands."

The answer only confirmed her suspicions. Jesse took a deep breath, struggling to talk herself out of bolting for the exit. Did she really have a choice? Flat out refusing to work with the first producer willing to take her on could jeopardize the project even more. That was assuming Ash agreed. Based on the exchange with Chance as they entered the building, he didn't even know why he was here.

If he passed, they never had to see each other. If he agreed, Jesse had a decision to make. Would Clay Benedict, the owner and president of Shooting Stars Records—and the only executive in town willing to give her a chance—consider a refusal her third strike and drop Jesse from the label?

The receptionist finally called them back, and Jesse could barely feel her feet as she followed Silas into the bowels of the building. She'd spent years thinking about what she would say if she and Ash ever came face to face, but she had never settled on a definite strategy. Go to hell had been on the list, but the current circumstances swept that opening off the table.

Considering how her heart was attempting to beat out of her chest, her only hope was not to pass out before learning her fate.

* * *

Ash didn't like surprises, and this mysterious meeting had *surprise* written all over it. Chance had been vague at best, only saying that the head of his label had asked that Ash attend a meeting at the Shooting Stars office. The purpose of the meeting had not been given.

Instead of heading straight for a conference room, Chance had gone to his wife's office. As the PR manager, Naomi had accomplished what many in the industry had considered impossible—she'd redeemed Chance Colburn, whose long list of sins included addiction, highly publicized run-ins with the law, and a lengthy stay in rehab.

Lucky for Chance, country music fans had a long history of forgiving the trespasses of their favorite artists. The recent success of his first new single in two years stood as proof that forgiveness had been granted in his case as well.

An affectionate greeting between the newlyweds, during which Ash had discreetly glanced away, was followed by a personal escort to the conference room. Ash had asked Naomi why he was there, but she'd dodged the question, offering a vague "Clay will fill you in."

That had been five minutes ago, and Ash's patience grew thin as he tapped out a melody on the large Mahogany table. About the time his patience ran out, Clay Benedict stepped through the door.

"Sorry to keep you waiting. That last call took longer than expected." Unbuttoning his suit jacket, the label head settled his broad frame into the opposite chair. "I'm sure you're wondering why you're here, so I'll get right to the point. I'm impressed with your production work on Chance's album."

Ash appreciated the compliment. "Good to hear."

"Have you considered producing an entire album?"

Not a question Ash expected. "For Chance? I thought the rest of the album was finished?"

Clay's expression revealed nothing. "Not for Chance. Are you interested? We'll offer triple the compensation we paid for Chance's three songs."

A nice offer but Ash hadn't gotten into this business for the money. He'd been tooling around Nashville for more than a decade, enjoying moderate successes until his songwriting career took off in the last five years. Now that he'd established a reputation for writing hits, Ash was more than ready to carry that success into producing. But whatever project he signed on for had to be worth his time.

"I'm on board." Shooting Stars had launched with Dylan Monroe the year before with incredible success, and he could only assume this was the chance to helm his sophomore effort. The perfect project to establish Ash's reputation in the studio. "When is Dylan set to record?"

The record exec shook his head. "We have other plans for Dylan. I'm looking for a producer for Jesse Gold. You mentioned at Chance's wedding that you two are from the same hometown, and I'm hoping that connection can work in our favor."

Ash's enthusiasm waned. Jesse was the one artist he *couldn't* work with.

Leaning back in his chair, he changed his previous answer. "I'm not the guy for that one."

"You haven't even heard the details yet."

Shoving back from the table, Ash rose to his feet. "I'm sorry, but I'll have to pass."

"Is the problem that she's a woman?" Clay asked. "If so, that's a shitty reason to pass this opportunity by."

"Jesse's gender has nothing to do with it." Ash shoved a hand into his hair. How was he going to explain this without revealing more than Jesse would want her boss to know? "Jess and I have a history. Did you tell her you were going to offer me the job?"

The big man leaned back in his chair with a narrowed gaze. "I didn't want to tell her until I'd talked to you. Two producers have already turned us down, and the others I've contacted are either booked or not returning my calls. All thanks to unfounded rumors that Jesse has strong opinions that make her difficult to work with."

Jesse had been a force of nature since birth, but she was no diva. Her drive for perfection was due to her passion for the things she cared about. Any producer would be lucky to work with an artist as talented and devoted to the craft as she was.

Ash had been following Jesse's career since he'd spotted her playing for tips at Tootsies in the Nashville airport five years ago. That's how he'd learned she'd moved to town, and he'd kept an eye on her ever since—always from the shadows.

Watching her and not touching her had been agonizing. She'd was eighteen the last time he'd held her hand. Bruised and battered and fighting for her life in a hospital bed. Ash had been driving the car that night. The night that his best friend was killed, and Jesse was thrown forty feet through the air.

While Tommy was the brother Ash never had, Jesse had never felt like a sister. Despite being a year behind them, she'd taken part in every adventure they ever took—from four-wheeling to fishing to risking life and limb flying off the rope swing over Old Man Willoughby's water hole.

Ash had been half in love by middle school but didn't worked up the courage to ask her out until years later, when she'd been a sophomore and him a love-sick junior. By the time he and Tommy left for college, Jesse had agreed to follow them to Kennesaw the next year, and once they'd both finished their degrees, a wedding would be the next step.

But in one tragic night, all that changed.

Ash was to stay away from Jesse and never contact the family again. Out of respect and suffocating guilt, he'd honored their decision, but he kept an eye on Jesse as best he could without crossing the line.

Producing Jesse's album would *obliterate* that line.

"Who's turned you down?" Maybe he could suggest a possible alternative.

"Walker and Matthews," Clay replied. "They've both launched careers in the past, but like I said, neither wanted the job after learning who the artist would be. To me, Jesse's spirit is what makes her a star, but neither producer wanted the challenge."

Challenge was Jesse's middle name. At ten she'd refused to wear the pretty pink dress her mom had picked for her school pictures, arguing that the color clashed with her red hair. Then, and many times after, Enid Rheingold had bowed to Jesse's rebellious leanings if for no other reason than to gain a little peace.

Ash debated how he could help Jesse *and* keep his distance, but he could see no way to do both. Teetering on the edge of rejecting the job, he heard Tommy's voice in his head.

Help her, buddy. Help her make this happen.

With a sigh of resignation, Ash sat back down. "It's up to Jesse."

"Excellent." Clay extended a hand across the table. "She's special, Ash. Play this right, and she'll put you both on the map."

She was special all right, but she also had a damn good reason *not* to work with Ash on anything. He only hoped Clay Benedict would keep looking after his artist turned down the only producer so far willing to take the job.

* * *

By the time they reached the conference room, Jesse had latched onto Silas's arm to keep her knees from buckling. Her reaction to the impending encounter annoyed her enough to let anger take the lead. After all this time, if Ash Shepherd thought he could waltz back into her life, he was sadly mistaken.

How to make that clear without ending her solo career before it began was the question. After the Daisies breakup, a rumor spread that Jesse was difficult to work with. The source of the lie remained a mystery—though she had her suspicions—but true or not, the damage had been done.

Not a single label head would even take a meeting with Silas to discuss his newly solo artist. The one Honkytonk Daisies song that had gotten radio airplay had been co-written by Jesse, but Taylor had been the voice, and that left Jesse with nothing on her resume except singing harmony on her own song.

Then, when she'd been on the brink of panic, Silas had received a call from Clay Benedict. The label head had ignored the rumors, recognized her potential, and offered Jesse a deal. She wasn't a weeper by nature, but she'd cried like a teething baby that Tuesday afternoon.

How far could she push Clay's patience? He'd remained supportive and optimistic when the other producers had fallen through, but would that attitude wane if Jesse shot this one down, too? Could she afford three strikes? And then, should she get another chance, what if no other producer took the job?

Stressed and nauseated, she swallowed the bile rising up her throat and prayed that Ash had turned down the offer. The room was empty, which Jesse took as a good sign, but just when her stomach began to settle, Clay and Ash entered the room.

Silas rose from his chair while Jesse struggled to breathe. "Good morning, Mr. Benedict. This must be the young man we're here to meet."

The three men exchanged handshakes while Jesse remained seated and silent. Her tongue felt like a wad of cotton in her mouth, and a drumbeat of anxiety pounded in her ears as she tumbled through a time warp. In an instant, she was eighteen years old, bandaged, floating on pain meds, and completely incapable of fathoming life without her brother. Ash was beside her, and she couldn't remember what he'd said that had coaxed a smile from her lips. The first time she'd smiled since learning that Tommy was gone. And the last time for several months.

Willing herself back to the present, Jesse tried to catch up with the conversation. As if from a distance, she heard Clay begin to introduce her and rose on shaky knees.

"As you know, this is our talented new artist, Jesse Gold."

"Hi, Jesse," Ash said. Hearing his voice again was like a punch in the heart. "It's nice to see you."

Throat clogged, she nodded and returned to her chair before her knees buckled.

Silas sent her a *What the hell was that?* look as he nervously messed with his coffee-stained tie.

The men took their seats, and Jesse warred with herself. The broad-chested man across the table bore little resemblance to the rangy boy she'd grown up with, but one thing was still the same. Long lashes framed muted gold eyes that sent memories washing over her. Tommy and Ash had rarely been apart from third grade on. If one was there, so was the other.

Seeing Ash again without his other half intensified Tommy's absence.

Jesse gripped Silas's hand and he whispered, "Breathe, child. We'll get a yes on this one."

Jesse didn't want a yes. She wanted the ground to swallow her up. Anything to be out of this room.

"We know you can write songs, Mr. Shepherd," Silas began, "but how do we know you can produce my girl's album?"

"I sent you the tracks that Ash produced for Chance," Clay said, clearly taken aback by the question. "They're some of the best cuts on the album."

Silas didn't miss a beat. "Now, Clayton, we both know that Chance Colburn had as much input on those songs as Ash here. He's an established artist with multiple albums under his belt and a distinct sound that sets him apart in the genre. Jesse doesn't have that—yet—which means we have to trust that the person who produces this album has the skill and knowledge to turn her vision into reality."

Super-manager to the rescue. At this rate, Silas would eliminate Ash as a candidate and save Jesse from having to say anything at all.

"That's why Ash is the man for the job," Clay replied. "He and Jesse grew up in the same town and have a personal history. He knows her, knows where she comes from, and can help mold her sound into something individually hers."

"Ash exaggerates," Jesse cut in. "Our *history* ended a decade ago."

The group fell silent as Silas and Clay exchanged glances. Ash didn't flinch, nor did he take his eyes from hers. "Could I get a minute with Jesse alone?"

She nearly cried out *No!* but held her tongue. Clay rose to his feet while Silas looked to his client for direction.

"It's up to you, child. Do you want me to stay?"

Did she? Jesse gnawed her bottom lip as she stared at the table. If she could keep it together long enough to convince Ash to walk away, this trial would be over, and Clay would move on to the next candidate.

"Go, Silas. I'll be okay."

The two men exited the room, and once witnesses were gone, Jesse unleashed the anger she'd been holding in for far too long.

TWO

"You can't really think I'd ever work with you," Jesse snapped, arms crossed, her blue eyes locked with his. "Not after what you did."

"I don't blame you for being pissed," Ash said, knowing he deserved whatever she threw his way. "I had no idea why they brought me here today. If I'd known, I wouldn't have come."

Fire flashed in her hard gaze as she leaned forward in her chair. "Of course, you wouldn't have come. Heaven forbid you be in the same room with me."

That wasn't what he meant, and she knew it. "You've got that backwards, don't you? You're the one who wanted me out of your life, and I've respected that for ten years."

Jesse bolted from her chair. "How can you say that? You were all I had left!" She slammed the butt of her hands against her eyes and let out a muted growl before crossing her arms as if holding herself together. "Why didn't you come back? You were the only other person who knew what I was going through. The only person who missed Tommy as much as I did. I needed you, damn it."

Ash still missed Tommy every day, but it was that loss that had forced him to stay away. "What about your parents?"

The russet ponytail swung as she shook her head. "Oh, they miss Tommy all right. They might as well have lost their *only* child the way they gnash and wail." Bitterness did little to mask the hurt and anger. "The whole house is a shrine," she added. "They couldn't be bothered to frame my senior picture, but we must bow at the altar of the beloved lost son."

Anyone else would read resentment in her words, but Ash knew better. Jesse had adored her brother, despite him being her parents' obvious favorite. A status he'd clearly retained after his death.

"I was honoring your request."

"Whose request?" she asked, eyes flashing.

"Your parents. Yours. They told me to stay away."

"When?"

"At the hospital. I came to see you after our last visit, and the staff wouldn't let me in." Ash remembered that day well. He'd already been drowning in guilt and his own grief. The confrontation in the hospital lobby had intensified both. "I thought it was a mistake, but your mom insisted that you didn't want to see me. I'd killed Tommy, and I needed to stay out of your lives."

Mouth agape, Jesse dropped into her chair. "You didn't kill Tommy. I've told them that a thousand times."

"I was driving the car," Ash reminded her, refusing to let himself off on a technicality.

"And if Tommy had been driving when that deer darted out in front of us, the same thing would have happened."

Ash had come through the accident with little more than a bump on the head, which had planted a thought that haunted him for years. "If Tommy had been driving, he might be alive today."

Jesse rolled her eyes. "And *you* might be dead. Do you really believe that would be better?"

He'd wished more than once that the results of that night had been the other way around. Though, rationally, Ash understood that accidents were random and deer dashing across country roads were common and frequent, he'd still been the one behind the wheel and couldn't shake the guilt.

Ignoring the question, he said, "I couldn't change what happened, but I could give the one thing you asked for. So that's what I did."

The leather chair rolled as Jesse leaned back. "That's why you weren't at the funeral."

Ash tensed. "I was there."

"I didn't see you."

"That was the point."

Blue eyes softened and her whole body seemed to deflate. "All this time, I thought you'd abandoned me."

"And I thought you pushed me away."

They stared in silence, both grappling with a new reality.

"Why didn't you fight harder?" Jesse asked. "Why didn't you insist on hearing those words from my lips?"

The pain and regret had been too intense—too raw—for Ash to even consider pushing back. Staying away from Tommy's family had been the *one* thing he could do to atone for their loss. Maybe this was his chance to atone for the rest.

"I thought I was doing what you wanted. Jesse, I can't undo the past, but I'm here now, and I'm ready to do this job. You're talented. If you give me a chance, I think we could make one hell of an album."

She needed to say yes. There was only so long Clay Benedict would try to make this deal work before cutting his losses and moving on.

"Do you know why the other producers turned down the job?" she asked.

At the risk of hurting her more, Ash answered truthfully. "According to Clay, they believed working with you would be too much of a challenge."

Her face fell. "You're the first person to answer that question honestly." She stared at the table for several seconds before lifting her gaze. "You don't have the same reservations?"

"I don't," Ash replied.

"What about our past?" she asked, the first to acknowledge the other elephant in the room.

Ash knew better than to expect a second chance for them, and not only because she was with someone else. "That was a long time ago."

"Yes, it was." Every thought shone on her face. Jesse didn't want to work with him, but she understood the damage walking away could do. The moment she accepted her fate, her shoulders fell. "You're the one who turned me into a musician in the first place. If you're game on this, then so am I."

He'd taught her some chords, but Jesse had turned herself into a musician. And from what Ash had seen, a damn good one. Grateful for the opportunity to make things right, he rose from his chair and went to invite the others back in.

* * *

"Are we all good then?" Clay asked as he lowered into the chair at the head of the table. Few people intimidated Jesse like her new boss. He'd never given her a reason to fear him, yet he carried an air of power that only men of his experience and stature could. Then there was the fact that he held her professional fate in his hands.

Jesse nodded. "Yes, we are."

She'd agreed for two reasons. Ash was the first person to be totally honest with her, so at least now she knew for certain that the hateful rumors had been the problem. The second reason had been the risk of *not* agreeing. Clay Benedict had been generous with her so far, but he was also a shrewd businessman who would not continue tossing money at a worthless cause. If Jesse wanted to stay in this business, she had to make compromises when necessary, and this was one of those times.

The more startling revelation of this meeting was that Ash hadn't truly abandoned her all those years ago. Not willingly, anyway.

Turning Ash away had been a cruel move by her parents. Cruel to their daughter, who'd cried for days when he hadn't called or come to see her, but also cruel to Ash. Like the rest of them, he'd lost Tommy, too, and then lost his second family at the same time.

Nothing her mother did should surprise Jesse at this point, and yet...

"Then we're set." Clay grinned, and Jesse felt Silas relax beside her.

She'd made the older man worry, and for that she was sorry. Silas had been her rock through this mess, and having Jesse as a client did not make his life easy. When she finally made it big, she would do something really special for the old man. Take him on a shopping spree and let him buy anything he wanted, which would probably be a new set of golf clubs. Silas loved that damn game.

"In light of how I'd hoped this meeting would go," Clay said, "and because Jesse made it clear at the time of her signing that she has a solid collection of songs ready to record, we've scheduled Treble Tone Studios starting a week from Monday. We're locked in for three months and can add more time if necessary."

Dana and Reggie, her bass player and drummer respectively, had been as anxious as Jesse to get this project underway, and she couldn't wait to give them the good news. Though there was someone else she would call first.

"Thank you again for this opportunity," Jesse said, mentally running through her song options to decide which ones should go on the album. This was the most important project of her life and had to be her best work. And then there was the other reality of the business—at her age, this was most likely her last shot as a solo artist. Breaking through after thirty was unheard of.

"No thanks necessary," Clay replied. "You and Ash are welcome to use the smaller conference room here to go over song selections next week, or if another location works, that's fine, too." Clay glanced around the table. "Any questions?"

"Who's the engineer?" Ash asked.

"The same one we used for Chance, Aiden D'Angelo."

Aiden was one of the best engineers in town, and she never expected to work with someone of his caliber so soon. Especially not on her debut.

"That's all I needed to know." Ash rose to his feet, as did the other attendees.

Everyone filed from the room with an optimistic murmur, and Jesse dragged the cell phone from the back pocket of her jeans. Once in the lobby, she dashed around Silas and pushed through the glass doors to find a private spot halfway down the sidewalk.

Ryan Dimitri, her boyfriend of fourteen months, had been with Jesse during the good days with the Daisies, and then provided regular pep talks to get her through the breakup. There were times she wondered how she'd landed one of the hottest lead singers in country music, especially on the rare occasions when they were photographed on the red carpet together. Their busy schedules rarely landed them in the same state, let alone at the same event, but they'd managed to fit in a few award shows along the way.

At barely five foot three, Jesse looked miniature next to Ryan's six-foot-four-inch frame, which made the pictures look as if he'd taken a member of the Lollipop Gang as his date. Where he was lanky and fit, she was squat and round. Before coming to Nashville, Jesse hadn't given her looks much thought. The red hair made her stand out in a crowd. The unexpected blue eyes often garnered her a second look. But in all other ways, she was average at best.

Which had always been fine with her.

Not until she'd paired up with Taylor Roper did Jesse's appearance become an issue. A former beauty queen, the other half of the Daisies looked gorgeous in anything she put on. For their first photo shoot, a stylist had provided a full rack of designer clothes for them to choose from.

Everything fit Taylor, but Jesse had discarded three outfits before finding a pair of jeans she could drag on over her abundant hips. Due to the length, she'd discarded those, along with the following two options, before finding something that didn't make her look like a little girl playing dress up in her mother's closet.

That had been an eye-opening day, and for every photo shoot after, Jesse provided her own clothes, tailored to her size and shape. She also accumulated a shoe collection and traded in her low-maintenance ponytail—which she still wore while not performing—to the highest, teased-to-the-heavens do possible in an effort to add a few more inches to her height. The transformation took her from stunted to less stunted, and still a head shorter than her duet partner.

Employing the same tactics when out with her man was tougher to pull off. Red carpets required *walking* in the five-inch heels, a feat Jesse had never actually mastered.

"Hey, baby," Ryan Dimitri drawled on the other end of the line. "What's up?"

Ryan's band, Flesh and Blood, was on a twelve-week tour with a month of shows left.

"I have a producer," she announced. Despite who that producer was, in her desperate race to beat Taylor to radio, Jesse was finally out of the gate, and that was worth celebrating. "We head into the studio a week from Monday."

"That's great. Who is it? Walters? Huff? Tell me!"

Ryan's mention of two of the top producers in the game dulled Jesse's enthusiasm. "I'll be working with Ash Shepherd.

He's written six number one hits in the last two years." That factoid was as much for her own benefit as for Ryan's. "That's a huge score."

"I didn't know Shepherd was a producer." A woman's voice murmured something in the background, and Ryan said, "They're calling me for a meet and greet, hon. I'm happy you're finally heading into the studio."

Eleven thirty in the morning seemed early for a meet and greet. "Who set up a fan meet more than eight hours before showtime?"

"It's for the local radio station," he replied. "I'll give you a call later."

"Wait," Jesse cut in. "I'm coming up there so we can celebrate." Tonight's show was in Cincinnati, only a four-hour drive from Nashville. "I can hit the road in a couple of hours and be there well before showtime."

"I don't know, babe. I'd hate for you to drive all this way and me not have time to spend with you."

"It isn't that far." Jesse nodded for Silas to hold on when he waved for her to hurry.

The woman in the background called again. "You stay there and celebrate with Dana and Reggie," Ryan countered. "We'll go out when I get home."

"But that's weeks from now." Of course, she'd be happy to celebrate with the only two band members who'd stuck with her —the rest having jumped ship along with Taylor—but it had been two months, damn it. Her boyfriend should *want* to see her.

"Jesse, come on. You know how it is. The band is running ninety to nothing. By the time we'd get twenty minutes together, you'd have to head back home."

No, she *didn't* know how it was. The Daisies had done a six-week stint opening for Davis Daniels in the spring, which was when Jesse had met Clay Benedict for the first time thanks to Dylan Monroe, another Shooting Stars artist, who had also been on the tour. But the Honkytonk Daisies hadn't lasted long enough to experience headlining arenas, multiple meet and greets, or endless radio interviews.

When she sighed, Ryan added, "I promise we'll do it up big. Balloons. Champagne. Anything you want. This will still be exciting a month from now."

"Fine," she said, conceding, "we'll wait. I miss you, though. Sleeping alone sucks."

"Tell you what. I'll do my best to make a quick trip home. First chance I get, okay?"

The promise lifted her spirits. "I'll take that. But don't be surprised if I tackle you at the front door."

He chuckled, and Jesse grinned at his response. Not having him around the last two months had been more difficult than usual since this time she'd had nothing better to do than stare at the walls and stress. First about not having a deal, and then about not having a producer.

"I'm looking forward to it, baby," he purred, and she could almost see the sexy grin dance across his full lips. "Now I really have to go. Kick ass in the studio and remember, you've got this."

Ryan had been repeating those words since the day of Taylor's betrayal. His positivity was one of the only things that had kept her going.

"Have a good show tonight," she said, walking toward Silas. "And don't let those fan girls turn your head."

"Never, babe. Talk to you later."

With a beep, he was gone, and Jesse returned the cell to her back pocket. Resigned to another night alone, she crossed the lot to Silas's Lincoln Continental and on the way spotted Ash talking to Chance Colburn inside the building. He looked completely at ease, as if he were talking to an ordinary person and not a former winner of the coveted Entertainer of the Year award.

When he caught sight of her through the glass, his face

curved into a tender smile that did funny things to her heart, so Jesse turned away, aware of the danger that lay ahead. Making an album with him would be the easy part. Not falling back in love with him would be the real test.

THREE

"ARE YOU KIDDING ME RIGHT NOW?" RONNIE ASKED, LOOKING UP
from the studio console.

Though they'd been divorced for years, Veronica "Ronnie"
Shepherd was still Ash's best friend. At the end of their brief
marriage, they'd both agreed that friendship was where they
should have stopped. Ronnie started producing albums four
years ago, so she was the first person he went to see after leaving
the Shooting Stars office.

"I'm as shocked as you are," he replied, spinning his chair
from side to side.

Not that he didn't deserve the job. Ash had been producing
his own demos for years, and working with Chance had given
him access to the best equipment and engineer in town. But, as
Silas Fillmore had pointed out, taking the helm on a debut
album was very different from producing three songs for an
established artist.

"I can't believe she agreed to this." Besides being his ex,
Ronnie was also the only person in town who knew the ugly
details of Ash's past.

Still a little shell-shocked, he nodded. "She was pissed the moment she saw me, which made sense, but not for the reason I expected."

The brunette shifted to tuck long legs beneath her bottom. "What other reason could she have? You've kept your distance like they wanted."

"That's the problem. Turns out, Jesse had no idea they cut me off."

Brown eyes went wide. "Really?"

After a dozen years of constant guilt, learning that Jesse didn't blame him for Tommy's death was going to take more than a couple of hours to process.

How different would his life be if he'd refused to believe her parents? If Ash had fought harder, as Jesse put it. He might never have moved to Nashville, at least not when he did.

Ash and Tommy had roomed together at Kennesaw State north of Atlanta, having both secured scholarships to play baseball for the school. After the accident, Ash couldn't make himself go back. His life had changed on December 23 and by the end of Christmas break, he'd withdrawn from school. In desperate need to be anywhere but their hometown, he'd packed up an old clunker bought from a high school buddy and headed for Nashville.

In Music City, Ash was able to start over without being constantly assaulted by memories of his dead best friend. Not that he would ever forget him, but he'd needed a clean start where people didn't know him as *the boy who'd been driving*.

Within months, he'd found himself welcomed into the songwriting community. Moderate successes followed relatively quickly with an unexpected result—the more accolades he earned, the more miserable Ash became as if what happened in the past made him undeserving of anything good. While staring at his first substantial royalty check, he'd heard Tommy's voice in his ear.

You did good, buddy. I'm proud of you. Now stop being such a shit and go celebrate.

Following his best friend's orders, Ash had hit the town hard that night, and many nights after. The combination of youth, regret, and heartache was as strong as the cocktails he was drinking, and soon a few beers on the weekend rolled into a few bottles through the week.

Lucky for Ash, Ronnie had put her foot down and pulled him out of the drunken spiral.

"Yeah, really," Ash said.

Lips pursed, Ronnie asked, "Why didn't *she* contact *you*? Jesse could have found a way to get in touch if she really wanted to."

Possibly, but Ronnie didn't know Jesse like he did. "She took my silence as rejection. If I didn't want her in my life, then she didn't want me in hers either."

Ronnie looked slightly appeased. "I've heard she's difficult to work with. No offense, but that's probably why they couldn't find anyone else to take the job."

Word traveled fast. One of the many ways in which Music Row was like a small town. "Clay used the term *challenging*."

"You up for that?" she asked, apprehensive on his behalf.

Ash leaned forward to rest his elbows on his knees. "Jesse isn't challenging so much as . . . determined." At twelve years old, she'd practiced for hours to learn every chord he taught her. Ash would take an artist with that kind of dedication any day. "If we can funnel even half of her passion into this album, she'll be unstoppable."

"And you'll be the most sought-after new producer in town." Eyes narrowed, she added, "I'm not sure how I feel about you cutting in on my territory."

"Considering your trophy case full of awards, I think you'll be all right." Ash rose from the chair. He had a songwriting session two streets over in ten minutes. "I'm not going to lie, I might be in over my head with this one. You available if I need to phone a friend?"

"I've got you, homie." She held up a hand for a high-five, and Ash pulled it to his lips to place a kiss on her knuckles. "You're a hopeless romantic, Shepherd," Ronnie scoffed, leaning back in her chair.

"You say that like it's a bad thing." Still holding her hand, he bent and kissed her cheek. "Being a romantic helped me win that single of the year award back in May. How else could I have written a song called 'Hugs and Kisses'?"

"That song is about two people kept apart by war."

"But it's still romantic," Ash argued. On his way to the door, he added, "Let me know if I need to come mow on Sunday."

Ronnie had let Ash have the house after their divorce, and in exchange, he took care of the yardwork at her new place. At least until she found someone else to do it for her.

"I'll check when I get home," she said before pressing a button on the board and filling the room with an upbeat banjo solo.

Strolling toward the studio exit, Ash felt better about the task ahead. Reconnecting with Jesse aside, this project was the break he needed to really shape the music that came out of this town. Writing the songs was one thing. Producing them meant controlling the final sound, and that's where the real creativity came in.

* * *

If Jesse couldn't be with her boyfriend tonight, then being with her friends was the next best thing.

Lunch with Silas had been fun. He knew everyone in town, which meant lots of visitors to their table. Each offered their congratulations after Silas bragged about his young client and how she was going to rule the airwaves.

Jesse hoped that was true.

She'd spent a couple of hours during the afternoon flipping through notebooks filled with every song she'd ever written. The early stuff was crap, of course, but you never knew when there might be a flicker of genius in a chorus or verse. Lyrics could be improved upon. Melodies sped up or slowed down, turning a dud into a viable tune.

By five o'clock, she'd showered and dressed for dinner, which Dana had insisted on hosting, and Reggie and his wife, Phoenix, had managed to find a last-minute babysitter for their twins, Tatiana and Arquette. The four-year-old girls adored Jesse, partially because she was the only adult who fit inside their playhouse. Even Silas had agreed to come. The elderly manager was often asleep by eight o'clock, so his willingness to stay up past his bedtime meant a lot to Jesse.

While brushing her damp hair back into a ponytail, she'd gotten the crazy idea to invite Ash but wasn't sure how to contact him. Naomi Colburn would probably have his number. Not only was she Jesse's new publicist and Clay Benedict's right-hand person, but Ash had worked with her husband and had even attended their wedding last month.

At least that's what Jesse had heard. The couple set the whole thing up as a Labor Day party, and then surprised their guests with the unexpected nuptials. The press had been thwarted, and the guests were still talking about the romantically sappy ceremony.

Jesse wasn't much of a romantic. Flowers died. Candlelight wasn't nearly bright enough to see what you were eating. And candy caused cavities and added bulk to her backside, neither of which Jesse needed more of. A root canal the year before had been traumatic enough to put her off the sweets, and she hoped *not* to resemble a baby whale in her first music video.

After firing off a quick text to Naomi, she completed her makeup routine of eyeliner and mascara—the only makeup she wore when not in the spotlight—and dug through the guest bedroom closet for her favorite boots. Ryan's sizable wardrobe had occupied the entire master closet well before Jesse moved in, so her more meager choices had been relegated to the only spare closet in the house. They'd discussed getting a bigger place, but their busy schedules never coincided enough to explore the options.

Thankfully, Jesse had been smart with her money, partially thanks to Silas and his conservative accountant who took penny-pinching to new heights, and her own frugal nature. Most of what she'd made with the Daisies still sat in the bank, and the signing bonus offered by Shooting Stars had padded her account nicely. When Ryan came home in a month, they'd narrow down a target location and put a real estate agent to work finding their perfect new home.

Jesse's cell phone dinged from the other room, and she hurried back, boots in hand, to find Ash's number in a text from Naomi. She sent back a grateful reply and dialed up her new producer, oddly nervous, considering their history.

"Hello?" Ash answered.

"Hey, Ash. It's me. Jesse."

"Oh."

He didn't sound all that happy to hear from her. "I'm sorry to bother you."

"No," he said. "The area code just threw me off. I haven't seen that one in a long time."

Jesse still used the number she'd gotten years ago while living at home. Keeping in touch with his mom should have meant seeing the area code regularly.

"Your mom doesn't call you?" she asked, unable to muzzle her curiosity.

"She lives here, and we don't have much reason to go back."

That explained why their paths never crossed back in Eton, despite her looking for him around every corner.

Tucking the phone against her shoulder, she pulled on a sock. "We're having a little get-together tonight to celebrate finally heading into the studio, and I thought you might want to join us. It's nothing fancy. Just dinner and drinks at my bass player's house." The nerves were making her ramble. "If you have other plans—"

"Are you sure you want me crashing your party?" he asked.

"It isn't crashing if you're invited." Sitting up, she took the phone in hand and tried swaying him with a little honesty. "The truth is, I'm never going to make it to Monday. I've been dreaming of this opportunity for so long that waiting another forty-eight hours is going to drive me nuts. You'll get a good, home-cooked meal, and we can talk shop. What do you say?"

She held her breath waiting for his answer. This was probably out of bounds from a professional standpoint, but if they were going to work together, they needed to connect on new ground. As long as she thought of him as the boy he once was, Jesse would never wedge him out of her heart for good. And that's exactly what she needed to do to survive the next three months.

"All right, sure. What time?"

"Six thirty. I'll text you the address."

"Sounds good." Ash hesitated, as if unsure of what to say next. "I'll see you then."

"Yes," she said, feeling like an awkward teen all over again. "I'll see you then."

Jesse ended the call, sent the promised text, and tossed the phone on the bed so she could finish putting on her socks. By the time she reached for a boot, the phone dinged with a reply that simply said *Thanks*.

She stared at the phone and doubts crept in. What if he didn't like her songs and changed his mind about doing the project? She should have worked on more songs over the last two months so she'd be more prepared for this moment.

"Get a grip, woman," Jesse mumbled to herself. "You couldn't be more prepared if you had another year."

FOUR

When the call popped up on his screen, Ash's heart lodged in his throat.

Jesse's number was only a few digits off from Tommy's old one, and he'd nearly answered with his best friend's name. That would have been an uncomfortable way to start their second conversation in ten years.

Ash checked his GPS to make sure he hadn't missed a turn. He'd had casual plans for the evening, but nothing he couldn't back out of. He, too, was anxious to get this project underway, and the more they talked about concepts and expectations, the more comfortable he'd feel creating a plan of attack.

Working with Chance had been a breeze. With a signature sound established long ago, he knew exactly what he wanted and how to get it. He'd been open to input, but producing the three singles had been a team effort, with Ash probably receiving more credit than he deserved.

Working with Jesse would be a much different experience. Not that Chance's album hadn't come with plenty of pressure— tasked with relaunching his career after a very public downfall— but the job ahead had the potential to decide Jesse's fate in the industry. The days of an artist being granted the time and support required to develop and build a following were long gone. Now you had to burst onto the airwaves with instant buzz, an overnight success that in reality was many years in the making.

The Honkytonk Daisies had established a respectable following and would have likely continued to gain momentum had they been given the chance. Jesse had been the majority songwriter on the Daisies' album, which meant their sound stemmed from her sensibilities, and that gave Ash a solid place to start.

The GPS said to turn left ahead, and Ash followed the order, pulling into a suburban neighborhood of large brick homes and tailored lawns. The houses weren't completely cookie-cutter, but close. There were a ton of these sorts of neighborhoods surrounding the city, most in areas like this—little towns in bordering counties populated by folks looking for a more family-friendly area to settle down. Many endured the grueling commute for good, if overpopulated, schools, manicured parks, and generic shopping centers that offered box stores and chain restaurants.

Budding families got more space close enough to enjoy the benefits of Nashville, yet far enough away to avoid the bright lights and noise of the city. But the lights and noise were what Ash loved.

Unless you were down on Broadway, where the tourists and locals gathered to sample the latest microbrew or scoot their boots while an underappreciated dreamer belted out cover tunes, Ash's adopted city was actually pretty normal. He knew his neighbors, held cookouts on the weekends, and attended a sporting event now and then.

The only difference was that most of his neighbors also worked in the music industry—which turned cookouts into jam sessions—and sporting events typically came with box seats courtesy of this label or that publishing company.

Nashville might not be small-town America, but the city was

more down-to-earth than an outsider probably expected, due in no small part to the transplants who brought their small-town ideals with them.

Locating the house number, Ash pulled into the long driveway to park behind a burgundy Jeep—the type of vehicle he would never own again. Phone and keys were slipped into his jacket pockets before he grabbed the bottle of wine from the passenger seat and made his way to the porch, noting the quiet setting. No horns blowing in the distance. No neon as far as the eye could see.

"I don't know how people live this way," he muttered, reaching for the doorbell.

Seconds later, the door swung open, and a young girl with dark eyes and a head full of tight curls stared him up and down.

"Who are you?" she asked, nose crinkled as if she were greeting a skunk instead of a freshly-showered man.

Great. He'd gone to the wrong house. Ash stepped back. "I'm sorry. I must have gotten the address wrong."

"Hold on!" yelled a voice from somewhere behind the child. A blonde woman pulled the door open wider, and the smell of grilled peppers filled the night air. "You must be Ash?" she asked with a European accent. Her pale skin and sunshine-colored hair stood in stark contrast to the child's warm brown tones.

Relieved, he nodded. "I am. Is this Dana's place?"

"Technically, it's my place, but Dana lives here." She extended a hand. "I'm Ingrid, and this is Angelica. She belongs to our neighbor, who had to make a quick run to the store."

Accepting the greeting, Ash nodded. "Nice to meet you both."

Ingrid escorted him into the foyer and closed the door as Angelica continued to give him the stink-eye.

"Are you Ms. Jesse's boyfriend?" the little one asked.

"No, ma'am. I'm her producer."

"Good," she replied, the crease between her brows softening. "Ms. Dana says Ms. Jesse's boyfriend is an asshole. Mama says that means he isn't a nice man."

Ash had met Ryan Dimitri on two occasions and agreed with Dana's assessment. When he'd heard the news that Jesse was dating the arrogant artist, he'd nearly broken his keep-his-distance rule just to shake some sense into her.

Ingrid slid her hands into her pockets as pale brows arched. "Angelica is in the repeats-everything stage." To the child she said, "Your mama also told you not to use that grown-up word, didn't she?"

"Yes, ma'am. Can you not tell her I said that?"

"I'll let you slide this time." Patting the wild curls, Ingrid added, "Run and tell the others our last guest has arrived."

The youngster took off into the house, sliding across the hardwood floor and darting out of sight.

"She's quite a character," Ash said. He volunteered with a mentor program for young kids and recognized the spunk and intelligence that would someday serve the little girl well. "I'm sorry if I kept you all waiting." Jesse had said six thirty, and he'd arrived right on time.

"No worries. We've just been sitting around talking about *you*."

He expected her to laugh and say she was joking, but her expression never changed. Unsure how to reply, Ash held his tongue and followed her into the house. High ceilings made the open space feel even larger, and the island to his right more than earned the name. An enormous slab of granite glimmered beneath a modern light fixture that would look even better over a pool table.

Five sets of eyes turned Ash's way, and he felt as if he'd invaded a private meeting. Jesse broke off from the group to greet him, though she looked confused about how to do so. Once upon a time she'd have run full-tilt and leaped into his arms, and then they'd sneak off for a more intimate greeting.

Shoving the image out of his mind, Ash held up the bottle of wine. "I didn't want to show up empty-handed."

Jesse took the bottle and passed it off to Ingrid. "You didn't have to do that, but no wine goes to waste in this house."

"Amen to that," muttered Ingrid.

An awkward silence took over until Ash leaned down to drop a kiss on Jesse's cheek. "Thanks for inviting me."

"Thanks for coming," she replied, not meeting his gaze. "Let me introduce you to the group." He followed her to the island where the rest of the gathering hovered in silence. "Everyone, this is Ash Shepherd, the man I plan to blame if this album flops." The joke broke the ice, and everyone seemed to relax. "You've met Ingrid and the terror next door, Angelica. Then we have bass player extraordinaire, Dana Mills, whipping up a batch of tasty fajitas at the stove." The cooking musician waved a wooden spoon. "Silas, whom you met this morning. And Reggie Summers, the best drummer in town, with his wife Phoenix."

"Reggie and I know each other," he said and moved in for a shake and a pat on the back. "Been a while, man."

"Yes, it has." The drummer pointed to Jesse. "This is my girl, now. You've got to help her make this album unstoppable. We're counting on you."

No pressure there. "I'll do my best." Ash turned to the others. "It's nice to meet you all."

When she'd said friends were gathering to celebrate, Ash had imagined a larger crowd. The music community was a tight-knit group, and Jesse had been in the mix long enough to build a significant crew. Even one of Ash's spontaneous cookouts brought out twice as many people, and something told him the lack of attendees was due to the fallout from the Honkytonk Daisies breakup.

Duos were like marriages, and when they didn't work out, friends were forced to choose sides. Lucky for Ash, his and Ronnie's divorce had been so amicable that their core group of friends had remained intact. Clearly, that hadn't been the case for Jesse.

"I have a good feeling about you." Silas smacked Ash on the back. "You're the one to take care of my girl."

A task Ash had undertaken long ago. "I'm looking forward to working with her," he said, and he meant it. Just being in the same room again made the ever-present hole in his chest a little less cavernous.

"Dinner is served!" called Dana from her side of the kitchen, and the attendees hopped into action. As Silas waddled off, Jesse stared up at Ash with a serious expression.

"I guess this is going to feel awkward for a while."

She always had been honest to a fault. "A little. Nothing we can't get past, though."

Jesse smiled, but the sentiment didn't reach her eyes. "I hope you came with an empty stomach because Dana makes the most amazing fajitas."

He gestured for her to lead the way. "If it tastes as good as it smells, I believe it."

Stepping into line behind the others, they waited to fill their plates from the array of ingredients spread across the counter, and Ash caught the scent of vanilla and orange blossoms. The scent brought back memories of warm nights in the back of his Jeep and cold mornings behind the school that had resulted in both of them being late for class.

Out of self-preservation, he stepped back, blinking the flashbacks away.

"You good there, buddy?" Reggie asked, reaching past him for extra napkins.

Ash tried to answer but had to clear his throat to find his voice. "Sure. Yeah. I'm fine. The peppers are a little strong, that's all."

Reggie chuckled. "You think they smell strong? Wait until you taste them."

The drummer walked off with his bounty, and Ash reached for an empty plate, reminding himself that Jesse wasn't his to sneak off with anymore. That pleasure belonged to another lucky bastard who didn't deserve her in the least.

* * *

Everyone loved Ash.

Due to him ignoring her for the last ten years—for reasons Jesse didn't like but now understood—she'd altered her image of him in her mind to one of a pompous ass who'd found success, and then couldn't be bothered with the little people he'd left behind. In one casual meal with her friends, he'd replaced that tarnished image with the kind, generous boy she remembered.

"Dana, that was amazing," Ash said, leaning back from his empty plate and wiping his mouth.

"I'm glad you liked it," she said, collecting Ingrid's and her own plates as she rose to her feet. "Did anyone save room for dessert?"

Groans echoed around the table as Angelica yelled, "I did!"

Ash flashed a full-on smile at the little girl, and Jesse was transported back in time to a Sunday afternoon in the Rheingold house. Tommy occupied the chair to Jesse's left while Ash sat to her right. The boys were picking at one another like an old married couple, and Jesse was caught in the crosshairs, as usual.

She hadn't thought about those days in a long time, but reuniting with Ash brought them roaring back. The good times. The laughter. The heartache. The loss.

"Time to take the party outside," Ingrid said, snapping Jesse back to the present. "Reggie, you're in charge of the fire pit."

The past summer in middle Tennessee had been brutal and long, making the cooler October nights a welcome reprieve. One by one, attendees carried their dishes into the kitchen, and then filed through the sliding glass doors out to Jesse's favorite part of the house.

The sprawling patio, the fairy lights draped around the white pergola and the winding concrete walk that led to a fire pit surrounded by five Adirondack chairs combined to form the perfect outdoor retreat. Musicians were supposed to be most content on stage, but this suburban oasis was Jesse's happy place.

"I call the swing!" Angelica shouted, dessert forgotten as she rushed for the hammock chair hanging from a hook stand at the edge of the patio. Standing before it, she clutched the seat. "Can someone help me get in?"

Ash did the honors, sweeping the little girl off her feet and plopping her into the swing. Much giggling ensued as dark eyes looked up adoringly. Watching the two interact, Jesse thought about what a great dad Ash would be. She knew firsthand how good he was with kids. They'd volunteered at vacation Bible school as teens, and he'd been endlessly patient with all of the little ones.

When his career took off and she started hearing his name more and more, Jesse did a little digging and learned that Ash had gotten married. For several seconds after reading the news, she'd sat numb, her heart breaking all over again. But then she read that the marriage hadn't lasted a full year. Jesse wasn't proud of her reaction to that little tidbit, which landed somewhere between *ha!* and *serves you right.* To be fair, back then he was still the rotten jerk who'd abandoned her without so much as a *have a nice life,* so she gave herself a pass.

Watching him now, Jesse couldn't help but admire the man Ash grew up to be. In their youth, he'd been tall and lanky with a boyish face and pretty hazel eyes. Ash was still tall, of course, but the once-thin frame had filled out nicely over the years. The once-spindly legs were now firm and muscled beneath the dark denim that accentuated the rather delectable bottom he was currently pointing her way.

The man was freaking gorgeous.

"You look deep in thought over here," he said, lowering into the chair beside her. Jesse had chosen one on the patio instead of near the fire pit, as the smoke bothered her. "What's going on in that dangerous little mind of yours?"

Jesse feigned innocence, not about to admit she'd been admiring his ass. "Me? Dangerous?"

"Yeah, you. The girl who put a whole jalapeno in a brownie, and then handed it to me without batting an eye."

She would remember Ash sticking his mouth under the kitchen faucet for the rest of her days. "That was payback for you filling the sugar bowl with salt and letting me put it on my cereal." Jesse would remember that awful taste for just as long.

"There was no proof that was me." Shifty eyes said otherwise. "So what had you looking so serious?"

Searching for a less-embarrassing answer than the truth, she said, "You look different."

A dark brow arched. "Different than what?"

"Than back when we . . ." Finishing that sentence would only make things worse so Jesse rephrased. "Than the last time I saw you."

Hazel eyes narrowed, and a corner of his mouth tilted up. "Is it a good different?"

The sexy grin dazed her enough to hinder her ability to lie. "Very good." Hearing the breathy tone in her voice, she looked away, certain that her cheeks were quickly becoming the shade of her hair.

Voice low, he said, "You look good, too, Jesse."

The words knocked the wind out of her, and she leaned forward in her chair, eyes locked on the concrete between her feet. "Thanks."

Emotions tangled into a knot she didn't know how to unravel. Grasping for a lifeline, she reminded herself that there was a man in her life. A man who loved her. A man who was much too far away in that moment.

FIVE

AFTER AGREEING THAT EACH HAD TURNED OUT WELL, JESSE GREW distant, turning noticeably colder than she'd been moments before. Eager to bring them back to neutral, Ash ventured into safer territory.

"Not a very big crowd tonight. I guess some people couldn't make it on such short notice?"

Jesse leaned back and focused on the fire across the yard. "Other than Ryan, who's on tour right now, everyone who matters is here." Jesse stared down at her lap. "I'm sure when Taylor throws a party, she still packs them in, but that means she got stuck with the leeches. I'll take my crew over hers any day."

So his assumption had been correct. Jesse put up a good front, but she was hurting and that pissed him off. "What happened with Taylor? I get the feeling you didn't see it coming."

She shook her head. "Nope. I thought we were in it for the long haul—climbing to the top together, and then sailing into the Hall of Fame in two or three decades—but Taylor had other plans." Tapping the side of her beer bottle, Jesse shook her head. "She had the nerve to tell me over the phone. *'I'm calling it quits on the act and going on without you'* is something you should tell a person *in person.*"

"Yes, it is," Ash agreed.

"Did you know that I'm the first person she met when she moved to town?" Jesse didn't wait for an answer. "*I* introduced her around. *I* took her to songwriting sessions and pushed her on stage for her first open mic night. If it weren't for *me*, she'd still be singing for tips on Broadway."

The anger was more than justified, but they needed to channel all that emotion into something more productive than a rant.

"Write it down," he said, shifting through melodies in his head. "Channel your inner Loretta and put that into a song."

Blue eyes blinked his way. "Bitching to you is one thing. Telling the whole world that I'm still pissed is another. I'd rather people think that I'm over it."

Since when did Jesse Rheingold pull her punches? "Songs connect with fans when they're authentic. You don't need to call her names or even aim the song directly at her. Write it like you're talking to a guy who did you wrong. Tell him exactly where he can stick it, and we'll have your first number one hit."

Jesse's jaw worked as she contemplated the idea. "I don't know," she said, clearly conflicted. "I want this album to be distinctly me, but I want it to sell, too. Whatever we put together needs to be radio and fan-friendly. Coming out as the bitter dumpee isn't the first impression I want to give."

Ash was happy to hear she'd put some thought into the record, but this sounded dangerously close to *overthinking*.

"Let's break it down," he said. "The only thing this album has to do is reflect the best music you can make right now. That's all. Record songs that speak to you, and the rest will take care of itself."

For a moment she only stared at him, and then uttered exactly what she thought of his advice. "That's bull."

Not an encouraging response. If they were going to make this work, he'd have to cure Jesse of a few delusions.

"You think you can crank out a record following some radio formula that has nothing to do with who you are?"

"I think I need to craft an album that country music fans want to listen to because if I don't, I might as well pack my bags and head back to Georgia right now."

Ash dug deep for patience. "So authentic doesn't translate to the fans, is that it?"

"Authentic me, maybe not."

Now she wasn't making any sense. "What's wrong with authentic you?"

Jesse lowered her voice and lifted the bottle halfway to her lips. "If I knew that, there'd be more people here, now wouldn't there?"

Well, shit. The break with Taylor had done the impossible—put a ding in Jesse's once-undingable confidence. This was the girl who'd belted out a Johnny Cash song in a fifth-grade talent show despite being told the song wasn't *age-appropriate*. And she'd blown the room away. She was also the woman who'd written the majority of songs on the Honkytonk Daisies only studio album, which had climbed into the top twenty on several charts.

Desperation and doubts were a lethal combination in this town, and more than one hopeful had learned that lesson the hard way. If Jesse didn't get her confidence back, she'd suffer the same fate. And take Ash down with her.

* * *

How could she let her cover slip like that? Especially with Ash.

So Jesse sucked at making friends. So what. She'd long ago accepted the fact that her core circle would be small but tight. Even as a kid, she'd struggled to connect with her peers. Especially the other girls. She could toss a football with the guys. Or shoot some hoops, holding her own despite her size. But fitting in with the girls had never come naturally.

That didn't mean there was anything *wrong* with her.

When the Daisies took off, everyone wanted to be her friend. The parties were crowded, the texts were flying, and Jesse had finally found her tribe. Until Taylor defected and took the tribe with her.

Annoyed with her wayward thoughts, Jesse felt a sudden urge to talk to the one person who liked her for exactly who she was. And right now, she needed to hear his voice.

"Excuse me," she said to Ash, exiting her chair and crossing to the wooden swing in the back corner of the yard. By the time her butt hit the seat, she'd dialed Ryan's number. On the fifth ring, someone answered, but the voice on the other end wasn't the one she expected.

"Hello?" a woman squeaked, lips smacking as if she was chewing gum.

"Who is this?" Jesse asked.

"Who are you?" the woman replied.

Laughter erupted in the background, and Jesse recognized the booming voice of Paul Rigley, the drummer of Flesh and Blood.

"Where's Ryan?" Jesse snapped.

"Ryan is… busy. Who is this again?"

"This is Ryan's *girlfriend*. Jesse Gold."

"Jesse who?"

Before she could answer, the voice on the phone changed.

"Hey, Jess," Paul said. "Sorry about that. We're, uh, having the bus cleaned, and Britney picked up the phone by mistake." Right. Having the bus cleaned an hour before showtime. Totally believable. "Ryan is grabbing a quick shower," Paul continued, "but I'll have him call you when he gets out."

A tiny voice in Jesse's brain whispered, *he's lying*, but she ignored it, as she had many times before.

"Sounds like a big cleaning crew," she said as female laughter nearly drowned out the drummer's voice.

Paul shushed the gathering. "Davie is making 'em laugh. You know how he loves to entertain."

Yes, Jesse knew how the guitarist liked to *entertain*. When she'd first moved in with Ryan, Davie Juniper had also lived in the house. In the one month the band had been off the road, Jesse had encountered more than a dozen women in various states of undress while fetching her morning coffee. Disgustingly, she never saw the same woman twice.

"Shouldn't you guys be getting ready for the show?" Jesse had taken on the mothering role with the band, though she doubted they appreciated her efforts. All of them were ridiculously talented, and she hated to watch them waste the gifts they'd been given. She also knew how quickly a good situation could go south. Despite their frat boy ways, she liked the guys as a whole and wanted them to succeed.

"Yes, ma'am." The ma'am part amused her since Paul was eight years older than she was. "We're on it," he said. "I'll tell Ryan you called."

The line went dead, and Jesse forced herself not to picture the real scenario she'd just interrupted. Eyes shut tight, she tilted her head back and exhaled.

"You okay?" Ash asked, startling her.

"I'm fine," she lied. Something she'd been doing a lot lately. *Fake it 'til you make it* had become her new motto. "Is the munchkin gone?" She'd spotted Angelica's mom step through the gate while on her call.

"Yeah. She's a sweet kid."

"You wouldn't call her sweet if you heard some of the things that come out of her mouth." The sassy, off-the-cuff nature was what Jesse liked most about Angelica.

Ash grinned. "I got a hint of that when she greeted me at the door."

This should be good. "What did she say?"

Hesitating, he sighed. "Mind if I sit?"

The swing wasn't big, but there was room for two. If the two didn't mind being cozy. Jesse scooted over, bracing herself for the forced intimacy. "I don't mind."

The biggest lie she'd told this evening.

Chains rattled as he settled in, his thigh firm and warm, pressing against hers. Ignoring the heat penetrating her jeans, she crossed her legs to put whatever distance possible between them.

"So what did the little firecracker say?" Jesse asked, desperate for a distraction.

"She asked if I was your boyfriend." Ash looked up and bounced as if testing the chains. "When I said no, she said that was good because she heard your boyfriend is an asshole."

Jesse knew where that little nugget had come from. Ryan was the only bone of contention between her and Dana. "Ryan is *not* an asshole," she replied, defending him out of habit.

Ash didn't share an opinion either way. "Is he good to you?"

"He is." Which was the truth. When they were together, Ryan was caring and affectionate, said all the right things that made her feel special and loved. The times they were apart were an issue, but Jesse wasn't about to discuss her misgivings with Ash. She'd already revealed one weakness this evening. She would not reveal another.

"If that ever changes, let me know, and I'll have a word with him."

She turned to see his face. "Are you serious right now?"

"What?" He had the nerve to look confused.

"My personal life is none of your business. Not anymore."

"I'm sorry—"

"Ten years of nothing and now you want to play protector," she mumbled. "I don't need your protection."

"Jesse, I told you—"

"You weren't there when I needed you, and I managed just fine on my own."

He tensed beside her. "If you'd have called, I would have been there."

She'd *wanted* to call him. She'd even tried to call at one point, sneaking behind her mother's back because she didn't want to hear the crap about how he'd taken their favorite child. A stranger had answered the call and claimed she didn't know anyone named Ash.

Shaking off the memory, Jesse slid off the swing. "You changed your number, remember? So don't put that on me."

He rose, too, towering above her. "I gave Enid my new number as soon as I got it. I didn't expect anyone to use it, but I gave it to her anyway, so you'd have it."

Good old Enid strikes again. Why couldn't she have gotten nice parents? A doting couple who cared as much about kid two as kid one. Jesse knew the answer to that one. Enid had lost three babies before finally carrying Tommy to term. He was her miracle baby. Four months after he was born, she'd gotten pregnant with Jesse and had a trouble-free pregnancy all the way through.

In some twisted way, the ease with which she'd come to be had made Jesse less special in her mother's eyes.

"She never shared that number with me." Tired of wading through ancient history, she returned to the original subject. "Ryan is a good guy, and he's good to me. So thanks for the delayed offer, but I don't need your help anymore."

Sadness etched in the lines around his mouth. "I'm sorry to hear that."

So was she.

"I should probably go." Ash slid his hands into his pockets. "We didn't get to talk about the album much. Are you busy tomorrow?"

Ignoring the instinct to lie, Jesse said, "Other than working on some songs, I'm free."

He pulled out his phone. "I'm going to text you an address. Meet me there at eight tomorrow morning."

"Eight?" she exclaimed. Who went anywhere at eight on a Saturday morning?

"Yeah, eight." When he lowered his phone, Jesse's dinged. "I have some friends I want you to meet."

If this hadn't been work-related, she'd have said forget it and stayed in bed, but Ash's friends were heavy hitters in the business, and those were the kinds of friends Jesse needed.

She checked the message in her phone and found an unfamiliar address. "What is this place?"

"You'll see." Leveling her with the grin that knocked her off-kilter, Ash leaned in close. "You're one of the most talented people I've ever met, Jesse. Don't forget that."

An odd note to leave on, and an exaggeration considering with whom he'd worked, but Jesse accepted the compliment anyway. "Thanks."

He strolled off and said his goodbyes to the rest of the group before giving her a wave from the sliding glass doors. Ingrid then followed him inside to show him out. Still holding her phone, Jesse dropped back onto the swing and looked up the address for her morning destination—a recreation center.

Must be a place where songwriters met up to write. Or a rehearsal space. Having a sizable room to set up and actually work out the songs before hitting the studio was a better idea than sitting around some boring conference room.

Convinced she'd solved the mystery, Jesse rejoined the party and forced herself not to think about cleaning ladies named Britney and what she and her friends were likely *cleaning*. She also told herself not to think about Ash and the look in his eyes when she'd said she didn't need him anymore. The first task turned out to be easier than the second.

SIX

"WHY DO YOU HAVE HAIR STICKING OUT OF YOUR NOSE?"

Ash twitched and struggled not to laugh. Sarah's tone was too serious not to answer with a straight face. "That happens when you get to be an old man like me. I'll do my best to trim them back before next week."

"You can't help being old, I guess, but I hope that doesn't happen to me. I don't want hairs in my nose."

He refrained from pointing out that she already had hairs in her nose and instead finished tying the six-year-old's shoe before sending her back to the swings where she would hopefully not ask Ms. Frieda about the hair coming out of her ears. Not that anything ever offended Ms. Frieda, but Ash didn't trust what the woman might say in response. The elderly volunteer had once told *him* that she'd have tickled his pickle if only she were forty years younger. Thankfully, no children had been around to overhear.

When Ash wasn't in a writing session or the recording studio, he most enjoyed his time at Sunshine Academy, which wasn't an academy in the traditional sense, but a recreation center in one of the more downtrodden neighborhoods in the city. As a child who never knew his father, Ash related to the kids who were navigating the world much as he had—predominantly alone and with little guidance.

Kathleen Shepherd had done her best, but supporting herself and her son had required holding down multiple jobs at a time that led to long working hours. By the age of nine, Ash had learned to cook, clean, and take care of himself with little adult supervision. Lucky for him, they'd moved to Eton that year, and he'd found the Rheingold family, who'd welcomed him with open arms.

Until the accident.

Checking his watch, Ash wondered if Jesse was going to show. She was already ten minutes late when he spotted a burgundy Jeep, much like the one he'd parked behind the night before, pull into the center parking lot. When Jesse stepped from the vehicle, anger ignited like a flash-fire.

"What are you doing driving a Jeep?" he asked as she approached. "And you're late."

Sunlight turned her swaying ponytail a fiery red while dark shades covered her eyes. Ignoring his question, she said, "Why are these kids out here so early?"

"Because their parents have to work and they need someplace to go." Still annoyed, he repeated the first question. "The Jeep. What the hell, Jesse?"

She slid the glasses onto the top of her head. "What? You used to own one."

"And I won't own one again."

Confusion clouded her blue eyes until the memory returned. "You cannot be serious. That was a random accident that would have happened no matter what vehicle we were in. Let it go, Ash." It wasn't that easy. "You said you have some friends for me to meet?"

Dropping the Jeep issue—for now—Ash said, "Follow me."

They were headed for the back of the rec center when Millie Hopewell stepped into the morning light with a child Ash didn't recognize.

"There you are," said the center director, cheeks pinker than usual.

Millie had been running the center for sixteen years and had never missed a Saturday as long as Ash had been volunteering. Loose strands of her shoulder-length, salt-and-pepper hair flew out in all directions as if she'd styled it by rubbing a balloon on her head, and her neutral-toned, oversized clothes contained as many wrinkles as tattered threads. Despite her appearance, Millie was the most calm, organized person Ash had ever met, and she lived for the children she served.

Always happy to lend a hand, Ash said, "How can I help?"

"We have a new attendee, and I thought maybe you could help her meet the other children." Noticing the woman beside him, she added, "I see you also brought us a new face today."

"I did. Millie Hopewell, meet Jesse Gold."

"Nice to meet you," Jess said, shaking the older woman's hand.

"Nice to meet you, too." Beside Millie stood a pixie of a child. Small, with fiery hair, discerning blue eyes, and freckles scattered across her button nose, she bore a striking resemblance to a younger version of Jesse.

Lowering her voice, Millie whispered, "I'm hoping you can work your magic for this one."

"I'd be happy to." Ash had a knack for pairing up the newcomers with another child already in the program. Dropping to one knee in order to greet the little girl, he said, "What's your name?"

"Grimelda," the redhead replied.

Ash glanced up to Millie, who shook her head. "Her name is Jane, but she prefers Grimelda."

"Grimelda is a witch's name," the little one informed him. "I like witches."

Interesting kid. "Okay, then, Grimelda it is. Are you ready to make some friends?"

Pink lips puckered as she shook her head in the negative.

"Smart kid," Jesse muttered. Ash shot her a not-helping look, and she dropped the sunglasses back to her own freckle-covered nose.

Pointing to an empty bench on the side of the playground, he said, "How about we go sit over there and talk? I bet you have some good stories to tell."

Every kid had a story. They just rarely found an adult willing to listen.

The bright-red ponytail swayed as she nodded in agreement, and Ash led her to the bench, ignoring Jesse's impatient sigh.

Once the three were settled, Grimelda opened with an unexpected question. "Are you two married?"

"No," Jesse replied a little too quickly, considering they'd once discussed walking down the aisle together.

"You don't have to make it sound like being married to me would be so bad."

Jesse eyed him over the little girl's head. "You're too pretty. I'd be insecure all the time."

"You *are* very pretty," Grimelda agreed. At least when *she* said it, the description sounded like a compliment.

"As Ms. Jesse says, no, we aren't married."

"Have you ever been married?"

"Once," he replied. "But not anymore."

"Did you cheat?" Grimelda asked.

"Good question." Jesse stretched an arm over the back of the bench.

Why had he invited her here again? "No, I did not cheat."

"Did she?" Before Ash could answer, the child added, "Or he. I know that boys can marry each other, too."

A worldly statement for a child her age.

"I like this one," Jesse said, removing the glasses once more.

"Thank you," Grimelda replied. Looking back to Ash, she said, "So?"

"My wife didn't cheat either," he answered. "We just decided to be friends instead."

"Are you still friends?"

"Yes, we are."

"Really?" Jesse asked, appearing genuinely interested.

"Yes. Really." To Grimelda, he said, "Are you sure you don't want to make a new friend today?"

Another quick shake of her head. "Kids are mean."

"Amen to that."

"Jesse," Ash warned.

"Come on. They *are* mean."

They could be, but there were plenty at Sunshine Academy who weren't. Running down the list of kids Grimelda's age, which looked to be about five, Ash remembered that one of the girls had dressed as a witch for Halloween *and* had given herself a unique nickname much as the redhead had.

"Will you let me introduce you to one little girl? I think you'll like her."

The bottom lip puckered again, but she didn't refuse outright. "Why do you think I'll like her?"

"Meet her and you'll see."

With a sigh well beyond her years, Grimelda agreed, and Ash felt as if he'd won a small victory. Locating the brunette near the giant blocks, he took his neighbor's hand and said, "Let's go."

As they stepped away from the bench, Grimelda slipped her other hand into Jesse's, who looked as if she'd been handed a live grenade and didn't know what to do with it. Ash couldn't help but smile at the picture they must have presented considering how much their small charge looked like the slightly taller version on her right.

Thirty feet later, they stood before a tower of teetering blocks. "Can I interrupt you for a minute?" Ash asked.

Shoving a curtain of black hair from her face, the small girl gave them her full attention. "Sure, Mr. Ash. Do you like my tower? There's a princess trapped at the top, and I'm going to rescue her."

"How are you going to do that?" Grimelda asked.

"Knock it down, of course." As Ash had hoped she would, the brunette added, "Do you want to help?"

The pucker returned. "I'd rather cast a spell to make it fall away instead."

A tiny finger tapped a dimpled chin. "That could work, too. I'm Belle Pepper. What's your name?"

"I'm Grimelda O'Riordan."

Belle took her new friend's hand and pulled her closer to the tower. "Okay, Grimelda, let's save Princess Flufferbutt together."

Mission accomplished, Ash backed away as Jesse whispered, "How did you know that would work?"

"You just find something they have in common. Belle was a witch for Halloween, and she has a great imagination. That seemed like the right fit."

They stood back and watched Grimelda wave a twig in the air seconds before Belle knocked the tower over.

"Wow," Jesse mumbled, "you're a kid whisperer."

Ash laughed and took her hand. "Come on. It's time to show you why you're here."

* * *

Jesse was still processing Ash's magical friend-finder abilities when he whisked her into the large brick building and down a narrow hall that instantly took her back to grade school. Rudimentary drawings decorated the walls, and a large bulletin board read, *If you can dream it, you can do it*, with a glittery rainbow arching bold and bright above the motivational saying. As they progressed farther into the building, she picked up the sound of tuning instruments.

So he *had* brought her here to meet musicians.

Jesse followed Ash into a large classroom to find half a dozen children of various ages and sizes, each with a guitar in hand.

"Good morning, everybody," Ash said, tugging her along behind him. "I brought a special guest with me today."

"Holy crap," said a young girl with striking blonde hair. "You're Jesse Gold."

Removing her leather jacket, Jesse said, "You know me?"

A smile split the young girl's face, revealing two rows of metal braces. "Are you kidding? The Honkytonk Daisies are my favorite. I've listened to your album, like, a million times."

Jesse looked to Ash who grinned back in that sexy-smug way. "Virginia is one of my guitar students."

"After seeing you in concert, I begged my mom for a guitar." The teen extended her Yamaha acoustic toward Jesse. "Would you sign this?"

"Of course." She looked around for something to use, and Ash produced a Sharpie from a cup on the small desk in the corner. After scrawling her autograph across the polished surface, Jesse stepped back and replaced the cap on the marker. "There you go."

As far as surreal moments went, this one was definitely at the top of the list. No one had ever recognized her in public before —a fact Jesse attributed to how different her stage persona looked from her everyday appearance—and she'd certainly never been asked to sign someone's guitar.

Virginia examined the signature from her upside-down view. "Oh my gosh. Mom is never going to believe this without a picture. Can we take a selfie?"

"After practice," Ash cut in. "We're already getting a late start."

Undeterred, the excited blonde returned to her seat, color high and eyes wide. She showed the boy next to her—an older-looking kid with dark, curly hair and wire-rimmed glasses—her shiny new autograph. If Ash brought Jesse here to boost her ego, he could consider it mission accomplished.

Hands itching to play, she realized she was missing something. "I didn't bring a guitar," Jesse whispered to Ash. "Why didn't you tell me I needed one?"

"I keep a couple here, so I don't have to carry one in every weekend. Or in case one of the kids forgets theirs." Whipping a set of keys from his pocket, Ash unlocked a door behind the desk, disappeared inside what she assumed was a storage closet, and then reappeared carrying two hard cases. "Here you go," he said, handing one to Jesse.

She set the instrument across a couple desks and opened the case, heart nearly stopping when she got a look at what was inside.

"This is a Takamine Pro Series 7."

"Yep," Ash replied, clicking open his own case.

Jesse blinked in astonishment. "You keep a three-thousand-dollar guitar locked in that closet? And you let these kids use it?"

Holding a Gibson Hummingbird, he said, "Normally, I'd use that one, but you're a special guest so you get it today."

Now he was messing with her. "You keep over five thousand dollars' worth of guitars here all the time? What do you keep at home?"

With a casual shrug, he withdrew several picks from his jeans pocket and passed one her way. "I have a solid collection. A few more Gibsons. Fender, Epiphone, Martin. Enough to fill out any spontaneous jam sessions that might come about."

Except for not being on stage, Ash was living the life Jesse wanted. She'd been part of the Nashville music scene for five years but had yet to fully wedge her way in. Granted, Ash had been here longer and had enough number ones to earn his credibility, but dang, she wanted what he had.

While Jesse was still admiring her guitar-for-the-day, Ash settled on a tall stool in front of the gathering and started the class. "Everyone warmed up?"

A collective yes echoed from the students.

"Good. First, let me introduce our guest." He turned to find Jesse hadn't lifted the guitar from the case. "What are you doing back there?"

"Working up the courage to pick this baby up."

Ash lowered his voice. "It's a guitar, Jesse, not a priceless work of art."

The heck it wasn't.

"You've been playing since you were younger than these guys," he reminded her. "Let's go."

Jesse did as ordered, loving the feel of the instrument in her hands. After taking the stool beside his, she gave the strings a quick strum and had a musical orgasm. "This is awesome."

"Keep it together, Rheingold," he mumbled, the use of her real name shocking her into paying attention. "Let's show Ms. Jesse what we can do. 'Brown Eyed Girl.' Everyone ready?"

After another collective response, Ash dove into the opening riff of the classic Van Morrison song. He'd used the same tune to teach Jesse nearly two decades before, and she remembered the chords well. Eight bars in, the kids joined him, every last one of them singing in harmony. The explosion of sound took her by surprise, but she recovered another bar in and picked up with the ensemble. Three minutes later, after several sha la las, the song ended with one final chord, and Jesse couldn't remember the last time she'd had this much fun.

"Great job, you guys," she said, unable to contain her enthusiasm. "Y'all are really good."

"You want to take lead vocals for one?" Ash asked her.

"What are my options?"

Holding her gaze, he said, "'Ring of Fire.'"

The song she'd sung in her first public performance ever, and one of Jesse's favorites. The look in his eyes said he remembered the fifth-grade talent show as well as she did. Jesse had forgotten that though neither of her parents could be bothered to watch, Ash had surprised her after the show, still dressed in his dirty baseball uniform, to congratulate her on the triumphant debut.

He'd been there from the beginning, and Jesse realized he was trying to remind her why she started playing music in the first place. The kids murmured their approval of the song choice, and Ash kicked them off. By the end of the song, Jesse knew without a doubt that this would not be her last visit to the Sunshine Academy.

* * *

"I can't believe how good those kids are," Jesse said as she returned the guitar to its case.

Ash was proud of his students, but even prouder of Jesse. She'd humored Virginia and posed for a series of pictures, even taking one on her own phone and sharing it to Instagram. The young girl had nearly passed out from excitement.

"They're a talented bunch," he replied.

"How long have you been working with them?"

"I've been teaching here for about six years, but this group averages around nine months or so." Of all that Ash had achieved since moving to Nashville, running the music program at Sunshine Academy was one of his most satisfying endeavors. "Butler—the older one with the curly hair—has been with me just over a year. He was falling into the wrong crowd, so his mom was looking for something to keep him out of trouble."

"And music was that something."

Ash nodded. "It was. The kid took to it much like you did. Like he was born to play."

"I don't know about that," she said. "I remember the early days when I couldn't find a chord to save my life."

"Nobody is great from day one." He let her close the guitar case, and then carried them both back to the closet. Returning, Ash said, "Once upon a time, Jimmy Page couldn't play a G-chord."

Jesse pulled on her leather jacket. "I can't imagine that."

"But it's true."

"Oh, thank goodness you're still here." Millie Hopewell burst into the room, more disheveled than usual. "I just received some wonderful news."

He'd never seen her so animated. "What is it, Millie?"

She waved the letter in her hand. "We've been invited to participate in a Christmas show at the Ryman. Our students are going to be on television!"

"That's a big deal," Jesse said with a genuine smile.

"Isn't it, though? They want both the choir and the musicians. I can't wait to tell the children."

Ash headed up both those groups. "How did they hear about the academy?" he asked.

Millie shrugged. "I have no idea, but who cares? This kind of exposure can do wonders for our programs." She hugged the letter to her chest. "The children are going to be absolutely thrilled. All of the parents are invited to be part of the audience, and you'll be center stage as their leader."

"I'll be what?" Ash didn't do stages. Not ones the size of the Ryman—which was sacred ground as the previous and still occasional home of the Grand Ole Opry. He definitely didn't do television. "I doubt they'll need me on stage."

"You're the musical director of Sunshine Academy. The children couldn't possibly go up there without you."

"You're the musical director?" Jesse cut in. "I thought you just a volunteer."

"Just a volunteer? Ash is an important part of this facility, and I don't know what we would do without him." Millie offered Jesse a warm smile. "I'm glad you joined us today, Ms. Gold. And I hope you'll come back."

"I plan on it," Jesse replied, surprising Ash, who was still shell-shocked from the TV news.

"You do?"

"Yeah." She gave a non-committal shrug. "This was fun."

He'd hoped to put Jesse's focus back on the music and not all the other distractions that came with trying to make it in this town. He'd never expected her to pay a return visit.

"Wonderful. Just wonderful." Millie straightened the letter she'd nearly crumpled and pushed her glasses up on her nose. "The taping is the middle of next month, and the producers asked to set up a meeting to discuss expectations and ideas. As soon as I have a date for that, I'll let you know."

"Sounds good," Ash replied, forcing enthusiasm into his voice.

Millie turned and nearly floated from the room. "We're going to be on television."

Jesse turned his way. "You're going to be on stage at the Ryman. I'd kill to do that."

Ash nodded and led her from the room with only one thought in mind.

Better you than me.

SEVEN

JESSE HATED SITTING STILL, WHICH WAS ONE OF MANY REASONS the last few months had been so frustrating.

To keep her skills high, she'd played a few local gigs, but the people she'd encountered, both fellow musicians and fans alike, all wanted to talk about the breakup. The questions hadn't been easy or comfortable to answer, and Jesse knew that from an outsider's perspective, *she* looked like the loser. At least sweet Virginia didn't see it that way.

The young girl had made Jesse's year, and not because she was a fan, but because seeing Jesse play had motivated her to pick up a guitar. *That* was something to be proud of. Also something Jesse never imagined would happen. She'd been so focused on the charts and the press and the accolades, that the true purpose of performing—to move and inspire people—had gotten lost along the way.

Nothing like an innocent teen to put Jesse's life back in perspective.

By Sunday afternoon, she'd finished three rounds of laundry, unloaded the dishwasher, vacuumed the carpets, and watered the plants. Plants that were quickly fading due to Jesse's incurable black thumb. She'd recently begun regular plant pep talks to convince them to stay alive for a few weeks longer until their loving owner returned. Though Ryan wasn't their *original* owner.

That was Helena, Ryan's previous girlfriend, who'd caught him in bed with another woman and made a hasty exit without the greenery. Ryan's track record with women was, in a word, *distressing*, but he loved Jesse, and in the year plus they'd been together, he'd never given her reason to doubt him. Was she ignoring what she didn't want to see? Perhaps. But when they were together, it was easy to pretend.

While scrubbing mildew off the shower door, Jesse focused on the things she loved about Ryan. His endless charm, wicked grin, and ice-blue eyes were an irresistible combination, but he was also quick to laugh and made her feel loved. The only thing Ryan took seriously was play, and he attacked life with abandon, something Jesse needed to do more of. Where Ash was safe and steady, Ryan was dangerous and unpredictable. One supplied comfort while the other was like playing with fire.

Stopping mid-wipe, Jesse stared through the soapy glass. Why was she comparing Ryan to Ash? It wasn't as if she were choosing between the two. Anything beyond a professional relationship with Ash was out of the question. He was her past. Ryan was her future. End of story.

Annoyed with her wayward thoughts, she finished scouring the bathroom and found herself with nothing else to clean. Which brought her right back to sitting still. Glass of sweet tea in one hand and her notebooks in the other, Jesse settled on the oversized swing on the back porch—*her* addition to the dwelling.

A porch swing was better than some fickle old houseplants any day.

She set the swing into motion and proceeded to flip through the notebooks, trying to predict which songs Ash might like. After dismissing three in a row, she remembered that this was *her* album and what Ash liked or didn't like shouldn't matter.

"Hey there, neighbor," called Geraldine Allsop from next door. "Are you going to give me an update or what?"

This part of town mostly consisted of bungalows built decades before, all close enough together to make avoiding your neighbors nearly impossible. Thankfully, Jesse adored Geraldine and never missed an opportunity to visit with the older woman.

"Come on over." Jesse hopped off the swing. "I'll get you some tea."

By the time Jesse returned with the drink, the neighbor had planted herself in the old rocker. Her black hair was teased high and hair-sprayed into an unmoving coif, and she still wore her church clothes—a white blouse and a long denim skirt that covered the tops of her sparkly cowboy boots, plus a trademark red scarf tied jauntily around her neck. At fifty-six, she was still a striking woman.

Like others before her, and those still arriving today, Geraldine had moved to town thirty-five years ago with a guitar and a dream, but she never made the big time. There'd been times after Taylor's betrayal that Jesse feared she might meet the same fate. If a woman as talented as Geraldine—a virtual powerhouse of a singer—couldn't make it, then what chance did Jesse have? To her credit, the older woman had scolded her for entertaining such ridiculous doubts, claiming that Jesse possessed all the ingredients to be a real star.

From Geraldine's ruby-red lips to God's ears.

With her typical, laid-back smile, she accepted the tea and set the rocker into motion. "Thank you, darling. I've been watching for you all weekend. Do we have a producer yet?"

Jesse grinned. "We do. He doesn't have a lot of experience, but he's written a bunch of hit songs, and that's what I need. Now I just have to figure out which of *my* songs to show him."

"I'm here for you, honey-child. Tell old Geraldine what you're thinking."

"You aren't old," Jesse admonished, and then held up her notebooks. "I've gone through these things multiple times, and I can't decide what is right for the album. Ash said I need to pick songs that *speak to me*, and the rest will fall into place."

Her friend snorted. "If he thinks it's that simple, then, baby, you're in trouble. Country radio doesn't give a shit about what speaks to *you*. They want songs that speak to their *listeners*. Today, that's more pop than twang, and a hook that will have twenty-somethings cranking their station at every kegger and bonfire north *and* south of the Mason Dixon Line."

"Exactly," Jesse's said. "Party songs. High energy, but sweet, too. That's what's working right now for female artists."

"Darn tootin'. Plug in that formula, and you'll have yourself a hit record."

Jesse didn't like the word formula, but that's all any song was, really. A couple verses, a chorus with an undeniable hook, and a bridge to bring it all together. Three minutes of magic, as Silas once called it.

Holding out her glass for a toast, Jesse said, "To hit records."

Geraldine tapped her own against Jesse's before flipping her hair over her shoulder. The hair didn't budge. "To hit records and lots of 'em."

In one more day, Jesse's solo career would finally be off the ground. Now she just had to take off before Taylor Roper did it first.

* * *

Clay Benedict was getting beaten by an old man.

Concerned about his newly signed artist, Clay had extended an invitation to Silas Fillmore for a Sunday round of golf, somehow unaware of how well the man knew his way around a course. The exec had no reason to regret signing the young artist—yet—but Jesse's initial reaction to Ash Shepherd concerned him. In the six weeks since they'd signed the contracts, every interaction Clay had with Jesse told him he'd made the right choice, but reputations were tough to live down, even when they were undeserved.

The rumor that Jesse was hard to deal with—likely spread by the Taylor Roper camp, though Clay had no proof of that—had hindered their progress. She'd never displayed a hint of temper or diva behavior in his presence, nor had any of his staff reported negative encounters. Yet Jesse had done a complete reversal when he'd announced Ash as her producer, and though after the two met privately, she'd been more receptive to the arrangement, Clay worried that any amount of tension could not only delay the project further, but derail it completely.

"Good shot," he muttered as Silas planted the ball well onto the green, positioning himself for yet another birdie. "How long have you been playing this game?"

Silas dropped the club into his bag and gave Clay a wink. "Probably about as long as you've been alive, Mr. Benedict." Grinning, he stepped back from the tee. More than once, Clay had suggested the older man use his given name, but Silas insisted on the formality.

They were six holes in and had yet to discuss the older man's client. A fact Clay suspected was his companion's doing. Silas had to know why he'd received the invitation but was following the cardinal rule of Business 101—never give anything away. If Clay wanted to discuss Jesse Gold, he would have to broach the subject himself.

"Do you know anything about Jesse's history with Ash Shepherd?" Clay asked. He'd posed the same question to the new producer and received a vague answer about them growing up in the same town. The one fact Clay already knew.

"They're both from Eton, Georgia, but that's the extent of my knowledge. I'm more interested in Jesse's future than her past."

And you should be, too was the unspoken ending to that statement. Clay was only interested so far as the past could affect her future and, in turn, the future of his label.

"She didn't seem happy to see him on Friday morning."

Swinging the driver, Clay made contact with the ball and sent it slicing right toward a bunker. "Shit," he mumbled, watching the ball touch down on the green, and then careen into the sand.

"Unlucky bounce," Silas said, knowing full well the bounce was not the problem. Heading off toward the cart, Silas offered no response to Clay's question.

Undeterred, Clay waited until they'd finished the hole—Silas finishing two strokes ahead of him—and were on to the next to try again.

"Are you certain she's willing to work with him on this album?"

Hand shading his eyes, Silas searched for the flag in the distance. "He joined us all for dinner Friday night, and they seemed friendly enough." After putting his ball on the tee, he met Clay's gaze, expression dead serious. "My girl is ready, willing, and able to make this record. So long as your boy knows what he's doing, there shouldn't be a problem."

There was a reason Silas Fillmore had been a staple in this town for nearly five decades. Clay had respected him from the moment they met, but today, he was starting to like him, too.

"I have faith in Ash," Clay replied.

"Faith in Jesse is more important," the older man pointed out. "*She's* your artist, not Shepherd."

Fair point. Like any producer, Ash could be replaced. So could Jesse, if necessary, but Clay wasn't the type to toss an artist aside without giving them his full effort first. Jesse's track record with the Honkytonk Daisies, her songwriting abilities, and her natural presence on-stage were all assets in her favor. Most other hopefuls in town didn't come with such credentials.

There was also her voice, which was as good as, if not better, than any female artist on the radio today.

Doubts put to rest, Clay leaned on his club and offered Silas a friendly smile. "I have complete faith in Jesse, or I wouldn't have signed her. I just want to make sure we have the right combination going into the studio. If we need to make a change, I prefer to find out now rather than later."

Silas relaxed and took his position behind the ball. "That's good to hear." The club made a whooshing sound before cracking the ball, sending the little white dot sailing over the green to land less than fifty yards from the hole.

This outing may have put Clay's fears to rest, but Silas's performance was putting a serious dent in his ego. Clay had played many a pro/am tournament and held his own. The next tournament invite he received, he'd be reaching out to Silas to fill out a foursome.

"That's a beautiful shot," called a woman from behind them. "Even for you, old man."

Clay turned to find Samantha Walters approaching with Clay's former partner, Tony Rossi. The sight of her, dressed in white pants that accentuated her long legs, a long-sleeve pink polo, collar high, and a white visor settled over dark waves sent the now-familiar surge through his system that hit whenever she was around. A surge of pure attraction. Now that she represented Dylan Monroe, their paths crossed often, and resisting the urge to pursue a more personal connection was proving difficult.

Seeing Tony caused a very different reaction in Clay. First was the ever-present guilt, followed by a hefty dose of jealousy. Clay had never been the jealous type, but the combination of these two individuals together was more complicated than he could untangle in a matter of seconds.

As Samantha embraced Silas, Tony approached Clay with an outstretched hand. They'd parted ways after a nearly twenty-year partnership and a friendship that went back even further. In the two years since, Clay had never been honest with his oldest friend as to why he'd removed himself from the label they'd built together.

"Good to see you, Clay," Tony said. "I hear you signed the other half of the Daisies. Looks like a score for both of us."

The Honkytonk Daisies had broken up because Taylor had been coaxed away to Foxfire Records as a solo act. A move Clay would not have tolerated if he were still part of the company.

"I consider it a score, yes." Clay didn't want to talk business. Not with Tony. "Silas and I were just moving up the green. We'll be out of your way shortly."

"We could make it a foursome," Tony suggested, and called to Samantha. "Do you mind if we join forces, Sam?"

Samantha met Clay's gaze. "I don't mind at all." There was an invitation in her eyes, and he considered his dilemma. The desire to spend time with the brilliant manager warred with the equal and opposite desire to spend as little time with Tony as possible. A feat he'd managed since following his conscience, ending his affair with Tony's wife, and walking away from their partnership.

"That's a nice offer," Silas said, "but Clay and I are mixing business and pleasure today. Afraid we'll have to take a rain check."

Their business discussion was all but over, and Silas knew it. Clay appreciated the out but wondered about the older man's motives.

Tony's smile wavered as he said, "Another time, then."

Samantha joined her golf partner without another glance in Clay's direction. As he and Silas strode to their cart, Clay made a bold decision.

"Samantha!" he called, and she looked his way. "I'd like to set up a meeting. Are you available this week?"

Though he hadn't included a reason for the request, she nodded with understanding. "I can make room in my calendar."

Clay failed to hide the smile as a feeling of accomplishment filled his chest. Two years was long enough. He could never undo his misdeeds, but the self-imposed hiatus from anything personal couldn't go on forever.

"Good," he said with a nod. "I'll call you."

Once the cart was in motion, Silas said, "Be careful there, boy."

An odd statement. "Careful about what?"

"I know why you parted ways with Tony, and I know he has no idea. Don't put Sam in a position to be caught in the crossfire."

No one knew why Clay left Foxfire except Joanna Rossi, Tony's wife and Clay's former lover. Therefore, there was no way Silas could know anything.

"What crossfire?"

Silas sighed. "I ran into Mrs. Rossi around the time we were negotiating Jesse's contract. She thought the information might give me an advantage. As you know, I didn't use the knowledge then, and I don't intend to in the future." His voice softened. "But I like Sammy. Don't put her in Joanna's sights. She doesn't deserve that."

They rode on in silence, Clay astounded that Joanna would sink to such depths, yet he should have been prepared for something like this. Not long ago, she'd warned him that she wouldn't take kindly to being replaced. Clay had written the threat off as a bluff, but he'd clearly miscalculated. If she'd shared the truth of their affair—a secret that could destroy Joanna as well as Clay—to put him at a disadvantage in a minor business deal, what would she do if Clay started *dating* Samantha?

Suppressing the anger rising inside him, Clay clenched his jaw and breathed through his nose. "Thanks for letting me know, Silas."

Silas gave a curt nod and kept his eyes on the path ahead.

EIGHT

FOR JESSE, REPORTING TO AN OFFICE ON A MONDAY MORNING WAS a completely foreign experience.

She'd worked retail, waited tables, bagged groceries, and even mucked out stalls at one point in her life, but had never worked in an office. The concept of spending eight hours perched in front of a computer, manipulating spreadsheets and answering inane questions when you'd rather staple your lips shut than explain one more time how the copier works, seemed unbearable.

Jesse would take drunks requesting "Free Bird" any day.

Upon entering the Shooting Stars building, the always-smiling Belinda let her know that Ash was waiting in a back conference room. Jesse shoved her sunglasses up on her head and set off down the long corridor behind the reception desk, stopping at the break room for a bottle of water. On the wall to the right of the fridge were two huge posters. One for Dylan Monroe's debut album, which had released the year before, and the other for Chance Colburn's forthcoming CD. Both artists were larger than life, and for the first time ever, Jesse considered Taylor breaking up the act a good thing.

Without that kick in the pants, Jesse wouldn't be on the verge of making her own debut album. And unless she got her butt moving, the verge was as close as she would get. Following the receptionist's directions, she ducked around a corner and spotted Ash waiting in a small, windowless room.

"It's nine o'clock," he said the second she walked in. "I thought we said eight thirty."

"It's a Monday morning. Cut me some slack." She set the guitar on the floor and dropped into a black leather chair.

"Still not a morning person?"

"Nope."

On the table in front of him rested a Fender acoustic. Ready to work, Jesse withdrew her prized possession—a Gibson Dove she'd found in a pawn shop six months after moving to town—from its light-brown case. Unaware of its full value at the time, she'd known enough to recognize that the two-hundred-and-fifty-dollar asking price had been a serious bargain.

Later, she'd done her research and put the value closer to twenty-five hundred.

This wasn't Jesse's only guitar, and she typically saved it for special occasions, but after getting a taste of Ash's collection on Saturday, she'd grabbed the Dove with the sole purpose of impressing her new producer.

"Wow," Ash said. "Where'd you find that beauty?"

"Hickson Pawn in Hermitage. I stumbled across it not long after moving to town. One of those right time, right place moments." Jesse gave the strings a strum. "Sounds as pretty as she looks."

"Nice. Give me a taste and play me something."

Jesse had six songs she was sure were album material, and four more that had potential. She kicked off the first option, titled "Baby Baby," with its simple melody and lyrics that told the basic girl-meets-boy story. The chorus was super catchy, and she could already imagine crowds singing along during live shows.

When the song came to an end, the last chord still hung in

the air as Ash said, "What else do you have?"

Right. Not the reaction she'd hoped for.

Jesse played the next one, which told the story of a girl who *literally* tripped over Mr. Right, that was titled "Fall For You." Not as upbeat as the one before it, but the song featured another catchy chorus, and Jesse had always enjoyed performing the tune live back in her days playing the local bars.

Watching Ash more closely this time, she tried to gauge his expression. No head bob. No toe-tapping as far as she could tell. He wasn't frowning, but he wasn't smiling either. Adding a little more oomph to her delivery, she finished with a dramatic high note and waited for an encouraging word.

Instead, she got a chin rub and a head tilt.

"Are you considering these songs for the album?" he asked, brows drawn.

"I was," she drawled, not feeling the love. "You don't like them?"

Ash shrugged. "They aren't bad, necessarily, but…"

"But what?"

"They're fluff."

Jesse blinked. "They're what?"

"Fluff," he repeated. "Musical cotton candy—sweet, thin, and one-dimensional."

The critique stung. "Tell me how you really feel."

Ash made no effort to soothe her ego. "What about the songs on the Daisies' CD?"

"I'm not re-cutting those songs."

He leaned forward in his chair. "I'm not suggesting you do. I'm asking if you have more songs like those? That's a great album, and I know you wrote most of the material."

Partially true. "I *co-wrote* those songs, and they didn't sound like the finished versions the first day we walked into the studio." Wasn't that why they were here? To take these raw ingredients and make them sparkle? "You don't think the two I played could be polished into something album-worthy?"

He sat back. "An arrangement can go only so far. What do you have with a little more substance?"

Substance? She wasn't writing symphonies here. This was a country record. Not that country music didn't have *substance*, but Jesse wanted her album to be fun. And more importantly, radio-friendly.

Determined to win him over, she tried another. "Here's one called 'Come See Me.'"

Jesse slowed the melody from how she'd originally wrote it and added a bluesy vocal as she sang about a woman suggesting to her ex that he should leave the bar and come see her. At the end of the song, when she thinks he's ignoring her text messages, the guy shows up at her door.

The song came to an end and again, Ash's face gave away nothing. Finally, he said, "That's a solid maybe, but is that all you write about? Women looking for guys?"

What kind of a question was that? Men sang about picking up women *all the time.* So why couldn't she sing a few love songs? Country music was built on love and heartbreak, for crying out loud.

"What would you like me to write about, Ash? World peace? Global warming? The eternal chicken-or-egg question? Tell me what you want."

Unmoved by her outburst, he crossed his arms and held her gaze. "We're three songs in, and you're already getting defensive. Did you think this was going to be easy?"

"I didn't expect you to make it so hard," she snapped. "And I don't appreciate the double standard. No one ever tells a guy he should stop singing about getting a woman."

"I'm not saying you can't sing about men, Jesse. I'm saying if you're going to sing about them, it should involve more than the woman saying *come over and you can have me*. What about all that anger from the Taylor stuff? Have you put that into a song like we talked about?"

Why was he so insistent that Jesse look like the bitter artist who couldn't get over being ditched? "Did it ever occur to you that if the first thing people hear from me is how Taylor left me high and dry, that *I'm* the one who'll look like a loser?"

"I told you, aim it at a guy. Make it a traditional breakup song and say everything you want to say to her." He arched a brow. "You won't look like a loser when your song becomes the hit of the summer."

Jesse liked the sound of that and stopped arguing long enough to consider the idea. She could load all of her anger and attitude into a tune, but she'd done that her first couple of years in town and gotten nowhere. Not until she'd met Taylor and softened her image to fit the duo did anything positive happen. Fiery Jesse had been stuck in small-time honkytonks. Sweet and smiling Jesse had gotten a record deal as part of a duet and managed to grow a modest fan base.

Did she dare mess with her image?

"I'm not interested," she said, determined to stick to her game plan. "Try this one."

She ripped into "Letting Loose," a song about blowing off steam on a Friday night, and though the last verse mentioned having a twirl around the dance floor with a cute guy, the song had nothing to do with *finding a man*. With a final strum, she looked up, certain to find approval in Ash's eyes.

"I don't get it," he said, knocking the wind out of her. "This isn't you. Where's the edge? The attitude? That's what sets you apart."

He could not be serious. "These *are* me. I wrote these songs, and I stand by them." This was Jesse's album, dang it, and she would cut the songs she wanted to cut. "I want the record to be fun and upbeat, and this is what will get me on the radio."

Jaw tight, Ash exited his chair, slid his own guitar into its case, and headed for the door. Was he really going to quit before they'd even started? How dare he walk away from her. Again.

"You can't—"

"So you want to be on the radio?" he interrupted.

The question confused her. "Of course, I do."

"Then pack up and let's go."

Before Jesse could form a response, Ash ambled from the room and disappeared around the corner. Fearing he'd leave without her, she packed up as fast as she could and hurried after him, catching up just before the receptionist's desk.

"Where are we going?" she asked, slightly winded.

Ash opened the door, and then held it for her to pass through.

"We're taking a research trip."

"To where?"

Pulling keys from his pocket, he headed for his pickup, forcing Jesse to hustle in order to keep up with his long strides. Casting a glance to her Jeep, she debated whether to leave it or not, but then she couldn't exactly drive herself when she didn't know where the heck she was going.

After lifting his guitar into the truck bed, Ash took hers—making the decision for her—and slid it into the cab behind the seats. Without another word, he walked around to the driver's side, leaving the passenger door open.

Jesse crossed her arms, determined not to be kept in the dark. "I'm not getting in until you tell me where we're going."

Ash buckled his seatbelt. "If you want to make this record, then get in. If not, take your guitar and go."

She ground her teeth, trying to decide if he was bluffing.

"In or out," he snapped.

Cursing a blue streak in her head, Jesse climbed into the Nissan, buckled her seatbelt, and stared straight ahead as the engine roared to life.

"Good choice," Ash said and set the truck in motion.

* * *

Ash pulled into the Music City Center garage, snagged the ticket from the machine, and waited for the bar to lift. Jesse hadn't spoken since they'd left the label office, which was fine with him. She'd find out his purpose soon enough. Nashville didn't have much of an off-season when it came to tourists, but October was a less popular month, so he managed to find a space not far from the entrance.

When they climbed from the truck, Jesse reached for her guitar.

"You don't need it," he said, closing his door and coming around the front.

As they walked toward the exit, Jesse found her voice. "Where are we going?"

"Next door."

"What's next door?"

Ash stopped, and it took Jesse two more steps to realize she was walking alone. Spinning, she said, "What?"

"Are you telling me you've never been to the Country Music Hall of Fame?" How did she plan to carry on the legacy of those who'd come before her without knowing anything about them?

Blue eyes rolled. "Of course, I've been there. I took Mom and Dad when they visited two years ago."

His teeth clamped tight enough to chip a molar. "Is that the only time you've gone?"

Jesse rolled her eyes. "No, but it's been a while since I played tourist. What's your point?"

Ash closed the distance between them and loomed over his clueless artist. "You're trying to step into a tradition that goes back decades. To do so, you need to study those who've paved the way, and there's no better place to do that than the Hall of Fame."

"I listen to the old stuff."

Ash resisted the urge to shake her senseless. "That isn't enough." He pointed toward the exit. "Walk."

"I *was* walking," Jesse mumbled, stomping through the garage. "You're the one who stopped to throw a tantrum."

They traveled the block down to the corner of 5th and

Demonbreun and waited for the light to change so that they could cross. The cool wind off the river cut between the buildings, and Ash noticed Jesse hug her jacket tight as they reached the other side. He picked up his pace to get her out of the cold quicker.

"Whoever designed this place deserves an award," she declared, eyes up.

Ash took in the windowed facade meant to look like piano keys. "Ralph Applebaum. He's pretty much a genius in museum design."

She spun his way, ponytail flapping in the breeze. "How do you know that?"

"I worked here when I first moved to town." He'd been hungry to absorb all the musical knowledge available, so working at the Hall had been an obvious choice. "You have to learn a lot to answer the visitors' questions."

They stepped through the entrance, and Ash watched her admire their surroundings with wide eyes. Jesse possessed the same raw talent and endless passion for her craft that those honored in this building had displayed over the years. Artists who'd built the genre and, in the process, made both his and Jesse's livelihoods possible. She needed to understand her place among the greats.

They reached the ticket desk, and Ash said, "One general admission."

"Just one?" Jesse asked.

He handed the ticket clerk his debit card "I have a yearly pass." Ticket in hand, he said. "This way."

"Why exactly are we here?" she queried as a young guy with thick glasses and a pointed goatee waved them in.

"For inspiration," Ash replied. "And I know the perfect place to start."

NINE

THEY PASSED SEVERAL DISPLAYS BEFORE ASH STOPPED. "HERE we are."

Jesse didn't see anything familiar behind the glass. The collection included a pair of colorful cowboy boots that had obviously belonged to a woman, a manual typewriter decorated in a feminine flower motif, and endless sheets of handwritten song lyrics. In the front was a handwritten copy of the classic song "You Don't Know Me."

"Who is this?"

"Her name is Cindy Walker."

Above the collection hung a black and white photo of a beautiful young woman in a cowboy hat. "Was she a songwriter?"

Ash sighed as if disappointed by the question. "Yes, she wrote 'You Don't Know Me' and about a hundred others."

Jesse knew the tune. "I thought that was an Eddy Arnold song."

"Arnold gets a co-writing credit, but legend says he only gave her the title. She came up with the rest."

"Really?" She studied the treasures before her. "Why have I never heard of her?"

"That's a good question, and the reason we're here. The first step in making this record is plugging the holes in your musical education."

She didn't appreciate the comment, but she couldn't argue either. She knew the main classics—hits by Cash, Jones, and Reba—but about this really old stuff, she was clueless.

"I admit, I haven't done my homework. But how are songs from the forties and fifties going to help me now?"

"A song is a song, Jesse. And a great song is still great in any era."

Again, she couldn't argue. But what worked in the past wouldn't necessarily work in the modern era. "Again, how does this help me pick songs that will get radio play *today*?"

Ash ran a hand through his hair and practically growled. "You're missing the point. The goal isn't to *guess* what some radio programmer will play. The goal is to make songs so good that they won't be able to *not* play them."

If only it was that easy. "You know as well as I do that there are countless talented artists writing *good* songs up and down Music Row, and they're getting zero attention or airplay. Good is subjective."

He crossed his arms. "If you're looking for guarantees, you're in the wrong business. Even if we spend three months piecing together the most formulaic, radio-friendly album we can, by the time the album gets released, radio will have found a new trend and passed you by."

"I don't think so," she said, convinced that recording the album without an eye to radio would be equivalent to putting the nail in her own musical coffin. "I'm competing here, remember? Not only do I need to get a single out as soon as possible to beat Taylor to the punch, I need that single to take off and prove that I'm not a talentless hack who spent two years riding the Blonde Wonder's coattails."

As soon as the words were out, Jesse realized she'd admitted too much. Again. What was it about Ash that compelled her to air every last flipping insecurity?

In a low voice, Ash said, "No one in their right mind would see you as a talentless hack. Look around this building. The people honored in these hallowed halls were talented and passionate and put their hearts into everything that they did." She glanced to the young girl smiling back from the black and white photo. "You have that same talent and passion, Jesse. Add your heart to the mix, and there's no limit to where you can go."

Her heart *was* in the project. That's why she was pushing so hard to get it right.

"How can you not see how invested I am in this album? Why else would I be trying to twist myself into a pretzel to be the artist that fans want?"

Ash grasped her upper arms and leaned down until they were nose to nose. "Stop twisting. The artist you *are* is better than any imaginary character you could ever become." He gave her a gentle shake. "Give them the fire and intensity that I know is in there. Don't bury it. Bring it out."

Could she do that? Better yet, could she do that and *not* fall on her face?

"What if I do what you say, and the album goes down in flames?"

"What if it doesn't?" Ash dropped his hands. "There's no point in making an album if the music on it doesn't mean something to you. Put *yourself* into the music. You won't regret it."

Doubts raced through her brain, but she held Ash's gaze in the dim light. He believed in her, just as he always had.

"You're sure that this will work?"

"As sure as I am that doing it any other way definitely won't."

Wanting to trust him, she shoved the doubts away. "Okay, then." She glanced around. "Other than Cindy here, who else should I know about?"

Ash grinned. "Have you heard of Marijohn Wilkin?"

Jesse felt the chasm in her education widen. "No."

"Then that's where we go next."

* * *

Jesse was like a sponge as they strolled through more exhibits, discussing artists like Hank Sr., Kitty Wells, and Billy Sherrill— arguably one of the greatest producer songwriters to have ever worked in country music. She was attentive, asked questions, and made connections between the individuals honored and the classic works of which she had peripheral knowledge.

But after an hour of exploring, Ash remembered that he'd have to cut the day short. If they were going to accomplish more than a museum tour, they needed to get moving.

"Are you ready to get back to work?" he asked.

Jesse nodded while admiring a Gibson acoustic on display in the Emmylou Harris exhibit. "I am, but do we have to go back to that stuffy conference room? Other than to get my Jeep, that is."

Ash agreed that the small space didn't foster much creativity. "We can go somewhere else. How about my place?"

"Your place?" she asked, turning narrowed-eyes his way.

"Sure. I have a small studio so if we come up with something good, we can cut a quick demo and see how it sounds."

Jesse's jaw twitched as she considered the idea. "We can do that. Do you think Clay will mind?"

"We'll let Belinda know where we're going, and if they need us, they have our numbers."

She didn't look convinced. "You don't think that would be strange? Us being alone at your house?"

Ignoring the real question, he said, "We were alone in the conference room."

Eyes snapping, she stared him down. "You know what I mean."

Yes, he did. There had been others at the office, and more to the point, there were no bedrooms. Not that they'd needed a bedroom back in the day.

"We're adults, Jesse, not randy teenagers anymore."

Lowering her voice, she looked away. "So that's all that was. Raging hormones and a lack of supervision?"

Ash pulled her away from a passing group. "That's not what I meant, and you know it. We aren't those kids anymore. If we're going to do this, we need to let the past go. At least that part of it."

Tugging her arm away, she straightened her jacket. "I let it go. I had to after you left."

Ash absorbed the words, not letting the hit show on his face. "Then we're on the same page."

They exited the museum in silence and made their way back to the garage. When they reached the truck, Ash started the engine and was surprised to hear a familiar tune on the radio.

"That's my song," he said, increasing the volume.

"You wrote it?"

Ash shook his head. "No, I produced it. They didn't tell me this would be the next single."

Jesse cranked the volume even more as Chance sang about a man meeting his match. "This is really good." She raised her voice to be heard over the song. "Was it your idea to lay in the steel like that?"

Whether or not to add the steel had been a major debate. "It was. Chance had his doubts, but he trusted my instincts."

Flashing a genuine smile, she nodded. "Then I guess I should trust you too, huh?"

Changing lanes, he shot her a grin. "Yes, you should."

* * *

Jesse ran into the office to tell Belinda where they were going while Ash waited in his truck so she could follow him.

"You guys taking a break?" Naomi asked as she set a stack of folders on Belinda's desk.

She turned back a few steps from the exit. "We went to the Hall of Fame."

"You left?" Naomi laughed. "Goes to show how much we pay attention around here. Did you find inspiration among the exhibits?"

"I did. It's encouraging to know that so many legends started with just a guitar and a dream."

With a tilt of her head, the publicist grinned. "That's still how most artists start out, isn't it? Chance. Dylan. You."

Being lumped together with two such established performers felt both flattering and terrifying. Chance had platinum records on his walls and top honors in his trophy case. Dylan's debut had taken off the year before, and he was still sitting high on the charts. That the label expected the same from Jesse was a boost to her confidence, and an added weight on her already stressed shoulders.

Not that she'd let Naomi see as much.

"That's a good point," she said, pretending they weren't having a casual discussion about Jesse's entire future. "We're heading over to Ash's house to work on some songs. He says he has a studio, so we can lay down a demo if we get that far. I'm going to follow him in my Jeep."

Great. Now she was babbling as if she needed to justify skipping class to the principal.

"By all means. Go make beautiful music together." Switching her attention to the receptionist, the publicist said, "I've marked up these graphics with several changes. Make sure Daphne gets them and let her know that we need them turned around as soon as possible."

Jesse used her butt to open the door and spun herself into the morning sun. Ash's truck idled behind her Jeep, and he waved through the open window as she approached.

"What took so long?"

"I was talking to Naomi," she replied, climbing behind the wheel.

"Stay close and we'll be there in about ten minutes."

Jesse nodded as she turned the key. Before putting the Jeep in gear, she dialed Ryan's number and slid the phone between her ear and shoulder. Two rings in, the call went to voice mail, and she tossed the cell onto the passenger seat with a sigh. After the cleaning ladies incident on Friday, Jesse felt a pressing need to check in more often. The band was in Charlotte tonight, too far away for a quick visit, but next week they'd be in Memphis, and Jesse had every intention of being there.

Only this time, there would be no warning call to give Ryan the chance to talk her out of coming. It was time to remind him of what he had waiting at home.

TEN

THIS WASN'T REMOTELY WHAT SHE'D EXPECTED. "I NEVER PICTURED you as the blue cottage and white picket fence type," Jesse said, admiring the cute A-frame with the wide, covered porch.

"I didn't either until I saw the place."

The home before them couldn't be more different from the single-wide trailer Ash had grown up in. The mobile home had sported a giant hole in the floor at the end of the hall, and the walls were so thin that the place was downright frigid during the winter months. Looking back now, she didn't blame him for spending so much time with her family.

"This is my dream porch," she said, running a hand along the white rail as they climbed the four steps to the top. "And the red door is perfect."

"That was Mama's idea. We put the same one on her house." He glanced at his watch. "Speaking of, I have to help her out this afternoon, but three hours should be plenty of time to get some work done."

Slipping a key into the lock, he pushed the front door open and stepped aside for Jesse to enter first. She walked through and stopped to wipe her boots on the black mat as her eyes were drawn to the vaulted ceiling.

"I did not see that coming." It was like an optical illusion. "The place looks so small from the outside, but it's huge."

"That's what I said when my agent showed me the house as a *potential project*. I was looking for a fixer upper and knew immediately that I'd be in over my head, but the place had great bones, and when you add in the location, I couldn't turn it down." He pointed to the room ahead. "Step into the kitchen, and we'll grab drinks on our way to the studio."

Jesse did as ordered, eyes still taking in every detail of his home. The place suited him. Warm but not overly fussy. Functional but charming.

"When was it built?" she asked. "Everything looks brand-new, but I know this is an older part of town."

"The structure was built in the 1940s," Ash replied, setting down his guitar before stepping around the island to reach the fridge. "I gutted it to the studs so now it lists as built the year of the reno." Perusing the options, he said, "I have Coke, water, and a couple Music City Lights. Pick your poison."

"Coke will work. So you fixed the place up by yourself?"

He handed her the drink and withdrew a bottle for himself. "Ronnie and I did, with a little help from our friends."

"Ronnie?"

"My ex-wife." Ash pointed to the small windows in the wall above the white cabinets. "Those were her idea, and she also picked out all the light fixtures. In addition to the door, Mama suggested the skylights here above the counter, as well as the pergola cover over the back porch. I'll show you that later if you want to see it."

"That would be nice." Jesse wanted to go back to Ronnie. "How long were you married?" She knew the answer but couldn't let him know she'd snooped into his past.

"Less than a year."

Despite the baggage between them, Jesse couldn't imagine why any woman would leave Ash. He was as steady as they came and didn't have a jealous bone in his body. The ex must have been the problem.

Treading into dangerous territory, she asked, "Did you love her?" The added phrase *more than me* almost slipped out.

"I did, and I still do." Before she could absorb that blow, he asked, "Do you love Ryan?"

A yes danced at the tip of her tongue, but for some reason, she couldn't say it. Opening her Coke, Jesse glanced around. "Did you design the rest?"

To her relief, Ash didn't push for an answer to his question. "Pretty much. It was my idea to vault the ceiling in the living room and to add the fireplace."

They'd built a tree house once, and Jesse distinctly remembered Ash taking the lead. The structure still stood, holding memories she didn't need to think about right now.

"It's a beautiful house." Head tilted, she offered a sincere smile. "You should be proud of it."

Ash accepted the compliment with a nod and pointed down the hall. "The studio is on your right. You can't miss it. I'll be there in a minute."

Happy to get to work, Jesse followed his directions and found a small room easily recognizable as a studio thanks to the combination of soundproofing and acoustic filters covering the walls. A built-in desk ran the length of one wall and held a state-of-the-art setup complete with two massive monitors and a small but impressive mixing board.

Ash had not cut corners. Jesse bent to open her guitar case and felt a nudge behind her, nearly sending her headlong into the open door.

"Hey!" she cried, turning to find an enormous black creature staring at her, pink tongue drooped over intimidatingly large teeth.

He could have mentioned that he had a dog. Unsure if the animal was friendly, Jesse rose to her full height, which wasn't much taller than the beast staring her down. His tail was wagging, and she took that as a good sign.

"Hello, Mr. Scary Dog. I promise I have permission to be in your territory." The canine stepped closer and nudged her hand until Jesse patted him on the head. "That's a good boy." She rubbed around his ears, and black eyes rolled shut in euphoria. "You aren't scary at all, big fella."

The tail was still wagging as Ash entered the room. "I see you've met Brutus."

"He's gorgeous." Jesse put her nose close to the dog's face. "You could have told me you have a giant dog, though. He scared me half to death."

Ash picked up a guitar on his way to the desk, where he set down a plate of sandwiches and lowered into the chair. "I don't own a dog. Brutus lives next door but uses the dog door to come visit."

That explanation made no sense at all. "Why do you have a dog door if you don't have a dog?"

"Because Ronnie wanted a dog, but we never got around to adopting one before the divorce." He gave a half shrug. "I never bothered to take the door out."

"Must be a pretty big door for this boy to fit through." She wiped a drop of slobber off her jeans. "Were you planning to adopt a St. Bernard?"

Brutus took another step forward, and Jesse lost her balance when her heels hit the open guitar case on the floor. Afraid of crushing her Gibson, she twisted to the side, and Ash caught her less than a foot from the hardwood. She looked up to see the soft lines etched at the corners of his eyes. Eyes that dropped immediately to her lips.

"You all right?" he asked, breath warm on her cheek.

Jesse's heart raced, but not from the tumble. "Yeah, I think so."

He held her a moment longer, eyes like crystallized honey

locked with hers. As she wrapped her fingers around his warm wrist, Jesse's world tilted once more as Ash lifted her back to her feet.

"Sorry about that," he said, turning away to click on the computer monitors. "Brutus doesn't know how big he is."

Dazed, Jesse straightened her jacket and ignored the sudden weight of disappointment. "Thanks for catching me."

"No problem." He pushed the plate her way. "I made us some sandwiches. Ham and swiss on wheat."

The sandwich was Jesse's favorite, and he'd even cut it diagonally the way she liked. "You remembered."

"Yeah," Ash replied, playing down the gesture. "So what other songs do you have?"

Jolted by his abrupt switch from hot to cold, she took a second to retrieve her notebooks from beneath the guitar, and then set them on the desk beside the plate. "That's everything I have."

While he perused her work, Jesse grabbed a sandwich and dropped into a rolling chair. Brutus plopped down at her feet and stared intently, but to his credit, refrained from openly begging. Ash flipped through the first book, which had her best stuff, and looked unimpressed. When he opened the more-tattered one, she cringed.

"Those are old."

He slowly turned the pages, showing more interest than before. "Is this one about your grandmother?" Ash asked, flipping the book around for her to see.

"It is, but the songs in there aren't album material."

Ash ignored her claim. "I haven't thought about Grandma Evie in years. How is she?"

Appetite waning, Jesse put the sandwich back on the plate. "She passed away four years ago." Though she'd meant to speak in a matter-of-fact tone, her voice caught on the *passed away* part. Unlike her parents, Grandma Evie had lavished Jesse with all the love and attention a young girl could possibly want. She'd often wondered how someone so loving and sweet could have raised a woman as frigid as Enid Rheingold.

"I'm sorry," Ash said, his voice laced with regret. "She was a special woman."

He'd get no argument there. "Yes, she was."

A beat of silence passed before he asked, "Will you play this for me?"

Jesse never played her truly intimate writings for anyone. Not even Taylor. "I'd rather not."

"Come on. I'd really like to hear it."

Caving, she lifted the guitar onto her lap and paused to recall the chords. Once she had the melody clear, Jesse closed her eyes and began to sing.

She had a smile that lit up a room
Her laughter was contagious
Blue eyes that sparkled bold and bright
Always shining when she saw us.

Lifting her eyes, she checked Ash's reaction and caught the gentle smile on his lips. With a quick nod, he encouraged her to continue.

I wanted to be like her
So strong and yet so soft
Her love for me was a precious gift
Her time on earth not long enough.

To Jesse's surprise, Ash began to play with her as she rolled into the chorus.

I had an angel in my life

One sent from up above
To fill the holes that others left
To fill me up with love
If she could see me here today
I wonder what she'd say
I hope that she'd be proud of me
Sweet Grandma Evie May.

She let the next chord fade and waved for Ash to stop. "That's all I have. I never finished it."

Ash propped his arms along the top of his guitar. "That's really good."

Brutus barked in agreement, and she laughed, giving the dog a quick scratch under his chin. "I had trouble sleeping in the weeks after she died. One night I heard a tune in my head, and those words poured onto the page."

Eyes alight, Ash scooted to the edge of his chair. "Let's finish it. This is perfect for the album."

Jesse closed the old notebook and dropped it back into the case. "I can't. There's better stuff in the other book. Besides, no one wants to hear a song about my grandmother."

Ash rolled his chair closer. "Jesse, that's exactly what people want to hear. Think of the listeners out there who feel the same way, but don't know how to express it like you do. That's a gift you can give them."

Jesse couldn't imagine singing something so personal in front of a real audience, but she recognized the determined look in Ash's eye. This was day one, and she was certain there would be plenty of other songs to knock this one out of the running. Letting him help her write a final verse couldn't hurt anything.

"Okay, then," she said. "Let's finish it."

* * *

"What rhymes with reminder?" Jesse asked, biting her bottom lip as her pen hovered above the notebook.

"Kinder?" Ash offered.

They'd spent thirty minutes working on the song, and Jesse had rejected all of his suggestions. He'd let her have her way, but only because her ideas were better.

"Not what I was going for," she replied, studying the page, "but if I reword the previous line, it could work."

The way she scrutinized every lyric made Ash wonder where the bubble gum songs had come from. They hadn't been all bad, but this short session alone revealed what Jesse was capable of, and it wasn't the shallow stuff she'd played earlier.

As she flipped the pencil to employ the eraser, her cell phone rang. She tugged it from her back pocket and checked the screen. "It's Ryan. I really need to take this. He's on tour, and I don't know if I'll get another chance to talk to him today."

They'd made enough progress to earn a break. "Go for it."

Ash expected Jesse to leave the room, but she stayed in her chair.

"Hey, baby," she purred in greeting. "How's it going?" There was a pause before she added, "I'm working with Ash at his house." A second later, she visibly stiffened. "What does it matter where we work?"

Glancing up, Ash caught the confusion in her eyes.

"I didn't like working in the label conference room, so Ash suggested we come over here. He has a studio and—"

Full lips clamped shut, and the voice on the other end grew loud enough for Ash to hear. He couldn't make out the words, but the tone was clear. Ryan Dimitri wasn't happy.

"You're being stupid right now," she said, spinning her chair to face the opposite direction. "Since when are you jealous of anyone?"

Jealous? Based on reputation alone, Dimitri had no business suggesting Jesse would be the unfaithful one. The man had cheated on every woman he'd ever dated.

"I am *not* giving you a reason to be jealous. He's my producer. We're working."

Ash fought the urge to snatch the phone from her hands and tell the asshole where he could shove his accusations.

"I tried to come see you over the weekend so we could celebrate, and you told me not to come. That's not on me."

Ash's leg bounced as his anger grew. Of course he'd told her not to come. Having his girlfriend around would only curb Dimitri's *extracurricular activities*. What was she doing with this dipshit anyway? Jesse knew better. She sure as hell deserved better.

"I can't come now, I'm working. We hit the studio next week, and I need to be prepared."

Why hadn't she hung up yet?

"Jesse," Ash said, voice loud enough to be heard down the line, "we need to get back to work."

She spun the chair and gave him a *hold on one damn minute* look. As if *he* was the problem here.

"Baby, I need to go, but I won't be here much longer. I'll call you back, okay?"

The placating tone infuriated him. She'd done nothing wrong, but Dimitri had her practically apologizing for his bullshit. And who said she wouldn't be here much longer? They still had nearly two hours before Ash had to be at his mom's place, and if Jesse thought they were cutting the day even shorter to please the insecure shit on the phone, she was sadly mistaken.

"I'm sorry," she mumbled, and Ash ground his teeth to keep from butting in. "We'll talk later. Love you." Jesse pulled the phone away from her ear, and he could tell the last sentiment hadn't been returned. Spinning back around, she dropped the phone into her guitar case. "Where were we?"

Leave it alone. Her personal life is none of your business.

Ash tapped a finger on the notebook as the muscle in his jaw twitched.

"What's wrong with you?" she asked, giving him the attitude she should have given her boyfriend.

That was it. Jesse *was* his business, and she always would be.

ELEVEN

"What's wrong with me?" Ash exploded. "What's wrong with *you*, Jesse? Why did you let him talk to you like that?"

Jesse was not in the mood to deal with another cranky man.

"My conversation with my boyfriend is none of your business."

"Bullshit," Ash snapped, and Brutus leapt to his feet with a whine. "Nobody gets to talk to you like that. Not when I'm around."

"You haven't been *around* for years, and I've taken care of myself just fine. I don't need you telling me what to do."

"He accused you of cheating on him."

"He has a right to ask," she snapped back, reaching for the notebook. "We're alone in *your* house. Ryan doesn't know you. How's he supposed to know if he can trust you with his girlfriend?"

"You cannot be serious. How about he should know he can trust *you*?" Ash shoved a hand through his hair, making it stand on end. "And where does a guy with his reputation get off even suggesting that?"

Jesse bolted from the chair, catching the guitar before it hit the floor. "What is that supposed to mean?"

Ash held her gaze. "You know what it means. Why are you with him, Jesse?"

Realizing her mistake, she fit the guitar into its case and clicked it shut. "I am *not* doing this. I don't have to sit here and be insulted."

"Your boyfriend is the one who insulted you. Why didn't you get this angry with him?"

"Why would I be angry with Ryan for caring about me?" Jesse snagged her jacket off the back of the chair. "That's more than I can say for you."

Without looking back, she charged from the room, hurt and shame clogging her throat. In her heart, she knew that Ash was right, but hearing him voice the reality she'd denied for so long raised her defenses. Jesse's vision blurred with the threat of tears, and she picked up her pace.

"You can't leave," he said, following behind her. "We have work to do."

"We're done." Wiping her eyes with her sleeve, she pushed on, blowing through the front door and rushing down the steps. Despite her best efforts, Ash reached the Jeep before she could start the engine.

"This album is too important to walk away because of a stupid argument." He leaned on the door. "I crossed the line, but I couldn't let him walk all over you like that. You deserve better than that asshole, Jesse. Don't let him ruin this for you."

Brutus barked from the porch, and she couldn't decide if he was yelling at her, too, or scolding them both for fighting. Neither made her feel any better.

Eyes locked on the steering wheel, she said, "You're the one ruining this. Thanks for nothing, Ash." Jaw tight, she finally turned his way. "Again."

Slamming the Jeep into gear, Jesse backed from the drive and with a quick shift, she peeled away, paying little attention to where she was going. Several blocks later, she pulled into a parking lot to pull up the GPS on her phone since she wasn't familiar enough with the area to find her way out. Once the lady in the phone started giving directions, Jesse got back on the road and tried not to think about what she'd just done. But, of course, that was *all* she could think about.

What was she going to do now? Obviously, she and Ash couldn't work together. Even *if* they managed to establish hard boundaries about where Ash did and did not poke his nose into her life, he'd already made his opinion on Ryan abundantly clear. His *reputation*, as Ash had put it, was in the past. Ryan was different with her. He was faithful, and there was no reason to think otherwise. Yes, she had her doubts, especially when he was out on the road, but if he was out there hitting up every eye lash-fluttering chick in a mini-skirt, Jesse would know.

The other members of Flesh and Blood weren't exactly the responsible type, and they certainly weren't good at keeping secrets. If there was evidence of infidelity, she'd have seen or heard about it by now. Davy alone lived on Instagram, and if he managed not to blow a secret like that, then the secret flat out didn't exist.

Drying her cheeks, Jesse approached a traffic light, and the phone told her to hang a left. A few more turns and she reached the interstate. Jesse closed the app with a deep sigh as reality set in. This was bad. Very, *very* bad. Clay Benedict was going to be furious, and she didn't blame him. Jesse was proving the rumors to be true—she was impossible to work with.

Desperate to save her career, she took the next exit and found a spot to pull off to use her phone. Silas would know what to do.

* * *

Clay spent Monday morning reviewing resumes. The label had been in operation for a year and a half, and thanks to the success of Dylan's debut record, followed by Chance's album entering the charts at number one, Shooting Stars was ready to hire an A&R Director.

Otherwise known as the Artist and Repertoire division, he was looking for an individual to handle talent scouting and artist development. Until now, Clay had filled the role himself. His first two choices had proved successful, and he had every faith that Jesse Gold would do the same. But as the label grew, so did Clay's responsibilities, and he needed someone on the task full time. A new batch of hopefuls arrived in Music City on a daily basis, and he didn't have the time needed to unearth the true stars.

That meant adding a new member to the team.

So far, he'd printed off three resumes for consideration. One in particular stood out from the rest, and he'd already scheduled the applicant for an interview the next day. As he checked his schedule for when he could schedule the others, the cell phone in his suit coat pocket vibrated to life. The screen revealed the caller to be Joanna Rossi. After the little revelation during his golf game with Silas, Clay had no desire to take the call, but he now knew not to underestimate her. Or tick her off any more than he already had.

Teeth grinding, he answered the call. "Hello, Joanna."

"Hello, Clayton," she purred, feigning the posh accent she'd donned in recent years. Clay, of course, knew she'd once been a country-bumpkin waitress with a thick Carolina drawl. "I hadn't heard from you in so long, I feared you might have deleted my number from your phone."

He'd considered taking that step but kept the number for this very reason. "I haven't had a reason to call you."

The purr evaporated. "Is that your way of saying you've replaced me?"

When would she give up this stupid game? They'd had an affair—a choice Clay would regret for the rest of his life—but he'd ended things two years ago. She lacked any semblance of a heart, so the endless pursuit was not motivated by undying love.

She'd also made her intentions clear when it came to her husband. Joanna would not divorce Tony for any reason.

So why the hell wouldn't she let this go?

"I'm not seeing anyone, if that's your question. I also haven't initiated any more *regrettable* affairs." Clay should have held his temper in check and stopped at the first statement, but he didn't like being manipulated and had endured enough of her threats. Up to now, he'd been firm without engaging in an all-out battle, but her decision to share their secret with Silas amounted to a declaration of war.

"You didn't seem to regret our affair when you were buried inside me on your desk at Foxfire. Or in that limo on our way to dinner in New York. I'm sure the driver would agree with me. Surely he heard the whole thing."

Clay's jaw tightened. "What do you want, Joanna?"

"You know what I want."

"Why?" he asked, truly perplexed. "We both know you can find someone else. Or better yet, try limiting your bedroom exploits to your husband."

The snap in her voice softened. "I'd rather have you, Clayton. It was always you."

A new tactic he hadn't expected. "I might have believed that two years ago," he admitted, the confession bitter on his tongue. "But we both know it's a lie."

The three of them—Clay, Tony, and Joanna—had gone from struggling nobodies to influential industry leaders *together*. They'd been the three musketeers from the moment Tony had picked her up in a small-town diner nearly twenty years ago. He and Clay had been headed to Nashville to chase a dream, and the pretty blonde with a quick wit had jumped at the chance to join them. From the moment she'd stepped into their lives, she and Tony had been inseparable. Any claims that she'd been secretly in love with Clay were utter bullshit.

"You loved me," she insisted, her voice shrill. "Don't deny it."

Love had never played a part in their relationship. Lust, yes. But not love.

"Tony loves you, Joanna. He always has. Do us both a favor and let it go."

Silence loomed, and Clay waited for the click that would signify the end of this pointless farce. But he wasn't that lucky.

"You'll regret this, Clayton. I'll make sure of that."

The line went dead, and Clay sighed as he tossed the cell onto his desk. Running a hand through his hair, he spun the leather chair to stare out his office window onto the patch of greenery beyond. When he and Tony had first started Foxfire Records, they'd barely been able to afford the small rental house on 17th Avenue where they'd shared an office view of two ancient Dumpsters. Now he had his own label with a corner office and a beautiful view. Could Joanna take that away from him?

Revealing their affair would damage Clay's reputation, but he wasn't the first executive to commit such an offense. A few invitations might mysteriously stop arriving, but his business would be secure. The real victim would be Tony. Could Joanna do that to her husband? Would she chance Tony divorcing her just to get back at Clay for having the nerve to tell her no?

Sadly, he believed she would. And short of traveling back in time to correct his mistakes, there was nothing Clay could do about it.

* * *

He couldn't believe she didn't come back.

Ash knew how badly Jesse wanted this dream. How hard she'd worked. Without him signing on, Clay might never have found a producer willing to work with her. At least not one worth hiring. For that reason alone, Ash had sat on his porch for thirty minutes, expecting to see her Jeep pull back into the drive.

So they'd had a fight. Disagreeing on her choice of boyfriend wasn't enough to derail the entire project.

Or it shouldn't have been anyway.

He didn't regret pushing her to stand up for herself, but he'd pushed too hard. Jesse wasn't his to protect anymore. Who she chose to date wasn't his call. But damn it, Ryan Dimitri was a scumbag, and everyone in this town knew it.

Except for Jesse.

Then again, maybe she did. Maybe that's why she'd gotten so defensive. Ash hoped that wasn't the case, because knowing she was *choosing* to stay in a bad situation was even worse than believing she was being duped by a professional cheater.

"You're early," his mom whispered as Ash strolled into the daycare center, careful not to wake the sleeping toddlers. "I didn't expect you for another hour."

He'd hunted for distractions at home, something to keep him from going in search of Jesse. Not that he knew where to look. He debated calling the label to see if she'd gone there, but the last thing they needed was for Clay to hear about this. Jesse may have been angry, but she wasn't stupid. Telling the label head that she needed a new producer after only one day would be career suicide.

"My day ended earlier than expected," he said, lowering himself into one of the tiny preschool chairs. "Who called out this time?"

Kathleen Shepherd pursed her lips and softly tapped a pen against the clipboard in her lap. "Marlene's grandmother fell again. I'm afraid they'll have to put her in a home for sure now. It's the third fall in two months, and it looks like a broken hip this time."

Ash grimaced. "I'm sorry to hear that. Is she going to be okay?"

"They took her to Vanderbilt so she's in good hands, but Marlene was a wreck on the phone. With both her parents gone, Ms. Louise is all she has left."

The statement reminded him of the song he and Jesse had been working on before the blow up. They'd been close to finishing, and he'd already had an arrangement in his head. "Sweet Evie May" would never be a single, but it carried the personal tone they needed on the album.

"I'm glad it's only a broken hip and not something worse." Ash glanced around and noticed a familiar set of eyes watching him. "How long have these guys been asleep?"

She checked the clock on the wall. "Nearly an hour. We'll get them up in another fifteen minutes or so."

"One of them is way ahead of you," he mumbled, well-acquainted with Buddy Winston's troublesome ways.

His mom had opened this daycare center nearly three years ago, and Buddy had been attending since opening week. Barely able to walk back then, he'd still managed to land in one predicament after another. To his credit, the little towheaded child had charm for days and a smile that could win over the hardest of hearts. Both of which had saved him on more than one occasion.

Overhearing Ash's statement, the young boy closed his eyes and pretended to sleep.

"You said you were starting a new project today," Mama said, her Georgia drawl as pronounced as ever. "Did my needing you mess that up?"

"No." Ash had messed up all on his own.

"Who is it this time?" she asked. "Anyone I know?"

Ash had put off sharing the details of this particular project for a reason, but he couldn't dance around the truth any longer.

"You know her," he replied. "I'm working with Jesse Gold."

The blue Bic stopped tapping. "You're working with the Rheingold girl?"

Mama had referred to Tommy's family in this way ever since the accident. Never first names, just the Rheingold this or that. After they'd shut him out, Mama Shepherd had declared the entire family miserable human beings who'd never deserved to have her son in their lives to begin with.

"Yes, I'm producing her debut album." Jesse might not think so at the moment, but they would hopefully be back to work tomorrow.

Mama's face puckered as if she'd caught the scent of something rotten. "I don't like you working with her. The whole family is heartless, the way they threw you away like that. As if you'd done anything on purpose. You were hurting, too."

They'd had this conversation countless times, and Ash felt no desire to rehash the subject. "Jesse didn't know that her parents turned on me. She thought I left on my own."

"Then why didn't she call you herself?" Mama asked, her increased volume causing the little ones to stir. Lips pinched, she held her tongue while they settled back to silence. "Like I said," she whispered, "they're all the same regardless of whatever sob story she fed you. I don't trust her, and neither should you."

Ash had never faulted his mother for her resentment of the Rheingold family. He'd resented them himself for many years. But he believed Jesse and had no intention of walking away from her again. Not for his mother or anyone else. He had a debt to pay, and producing her record was a small price compared to the hurt he'd caused her.

"This is a job, Mama. A good one. Jesse needs my help and, in the process, I'm getting my foot in the door to being seen as a capable producer. Writing songs is fine, but shaping the sound that comes out of this town is what I really want to do."

As he knew it would, the statement softened her features. "Can't you get your foot in the door working with someone else? What about that nice man you worked with over the summer? What was his name?"

"Chance Colburn, and that job is what led me to this one. I only produced a few songs on Chance's album, but now I get to create an entire record. If I can pull this off, I'll earn my place, and the projects will keep coming."

The brunette one mat over from Buddy leaned up and rubbed one eye. "Ms. Shepherd, is it time to get up?" she asked.

"Yes, it is, Madison. Go ahead and visit the little girl's room." To Ash, she said, "You wake the boys, and I'll take care of the girls. Julia prepared the snacks before she left so once they're in their seats, we'll get them fed."

As more children opened their eyes, the chaos of the afternoon kicked in, and Ash had no time to worry about Jesse or their stalled project. Once the kids had gone outside to play, he'd found a second to check his phone, but there was no word from his wayward artist. For the next several hours, the kids required his full attention, offering a much-needed distraction, and leaving Ash exhausted as the last child exited with a parent just before six. But the day wasn't over. As he mopped the floor, he found himself whistling while he worked, filling the air with a tune he quickly realized wasn't his own.

The melody was from a song Jesse had played him back in the conference room. He had to admit, the tune was catchy, and that wasn't always a bad thing. Struggling to remember the words, he tapped out a rhythm on the mop handle and considered several ways to expand the song.

Formulating a plan, Ash would spend the rest of the evening on the instrumentation and have something to start with the next morning. He hadn't been immune to her disappointment when he'd shot down her original ideas, and admitting that at least one had merit would go a long way to mending the rift between them.

TWELVE

"HAVE YOU LOST YOUR MIND, CHILD?" SILAS BOOMED, DRAWING curious stares.

They'd met at a small diner in Hillsboro, southwest of the city, where Silas had been a regular for longer than Jesse had been alive. If she'd thought he'd take her news so poorly, she might have shared it in a less public location.

"I can't work with him." She shoved a crispy fry into a puddle of ketchup. The place was dark and old and a bit dingy, but they knew how to make burgers and fries. "It's not as if we're in the middle of the album and I'm asking to start over with someone new. All Ash and I have done is work on one song that I had already started. And I don't really want to put that song on the album anyway."

The more she thought about including something so personal, the less she liked the idea.

Silas wiped his mouth. "Are you forgetting what we went through to get to this point? What makes you think Clay Benedict won't pull the plug the moment we tell him you refuse to work with the only producer willing to take the job?"

That one hurt. "I thought only two turned us down."

"And this makes strike three," he said, holding up three

fingers. "Jesse girl, we can't risk losing this deal, and *that's* what will happen if you tell Benedict to find another producer. I'm sure of it." His shoulders sagged. "I've sheltered you as much as I can, but this is your last shot. I guess I should have made that clear before, but I had faith that if someone gave you a chance, you'd prove the rest of them wrong."

By *the rest of them*, he meant those who believed the rumors. Jesse's jaw tightened, and her appetite vanished. Shoving her plate away, she simmered in her own reality, chest aching.

Disappointing the sweet man across the table was nearly as shameful as knowing that her dream hung by such a thin thread. What had she done to deserve any of this except work her butt off from the day she'd first picked up a guitar?

And for what? To toss it all away because Ash insulted her boyfriend?

"Forget it," she said, willing to swallow her pride for both their sakes. "I'll work things out with Ash. We'll make this album, and it'll be great."

The light returned to Silas's eyes. "That's my girl. By this time next year, they'll all be sorry they turned us away."

Jesse flinched. Nothing like being reminded of overwhelming rejection to boost a girl's ego.

After waving for the waitress, Silas patted the back of Jesse's hand across the small, weathered table. "I have faith in you, little one. You can do this."

"Thanks, Si. I won't let you down."

"Of course, you won't." The waitress arrived, and he flashed her his brightest smile. "Dorothy, darling, bring us two big pieces of apple pie. And don't skimp on the whipped cream."

Shifting the gum from one side of her mouth to the other, the woman stuck her pen behind her ear. "Anything for you, sweetie." She dropped her notepad into the apron slung low on her hips and reached for Silas's empty plate. To Jesse, she said, "Are you still working on that, doll?"

"No, you can take it."

"But you still have a mountain of fries there," Silas pointed out.

Jesse's stomach lurched, but she pulled the plate closer. "You're right. I'll nibble on these until the pie comes."

Silas looked pleased as she dipped a fry in ketchup. The greasy goodness had lost its appeal, but she ate on, trying not to think about the call she'd have to make when this meal was over. Would Ash be willing to stick with her? Or had her tantrum changed his mind? He'd tried convincing her to stay, so maybe they could start over. A simple conversation about boundaries, and then they could put the focus back where it belonged—on the work.

The bell over the door jingled, and the man who entered headed straight for their table. Jesse had met him on three occasions, but he never remembered her. She doubted this encounter would be any different.

"Heya, Si. How are you doing, old man?"

Paul Parsons had been Silas's client since the sixties and was likely as old, if not older, than his manager. He'd obviously had plastic surgery, and his false teeth glowed so white, Jesse wouldn't be surprised if they were visible from the space station.

"I'm good, Paulie. You remember Jesse Gold."

The bloodshot eyes held no recognition. "Yeah. Sure. How you doing, little lady?"

She hoped the distaste didn't show on her face. "I'm good, thanks."

"Jesse is making her debut album for Shooting Stars Records. She'll be a household name before we know it."

Some would see the statement as empty flattery, but Silas believed every word he uttered, and Jesse knew it. All the more reason to make things right with Ash.

"Good for you, darling. When you get it done, come play for us on the Opry." Paul tapped Silas on the shoulder. "Make sure I'm on the same night so I can show her around."

Jesse perked up. "I'd love to play the Grand Ole Opry."

Silas had been close to getting the Honkytonk Daisies into the lineup when Taylor left the duo.

"Then we'll make it happen." Paul swiped a fry from Jesse's plate as Dorothy returned with their pie. "I'll get out of the way so y'all can enjoy your desserts. Si, give me a call about that Country Gold special. They're messing with the slots again, and I'm hearing rumors about them cutting down the time for each act." Backing away, he added, "Good to see you again, Jackie. And good luck with the album."

She sighed as the waitress set the pie in front of her. "Why can't that man ever remember my name?"

"He's been calling me Denise for fifteen years," Dorothy drawled. "And I wear my name on my shirt."

Unable to contain the laughter, Jesse covered her mouth as Silas added, "Old Paul has been singing the same five songs for forty-five years, and they had to give him a teleprompter for his Opry appearances because he can't remember the words. Don't take it personally."

"He remembers *your* name," Jesse pointed out.

"That isn't always a good thing." Lifting his fork, her manager said, "To the first of many number one albums."

Seconding the sentiment, she touched her fork to his. "I'll eat to that."

Visions of platinum albums and her name in the Opry lights brushed her earlier thoughts away. So Jesse hadn't landed on solid ground yet. That didn't mean she wouldn't. As the cliché went, if it was easy, then everyone would do it. Making it in this business was hard, especially for a woman, but that didn't mean it couldn't be done. Jesse was going to make this happen, and hopefully, Ash was still along for the ride.

* * *

Ash was loading the dishwasher when the call came. He'd begun to fear that Jesse really would walk away from the project so long as he was involved, and knowing the damage the decision would do, he'd resolved to ask Ronnie to take over, prepared to take full blame for the fallout.

"Hello?"

"Ash," Jesse began, "I'm calling to apologize."

Not the greeting he expected. Though relief flooded through him, she had this conversation backwards.

"I'm the one who needs to apologize. I shouldn't have crossed the line like that."

Jesse sighed as if she'd been holding her breath. "I should have handled things better. Can we try this again?"

"That's what I was hoping." Remembering what he'd started before breaking for a late supper, he said, "I've been working on one of those songs you played me this morning."

"I thought you didn't like those ones."

Ash was a big enough man to admit when he was wrong. "The last one you played—the one about the woman texting her ex—has some good lines. I've been messing with the arrangement, and I think you'll like it."

"That's great. I can't wait to hear it." He could almost see her smile and knew that they'd weathered an early storm. There were bound to be others, but Ash felt confident they'd get through them together.

"Be here by nine and I'll have the demo ready."

"You already made a demo?"

"Just a rough cut. We'll change out my vocals for yours, and then get back to finishing your grandmother's song."

"About that…" Excitement changed to indecision. "I don't think that one should go on the album."

Ash disagreed, but they were early enough in the process that every song was still a maybe. "Let's just get as many songs together as we can and worry about the final track list later."

"I can live with that."

Leaning his bottom on the counter edge, he noticed Brutus

waiting patiently at the end of the island. "I'll let you go then. Brutus is sitting here waiting for a treat."

"I thought he wasn't your dog."

"He isn't, but I'm a sucker so he has a treat jar on my counter."

Her husky laugh brought back old memories. "Why don't you just admit that he's your dog?"

Ash closed the dishwasher and reached for the clear jar in the far corner of the counter. He'd moved it there after Brutus figured out how to reach it in its previous location. "Because Nancy would argue differently since she's the one who rescued him two years ago and pays all his vet bills."

"Sounds like shared custody to me." Ash heard a beep, and Jesse said, "I need to take this other call. I'll see you in the morning."

He resisted asking if the call was from Dimitri. *No more crossing that line.* "I'll be ready."

"And, Ash? Thank you."

A sigh left his lungs as the tension eased from his shoulders. "No problem."

She bid him good night, and Ash did the same before ending the call and setting the phone on the counter. Reaching into the jar for one of Brutus's treats, he said, "That was a close one, big guy. Too close."

The canine swiped the treat from his fingers, and Ash watched him prance off down the hall. A second later, he heard the swoosh of the dog door and smiled. Shared custody. The phrase could make an interesting song title.

Filing through melodies in his mind, Ash strolled back to the studio to play with the idea.

* * *

Usually a night owl, Jesse found her eyelids drooping well before midnight. The emotional roller coaster of the day had left her feeling as if she'd run a marathon. With a yawn, she dropped her toothbrush into the cup and headed for bed, too tired to be upset that Ryan hadn't called after the show. She'd hoped the call that beeped in on her chat with Ash was him, but no such luck. Instead she'd gotten a robocall for a survey and hung up at the start of the pitch.

Jesse wasn't sure how she felt about her boyfriend in that moment. Crawling into bed, she hugged his pillow against her chest and felt guilty for second-guessing him. Throughout the drive home from meeting Silas, she'd considered their relationship and why she was still in it. *Was* she fooling herself? Or was she letting Ash's opinion cloud her judgment?

Yes, Ryan had a bad reputation, but wasn't that the same thing Jesse was fighting against? People believing what they heard about her when they didn't even know her? Granted, parts of Ryan's reputation had been earned, but people could change. When they found the right person, *everything* changed.

That's how life had been for Jesse. Throughout her nearly three decades, everyone who was supposed to care about her either ignored her or walked away. Her parents had reminded her often enough that she'd been an oops they never wanted, and even Ash had left her behind. Knowing now why he'd done it didn't change the hurt she'd lived with for all those years.

A year after Tommy's death, Jesse had been convinced that no one would ever love her. Not until Ryan had she even considered the possibility.

He'd been there before the Daisies took off, stuck with her through the good *and* the bad times that followed, and had never wavered in supporting her dreams. *That* was the real Ryan. The one no one else got to see.

With a sigh, Jesse made sure the alarm was set on her phone before switching off the bedside lamp and tugging the blankets up close around her neck. She drifted off to sleep, but what could have been minutes or hours later, awoke when a loud thud sounded from somewhere in the house.

Eyes half open, she stayed still, waiting for the sound to come again. When there was nothing but silence, she assumed she'd been dreaming and closed her eyes once more, but a crash from the kitchen made her bolt upright.

Wide awake now, she debated what to do. Lying there waiting to be murdered in her bed didn't hold much appeal. Jesse's mind raced as she considered what she could use as a weapon against an intruder. No doubt the idiot would best her in size, but she had the element of surprise on her side and that gave her an edge.

Remembering the baseball bat in the closet, she slowly left the bed and crawled across the floor, careful not to make a sound. Sliding the door on the track, she felt around until cold aluminum brushed her fingers. Armed and annoyed enough to be dangerous, she hovered near the bedroom door, listening. The house wasn't huge, and she needed to figure out where the interloper was in order to sneak up on him.

On high alert, she heard a click that sounded like the refrigerator door. Who broke into a house to raid the refrigerator? That was all she needed. Some dude high out of his mind looking for snacks and not realizing he'd wandered into the wrong house.

If that was the case, she had no intention of bashing the guy's head in, but that didn't mean she'd put the bat down either. Tiptoeing down the hall, a voice in her head said this is how the too-stupid-to-live chicks died in horror movies. Somehow, the absence of eerie music made the situation less scary. If only real life came with a soundtrack, then she'd know what lingered in the darkness.

Another noise came from the kitchen, this one followed by a muffled curse. Maybe the jackass had cut himself. Good. He deserved whatever he got for invading someone else's space.

When Jesse was halfway down the hall, heavy footsteps echoed through the living room, and she realized the intruder was coming her way. Adrenaline kept the panic at bay, and she raised the bat high to defend herself, prepared to do as much damage as necessary to save her own ass.

The steps grew louder, and a dark figure appeared, silhouetted by the light from the microwave clock behind him. Jesse's grip tightened on the bat as she reared back, ready to let fly. Heart racing, she waited until the man was close enough for her not to miss and as she started to swing, the prowler flipped on the hall light.

Momentum carried her forward, and a leather clad arm shot up to catch the bat before it connected with his skull. Chest heaving, Jesse froze as her mind struggled to process what she was seeing.

"Ryan?" she breathed, fear quickly transforming into anger. "What the hell are you doing here?"

THIRTEEN

"You nearly killed me!" Ryan slurred, and the scent of liquor hit Jesse in the face.

Blood boiling, she tugged the bat from his grasp and waved it in the air between them. "You scared the shit out of me sneaking around like that. How was I supposed to know that was you making all that noise in the kitchen?"

He took a step back and leaned against the wall. "Well, who else would it be?"

His inability to stand without assistance sent her over the edge. "You're supposed to be in Charlotte right now, remember?" Jesse stormed past him to see the clock in the kitchen. "It's nearly two in the damn morning. What are you doing here, and why are you freaking drunk?"

"I couldn't stop thinking about you and Shepherd. The minute the show ended, I left for the airport and caught the last flight out." Pressing his shoulders to the wall, he swiped a hand across his nose. "I had a couple drinks on the plane to take the edge off."

Jesse fought the temptation to use the weapon in her hand. To think, she'd considered his reaction on the phone as a positive sign of how much he cared about her. This ridiculous encounter eliminated any romantic notions she had about jealous men.

"You need a shower and some coffee." When he'd said he left right after the show, he wasn't exaggerating. She could smell the sweat from halfway down the hall and felt sorry for whoever had had to sit next to him on the flight.

"Come on, baby. Aren't you happy to see me?" He attempted to saunter toward her and failed miserably.

She caught him before he could take a nosedive and swung him into the hall bath. Dropping him onto the toilet, Jesse propped the bat behind the commode and reached over him to turn on the water. Ryan wrapped his arms around her waist.

"I missed you, baby. Why don't you get in the shower with me."

Disengaging his arms, she adjusted the water temperature to be cool enough to begin the sobering process. "You're on your own, lover boy. I'll throw some clothes in and have the coffee ready when you get out. Try not to drown yourself."

She didn't truly wish him harm, but Jesse wasn't feeling all that charitable either. He'd shaved a good five years off of her life and had yet to offer a better explanation for his unexpected return.

"I told you I'd come home so we could celebrate. Why aren't you happier to see me?"

Jesse helped him out of the leather jacket and tossed it over her arm before retrieving a towel from the shelves behind the door. "Maybe I'll be happier when my heart rate returns to normal and you don't smell like a drunk sweat sock."

Ryan reached for her again. "Come on, now, baby. Don't be so grouchy. I came all this way to be with my girl."

Ruffling his hair, she stared into his earnest, bloodshot eyes. "Your girl is going to make coffee while you clean yourself up." She dropped a kiss on his forehead. "Then we can talk about this sudden jealous streak of yours."

Strong arms pulled her close, and he pressed his forehead

against her sternum. "I kept picturing you with someone else, and I hated it." Ryan looked up, and the distress in his gaze tugged at her heart. "Promise you won't leave me."

This. This was the Ryan that others never saw.

"I'm not going anywhere except to the kitchen. Take your shower and maybe I'll have more than a cup of coffee waiting when you get out."

A sexy grin curled his lips, and he squeezed her bottom. "I'll be out in five."

Jesse pulled away. "Don't forget to brush your teeth. You know I can't stand the taste of rum."

"Anything for you, baby."

He was pulling his shirt over his head as she left the room and shuffled toward the kitchen. As she draped the leather jacket over a chair, a ding sounded from the pocket, and Jesse dug for his phone. Checking the screen, she found a notification from someone identified only as Boston. She entered his password and touched the messages icon to read the text.

I can't wait to see you tomorrow night. It's been too long, baby. I've bought some new toys and the nightstand is stocked with Magnums for my big boy.

Jesse stared at the phone as the words penetrated her brain. Attempts to decipher the message as something innocent and easily explained were pointless. She'd unconsciously asked the universe for absolute proof and here it was.

It didn't get more absolute than this.

As if wanting to torture herself, Jesse exited the text to search for others and found an assortment of similar sentiments, all from individuals identified solely by city names. In addition to Boston, there was Buffalo, Tallahassee, Denver, and Albuquerque. All anticipating an impending visit, and a few expressing their appreciation for services rendered.

Still holding the phone, Jesse dropped into a kitchen chair and kept scrolling. Seconds later, the phone buzzed in her hand

and the name Charlotte popped up on the screen. With a white heat spreading through her chest, she checked the message.

Where did you go? I waited by the bus for an hour, but the guys said you left. What the hell, Ryan? I thought we had a date.

Jesse threw the phone across the room, furious with herself as much as with Ryan. Storming into the bedroom, she ripped off her nightgown to pull on a pair of jeans and a Georgia Bulldogs sweatshirt. Slamming her bare feet into her boots, she grabbed a tote from the closet and stuffed it with a couple of days' worth of clothes. Tossing in her hairbrush and some ponytail holders, she grabbed her phone from the nightstand before rushing back down the hall. Without shedding a tear, she snagged her keys off the hook on the wall and left the house.

* * *

Unable to sleep, Ash threw his legs over the side of the bed and sat up. He checked the time on his phone. Two thirty in the morning. An hour he didn't see often. Most musicians tended to be the stereotypical night owls, but not Ash. He'd hated playing bars because his body clock rarely let him sleep past 7 AM no matter what time his head hit the pillow.

Playing in front of crowds had been another issue. His move to town had not been about finding stardom or fame. He'd simply wanted to write music. Finding success as a songwriter had allowed him to do what he loved on a regular schedule without spending his nights in crowded honkytonks.

Thirsty, he plodded to the kitchen, filled a glass from the dispenser on the fridge door, and made his way back to bed. But instead of turning left, he turned right and stepped into the studio. If he wasn't going to sleep, he could do something more productive than stare at the walls. Leaving the water on a table by the door, he crossed to the desk and turned on a monitor. The song he'd been working on—Jesse's song—was still on the screen, but a notification along the bottom bar caught his attention.

A couple clicks and an email from Millie Hopewell popped up with the subject line *Meeting scheduled.* Ash steeled himself as he scrolled down to the message.

Dear Ash,

The producers of A Nashville Country Christmas called today and have requested a meeting on Friday morning. As I'm sure you'll agree, it's important that we work out the details quickly so that the children have plenty of time to rehearse.

The meeting is scheduled for ten o'clock Friday morning, and I've included the address below. I apologize for the short notice, but I do hope you can attend. I don't want to tell the children about this until everything has been finalized, so hopefully we can tell them together on Saturday morning.

With great excitement!

Millie Hopewell

Ash sighed as he read the email again. Other than working with Jesse, there was no reason he couldn't make the meeting. He doubted it would last more than an hour, and with luck, they'd be far enough along by then to be ready for Monday.

Millie's insistence that Ash accompany the kids on stage was his only real issue. He wasn't bashful so much as preferred to stay behind the scenes. The choir was good enough to run without his direction. Zoe, the oldest of the group, could take the lead and handle any direction needed on stage. The musicians were a different story. They were good, but not ready to fly on their own. Another sigh escaped as Ash clicked to reply. He let Millie know he would attend the meeting and looked forward to sharing the good news on Saturday.

Resigned to his fate, he shut down the monitor, grabbed his water on the way out, and went back to bed.

* * *

Jesse lingered in her Jeep, staring at Ingrid's house through a wall of rain. Waking her friends in the middle of the night wasn't her favorite idea, but she hadn't been sure where else to go. She could have checked into a hotel, but she didn't want to be alone. Not tonight. She needed someone to assure her that this wasn't all her fault for being an ignorant coward and not leaving Ryan a long time ago. Despite Dana's feelings about Jesse's significant other—make that *former* significant other—she wasn't likely to throw an I-told-you-so around.

Not for at least a week, Jesse hoped.

Cursing herself for not grabbing a jacket on her way out of the house, she snatched the canvas bag from the passenger seat and made a break for the front door. Thank heaven the house had a covered porch because, in this downpour, Jesse would be soaked through by the time anyone answered the door. She rang the bell and waited, rubbing her arms against the cold. The sweatshirt was proving inadequate, and the old boots were doing little to keep her bare toes warm.

Shivering, she listened for a sound inside but heard nothing. She rang the bell again, planning an apology speech in her mind for dragging them out of bed. Hopefully, Dana would answer, and Ingrid would sleep through the disturbance without a clue.

The second ring went unanswered, and Jesse pondered her options. Withdrawing her phone, she opened her messages app to text her bass player and spotted the earlier message she'd forgotten about. Dana and Ingrid had gone out of town to visit the homeowner's ailing sister in Atlanta.

"Shoot," Jesse muttered. *What now?*

Driving to Reggie's house was out of the question. Waking up adults at nearly three in the morning was one thing. Waking up Reggie's twins was another. That left Silas, who slept like the dead and lived well over an hour from Hendersonville on the south side of Nashville. Defeated, Jesse plopped down on the wooden glider and fought back tears. Despite her determination *not* to cry over Ryan Dimitri and his philandering ways, her cheeks remained damp from more than the rain.

Bracing herself, she raced back to the Jeep as the wind howled around her. Forehead on the steering wheel, the last threads of control snapped, and all the anger and hurt poured out.

"Why?!" Jesse screamed, rearing back to smack a hand against the wheel. *Why had she been such an idiot? And why couldn't Ryan be faithful for once in his daggone life?*

Then again, why had Jesse ever believed he *would* be faithful? She'd known his history. The better question was, why had she floated in this pathetic delusion for so long? Sobs racked her body until her sides hurt, and the harder she struggled for control, the harder she cried. Jesse forced herself to take deep breaths—in and out—until her breathing steadied.

Watching the rain slide down the windshield, she considered her options. Sleeping in her Jeep held little appeal, and the last thing she needed was for a neighbor to call the police on the interloper trespassing in Ingrid's driveway. The clock on the dash read three thirty. Jesse could be at Silas's place before five, if the rain didn't slow her down too much on the interstate. But she really didn't want to make that drive.

There was only one other place she could go. One other person who cared enough—or had at one time—to let her in out of the rain.

Desperate times called for desperate measures, so Jesse put the Jeep in reverse to make the late-night journey back to the city.

FOURTEEN

STILL MOSTLY ASLEEP, ASH TRIED TO FIGURE OUT WHERE THE booming was coming from. At first, he thought it was thunder, so he rolled over and put a pillow over his head. But then the pounding came in a steady beat, more like someone driving a nail into a wall. Must have been a neighbor hanging pictures. The noise continued, and Ash opened one eye, remembering that he didn't live in an apartment anymore so anyone driving nails into walls was doing so inside his house.

Sitting up, he blinked several times and listened for the source of whatever had interrupted his sleep. Only silence came. With a sigh, he dropped back to the pillow only to be jerked upright when the pounding resumed. Too sleepy to remember he wasn't wearing anything but boxer shorts, Ash shuffled through the house, stubbed his toe on the corner of the kitchen island, and cursed his way across the living room. Seconds before he reached the doorknob, lightning lit up the room, and a scream echoed from his porch.

Wide awake now, Ash yanked the door open to find a soaked and frightened Jesse shivering in the darkness.

"What the…"

Shoving wet hair out of her face, she said, "I didn't have any place else to go."

The quiver in her voice indicated she'd been crying, and Ash went on high alert. "Are you okay?"

Jesse shook her head and as the sky lit up again, she leaped into his arms. Shifting them both out of the way, he closed the door before hugging her tight against him. She was wet and cold and soaking his chest, but he didn't care. He was just relieved to be holding her again. Questions raced through his mind, but asking them could wait. A puddle formed at his feet and even as Jesse's sobbing eased, she continued to shiver.

Pulling away, he gently pressed on her shoulders until she released her hold. Her cheeks were streaked with a combination of rain and tears; her hair was flattened against her head, and her teeth were chattering.

"We need to get you dried off."

Jesse sniffled and brushed at her cheeks. "I'm sorry for waking you."

Ash ignored her needless apology and bolted into action. "Wait here and I'll get some towels."

He used the remote to turn on the gas fireplace, and then rushed down the hall to his room. After pulling on a T-shirt and sweats, he gathered several towels from the closet in his bathroom before returning to Jesse. There were only two circumstances that might have landed her at his door in tears. Either something happened to one of her parents, or Dimitri had done something stupid. Ash hoped for the second only because Jesse's family didn't deserve another tragedy.

As he rounded the corner, he found her still shivering in the same spot where he'd left her and was struck by the devastation in her puffy eyes. She'd been crying for a while.

"Here," he said, handing her one of the towels. "Dry your hair and come closer to the fire."

Sniffling, she did as ordered, squeezing water from her drenched curls as she shuffled toward the fireplace. Ash noticed her fingertips were blue, and there wasn't a dry thread on the Georgia sweatshirt.

"We need to get you out of those clothes."

Blue eyes went wide. "I left my bag in the Jeep."

Tossing the other towels onto the couch, he said, "I'll get it." Ash opened the door to a deluge of water falling sideways. In a few seconds, they would both be drenched, but she needed her things. He'd set one bare foot over the threshold when Jesse stopped him.

"Wait!" she yelled. "Don't do it. There's no sense in both of us being soaked."

"You can't stay in those wet clothes."

Jesse shook her head. "If I stay close to the fire, they should be dry in a little while. I'll be okay until morning." She dropped to her knees in front of the hearth and continued to towel the water out of her hair.

If he couldn't get her things from the car, Ash would have to provide his own. "I'll be right back," he said before making another quick trip to his room. Upon returning, he joined her at the fireplace. "I don't have much that won't swallow you up, but here are a couple options." He set a small pile of clothes beside her. "There are clean towels in the guest bath attached to the back bedroom. You'll feel better after a warm shower, and then we can talk."

It would be up to Jesse how much to tell him. Relief softened her features, and her eyes misted again. "I *am* really cold."

Ash extended a hand to help her up, and the moment her palm touched his, time fell away. His sweet Jesse stood before him, eyes wide, nose red, and lips parted. Her hand remained in his, and his body warmed from more than the fire.

"Thank you," she said, her voice barely a whisper. "I wasn't sure if you'd let me in."

How could she ever doubt him?

"I will always let you in, Jesse." Not trusting what he might do next, Ash nudged her toward the hall. "We'll talk when you come back."

Lashes lowered, she stepped away, padding softly toward the hall. Before turning the corner, she cast him one last glance over her shoulder, and then disappeared out of sight.

Expelling the breath he hadn't been aware of holding, he stared into the fire as the warmth from Jesse's touch still lingered on his skin. Recalling the look in her eyes, his mind wandered into dangerous territory. Territory he had no business getting near. Shaking the thoughts away, he crossed to the kitchen to put a pan of water on the stove. Jesse was going to need something hot to drink and a shoulder to cry on. Ash would provide both, and nothing more.

* * *

The hot shower was blissful, the towels warm and fluffy, and the clothes smelled like the man who owned them. The scent hurled Jesse back in time to high school dances and midnight kisses on her parents' front porch. If only her life was still that simple.

Forcing herself to stay in the present, she rolled the dark-gray sleeves of the crew neck several times so they wouldn't dangle over her hands. If the pants hadn't come with a drawstring, even her generous hips wouldn't have been enough to hold them up. The legs had taken some rolling as well to keep her from tripping when she walked.

Looking in the mirror, Jesse longed for her brush and was all too aware that vanity was the cause. It wasn't as if she hadn't burst into the house looking like a drowned rat. Yet she couldn't suppress the instinct to make herself presentable for Ash. Coming here with her defenses down had been a dangerous idea, but there was no going back now. If only the little voice in the back of her mind would stop whispering that this was where she should have been all along.

"No," she snapped to the wistful girl in the mirror. That path had been obliterated long ago, and if this night had taught her anything, it was that she needed to work out her current mess before stepping into another.

After running her hands through her hair as best she could, Jesse wrapped a towel around her shoulders to keep the shirt dry and exited the bedroom. She wasn't looking forward to sharing the details of her evening, but after waking Ash in the middle of the night, she owed him an explanation. Reaching the kitchen, she found him stirring something in a dark mug.

"What is that?" she asked, coming up behind him and peeking around his arm. "You're making hot chocolate?"

He set the spoon in the sink before sliding the mug her way. "I thought you might want some."

The gesture weakened her resolve, and Jesse had to force herself to take the drink and put some distance between them. Blowing on the chocolate concoction, she settled on the end of the couch closest to the fire and curled her legs beneath her, steeling herself for the conversation ahead.

Ash wasted no time after joining her. "What happened tonight, Jesse?"

Eyes on her drink she said, "Ryan surprised me by flying home after their show in Charlotte."

"Okay."

She cleared her throat and gave the real answer. "He walked in drunk and said he couldn't stand the thought of me being with someone else. I put him in the shower, and then went to the kitchen to make some coffee. That's when his phone chimed." Grateful for Ash's silence, she took a steadying breath and pressed on. "The text was from a contact named Boston. That's where they play tomorrow night. The woman—at least I assume it's a woman—wanted him to know that she's looking forward to seeing him and that she'd stocked up on condoms for the visit."

Ash growled a profanity but didn't interrupt.

"I should have put the phone down, but I couldn't help

myself. I looked through the rest of his messages, and there was more of the same. He literally has a girl in every city." Anger mounting, she blurted out the rest. "He didn't even bother to use their names. Denver. Cleveland. Tallahassee. That's how he tracks them in his phone. How disgusting is that?"

"I'm sorry you had to find out this way."

"I know I shouldn't care about any of them," Jesse added, "but it's so . . . insulting. He didn't even have the decency to use their names. Like. . . they aren't even people to him."

She'd never been so ashamed in her life. Jesse had given her heart to a man who used women, and then tucked them away until his next pass through town. Setting her mug on the coffee table, she bolted off the couch, too infuriated to sit still.

"I knew," she growled, no longer able to hide behind denial. "I knew, and I still stayed. I was *so desperate* for someone to love me that I ignored what was right in front of my nose. I *let* this happen."

"Whoa." Ash came to his feet. "You aren't responsible for his mistakes. He made the choice to cheat, Jesse. That's on him."

"*But I knew!*" she cried. "*You* knew. *Everyone* knew, and I looked the other way because I had convinced myself that things would be different with me. Loving me was going to keep him faithful." A bitter laugh nearly choked her. "I was never going to be enough to change him. I've never been enough for anyone."

Ash gripped her upper arms, his face close to hers. "Don't say that ever again. You're more than any man deserves, and just because Ryan Dimitri couldn't see that doesn't mean it isn't true."

Jesse shook her head, unconvinced. "But it isn't just Ryan. It's my parents. It's my friends." She crumbled against his chest, her forehead pressed to his sternum. "It was you."

Ash pulled her in and kissed the top of her head. "I'm so sorry. I swear I never wanted to leave you."

She gripped his shirt as the tears returned. "But you did. Everyone does. What is *wrong* with me?"

He pressed her back far enough to tip her chin up, forcing her to meet his gaze. "Nothing, Jesse. Absolutely nothing."

Hazel eyes held hers, and she wanted to believe him. "I wish you were right."

"I *am* right." Ash brushed a curl off her forehead. "I messed up. Dimitri messed up. But like I said, that's on us. You're everything, Jesse. Beautiful, smart, kind, talented. I was lucky to love you once. Damn lucky."

Ash had always seen more in Jesse than she'd seen in herself. Maybe, if he'd stayed in her life, things would be different.

She would be different.

"I was lucky, too."

Her eyes dropped to his mouth, and Jesse brushed his lips with her thumb. When his body tensed, her heart rate doubled. She caressed his scruff-covered jawline, the whiskers sharp against her hand, and she wondered how they would feel pressed to other parts of her.

"Jesse," he murmured. "What are you doing?"

Excellent question, but answering would require thinking, and she didn't want to think right now. She wanted to feel.

"You're so beautiful," she whispered.

Stepping away from her, Ash crossed his arms. "You need some sleep."

"Sleep?" Sleep was *not* what she needed.

"Yes, sleep. The sun will be up soon."

Jesse didn't see what the sun had to do with anything. "But—"

"If we do this, it can't be because some guy just broke your heart." Ash put more distance between them. "Good night, Jesse."

His words penetrated her tired mind. *If we do this…*

She looked away, embarrassed and exhausted. "Good night, Ash."

Dragging the towel from her shoulders, she hugged it against her chest and shuffled toward the hall with her head bent low.

"Jesse," Ash called, and she turned his way. "Don't think I don't want to. I just can't be something you regret. Not again."

Painfully aware of how much she'd lost all those years ago, she nodded and hurried away before he could see the tears.

* * *

Ash dropped onto the couch, his body buzzing like a live wire. What the hell had just happened?

Jesse had just suggested they go to bed—together—and Ash sent her off alone. Not that he regretted the decision, but his body didn't seem to get the rationale.

That was the odd thing about leaving someone the way he had with Jesse ten years ago. You don't know the last time you have sex that it's the last time you'll have sex with that person. He and Jesse had managed to sneak off just two nights before the accident. For years, he'd dreamed of that night, and hoped against hope that he'd hold her again someday. But eventually, Ash had accepted that she was out of his life for good.

Now she wasn't and that was setting off all sorts of conflicting signals.

Taking her up on her offer would have been so easy. Hell, even now he was ready to race down the hall and provide whatever she needed. But it couldn't be like this. Not because some asshole she'd been in love with—a circumstance that set his teeth on edge—had been stupid enough to lose her. Ash couldn't blame her for seeking solace any way she could get it, but he wasn't interested in being a consolation lay. Not with Jesse.

Leaning forward, he tapped the table beside the still-full mug. The last time they were together, they'd been kids. Ten years apart meant they didn't even know each other anymore. From their first meeting at the label office, Ash had noticed the differences. She still had the spunk, but the confidence was shot. The talent was there, but she had no idea how to harness the gifts she'd been given. And Jesse still had the smile that turned him inside out, but now it rarely reached her eyes.

Ash's first job was to correct the first two, and if he managed that, the third would surely fall into place. After turning off the fireplace, he carried the mug into the kitchen and lamented the one issue he was powerless to fix.

It's even my parents.

At one point in his life, Ash had seen Vince and Enid Rheingold as the most generous people he'd ever met. They'd opened their home and their hearts to a lonely little boy that their nine-year-old son had dragged home from school like a lost puppy. He realized now that their love for Tommy had been the only reason they'd let him in at all. And even at such a young age, Ash had noticed the difference in how they'd treated their children. Their world revolved around Tommy, and Jesse had been an afterthought, if thought of at all.

Losing Tommy should have compelled them to focus their energy on the child that remained, if for no other reason than the fear of losing her, too.

That had clearly not been the case, and now their beautiful, talented daughter saw herself as less than. Unworthy of being loved. The concept enraged him, and Ash cursed into the void, careful to keep his voice down. Glancing out the front window, he watched the clouds turn a muted pink as the sun began its ascent. A thick haze hovered in the air, and he noticed the rain had stopped.

Seizing the opportunity, he hurried out to Jesse's Jeep barefooted and returned with the large duffel off the passenger seat. She would likely sleep several more hours, but he wanted her to have her things when she woke. After a quiet trek down the hall, he listened to hear if she was moving around, but caught only the sound of a soft snore. At least one of them was getting some rest.

Leaving the bag just inside the bedroom, he crossed to his own and dropped onto the bed. Floating between arousal and anger, Ash knew he couldn't act on the first, but he wouldn't rule out doing something about the second. Like kicking the shit out of Ryan Dimitri. He wouldn't—for now—but he'd keep the option on the table.

Head on the pillow, he listened to the birds chirping outside and closed his eyes. Tomorrow, they would get the rest of her things and figure out a temporary living arrangement. She was welcome to stay at his place as long as she needed, but something told him that once Jesse had some sleep, staying with Ash would not be at the top of her list.

Maybe, if he played his cards right, that would eventually change.

FIFTEEN

Tuesday dawned damp and dreary after a major storm had passed through during the night. Clay was still tense from the call the day before. Joanna's threat left him feeling as if she'd pulled the pin on a grenade, and now he awaited the explosion that was sure to follow. At the same time, she might do nothing at all. Once she'd recovered from her snit, Joanna could have booked a pedicure and considered another tactic to lure Clay back to her bed.

At this point, who knew what the woman would do?

What Clay *did* know was that he had an interview to conduct. The candidate's resume put her at the top of his list for the A&R position, and he hoped she wouldn't disappoint. The information he'd been able to gather said she possessed a knack for recognizing talent, and a sixth sense about how to maximize their potential. Two required traits for the person who would play a key role in growing his label.

As he reviewed his notes, the phone on his desk buzzed. "Ms. Garcia has arrived," Belinda said through the speaker. "Are you ready for her?"

Clay picked up the receiver. "Yes, bring her back, please."

Seconds later, a knock sounded at his door. Belinda opened it and said, "I have Ms. Garcia."

Circling the desk, Clay welcomed the interviewee, noting that she appeared younger than he'd expected. Her references gave the impression she'd been active around town for a couple of decades, yet she hardly looked old enough to be out of her twenties.

"Thank you for coming in today," he said, offering his hand.

The woman offered her own and presented a firm shake. "Thank you for having me."

He motioned for her to have a seat as the receptionist closed the door behind her. "Did Belinda offer you something to drink?"

Ms. Garcia nodded. "Yes, but I'm fine, thank you. So you're looking for an A&R director?"

Right to the point. Clay liked her already. "That's right. According to your resume, you started in radio and have worked as a talent scout for two small labels in town."

"Technically, I started in my grandmother's Tejano club in San Antonio. By the time I was fifteen, I was working the booking office and deciding who would play and who wouldn't. I didn't move to radio until I was nineteen, but I list that first since the club work was in a more unofficial capacity."

"In other words, you weren't legally old enough to work in that environment," Clay surmised.

"Correct. But the experience contributed to what I do today."

Clay leaned back, intrigued. "Which is?"

Ms. Garcia held his gaze. "I find stars. I've had an ear for a hit song since I was young—well before I started running the booking office—and I've put that talent to work tracking down artists who have what it takes to be successful. Those who possess the inexplicable quality that few are born with and even fewer learn to exploit. Once I find them, I give them the tools and support necessary for them to break out and be successful."

She'd just reiterated every duty he and Naomi had listed on

the director job description the week before. The one they *hadn't* posted online. Emily Garcia knew her stuff, and Clay had every confidence she could back up her claims. But he had to be sure.

"Who have you discovered during your time in Nashville?"

Dark-red lips pursed. "I've had three relative success stories, but all have been limited by the resources afforded through my employers. Brandon Thompson scored a top fifty hit before the marketing budget ran out. Monica Whitcomb penned and recorded a song that, unbeknownst to myself and the label, she'd also given to another artist, who then recorded and took the song to number four the week before Ms. Whitcomb's version was scheduled for release. The label proceeded to pull the plug on the artist's deal."

When she stopped there, Clay asked, "And the third?"

"A band," she replied, her voice clipped. "They showed great potential, but the lead singer couldn't set his ego aside long enough to take advantage of my expertise. That deal fell through as well, and now I'm in search of a more suitable position with a label who is committed to the artists they sign. One willing to dedicate the resources necessary to see those artists not only succeed but thrive in such a competitive market."

So she'd actually had three failed attempts at signing new artists and had been relieved of her duties. Ms. Garcia talked a good game, but the track record didn't back up the bravado. Enthusiasm waning, Clay asked one more question. "What do you think of Jesse Gold?"

Dark brows drew together. "Of the Honkytonk Daisies? Haven't you already signed her?"

"I have. But I'd still like to hear what you think of her. Would you have recommended I sign her?"

Ms. Garcia tilted her head in contemplation. "Having never met her, I can only base my assessment on what I know of the duet, and what I've heard since the pair parted ways. I know she co-wrote many of the songs on the Honkytonk Daisies album, which had a moderate level of success. She has a good voice and a natural stage presence, two important skills in any performer. She also has a reputation for being difficult, though I've never heard this firsthand from anyone who has actually worked with her, so I'd be interested in testing the assertion." Crossing her arms, she added, "Women are inordinately accused of being difficult as compared to men, especially in this industry, so I would have suggested setting a meeting to see if Ms. Gold has the composure and wherewithal to pursue a solo career."

A good answer and one that put Clay squarely on the fence. Ms. Garcia's history was questionable at best, but she managed to employ both common sense practicality and open-minded intuition in making a determination about Jesse. In doing so, she'd come to the same conclusion Clay had via the same thought process. Except for the fact that he'd actually met Jesse and been able to confirm his gut feeling that she would prove to be worth the investment.

"I like your approach." Time to see if she'd done her homework. "How much do you know about Shooting Stars?"

Without hesitation, she said, "I know it's your second label after founding and running Foxfire Records with Tony Rossi for nearly two decades. You operate with a small but capable staff, have achieved impressive success with the first two artists signed—Dylan Monroe and Chance Colburn—and because of those two choices, I know you're willing to take calculated risks when it comes to choosing talent."

Ms. Garcia balanced on the edge of her seat. "I would also like to think that you apply those same tactics when adding new members to the staff. I'm well aware of my track record, Mr. Benedict, but I also know that I *am* the person for this job. If you'll give me the same chance you've afforded your artists, you won't regret it."

She'd beat him to the "Why should I hire you?" punch, and she made a valiant argument in the process. All of his artists so far *had* been calculated risks, and two of the three had paid off.

The risk with Ms. Garcia would not be as high since Clay would still be making the final call on who was signed.

He appreciated her honesty and confidence in her own abilities, but there were two candidates yet to be interviewed and if either had a better track record, Ms. Garcia's *search for a more suitable position* would continue.

Clay rose to his feet, buttoning his suit coat as he went. "Thank you. I appreciate you coming in today, and you'll be hearing from us soon."

Ignoring the obvious dismissal, she stood and stepped closer to the desk. "I know what it looks like, Mr. Benedict, but the acts I chose I would choose again today without hesitation. Most of them, anyway. I still believe that they have what it takes, but sadly, I cannot say the same for the labels with whom I've chosen to work. When I saw this opportunity, I knew that *this* is where I need to be. I hope you'll come to believe that as well."

The words implied a desperation not reflected in the woman's eyes. There Clay saw unflinching determination, a trait he recognized well. Without the same belief in himself, he wouldn't be where he was today.

"You've pled a solid case, and I can assure you that I haven't ruled you out. But there are other candidates vying for the position, and no decision will be made until all interviews have been conducted."

Expression tight, she nodded. "I understand. Thank you again for this opportunity."

Though nothing in her demeanor changed, Clay sensed a thread of resignation as she crossed to the door. "Ms. Garcia," he said, and waited for her to turn his way. "You've set a high bar for the other candidates. They'll need stellar credentials in order to outpace you for the position."

Intelligent brown eyes held his gaze. "Credentials aren't everything, Mr. Benedict, and instinct can't be gleaned from a resume. I hope you'll remember that."

The response put a smile on his face. "Duly noted."

Shoulders high, she left the office, and Clay remained standing behind his desk. Regardless of what Emily Garcia had achieved thus far, he had a sneaking suspicion that she would one day run this town. If that was the case, she would need a worthy mentor. He knew immediately he wanted that role.

Returning to his seat, he pressed the intercom button on the desk phone. When Belinda picked up, he said, "Cancel the other interviews, please. A decision has been made."

* * *

Drifting to consciousness, Jesse stretched her arms above her head and smacked her knuckles on a hard surface. Jerking them back down, she gripped the unfamiliar blankets as her eyes scanned the dimly lit room. Nothing looked familiar.

Fending off panic, she brushed the hair from her face. Dark curtains blocked the sun, making it difficult to tell what time it was. Sitting up, Jesse spotted her bag near the door, and reality came rushing back.

Ryan's drunken homecoming.

Finding the text messages.

Showing up at Ash's door in a rain storm.

And then another memory hit, and she pressed fleece-covered hands to her warming cheeks. Jesse had tried to seduce Ash. Part of her was relieved that he'd turned her down, while another felt insulted. Once upon a time, they'd created many elaborate ways to sneak off together. Now he'd had no trouble patting her on the head and sending her down the hall like some child with a silly crush.

Jesse pulled the covers over her head, chanting, "Stupid, stupid, stupid."

Eyes shut tight, she breathed through the ache in her chest, suffocating in mounting layers of humiliation. How had her life become such a colossal mess? On top of having to collect her meager possessions from Ryan's house, there was the minor problem of where the heck to put them.

She was, for all intents and purposes, homeless.

Another moment of panic set in. Would Ryan still be there? She didn't dare call him. That was out of the question. He'd presumably catch a flight to Boston at some point, but would he be gone by now? Desperate to know the time, she looked around for a clock and didn't see one.

Climbing from the bed, she tiptoed across the room to rummage through her bag for her phone, which was dead. Ryan had called several times as she'd searched for a place to land so she'd silenced the ringer and shoved the thing in the bag to avoid answering it. The sad truth was, Jesse didn't trust herself not to be sweet-talked into going back to him. A pathetic truth, but if she'd learned anything in the last twenty-four hours, it was that she had to stop lying to herself.

In her heart she knew that Ryan's betrayal was painful, but not surprising.

Digging deeper into the bag, she realized she'd forgotten to grab her charger. Ryan had most likely called around looking for her, and that meant several of her friends could quite possibly be freaking the heck out right now. Would he call her parents? They'd never liked him much, and she had no recollection of ever giving him their number. Why would she? Jesse rarely talked to them, and she'd long ago stopped using them as an emergency contact.

No, her parents should still be blissfully ignorant of the mess their daughter was in. A blanket text to the right contacts should put everyone else's fears to rest, but the phone had to be charged for her to do that. Her only option was to use the car charger in the Jeep, but that would require leaving the room. Which would mean facing Ash. Gut turning at the prospect, she carried the bag into the bathroom. If she was going to suffer the indignity of her actions, Jesse would not do so looking like the star of a *Honey, I Shrunk The Kids* reboot.

Another quick search of the bag revealed one more essential item she'd forgotten—a toothbrush. Thankfully, she found a travel-size bottle of mouthwash under the sink and gave her teeth a good rinse. She quickly changed into her own clothes, and then looked in the mirror.

"Good morning, Medusa."

This was why Jesse never went to bed with wet hair. Returning to the bag for the hairbrush she'd gratefully remembered, she tamed her fiery locks into a ponytail as best she could while she struggled with what to say to Ash. She obviously hadn't been thinking straight and could only pray that her bumbling attempt at seduction hadn't ruined their tenuous working relationship. Despite her personal life being a complete shambles, she had no intention of letting her professional one go the same way.

Settling on a simple plan—thank him for putting her up, apologize for the intrusion, and promise to return tomorrow when she'd, hopefully, secured some temporary lodging—Jesse stepped into the hall and caught the faint sounds of a guitar coming from the studio. The melody sounded familiar, and she realized it was one of hers.

Leaving her bag in the hall, she opened the door and stepped inside to find Ash strumming away with headphones covering his ears. Eyes closed, he was lost in the song, adding a yearning tone she hadn't come close to in the original version. It was a lonesome sound, and it complemented the lyrics perfectly.

When he finished recording, Ash removed the headphones, and Jesse said, "I thought you didn't like my songs."

He spun around, clearly surprised to no longer be alone. "And I thought you were going to sleep all day. Do you feel better?"

Jesse still didn't know what time it was. "How late is it? Why didn't you wake me up?"

He set the guitar in a stand to his left. "You had a tough night and needed the sleep." Rising from his chair, he closed the distance between them, and his nearness sent butterflies flitting around in her stomach. He was the only man who had ever had that effect on her. "I'll make you something to eat."

"I'm okay," she said, stepping back at the same moment her stomach growled loudly. One more betrayal she didn't need. "I don't want to put you out any more than I already have."

With a gentle smile, he ignored her words. "You need food. Come on."

Seeing the futility in arguing, she followed him to the kitchen and took a seat on one of the island stools. Ash went to work, drawing a small frying pan and a sauce pan from a lower cupboard before retrieving a can of tomato soup and a loaf of bread from the pantry. Next, he snagged a package of cheese from the fridge.

Jesse recognized the plan immediately.

"You remember that, too," she said, unable to keep the shock from her voice. First her favorite sandwich. Now her favorite gloomy-day meal.

Ash never broke stride. "I figured you could use some comfort food. The canned stuff isn't as good as Granny's homemade, but it's the best I can do today."

With a sigh, Jesse watched him work, graceful and efficient as he whipped the meal together. No man had ever cooked for her, not even her own father. When Ash paused long enough to offer a friendly grin, a tiny voice in the back of her brain whispered *if you leave this house, you're an idiot.*

SIXTEEN

"I can't stay here," Jesse said as Ash poured the soup into the pan.

Exactly what he'd expected her to say. "You're welcome for as long as you need a place, but that's up to you."

"About last night . . ."

"You mean this morning?" he said, trying to keep things light. He knew she was likely embarrassed, and he wanted to put her at ease. "Don't worry about it."

"I don't know what I was thinking."

Ash sighed. "You were hurt and tired, that's all."

"I made a fool of myself and put you in an awkward position." Face in her hands, she mumbled, "I feel like an idiot."

Ash leaned on the island, but she kept her head down. "Jesse, come on. Look at me." The ponytail swayed as she shook her head. "You're being a little hard on yourself, don't you think?" That got her attention and she lifted just enough for him to see her eyes. "You took a big hit last night. He hurt you, and you reached out for comfort. There's no harm in that. I'm just glad it was with me."

Dark brows drew together. "Glad it was with *you*?"

He stirred the soup. "Coming here was better than ending up

in some bar looking for a one-night stand. There aren't many men who would turn down that kind of an offer from a beautiful woman."

"And yet you had no problem saying no," Jesse snapped. "For your information, I've never been desperate enough to have sex with a stranger."

At some point, he'd taken a wrong turn, but Ash had no idea where. "I never said you were desperate. You just weren't thinking straight."

"Clearly," she snorted.

Was she pissed because he'd turned her down? "Luckily, I was thinking for both of us and made sure you didn't do anything you'd regret."

Jesse left her stool and slung the heavy bag over her shoulder. "Too late." Without another word, she stormed toward the door.

"Hey! Where are you going?"

"I have to get my stuff and find a place to stay. I'll be back tomorrow."

Ash reached the door before she did and cut off her exit. "Do you really think I'd leave you to deal with this on your own?"

"You've done enough."

"Let me rephrase that," he said. "There isn't a chance in hell I'm letting you handle this alone. So sit down and eat something, and then we'll get your things. I assume there's more than what's in that bag."

She hesitated, jaw tight. "I... I don't know if he's still there. But you don't—"

"I know I don't. You said he has a show tonight. Do you think he'd skip it?"

Jesse shook her head. "No. He'll catch a flight to Boston whether he finds me or not." Her voice cracked when she mentioned the city, and he remembered what she'd said about the text messages on Dimitri's phone. Someone was waiting for him in Boston.

Saving his anger for when he found the shithead in a dark

alley, Ash took the bag from her shoulder, dropped it by the door, and nodded for her to return to the kitchen. "He'll need to catch a flight soon, if he hasn't already. We can wait until this evening to make sure he's gone."

"I guess that could work." As he returned to the kitchen, Jesse surprised him with a question out of left field. "Why did you get divorced?"

"Like I told Grimelda, Ronnie and I were better as friends. We just figured that out a little later than we should have."

"But you said that you still love her."

Ash dropped the first sandwich into the pan, and it sizzled loudly. "There's a difference between loving someone and being *in love* with them." He pulled a spatula from the utensil jar and leaned his hip on the counter. "Ronnie and I love each other, but we were never really in love."

Arms crossed on the island top, she asked, "Were we in love?"

He could only speak for himself. "I was."

Jesse stayed quiet for several seconds. "We were just kids, though."

"Plenty of high school sweethearts make it for the long haul. We could have, too."

"If things had been different," she added. "I guess we'll never know."

He wanted to argue that it wasn't too late, but Jesse clearly didn't agree. Ash slid the grilled cheese onto a plate and set it and the bowl of soup on the island in front of her. "Eat up and then I'll show you what I've done with your song."

Pulling the food closer, she nodded, and he turned back to the stove to make his own sandwich.

"Ash?" she said. "I was in love with you, too."

Keeping his back to her to hide the sudden grin, he muttered, "Good to know."

* * *

What was it about Ash that made Jesse incapable of keeping her dang mouth shut?

And where did she get off being cranky about him *not* having sex with her? The last thing Jesse needed was to fall into bed with her ex-boyfriend immediately after learning that her current boyfriend was falling into bed with enough women to field a national beauty pageant.

That was not her finest hour.

And then she'd asked about his divorce—which was none of her business—and somehow rolled right into their best-forgotten history. Not that Jesse had ever forgotten those early days of first love. Ash had been her first kiss, her first date, her first boyfriend, and her first lover. He'd seemed perfect until the day he walked away. Was that why she'd made such lousy choices since?

If she picked a guy she knew deep down wasn't a keeper, then she wouldn't be so devastated when he left her. Is that what she'd been doing? Sabotaging her own happiness by settling for the worst men she could find?

That little nugget of self-realization came as Jesse finished her soup, and then watched Ash clear the plates and load the dishwasher. Had she ever seen a man load a dishwasher before? Heck, had she ever seen a man do any household chore without her having to throw a fit or hold his hand?

No. No, she hadn't. She was officially the worst boyfriend-finder ever.

Thankfully, she managed not to share *this* revelation with Ash, but only because they'd gone to work as soon as the kitchen had been cleaned. The distraction of laying down the early demos of not one, not two, but *three* of her songs kept Jesse from wallowing in the wreckage of her personal life. One of the songs had been an older tune titled "Save Yourself" that Ash dug out of her tattered notebook.

Upon finishing the cut—a female anthem about a woman wising up to her mistakes—they discussed naming the album after the song. Never had a tune been more pertinent to Jesse's life, both professionally and personally.

The bridge alone said it all…

Stop tossing your heart at the liars and losers
Stop playing the victim ignoring the bruises
You're worth more than this
You deserve to be kissed
By a man who knows what the truth is.

The lyrics had been inspired by a college roommate who'd married her abusive boyfriend after graduation, despite her friends' pleas for her to leave him. Within two years, her husband had put her in the hospital, and she'd needed reconstructive surgery just to breathe properly.

Lucky for Jesse, none of her boyfriends had been physically abusive, but that didn't mean they hadn't left her with scars.

"Which house is it?" Ash asked, jerking her back to the present.

"It's the one ahead on the left," she said as they turned down her former street. "The one with the orange flower pot on the top step."

To her surprise, Ryan hadn't called Dana looking for his errant girlfriend. He hadn't called anyone as far as Jesse could discern. Apparently, her one text reply that simply said, "You should have kept your date with Charlotte," must have been enough for Ryan to move on with his life.

Which made sense in a sick, twisted way. For him, this was the same scene played out many times before, only with a different girlfriend.

"How do we know if he's here?" Ash asked, parking his truck on the curb in front of the bungalow.

"The last message came four hours ago, and it sounded like airport noise behind him." Jesse stepped out of the truck and waited for Ash to come around the front. "I'd have heard from his manager by now if he wasn't in Boston."

There had been nearly a dozen voice mails in total, plus

another ten or so text messages. The first few of each had been frantic. The next half-dozen half-hearted pleading that evolved into whining. The last ones bordered on good riddance and make sure you get your crap out of my house. Fourteen months of her life and that's all she'd gotten.

Excellent life choices, indeed.

Staring at the house that had been her home the day before, Jesse was surprised to feel no connection to the place. Just sadness and the bitter taste of betrayal. Maybe there had been a reason why she'd never put in more effort to make the place feel like hers. None of the women who passed through Ryan's house ever did. A plant here. A picture there. Jesse had made the largest contribution with the swing on the back porch.

Once on the curb, she sized up Ash's truck. "Do you think we can fit a porch swing in there?"

"You're taking his porch swing?" he asked.

"It isn't his. It's *mine*."

Ash tucked the keys into his jacket pocket. "Then we'll make it work."

They'd picked up a few large moving boxes on the way over. All Jesse really had here was clothes, but she'd amassed a sizable collection of stagewear. After unlocking the front door, she removed the key from her key chain and left it on the counter.

"Where do we start?" Ash asked, stepping in behind her and closing the door.

"My stuff is in the spare bedroom." She led him down the narrow hall to the second door on the right. In truth, her everyday clothes were in the main bedroom, but Jesse wasn't ready to be in that room again. "The suitcases are in the back of the closet. We can pull them out and if you'll load the clothes onto the bed, I'll pack them."

Ash did as asked, hauling out the largest of the cases, a dark-blue hard-shell number covered in gray flowers. "You could fit a body in here."

She'd thought the same thing when Silas had gifted her the

case. "A woman needs a lot of crap out on the road." Opening the suitcase on the bed, she waited for the first load, but as Ash returned to the closet, a knock came from the front door.

They froze, staring at each other as if they'd been caught robbing the place.

"Who is that?" he asked.

"How should I know?" she whispered.

"Why are you whispering?"

"I don't know."

The knock came again, and Ash said, "Do you want me to answer it?"

The only person Jesse *didn't* want to see was currently in another time zone. "No, I'll get it. Keep pulling stuff out and pile it on the bed."

Jesse hurried to the front door as the knocking grew more insistent. Yanking it open, she found a harried Geraldine hovering on the doorstep. Maybe Ryan had called someone after all.

"My God, woman. I thought you were dead!" Geraldine cried, engulfing Jesse in a bear hug.

"Why would I be dead?" she asked, struggling to breathe.

The older woman jerked back. "Ryan showed up at my house in the middle of the night last night ranting that you were missing and demanding that I let him in to find you."

And people called Jesse a drama queen. "I wasn't missing. I left him."

To be fair, she'd left him without so much as a note, but the damaged phone—which clearly hadn't broken to bits since he'd managed to call her from it—should have been a good clue.

"Why would you leave him?" Without waiting for Jesse to answer, she added, "He cheated, didn't he? That boy couldn't keep his pecker in his pants if his fool life depended on it."

Confirming the assumption seemed unnecessary. "I'm sorry he scared you. I'm just here to get my things, and then I won't be coming back."

Hot-pink lips pursed. "You aren't going to give him another chance?"

The question felt disloyal. "*Would you?*"

Geraldine shrugged. "Wouldn't be the first time I went the extra mile believing I could fix a bad boy."

"Then you move in with him, because I'm done. I need to go help Ash in the bedroom. Again, I'm sorry that Ryan frightened you, but I'm fine."

"Ash?" she asked, concern pivoting to curiosity. "As in your producer, Ash Shepherd?"

Well, crap. Geraldine was a ninja-level gossip, and their little music community operated much like a small southern town. One word from the older woman's talkative lips, and within days—if not hours—Jesse would be having a mad affair with her brand-new producer. She'd be one of *those* artists. The kind who was willing to dabble in the sheets with anyone they believed could make them a star.

Jesse was not one of those artists.

"Yes, that's him. He has a truck and offered to help move my things." No need to add that her things would be moving to Ash's house, even if only temporarily.

"Can I meet him?" she whispered, looking like a child who'd learned Santa had just swept down her chimney.

Denying the request would only lead to speculation, so Jesse stepped back and motioned for her to come in. "Sure. He's down the hall."

So much for getting in and out without drawing attention from the neighbors. There were at least three other musicians and probably twice as many songwriters on this street alone. This meant killer block parties, but also lots of eyes always watching. And Jesse knew Ryan's house often put on the best shows. More than one story featuring Ryan chasing a departing woman-of-the-moment to her car had been told around a fire pit.

Jesse had lasted longer than any of Ryan's previous

relationships, which had contributed to her delusions that he was different with her. What a joke the neighbors must have thought her. The silly little girl who couldn't see the truth.

She could see it now, but that didn't lessen the humiliation one bit.

SEVENTEEN

"How does anyone own this many sequins?"

Ash dropped yet another pile of glittery clothes on the bed beside the suitcase. So far, he'd found an endless supply of jeans, boots, and dresses all covered in the shiny little dots. There was also a denim jacket that could double as a disco ball, and enough high heels scattered around the bottom of the closet to fill a runway show.

As he waded back in for another pile, Jesse returned. "How's it going?" she asked.

"Who owns this much crap?" he answered over his shoulder. "It looks like you stole some pageant queen's wardrobe."

"Then you won't like the *crap* in my closet either."

That had not been Jesse's voice. Ash backed out of the mess, nearly tripping over three pairs of shoes. "I didn't know anyone else was here."

"Ash, this is Geraldine Allsop," Jesse explained, brows furrowed in a way that said she wasn't happy about their visitor. "She lives next door."

He nodded in greeting. "Nice to meet you, Geraldine."

Skipping the traditional reply, the older woman leaned close to Jesse, her eyes sizing Ash up from head to toe. "You didn't tell me he was so pretty."

Ash raised a brow in Jesse's direction as she said, "He isn't *that* pretty."

"Excuse me?" Not that he wanted to be called pretty, but still.

"If I were twenty years younger and looking for a husband," Geraldine said, "this boy would be a danger to my singlehood. Good thing I'm at the perfect age to just play with him a little."

She knew he could hear her, right?

Jesse didn't flinch at the bold statement. "You can't play with him until he's done helping me get this stuff out of here."

"No one is playing with me at all." Turning to the admirer, he added, "No offense, ma'am."

Geraldine hit him with a haughty glare. "Suit yourself, stud. But it's your loss." She shifted her full attention to Jesse. "Where are you staying? You're welcome to my spare bedroom, but I suppose you'd rather be as far away from this house as possible."

"Thanks, but I'm good. I'm staying with a couple of friends in Hendersonville until I can find an apartment."

This was news to Ash. He assumed she meant Ingrid and Dana, but they'd been together all day, and she hadn't mentioned the move. There was no reason she couldn't stay with him. Between the work they were doing this week, and the proximity of his house to the studio, staying put made more sense. The drive from Hendersonville was going to be a bitch in traffic and burn twice as much gas.

"Good to hear," the neighbor said. "So long as you won't go homeless."

"I wouldn't let that happen," Ash cut in, dropping the last pile of clothes on top of the others.

Geraldine's penciled-in brows arched. "That's more hospitable than any producer I ever met."

"I'm not—"

"We're in a hurry," Jesse cut in, flipping open the case on the bed. "I want to get out of here before dark."

Dark would be in less than thirty minutes. They would never get all of this in the truck by then.

"I can help," the woman offered.

"No, thanks. We've got it." Jesse nudged the neighbor toward the door. "I'll call you with my new address as soon as I have one."

"You better," Geraldine said as the two women left the room.

Ash returned to the closet for the shoes, wondering why Jesse had been in such a hurry to get rid of her guest. And why had she cut him off from explaining that he wasn't *only* her producer?

When she returned alone, he said, "What was that about?"

"What?" Eyes down, she started loading clothes into the suitcase.

"You couldn't get her out of here fast enough. And since when are you staying at Ingrid's place?"

"I talked to Dana this afternoon. They're letting me stay in their guest room until I can find my own place."

"You're already in a guest room. One that's a few miles from the studio instead of thirty minutes away. What am I missing here?"

The stack of jeans packed, she moved to the dresses. "I can't stay with you."

"Why not?"

She wadded up a dark-green number and finally met his eye. "For the same reason I needed to get Geraldine out of here. Gossip."

Now she'd really lost him. "What gossip?"

"I'm already being called difficult. The last thing I need is rumors that we're sleeping together."

Ash had to sift through that one. "For starters, we aren't sleeping together." He resisted the urge to add a *yet* to the end of that statement. "But if we were, that would be our business. I signed on to do the album before any of this happened, and I don't have the credentials or the clout for people to believe you'd screw me to get ahead. So what exactly are we trying to avoid here?"

Jesse dropped onto the bed. "Don't you get it? It doesn't matter what we are or aren't doing. It only matters what people assume, and between my teetering career and the breakup with Ryan, I don't want to look any worse than I already do."

The female brain could make leaps and bounds with the agility of an Olympic gymnast.

"Hold up. Your career isn't teetering, and the fact that you're having to start over as a solo act isn't your fault." Ash couldn't believe he even had to explain this. "The crap with Ryan isn't your fault either. Based on Dimitri's reputation alone, people will know that as well as you do."

"Taylor ditched me to cut her own album," she said, ignoring his logic. "Ryan slept with other women while dating me. There's one common denominator in both of those scenarios, and it's me as the loser." Jesse rose to her feet and returned to packing. "I can't keep a duet partner, and I can't keep a boyfriend faithful. No matter how you spin it, that's the reality."

Ash bristled. "How do you not see that their actions say a lot more about them than they do about you?" Kicking a shoe out of his way, he swept around the bed and spun her to face him. "You're the victim here, Jesse. They're the assholes. To hell with anyone who says differently."

"That isn't how it works," she argued. "I've never done anything to earn that stupid difficult crap, but people still believe it. And if I stay with you, they'll believe that the only way that I got a producer is by sleeping with one."

"Then let them believe it. You can't live your life worrying about what people will think."

Jesse shook her head. "I'm a woman trying to make a living in the entertainment industry, Ash. Every decision I make has to be based on what people will think. My peers. My fans. My label.

They all decide if I get to keep doing this, so I don't have the luxury of saying to hell with anyone."

The reality of her words finally penetrated his thick skull. As a man, no one would ever accuse Ash of sleeping around to get ahead. No one would judge him on how shiny his clothes were or how small his waist was. But Jesse faced those assumptions and judgments every day. For no other reason than the misfortune of being born a woman.

Stepping back, he said, "If we're going to get all of this up to Hendersonville, we should get moving."

Jesse grasped his arm. "I'm not going because I want to."

The confession only heightened his frustration as he accepted her decision. "Good to know."

* * *

"That asshole never deserved you." Dana had refrained from doing an actual happy dance, but her joy at the change in Jesse's relationship status was clear. At the same time, she was angry on her friend's behalf. "You were the best thing that ever happened to him, the jerk."

She and Ingrid had welcomed Jesse with open arms, and an open bottle of wine.

"I'm not sure I happened to him as much as he happened to me." Swirling the red in her glass, Jesse leaned back and glanced up at the stars. "I feel like a moron."

"Ryan is the moron," Ingrid assured her, tossing a small log onto the fire.

Yes, he was. But that didn't diminish Jesse's humiliation. "Thanks again for putting me up. I promise I won't be here long."

"Stay as long as you need." The homeowner rose from her chair. "I have an early photo shoot in the morning so I'm off to bed." She dropped a kiss on Dana's forehead. "Do you want me to bring out another bottle of wine?"

"Jesse?" Dana said.

"No, I'm good."

The ladies settled into silence as the sliding glass door clicked shut. This was the first time Jesse had been able to relax in days, and she breathed the cool night air from her spot several feet from the fire. As often happened in the last few days, Ash filled her mind. He'd grown quieter once she'd finally gotten through to him about the tightrope that was her life. Ignore what people thought? If only. This was Jesse's profession of choice, and that meant taking the good with the bad.

The good was getting to do what she loved for a living. The bad was the precarious nature of that choice. One day you were up. The next you were playing for tips, dodging flying beer bottles, and relying on the kindness of strangers to fill your bucket. Some months the lights stayed on. Other months you found yourself homeless and living in your bass player's guest room.

"Can I ask you something?" Dana said.

Jesse opened her eyes. "Ask away."

"Why did you go to Ash instead of Silas?"

With a sigh, Jesse sat up. "Ash Shepherd isn't a producer I met last week. We grew up together. He was Tommy's best friend, and we were together in high school."

Her friend leaned forward. "Together?"

With a nod, she said, "Together. Ash was my first boyfriend, my first kiss, my first . . . everything."

Silent for several seconds, Dana eventually muttered, "Damn. Why didn't you tell me?" Putting the pieces together, she added, "Wait. He was driving that night?"

Only three people in Nashville knew about the accident, and Dana was one of them. Taylor and Ash were the other two.

"Yes, he was driving. All this time I thought he'd walked out of my life, but when I met him again the day he took this job, I found out my parents had sent him away." With a catch in her voice, she said, "He didn't leave me because he wanted to."

The same words Jesse had uttered to Ash earlier in the day. A little history repeating, though Jesse wasn't walking out of his life, just out of his guest room.

"That explains a lot," Dana said before tipping up her glass.

"What do you mean?"

"Last week at dinner, I caught him watching you more than once. He looked at you the way Reggie looks at Phoenix."

Jesse wasn't comfortable with the analogy. "I doubt that. What we had is in the past."

"Does it have to be?"

"Of course it does. He's my producer now."

She scoffed. "Like you'd be the first artist to fall for your producer."

"We need to change the subject."

Dana pressed on. "Come on, Jesse. I'm not blind. You looked at him the same way tonight. Maybe all of this is happening now for a reason?"

"All of what?" Jesse asked through clenched teeth.

"Ash getting hired to produce your record. The truth coming out about Ryan. There's a higher power at work here."

"Then that higher power needs to focus on helping me instead of turning my life into a complete cluster." She rose from her chair. "I need to go look up apartments."

"What are you afraid of?" Dana asked.

"You don't understand what it's like to have everyone talking about you behind your back," Jesse snapped.

The bass player raised a brow. "I'm a lesbian bass player in country music. I think I might understand what that's like."

Jesse dropped back into her chair. "That was a horrible thing to say. I'm sorry."

Her friend patted her knee. "I get it. These rumors about you being tough to work with aren't fair. But what does that have to do with you and Ash?"

Ignoring the question at hand, she said, "Do you know anything about Taylor's new manager?"

"Dennis Kohlman? Only that he's sleazy as hell and is probably the person spreading those rumors about you."

"You think so, too?" Jesse asked.

Dana shrugged. "Doesn't take a genius to figure it out. Everyone knows you were the more talented half of the duo, and that makes you Taylor's biggest competition."

Though Jesse had told herself as much on more than one occasion, she hadn't realized anyone agreed with her. "Do people really think that?"

With a hard eye-roll, the woman shook her head. "Yes, they do. But again, what does this have to do with you and Ash?"

She was getting to that. "Back when our second single didn't take off as fast as the first, Taylor said she was afraid that we would be one-hit wonders."

"She made sure of that now," Dana grimaced.

"She also told me that Kohlman had contacted her and claimed he could take us to the next level. He wanted to meet with us to discuss a change in management, but I refused. A week later, Taylor dragged me over to meet him at a party, and it was obvious that the two of them had done more than just talk."

"Ew," her friend muttered, her face twisted as if a skunk had entered the yard.

"Exactly what I thought," Jesse said. "But it gets worse. He sent Taylor off to get us drinks and immediately made a move on me, suggesting a little *you scratch my back, I'll scratch yours* arrangement, and I think the word threesome was thrown around."

Dana visibly flinched. "That's disgusting. I can't believe she'd still sign with him after knowing that." When Jesse made a face, she added, "You didn't tell her?"

"Not the details. I let her know I didn't like him and that we were fine with Silas. A week later, I got the text that she was going solo."

"Wow. I knew she was insecure, but geez."

That had been the irony of their partnership. Taylor had

been the long-legged blonde-bombshell of the duo, and yet she'd also been the least confident.

"And that's why I won't cross the line with Ash," Jesse said. "Whatever success I have, it's going to be on my terms, and no one will be able to say that I made it because of who I slept with."

Dark brows drew together. "But you just said you and Ash go back to high school. It isn't as if you met him at a party and fell into bed with him to get ahead."

"No one knows that, and even if they did, he'd still get the credit for my success."

Her hostess processed that statement for several seconds. "So Taylor is willing to sleep with a slimeball to get her chance, while you're giving up what could be the real thing to get the credit for yours. I have to be honest, Jesse. I don't think either of you are making the right choice."

Convinced otherwise, Jesse once again rose from her chair. "Maybe. Maybe not. But at least I can look myself in the mirror at the end of the day." After finishing the last sip in her glass, she said, "Now I really am going to look up apartments. If I can get some viewings for Saturday, you want to come with me?"

Dana rose beside her. "I can do that. Will you promise me one thing, though?"

"I can try."

"Don't let your ego get in the way of your heart."

The cryptic request made no sense. "What does that even mean?"

With a caring smile, she tapped her glass against Jesse's. "Just think about it." With a nod, she added, "Go on and do your research and I'll take care of the fire."

Jesse followed the suggestion with Dana's words still playing through her mind. By the time she reached her room, she opted to ignore her hopeless romantic friend and stick with her plan— concentrate on the music. If she let her focus slip for one second

—which is what would happen if she crossed the line with Ash—
the sharks in this town would eat her alive.

She would not let that happen.

EIGHTEEN

Ash met Millie Friday morning in the production company parking lot off of 18th Avenue. She wore a pressed, if ill-fitting, business suit, and he'd never seen her look so put together. Even her hair was neatly styled.

"Good morning," she said, her smile wide. "I'm so happy you could make this meeting. I truly wouldn't have been able to do this on my own."

She'd have been fine, he was sure. "No problem."

They proceeded into the building and were greeted by a male receptionist who offered them an assortment of drinks. Ash accepted a bottle of water while Millie passed.

"I'm way too nervous to drink anything," she whispered as the man returned to his post. "I've never been around television people before."

Ash had participated in a couple of locally televised programs. The first had been for charity, and the other had featured up-and-coming songwriters in town. Neither had put him in the spotlight, which was why he'd participated at all, but watching the behind-the-scenes action had been interesting.

"You'll be fine," he assured her. "All we have to do is listen to what they have to say."

"Yes," she agreed, nodding vigorously. "I can do that. But what if they want the children to wear fancy outfits? Their parents can barely afford food. I can't ask them to spend money like that."

That was a problem he hadn't considered. "If they want fancy, they'll have to pay for it. If that isn't an option, then they'll have to be happy with whatever the kids can put together."

"We did black pants and white shirts for the recital last spring. Maybe that will work." Millie squirmed on the edge of her seat. "I'm sure the center could pitch in for some sort of Christmas-y accessories. Red ties for the boys and pretty bows for the girls."

"That's a good idea." Ash could already hear the boys moaning about having to wear ties, but there was no need to burst Millie's bubble right now.

"Ms. Hopewell, Mr. Shepherd, they're ready for you now."

The receptionist led them into the bowels of the office, which was quieter than Ash would expect. Then again, this was the executive floor. Most activity likely took place on the lower levels. They were seated in a conference room twice the size of the one at Shooting Stars and waited several minutes before the producers joined them. The moment the suits walked into the room, Millie stopped squirming.

"Thank you again for taking the time to meet with us, Ms. Hopewell. I'm Jacob Holmes and this is Melissa Darby, who spoke to you on the phone last week."

"I remember, yes. It's nice to meet you both. And this is Ash Shepherd, our music director at Sunshine Academy."

"So you're the source of the children's talent," said Ms. Darby.

Ash shook his head. "The talent is all theirs. I just help them learn how to use it." Curious, he asked, "How did you hear about the academy?"

"Samantha Walters raved about your group. She saw them perform last spring through her connection with the Kids & The

Arts charity." The friendly brunette turned to Millie. "I believe they're a big contributor to your facility."

"Yes, they are. We're excited about this opportunity, but we need to make sure this is a proper venue for our students." Millie crossed her arms, looking every bit the shrewd negotiator. "What exactly are you wanting the children to do?"

Darby and Holmes exchanged a glance that Ash read loud and clear. They hadn't expected the mousy director to transform into a lion. Smiling, he sat back, happy to be the silent observer.

"The program will last two hours, and we'd like to feature the choir during the first hour, singing at least two traditional Christmas songs, though we can't be sure if both performances will make the final television cut."

"And the musicians?" Millie asked, her expression revealing nothing.

"They would appear in the second hour, and we were hoping they might play something more contemporary. Is that possible?"

Millie turned to Ash. "What do you think?"

He didn't see why not. "If you can get the performance rights for a modern Christmas tune, the kids will play it. But we'll need to know which songs as soon as possible so they have plenty of time to learn and practice. Will they need to play two as well?"

"Just one for the musicians," Holmes said. "We're packing more acts into the second hour so that limits the time allotted to each."

Learning a three- to four-minute song in a month's time was more than doable. "Who will they be performing behind?" he asked.

The producers exchanged another glance. "They'll have the spotlight all to themselves."

Confused, Ash said, "Then who is doing the singing?"

"Who did the singing in the spring?" Ms. Darby asked.

His gut dropped.

"That was Ash," Millie replied. "He's a wonderful singer."

"I'm a songwriter and musician, not a singer," he corrected. "We have plenty of talented kids in the choir who can handle this performance."

"Singing with a choir is quite different from taking lead on national television," Mr. Holmes pointed out. "If the kids are used to playing behind you, we should probably stick with that."

Ash was about to argue until catching the hint of panic in Millie's pleading gaze. This was important to her and would be equally important to the kids. His refusal to sing wasn't likely to be a deal breaker, but if it was and they lost this opportunity, he'd never forgive himself.

"Fine," he conceded. "But we'll expect final approval on song choice."

"That was always the plan since you know best what the children are capable of." Ms. Darby slid a sheet of paper their way. "We've compiled a list of options for both groups and hoped we could lock in the choices today. Since, as you mentioned, we'll need time to make sure we have all the rights we need."

Millie accepted the list and immediately handed it over to Ash. Within minutes, three songs were chosen—two for the choir and one for the guitar troop—and the Sunshine Academy performers were locked in as official participants in the November taping of a Nashville Country Christmas.

Ash still wasn't happy with the role he'd agreed to play, but there was no way around it. In the end, Millie was happy, and the kids were going to have a once-in-a-lifetime experience. That was really all that mattered.

* * *

Burger Republic was already packed with the Friday lunch crowd, but that was typical of this part of town. The Gulch, a development just off the downtown business district that had once been a railroad yard, was currently the trendiest neighborhood in town.

In fact, Jesse would trade all of her fancy outfits to live in one of the high-end condos with their modern décor and endless amenities.

Not only were they insanely pricey, but they were harder to get into than Harvard Law School. The waiting lists had waiting lists. You had to know someone who knew someone or dream on. Since Jesse lacked the right connections, dream on it would be.

"Look at it this way," Dana said as the hostess led them to their table, "That's less tourists milling about outside your metaphorical front door."

A stretch for a silver lining, but Jesse would take it. She'd scheduled three apartment viewings for the next day, but one had only been available to see this morning, which had worked out well with Ash off at his meeting with Millie. Unfortunately, the studio apartment had been less than attractive and during their short tour, Jesse had heard voices through the walls on both sides. That meant option number one got a hard pass.

"Here you go," the brunette said with a smile, indicating a booth against the back wall. "Deonne is your server, and he'll be right with you."

"Thanks," Jesse said, sliding into the seat and not bothering to open the menu. The sliders were her regular order, and she saw no reason to change things up.

"I always say I'm going to get one of these spiked milkshakes, but I never do." Dana scanned the list of boozy concoctions. "Ooh, there's a new one called Kentucky Thunder."

That sounded dangerous. "What's in it?"

"Stout, bourbon, and chocolate ice cream." She looked up with a wiggle of her brow. "We should do it."

Tempting but Jesse really wanted to make her solo debut at least twenty pounds lighter than she currently was. "I better not. I've eaten enough conciliatory ice cream this week to gain back the five pounds I managed to get off last month." Five pounds in a month was nothing to brag about, but Jesse had never dropped weight easily. The passing on of her mother's non-moving metabolism had been a cruel twist of fate.

"You look great," Dana assured her as an attractive black man approached the table.

"Hello, ladies. How are we doing today?"

"Good," they said in unison.

"All right. My name is Deonne, and I'll be your server today. Have y'all been here before?"

"Many times," Jesse replied.

"Cool. I'll get your drink order in and give you a little time to peruse our menu. What are we having?"

Dana ordered first. "I'll take a Diet Coke."

"Same for me," Jesse said. As Deonne left the table, she said, "What happened to the Kentucky Thunder?"

"You reminded me that the Thunder would go directly to my thighs."

The bass player was taller than Jesse—though who wasn't?—but of a similar size.

"When we celebrate our first number one, we'll come back for the Thunder and say screw the extra calories."

"That's a deal."

Crossing her arms on the table, Jesse glanced up to catch a headline scroll across the bottom of the screen on a mounted television. "Another hurricane. This season needs to freaking end."

"Oh, shit," Dana muttered, pulling Jesse's attention from the impending storm.

"What?"

Chin low, she whispered, "Don't look now, but Taylor is headed this way."

Jesse had no time to prepare before her former duet partner stepped up to the table.

"Hi," Taylor said as if they were still the best of friends.

"Hi," Jesse echoed, stomach roiling. She wanted to throw a

punch, burst into tears, and puke on Taylor's fancy boots all at the same time.

"How's it going, Taylor?" Dana asked, thankfully taking the traitor's attention away from Jesse.

"It's good," the blonde replied. "Different, but good. How about you guys?"

"We're great," her bass player answered. "We're going into the studio on Monday. Shooting Stars has lined up a great team for the album. Only the best for their newest star."

Dana won herself a job for life with that response.

"Oh." Taylor's voice cracked. "That's good to hear. With Jesse's talent, I'm sure the album will be great."

"Really?" Jesse said. "If I'm so talented, why did you ditch me like I was some loser sidekick you couldn't wait to get rid of?"

Taylor looked stunned as a hush fell over the tables around them. With more warning, Jesse might have curtailed the outburst, but the rage that had been building for months, combined with the simmering anger at Ryan's infidelity, merged into a perfect storm, unleashing Hurricane Jesse.

"Maybe we should discuss this outside," Dana suggested, but Taylor found her voice.

"I didn't ditch you, Jesse. This was an opportunity I couldn't pass up."

"*We* had opportunities," she reminded her. "Like the tour we should be on right now. You remember that?"

"Everyone can hear you," Dana muttered.

Taylor's eyes lowered. "I didn't come over here to cause a scene. I just wanted to say that I miss you. And I'm sorry about you and Ryan."

Jesse was on her feet in an instant. "What do you know about me and Ryan?"

"Just that you broke up," she said, taking a step back.

Stupid gossips. "That's *my* business, not yours. And you don't get to say that you *miss* me." Jesse poked her in the shoulder. "Not after what you did."

"That's enough." Dana put herself between the two women. "Taylor, go back to your table."

"What's going on over here?" growled Dennis Kohlman as he approached the table.

"Nothing," Taylor replied. "I was just leaving."

"Because that's what you do best," Jesse snarled.

Keeping Jesse behind her, Dana nodded toward the exit. "Go on."

"Come on, baby," Dennis mumbled, taking his client by the elbow. "I told you she wasn't worth your time."

Jesse lunged as they walked away, but Dana pressed her back into the booth and spun to face her. "What the hell is wrong with you?" she whispered.

"She—"

"She nothing. You know half this place is filled with industry people. How could you let her get to you like that?"

So much for loyalty. "Are you serious right now? She acted like nothing happened."

"And now everyone in this restaurant knows *exactly* what happened. Is that what you wanted?"

The message hit Jesse like a runaway bus. What had been only gossip before had just been confirmed. *By* Jesse. *She* was the one left behind. And now *she* was the crazy one attacking Taylor in a restaurant.

"I'm going to be sick," she mumbled, dropping her forehead onto the table.

"Let's just get out of here." Dana grabbed her jacket off the seat. "Come on."

Jesse followed blindly, avoiding eye contact with the other patrons as they marched toward the exit, but the hum of whispers couldn't be ignored. If Jesse hadn't been the most pathetic artist in town already, she definitely was now.

And this time, she had only herself to blame.

* * *

"Mr. Shepherd, could I speak to you a moment?"

Ms. Darby's request took Ash by surprise. Anything she wanted to discuss about the academy should include Millie.

"Do you have more questions about the kids' performances?"

She shook her head, and dark waves twirled around her face. "No, I wanted to ask about something else."

Millie cut him a sly smile. "I'll wait for you in the lobby." With that, she left the pair alone as Mr. Holmes had already departed.

"Okay, Ms. Darby. What can I do for you?"

"I've heard you're working with Jesse Gold."

Not sure where this was going, he replied, "Yes. I'm producing her debut album."

The television producer stepped to the door, looked both ways down the hall, and then closed them in. "Do you think she might be interested in being part of the Christmas show?"

Would she? Making her solo television debut before Taylor would not only help Jesse's career, but quite possibly make her year.

"I don't see why not. Have you contacted her manager, Silas Fillmore?"

She made a sour face. "Jacob scratched her off the invite list. In fact, he's scratched off nearly every female artist I suggested." Ash sensed a revolt in the air. "Most of them weren't likely to accept anyway, but I met Jesse when the Honkytonk Daisies first came out, and I really liked her. With the rumors floating around, I don't think she's getting a fair shake."

If Ms. Darby was looking for allies for her mutiny, she'd just found one.

"I can almost guarantee that Jesse would accept if she was asked, but will your Mr. Holmes let that happen?" The last thing he would tolerate was Jesse receiving an invitation only to have it revoked in short order.

Green eyes twinkled as a dark brow arched. "I'll handle Mr. Holmes, if you'll put in a good word with Jesse."

Extending a hand, Ash said, "Consider it done."

Instead of the quick shake he'd expected, Ms. Darby held on. "Now for a more personal question. Would you like to have dinner sometime?"

So this is what Millie's smile had been about. Somehow Ash had missed the signs and was caught off guard. Melissa Darby was pretty, with a nice smile and emerald eyes that sparkled as she held his gaze. The tailored suit accentuated shapely curves, and more importantly, she'd displayed intelligence, ambition, and excellent instincts where Jesse was concerned. He'd be an idiot to turn her down.

"I'm afraid I can't," Ash heard himself say, watching the green eyes dim. "But I appreciate the offer."

Ms. Darby didn't ask for a reason, which he appreciated since Ash didn't have one.

"Well, it was worth a shot." Whipping a business card from her pocket, she pressed it into his hand. "In case you change your mind."

Ash nodded as he slipped the card into his back pocket. "You'll be the first to know if I do," he muttered lamely.

She flashed an attractive smile as she opened the door. "Until next time, then."

A bit befuddled, he replied, "Until next time."

He found Millie waiting in the reception area, and she pressed the button for the elevator as he approached. The doors slid open, and they stepped on together. As they closed, she said, "So?"

"So what?" he asked, still trying to figure out why he'd turned down the invite.

"What did Ms. Darby want?"

"To know if Jesse Gold would be interesting in participating in the show." Ash saw no reason to share the other part.

Millie looked confused. "Jesse Gold?"

"You met her last Saturday at the center. I brought her in to play with the kids."

"Oh, yes. That pretty little redhead you're working with." The director tilted her head. "Is that all she wanted?"

Ash ignored the obvious suggestion in her tone. Millie knew what Ms. Darby had really wanted, but he had no plans to confirm her suspicions.

"Yep. That was it."

"I could have sworn…" she whispered more to herself than to him.

Which provided Ash the perfect opportunity to embrace his right to remain silent until they reached the parking lot and went their separate ways. The duration of the drive home was spent pondering his unexpected response. Why not go to dinner with a beautiful, successful woman? No answer came until he pulled into his drive to find Jesse waiting on his front steps.

"Right," he mumbled to himself. "That's why."

NINETEEN

JESSE SAT CROSS-LEGGED ON HER SWING WITH BRUTUS'S HEAD IN her lap. They'd put the swing on Ash's back porch, uninstalled, of course, until Jesse found a new home for it and herself. After the Daisies breakup, this had been Jesse's safe place. Where she'd written some of her best songs and cried the most tears. Even without the swaying motion, the swing was still her port in a storm, and the only place she wanted to be today.

Within minutes of arriving at Dana and Ingrid's, Jesse had hopped in her Jeep with no destination in mind. She'd made an ass of herself today, with Dana—and anyone spending their Friday lunch hour at Burger Republic—to bear witness. When was she going to wake up and stop acting like a helpless victim?

Until today, Jesse had blamed everyone else for her downfall. Taylor's desertion screwed up her career. Ryan's cheating broke her heart. The unknown source of gossip—be it Dennis Kohlman or someone else—had ruined her reputation. But the common denominator in all of these messes was Jesse. Why would her duet partner walk away? Why would her boyfriend cheat? Why would anyone call her difficult?

What was Jesse doing to make all of these things happen?

"I'm a basket case, Brutus," she said, stroking the dog's head. "A complete basket case."

"But you're a cute basket case," Ash drawled from the doorway. When Jesse didn't laugh, he strolled over and lowered himself onto the seat beside her. "Want to tell me about it?"

Jesse was surprised he hadn't heard the story by now. "I ran into Taylor today."

Ash whistled through his teeth. "Didn't go well, huh?"

She cut him a droll look. "No, it didn't."

"Let me hear it," he said, leaning back and taking her with him.

Jesse surrendered and laid her head on his shoulder. "It was awful. I don't even remember what all I said, but it was loud enough for the entire restaurant to hear."

"So you had an audience?" he asked, his thumb rubbing up and down her arm.

"Yeah. Dana and I went to Burger Republic after seeing an apartment. Taylor said she missed me and that she was sorry to hear about me and Ryan. I snapped and even poked her in the shoulder, which was ridiculously lame. Then Kohlman walked over and made some snide comment." Jesse ground her teeth. "I can't stand that man."

"Did she fight back?"

"What?" she said, turning to look into his face.

"Did she fight back?" he repeated.

Taylor had defended her choice to say hello, but she hadn't met Jesse jab for jab. "No, she didn't. She said she didn't mean to cause a scene, and she claimed that she left the act because of an opportunity she couldn't pass up." That one still hurt. "An opportunity that required leaving me behind."

They sat in silence for a while, the dog's fur soft beneath her hand and Ash's steady breathing beneath her cheek. They'd spent many nights this way. Either looking at the stars from the hood of a car or huddled under a blanket on the couch watching movies. Life had been so simple back then. With Ash by her side, anything had seemed possible. Now, everything felt endlessly complicated.

"There's something wrong with me," she mumbled.

"No, there isn't," he assured her with a gentle squeeze of her shoulder.

"Yes, there is. The rumors are right. I *am* difficult. And cranky and defensive *and* my own worst enemy." Pressing her nose into his shirt, she murmured, "I suck." A split second later, Jesse's view of the world changed as she found herself perched atop Ash's lap. "Wha—"

"This crap of blaming yourself for other people's actions has to stop. None of us are perfect. We have bad days and lose our temper. We make bad choices and suffer the consequences. On other days, we do extraordinary things and make the world a better place." He ran a finger across her brow. "This distorted idea that you are somehow fatally flawed, and therefore deserve all the bad that's happened to you in the last few months, is *bullshit*. Stop blaming yourself for everything, Jesse. The only mistake you made was to care about the wrong people. And lucky for you, they're both out of your life."

Dazed by the warm body beneath her and the passion in his speech, Jesse could only stare in silence into his beautiful amber eyes.

"Are you hearing me?" he asked, giving her shoulder a gentle shake.

"Yes," she replied, full sentences still illusive.

"Good. Because there *are* people who care about you. And I, for one, am tired of hearing you beat yourself up."

As his words sank in, a warmth spread through Jesse's chest. "You care about me?" she whispered, though he'd proven as much every minute since they'd reunited.

Ash trailed his thumb along her jaw. "I never stopped caring about you, Jesse. You have to know that."

She did know that. And as her heart kicked in her chest, Jesse leaned in to show him that she'd never stopped caring either.

* * *

The moment Jesse's lips met his, Ash pulled her in close, and she melted in his arms. She was as familiar as his own name, and as foreign as a strange new language on his tongue. His hands explored soft curves, warm skin, and silky copper curls. This is what he'd missed and feared he'd never have again. Jesse twisted to straddle his thighs and when she ground her core against him, his body went hard.

Ash deepened the kiss, his hands cupping her bottom as she purred with pleasure. She spread her knees to settle hot and desperate against his erection seconds before Ash found himself nearly deafened.

Jesse jerked back, wide-eyed and red-lipped, and Brutus nudged her shoulder before barking again. For several seconds, they stared at each other as if surprised by their unexpected proximity. And then Jesse covered her mouth to hold in the laughter. Ash wasn't feeling all that amused.

"This mutt needs to go home."

The mirth escaped then. A sound that was music to his ears. "I think he's trying to protect me."

Ash shifted her onto the swing and rose to his feet before dragging her up with him. "He's going to need protection if he doesn't go home." After giving the dog a quick scratch behind the ear, he said, "Go on, boy. Go see your mom."

In defiance, Brutus planted his butt next to Jesse's leg and growled. The sound wasn't menacing, but he was definitely showing a change of allegiance.

"I need to start closing that gate," Ash murmured.

Jesse poked him in the gut. "You will not. This dog loves you."

"Then why'd he interrupt the best kiss I've had in years?"

He hadn't meant to make such a confession, but he regretted nothing when Jesse flashed a heart-stopping smile. "It wasn't so bad for me, either."

Knowing the moment had passed, Ash ran a hand through

his hair. "I guess he can stay. You want something to eat before we get back to work?" Not that he wanted food in that moment, but he was his mother's son and that meant no one went hungry in his home.

"Since we left the restaurant before eating, a little food would be nice." As Ash turned to walk away, she wrapped slender fingers around his wrist. "Thank you for being such a good guy."

He didn't feel like a good guy. Dimitri had broken her heart less than a week ago, leaving Jesse vulnerable and alone. Any guy would have to be an asshole to take advantage of her right now.

As if reading his thoughts, she added, "Nothing that just happened was because of Ryan. I need you to know that."

Ash hoped that was true. If he was going to step back into her life, Dimitri needed to be completely out of it. "Are you sure of that?"

She nodded, eyes dark and locked on his as all the years between their last kiss and this one fell away. They lingered there, bodies inches apart, and he fought the urge to carry her inside and explore every delicious curve she had to offer. Ash reached to pull her in when a phone rang, the chime muffled as if coming from under something.

Jesse looked down. "My phone must have come out of my pocket." Retrieving the cell from beneath the swing, she checked the screen, and her face fell. "It's Silas. He must have heard about what happened."

The mention of her manager's name reminded Ash of the morning meeting and Ms. Darby's initial inquiry.

"Maybe not," he said. "Answer it."

She shot him a doubtful look as she followed the order. "Hey, Silas." Ash couldn't hear the voice on the other end but could tell by Jesse's expression that the old man wasn't scolding her. "Are you serious?" she said, her face lighting up like a Christmas tree. "Did you tell her yes?" Another pause and her face brightened even more. "That's fantastic! Send over the list of songs, and I'll narrow it down by Monday.

Thanks, Si," she added before cutting off the call and bouncing up and down. "I'm going to be on a Christmas special!"

"That's great," he said. "I'm glad they called."

Jesse halted her celebration. "You don't sound surprised. Did you know about this?" Before he could speak, she put two and two together and got the wrong answer. "Oh my gosh. This is the same special you had a meeting about this morning. You got me onto the show."

Ash held his hands up in front of him. "I had nothing to do with it. One of the producers caught me after the meeting because she heard I was working with you. Do you remember meeting Melissa Darby?"

Red brows drew together. "The name sounds familiar."

"Then you made a bigger impression on her than she did on you. She said she doesn't like the things people are saying about you."

Blue eyes went wide. "She did?"

"Yes, ma'am. Then she asked if I thought you'd be interested in joining the cast."

"What did you say?"

"That I thought you would, but that she needed to contact Silas to find out."

Her expression filled with wonder. "I'm going to make my first solo television appearance." Joy switched to panic. "I'm going to make my first solo television appearance. Holy crap, I have to go up there alone." Terror flitted across her face as the color drained from her cheeks. "I don't know if I'm ready."

"You were born ready," Ash assured her. "And I'll be in the wings for moral support. You'll be so good, the fans will be searching for more Jesse Gold music by the time the show goes off the air."

"But there isn't any Jesse Gold music."

He lifted her hands to kiss her knuckles. "Then we'd better get to work and change that."

A nervous giggle escaped her lips as she bounced on her toes. "Yes, let's change that."

* * *

By six that evening, Jesse's day had made a complete turnaround. Mostly.

To Ash's great satisfaction, Jesse finally wrote a song about Taylor, and oddly enough, the tune carried echoes of gratitude rather than anger. As she'd already concluded, if Taylor hadn't left the duo, Jesse wouldn't be cutting her own musical path. And without the current opportunity, she and Ash might never have reunited.

Considering their encounter on the back porch, that would have been a crying shame. Not that she was ready to pick up where they'd left off. They were different people now, and she needed to deal with her feelings for Ryan before diving into another relationship. When thinking of her now ex-boyfriend, Jesse mostly felt anger, hurt, and humiliation. But she also still loved him. A fact she'd realized during the week.

When Jesse hadn't returned his calls or texts, Ryan had sent one final message on Wednesday morning that simply said, "I'm sorry, baby."

She'd stared at the words, wanting to feel nothing. That was unrealistic, of course, but she would have settled for relief. That it was over. That he'd finally given up. Instead, Jesse began questioning her decision to leave. Three little words on her phone screen, and she'd nearly called Ryan to apologize. As if the tables had turned and *she* was the one in need of forgiveness.

A sure sign that what Jesse needed most was to be alone for a while. She needed to learn to trust herself, and to figure out who she was without a man in her life. It had been years since she'd been single for more than a week or two. A pattern she should have recognized sooner. Why couldn't she be alone? The answers that came to mind—that she didn't like herself or didn't feel complete without a man in her life—revealed a truth Jesse had avoided facing for far too long.

She was so desperate for the love and affection that her parents had failed to provide, she'd spent her adult life attaching herself to anyone willing to fill the void. Sadly, her standards had been low, and that's how she'd ended up with a string of ex-boyfriends, each as shallow as the one before. And now she was doing it again. Leaping from one man to another without even coming up for air. But then, this man wasn't like the others.

This was *Ash*. Responsible, generous, and the opposite of bad boy yet just as sexy. Like many women, Jesse had her typical turn-ons when it came to men. Playing guitar, of course, would always melt her panties, and there was something about watching a guy play pool. That intense gaze and the quick strokes as he sunk another ball in a corner pocket. But with Ash she'd found a new turn-on.

Cooking.

Who knew that watching him masterfully chop an onion could be so sexy? As he dribbled soy sauce over the stir fry, she struggled not to tackle him to the floor and rip his clothes off.

"Is there anything I can do?" she said, needing a distraction.

"You can grab the wine from the pantry." He lifted the frying pan to shift the veggies with a flick of his wrist. "This is just about done."

Though she could have swung around the opposite side, Jesse took the route that forced her to squeeze between him and the island. Unable to resist, she copped a feel on her way by, and Ash shot her a grin over his shoulder.

"Subtle, Rheingold."

"You know you can't call me that around other people, right?" she said, stepping into the pantry.

"Why not?"

Jesse stuck her head out. "Because I changed it to Gold for a reason. Which wine should I be getting?" She never knew what paired with what.

"The Riesling. What's wrong with the name Rheingold?"

She grabbed the right bottle and exited the pantry. "It sounds like a character in a World War II history book, and not one of the good guys."

Ash pulled two plates from a top cabinet. "I get using a stage name, but you shouldn't be ashamed of your heritage. What do your parents think of the change?"

"Where are the glasses?" she asked, avoiding the question. The last thing she wanted to talk about was her parents.

"Top far-left cabinet," he replied, splitting the stir fry between two plates. "Now answer the question."

Rising on her tiptoes, she dragged two wine glasses off the second shelf. "I told them that I changed it to protect them. If I'm a failure, then they're friends won't have any idea that their only remaining child is the loser they always knew she'd be."

Ash set the pan in the sink and grabbed silverware from the drawer. "Your parents have their faults, but they never thought you were a loser."

"Do you know what Mom said when I told her about the Daisies record deal?"

He stuck a fork on each plate and carried them to table. "What?"

"And I quote, 'That's nice, dear, but I hope you're still considering nursing school.'" Jesse carried the glasses and wine to join him. "I have *never* considered nursing school. I can barely stand the sight of blood, and I only passed my high school anatomy class because my lab partner was our future valedictorian. Thankfully, Freddy didn't mind doing all the work."

"But I'm sure they're proud of you now," Ash said, clearly delusional.

"The night after our celebration party for cracking the top twenty, I got home to find brochures to three Atlanta-area nursing schools in my mailbox. And the party was nearly a week *after* I called home to share the good news that we'd hit the charts."

Ash took his seat with a serious look on his face. "What do you think they'll say if we pursue what we started on the back porch?"

Jesse didn't even know how *she* felt about what happened on the porch, but her parents' opinions hadn't played a part in any of her other relationships, and she saw no reason to change that now. "My personal life is none of their business."

"My mom wouldn't like it," he admitted, shocking Jesse as she dropped into her seat.

"What? Why?"

"She doesn't trust you."

What had she ever done to Mrs. Shepherd?

"Since when?"

"Since your family cut me out of your lives after the accident. I've told her that you didn't know what your parents did, but she still holds a grudge." Ash poured the wine and slid one glass closer to Jesse. "I don't blame her. I held a grudge for a long time, too."

Jesse stared at the wine glass. All the years of running from the past—from her selfish and uncaring parents—only to have them once again screw with her life.

"What if your mother told you to leave me alone? Would you?"

Ash pushed vegetables around on his plate. "She already did, and you're still here."

The vice around her chest loosened. "The same goes for me. I stopped caring what my parents thought a long time ago."

"Okay, then," he said before popping a green bean into his mouth.

Jesse blinked. "What did you say?"

"Just okay, then," he repeated, and a slow smile curled his lips. "Dig in before it gets cold."

Due to practically growing up together, Ash and Jesse had

bickered like siblings as children, until her sophomore year of high school when Ash began ending their arguments with those two simple words. She'd been sixteen, him seventeen, and it had taken Jesse months to realize that Ash was pulling a Princess Bride on her. Only instead of *as you wish*, he would say *okay, then*. The innocent phrase became code for a number of messages between them, including the times they'd sneaked away to be alone together.

Hearing him say the words again, with that tell-tale grin that offered all sorts of promises, Jesse's heart stuttered in her chest. The man wasn't playing fair, and in an effort to buy herself more time, she opted to ignore the subtle message.

They ate in a comfortable silence, and Jesse's scattered thoughts eventually settled. Ash had that effect on her. He always had. With him, she was safe. She could breathe. But she needed to feel those things on her own, and that meant putting off anything between them that went beyond the making of the album. At least until Jesse figured out how to be by herself.

Because if she couldn't do that, then a relationship with Ash would be as doomed as all of her others.

TWENTY

CLAY HAD BEEN IN HIS OFFICE LESS THAN TWENTY MINUTES WHEN Naomi knocked on his open door. "Good morning," he said. "How was your weekend?"

"Good," she replied, crossing the office to set a folder on his desk before settling into a chair. "I managed to get the last of the info you requested. The band name was tougher to track down, but it landed in my email last night."

Retrieving the manila folder, he flipped it open. "Does the information match what she claims?"

Naomi nodded. "It does. Did you check my credentials this thoroughly?"

"I was already familiar with your work. That's why I recruited you."

"I'm going to take that as a compliment. The band Ms. Garcia *didn't* name is called The Hard Way, made up of Liam Bradshaw on lead vocals, Bobby Shaw on bass, Matt Keys and Eugene Pepper on guitar, and Olive Cindowski on drums. They did a short stint at Six String Records, the label for which Ms. Garcia worked, before leaving their contract."

"When did they leave?"

She leaned forward in her chair. "That's the interesting part.

They were released less than a week before Ms. Garcia left the label."

Clay opened the folder. "She left or was she let go?"

"From everything I've been able to gather, the decision was hers. That was a month ago, and they've yet to replace her. Word is the label will likely fold soon, and a bankruptcy filing is imminent."

That explained what she'd meant by looking for a label willing *and able* to put resources behind their artists. Without a successful act to bring money in, there likely hadn't been much in the way of development budgets. The story was a common one on Music Row. Small-time executive wannabes set up shop and lure in one or two of the thousands of acts seeking any deal they can find. Promises get made. Contracts get signed. And nothing ever comes of them.

Some artists lose a year or two, believing that eventually their career will be launched. Meanwhile, they're still working a day job and playing for tips to survive. In this particular case, not only were artists duped, but Ms. Garcia's talent had presumably been wasted.

"Thanks for putting this together."

Naomi rose from her chair. "I know you were only gathering information on the new recruit, but the band has a YouTube channel you should look at. Chance and I checked them out last night, and we were impressed."

"Are you vying for the A&R position?" Clay asked, setting the folder beside his laptop.

"I'll stick with publicity, thanks. And don't forget Jesse hits the studio this morning."

Speaking of Jesse. "I heard she and Taylor Roper put on a different kind of show last Friday. Have you gotten any calls on that?"

"Four emails on Saturday and two more yesterday. I replied that Shooting Stars did not comment on their artists' personal lives, but that Ms. Gold is working hard on her debut album and as soon as we have new music to share, they'd be the first to know."

That was why he'd hired Naomi. "Has there been anything reported from the Roper camp?"

"Only that the former duet partners are still friends and supportive of each other's solo projects."

Clay raised a brow. "Really?"

The publicist nodded. "Really. I figured they'd take the opportunity to bad-mouth Jesse since eyewitness reports cast her as the aggressor, but to my surprise, Roper took the high road."

Maybe Jesse's former partner wasn't the source of the rumors after all. "Good. Then we'll let it blow over." Tapping the folder, he added, "Thanks again for this. I plan to call our new hire today to give her the good news. She'll have the office beside yours."

"I'll get with Belinda and make sure it's stocked and ready when she arrives."

Naomi exited the office, and Clay did a quick search in his computer to locate The Hard Way on YouTube. There were plenty of songs to choose from, and he clicked the first option. The lead singer possessed a strong baritone and a growl that would appeal to female fans. The sound was retro but relevant and just different enough to stand out on modern radio.

With a few more key strokes, he found a website that provided the history of the band, the lineup, links to buy a self-financed EP, and a list of tour dates, all in small clubs around the country. The more he listened and read about the group, the more Clay felt Shooting Stars was ready to add a band to the roster.

Ms. Garcia would be happy to hear that she'd already found the label's next act, and she hadn't even started yet.

* * *

Sleep had been impossible.

This was the day. Her first day in the studio as a solo artist, and unlike a lot of hopefuls in her position, Jesse knew for certain that not only would her record be released, she had a label behind her, ready to provide all the push she needed to be successful. There was no better position to be in when it came to chasing this dream.

"Can you get the mandolin for me?" Jesse asked Dana as she unloaded her guitar and banjo from the SUV. They hadn't talked about adding the mandolin to anything, but she wanted to be prepared.

"Got it, boss."

The women entered the 1970s-era building, and Jesse told herself not to spaz out. This just happened to be one of the most historic studios in town. Legends had recorded here. Some of the greatest songs *ever* had been cut in these hallowed halls.

No big deal, she thought, as her stomach twisted into one gigantic knot.

Thankfully, Dana had done studio work at Triple Tone and knew her way around. She led Jesse to a large lounge not far from the entrance where they found Ash on a black leather sofa scrolling through his phone.

Jesse's heart did a cartwheel the moment he flashed the smile she'd become a bit addicted to lately.

"Morning, ladies," he said, rising to his feet. "Are we ready to make an album?"

"Yes, sir," Dana replied. "But where's the rest of the crew?"

"Reggie is setting up his kit, and Mason is on his way."

"Mason?" Jesse asked, certain he didn't mean *the* Mason Dexter.

"Mason Dexter, the guitar player," Ash replied, taking the banjo case from her grasp. "I called him for the session."

The knot in her stomach tightened. "He's playing on my album?"

Amber eyes narrowed. "Is that a problem? We have the

budget, so we might as well use it to get the best musicians available."

As if having the musician of the year seven years running playing on her debut record would be a problem. "No. I'm good with that."

"Holy crappola," Dana whispered behind her as they followed Ash out of the room and down a narrow hall. "Mason-Freaking-Dexter. He's played on every top album in the last decade."

This was not helping Jesse's nerves. She spun, nearly smacking Ash in the back of the knees with her guitar case. "I know," she whispered back. "But if you keep talking like that, I might throw up, and I do not want to puke in front of a living legend."

Dana schooled her features. "You're right. We can be cool about this."

"Are you two coming?" Ash asked, and Jesse plastered a smile on her face as she spun back around.

"Right behind you," she trilled, shuffling through the door he'd just stepped through. Inside Jesse found the longest control board she'd ever seen, with engineer extraordinaire Aiden D'Angelo behind the console.

This just kept getting better.

"Which one of you is the lady of the hour?" Aiden asked.

As Jesse shyly raised her hand, she realized this entire day was going to be an out-of-body experience. "That would be me."

"I'm Aiden D'Angelo," he said with a wide smile and one dreadlock hanging over his left eye. "Nice to meet you." His powerful black hand engulfed hers in a warm shake. "Ash says you can play anything with strings."

"Not anything," she corrected. "Just guitar, banjo, and mandolin."

Dark brows arched high. "Is that all?"

Despite understanding the rhetorical nature of the question, Jesse rambled off an answer. "I toyed with piano as a kid but didn't stick with it."

Ash hid a smile as Aiden grinned and returned to his seat.

"The drums are ready to go," Reggie announced as he entered the room. "Phoenix wanted to show her support, so she sent her homemade muffins. I dropped them in the lounge for anybody who wants one."

"Did someone say muffins?" Mason Dexter entered the room with one of the goodies in hand. "I'm already on it." Setting down his guitar, he greeted Ash with what Jesse referred to as a bro-shake—hands clasped and a quick pat on the back.

"How's it going, bud?" Ash asked. "Thanks for coming out today."

"My pleasure. Which one is Jesse?" Mason asked, glancing from one face to the next.

"I am," Jesse said, feeling as if she should have worn a name tag. Not that she was famous, but it wasn't as if she were a complete unknown. "I appreciate you playing on my album."

"I'm always up for working with Ash," he said, turning his attention to the producer. "You have some song sheets for me?"

"They're in my bag over here."

The two men crossed to the other side of the room, and Jesse caught a look from Dana. Neither was impressed with the award-winning musician, nor did they miss the meaning of his comment. Mason wasn't here because of Jesse. In fact, she got the impression he wouldn't be here at all if it weren't for Ash's involvement.

Her annoyance ebbed as Ash distributed the song sheets, and she spotted her name at the top. Regardless of why anyone was here, they all shared one goal—to make the best album they could. And that album would have Jesse's name on it.

Riding a wave of excitement, she and Dana followed Reggie out to his kit where they hashed out the first song. After so many months, Jesse was relieved to finally get this project underway.

* * *

"I really appreciate you doing this," Ash said as Mason withdrew his Fender Stratocaster from its case. "Especially on such short notice."

"You caught me with an opening." He dropped onto the leather sofa and propped the guitar on his knee. "Though I almost passed when you mentioned who this is for."

Ash tensed. "What do you mean?"

Dark eyes met his over wire-rimmed glasses. "The girl has a rep, man. You can't pretend you haven't heard it."

"That's idle gossip. You know how this town is."

Mason tuned his guitar. "I'd have ignored it if I'd heard conflicting stories, but when this many people are all saying the same thing, I tend to believe them."

"What exactly are they saying?"

"You haven't heard it?" he asked, glancing up from the tuner.

"Humor me," Ash replied.

"That she's difficult, mostly." Mason returned to his task. "Bossy. Likes things her way. Doesn't play well with others, which explains why that duet thing didn't work out."

All utter bullshit.

"The duet didn't work out because Taylor Roper got sucked in by a pretty talker with the age-old promise that he could make her a star all by herself. And if you heard that same description of a male artist, you'd be lining up to work with him. Being passionate about the music you want to make isn't a character flaw, and the only reason Jesse gets shit about her perfectionist tendencies—which she aims at herself more than anyone else—is because she's a female artist." Ash rested his arms on the top of the acoustic in his lap. "If you don't plan to put as much into this job as you would for anyone else, tell me now and I'll line up another picker."

Leaning back, Mason gave Ash a hard stare before his face split into a grin. "You seem pretty passionate about this project yourself."

"I believe in Jesse. She deserves this break, and I plan to do all that I can to make sure we turn out the best debut album this town has seen in years. Are you in on that mission or not?"

"When you put it that way, hell yeah, I'm in. But what makes you so sure this chick has what it takes?"

Ash remembered Jesse's reluctance to offer the rumor mill anymore fodder and opted to keep their past connection to himself. "She can play circles around half the musicians in this town—on multiple instruments—and she has a voice that doesn't sound like anyone else. Her songwriting is just as good, and more importantly, she's a true artist—musician, singer, songwriter—which is more than I can say for her former duet partner."

"She's really that good?"

"Stick around and you'll see for yourself."

After a brief hesitation, he nodded. "Okay, then. Which song is first?"

Relieved, Ash made an executive decision and changed the order they'd decided on the week before. "'Save Yourself.'"

Mason shuffled the papers until he found the song. "What's the tempo?"

"I'll show you."

Ash played the song on his acoustic and several bars in, Mason joined him. Ash wouldn't be playing on the album, but since he'd worked out the songs with Jesse, he'd taken on the task of getting the session musician up to speed. They worked through the verses, made an alteration to the chorus, and then the hired gun let fly on the solo before the bridge. As they strummed the last chords, Mason looked up with a genuine smile.

"You two wrote this?"

He shook his head. "She wrote this one by herself."

"Damn," the man murmured. "If this is what we're working with, I'm here as long as you need me."

Shoulders relaxing, Ash reached for another song sheet. "Good. Because it only gets better from here."

TWENTY-ONE

THIS. WAS. *HEAVEN*.

Hearing her song come together, note by note, verse by verse, played by the best musicians she could hope for meant Jesse spent the first part of the day pinching herself, and the other half stressing over whether the rest of her songs were as good as this one.

The session had begun with some shuffling since Ash changed the recording order from "Come See Me" first to starting with "Save Yourself." Jesse had nearly argued, but remembered that though it was *her* record, Ash was in charge. And really, what did it matter in what order they recorded so long as they were *recording her songs*.

Reggie and Dana had learned the new tune, and Jesse tried not to choke on her nerves once it came time for vocals.

The session had run smoothly from that point on, a dream come true sort of day. Only one thing felt off for Jesse. Ash had been all business. He gave no hint of their history together, nor cast her a warm glance that said he hadn't forgotten the kiss they'd shared three days before. Not that she wanted him to act any differently. After all, she had been the one worried about more rumors. The one who'd decided that ignoring the kiss was the smart thing to do and that she needed to be alone to break her unhealthy habit of jumping from one relationship to another.

All of which her head agreed with, but her heart had been voicing a dissenting opinion since she'd crawled out of bed Sunday morning following a very vivid dream in which Ash had done more than just kiss her.

Jesse had spent the rest of the day much as she had the one before—looking for an apartment and coming up empty. The options were either too modern, too expensive, or came with the kind of roommates that scurried under walls when the lights came on.

The apartment hunt had done little to keep her mind off Ash. After the accident, when he'd disappeared from her life, Jesse had spent months crying, and then a year convinced that he would come back. Hope had eventually been replaced by heartbreaking acceptance, and at some point, devolved into righteous indignation. The last had simmered for nearly a decade and had sustained her so long as Ash was the villain in her memory.

Now that he was the villain no more, Jesse found herself pondering a plethora of what-ifs that would lead her right back down the same road she was trying to get off. Maybe if he'd come back into her life at a different time, when she hadn't been with someone else and subsequently dealing with a bad breakup.

Then again, when would that have been? Jesse took a mental stroll through her dating history and couldn't find a time when she wasn't either with someone, getting over someone— typically an embarrassingly short period of time—or getting involved with someone else.

The therapist her parents had *forced* her to see when she'd nearly flunked out of her freshman year of college due to a lack of effort had been right. Jesse was trying to fill a hole and so far, she'd only managed to widen the gap.

"Did you want to take another run at the vocal?" Ash asked, interrupting her revelatory moment.

He'd been working on the drum track with Reggie, which had allowed Jesse time for her mental meanderings. Mason Dexter had left nine hours into what was now a ten-hour day, and Dana had stepped out to take a call from Ingrid.

"Yeah," Jesse said, snapping back to the present. "I can do that."

Before she could drag herself off of the comfortable leather sofa, Dana returned from her call. "I'm afraid we need to go. Ingrid's car won't start, and I have the jumper cables."

"Oh." Without her own vehicle, Jesse had to leave with her ride. "I guess we can work on the vocal tomorrow."

"You don't have your Jeep?" Ash asked.

"Dana's SUV was bigger to hold all the gear, and it seemed pointless not to ride together."

The bass player flashed an apologetic expression, and Ash said, "I can take you home."

She couldn't let him do that. "No," Jesse said. "That's too far out of your way."

"I don't mind," he said, his tone insistent. Ash turned his focus on Dana. "You go and if the jumper cables don't work, let us know, and I'll come see what I can do."

Brows high, the bass player looked to Jesse. "Do you care?"

Before Jesse could answer, Ash waved her on. "We need to start on the next song tomorrow so knocking the vocal out tonight will keep us on schedule."

Decision clearly made, Dana said, "Okay, then. See you guys later."

"See you at home," Jesse said, annoyed. While she *did* want to work on the vocal, she didn't like the decision being made for her. Once her friend was gone, she asked, "Where's Aiden?"

"I sent him home," Ash said, grabbing a bottle of water from the fridge. "Go on into the vocal booth, and we'll start from the top."

There was only so much being dictated to that Jesse would tolerate. "Is this what every session will be like? You barking out orders, expecting me to jump like a trained puppy?"

Now she had his attention. "I didn't bark anything. Do you *not* want to work on this?"

As if she had a choice. "Since my ride just left, I guess I might as well."

"Hey," he snapped as she vaulted from her seat like a bratty teenager. "What's wrong with you?"

"I don't like having decisions made for me."

"You said you wanted to stay, so I offered to take you home. What's the problem?"

Jesse was determined to contain her anger. She would not prove them right. She would not be *difficult* to work with.

"Nothing. I'm fine." She marched toward the door, wishing they were doing a song that required more rage than sympathy.

Ash reached the door before her. "You aren't fine."

"Just let me by. I don't want to be here all night."

"It seems more like you don't want to be here at all. What's the issue?"

"The issue is that I feel as if I've been ordered to stay after school like some misbehaving child. You let everyone else go and then made it so that I can't leave until you say I can."

"I sent everyone else home so that I could stop pretending that I don't want to kiss you every time we're in the same room. But by all means, call Dana back and go home if that's what you want."

His words doused her anger like running water on a lit match. "You want to kiss me?" Jesse asked, forgetting her vow to stay single.

Ash locked his hands on his hips. "That's all I've wanted to do all damn day."

Melting like a snow cone in a sauna, Jesse trailed a finger down his chest. "You were really good at hiding it."

Taking her hand, he said, "There are cameras. They record video, but not audio. For obvious reasons."

She glanced around and spotted a small, round device in the far corner of the room. She'd wanted to avoid more rumors, and Ash seemed ready to respect her wish. Turning back, she asked, "So that's why you've kept me at a distance? Acting like we barely know each other?"

He nodded. "Yeah, that's why."

The man knew how to take the air out of a woman's argument. "Oh. I didn't realize."

"That was the idea."

Jesse took a half step forward, and Ash nodded up toward the camera again. "Right," she said, shifting away from him in what she hoped looked like a normal movement. "Strictly business."

Amber eyes darkened as he visibly relaxed. "Okay, then."

How was she supposed to ignore their code when he looked at her like that? The sentiment, combined with the confession about wanting to kiss her, struck Jesse momentarily speechless, and after what felt like an eternity of staring silently into each other's eyes, Ash swept past her and across the hall to the control room.

"I've got everything cued up so let me know when you're ready."

Not sure what to do with the memories flooding back, or the conflicting emotions threatening to overrule the firm decision she'd made to stay single, Jesse stepped into the hall with the lyrics she was about to sing playing on a loop through her mind. Save yourself, indeed. She needed to save herself from the temptation of Ash Shepherd.

But did she want to? No. No, she did not.

* * *

This. Was. *Agony*.

Ash had been fine working with Jesse until that damn kiss on

Friday. She'd played cool through their lunch and the rest of the afternoon had been about work, but she was all he could think about throughout the weekend. When she'd walked into the studio lounge this morning, practically glowing with excitement, it had taken every ounce of control he possessed not to kiss her senseless. Controlling that urge had put him on edge all day until he'd found an excuse to get her alone.

He hadn't expected the pushback once he'd managed to do so, but the softness in her eyes when he'd revealed his true intentions gave Ash hope that he wasn't wading back into this particular pond alone. Jesse was still fresh off a breakup, so he knew the timing wasn't right, but they had months to go in the recording process. By the time the album was finished, they'd be into the new year. A perfect time for new beginnings.

And second chances.

"Do we have to eat here?" she asked as Ash turned into a parking lot off Trinity Lane.

They'd agreed to grab dinner on the way to her temporary home, and in front of them sat the unassuming gray building that housed the East Nashville Beer Works Taproom restaurant. One of Ash's favorite places to eat, though he didn't get up here as often as he'd like.

"What's wrong with this place?" he asked. "They serve the best pizza in town."

She sank down in the seat. "Five Points is better, but the pizza isn't the problem."

Jesse looked as if she were going to ooze onto the floorboard. "Then what *is* the problem?"

Sighing, she straightened in the seat. "A guy I used to date worked here."

"How long ago was that?" Ash knew she'd been with Dimitri for more than a year, so she presumably meant someone else.

"About the time I met Ryan so . . . fifteen months ago."

"Then he probably isn't here now."

The sinking resumed. "I don't know if I want to chance it."

Growing concerned, he asked, "Did this guy hurt you?"

"What?" She spun his way. "No. Nothing like that. I mean, he wasn't the best boyfriend ever, but Frankie never hit me."

Not exactly a glowing review. "Then why do you look scared to go in there? What aren't you telling me?"

"Well . . ." she hedged. "We didn't end on the best of terms."

"Meaning?"

"Meaning I sort of . . . disappeared."

"You ghosted?" Ash asked.

"Was ghosting a thing back then?"

"Answer the question, Rheingold."

"Before you get all judgmental on me, I had a good reason."

Doubtful. "And what was that?"

"I found out that I wasn't Frankie's only girlfriend. I was just the only one who *wasn't* sporting a big fat engagement ring."

That *was* a good reason. "Then I doubt the guy is still holding a grudge, and the odds that he still works here are slim." Ash reached for his door handle. "Let's eat."

She was slow to meet him around the front of the truck and plodded to the door as if marching to her own execution. Ash took her hand and tucked her close against his side. "Don't worry. I'll protect you," he said, joking to lighten the mood. He seriously doubted the dude would be here.

Within seconds of stepping inside, a booming baritone echoed off the metal walls. "You've got some nerve coming in here, Gold."

Jesse tensed, and Ash went on alert, searching the room for the source of the voice. A mountain of a man, covered in tattoos and sporting a leather vest that could double as a keg Koozie, charged their way. As he drew closer, Ash tensed for a fight he had no chance of winning, but instead of throwing a punch, the big guy whisked Jesse off her feet and spun her in a circle as laughter rolled from deep in his chest.

"I thought you were dead or left town until I recognized that gorgeous voice of yours in a Honkytonk Daisies song. What are you up to now, little darling?"

Ash bristled at the endearment but was smart enough to keep the irritation to himself.

"I'm recording my solo album," she replied, returning to Ash's side. "How is Savannah?"

He assumed Savannah was the one who'd gotten a ring.

Frankie snorted. "She left me six months ago." Brown eyes narrowed as he assessed Ash. "I see you've got another pretty boy. Didn't that Dimitri asshole teach you anything, doll? The pretty ones can't be trusted."

"*You* couldn't be trusted," Jesse reminded him. "And this isn't my boyfriend. He's my producer. Ash Shepherd, meet Frankie Snow."

Despite declaring Ash *not* her boyfriend, she slid her hand into his while making the introductions. Extending the other hand in greeting, he said, "Nice to meet you, Frankie."

"You, too, dude." Turning his back to them, he yelled toward the counter in the back. "Hailey, these folks need a table. And get them a flight on me."

"On it, boss," said a tall blonde with as many tattoos as the man who'd just bellowed her name. "Right this way, folks."

"It's good to see you, Jess," Frankie said with a lopsided grin and eyes locked on the petite redhead who refused to meet his gaze.

So Ash wasn't the only one interested in a second chance. Thankfully, Jesse's body language indicated Frankie's chance had passed.

"Here you go," Hailey said, showing them to a booth along the back wall and dropping a menu in front of each of them. "Do y'all want something to drink besides the flight?"

"Water, please," Jesse said, burying her nose in the menu.

"I'll have a Coke," Ash replied.

"Water and Coke, coming right up."

When they were alone—relatively speaking as the tables on

each side of them were occupied—he said, "You and Frankie, huh?"

She didn't come out of the menu. "Yep."

He pushed the barrier down with one finger. "Were you going through a biker phase?" Not that he knew for sure that Frankie Snow owned a motorcycle, but based on appearance alone, Ash felt the odds were good.

"As you can see, he's a really sweet guy. He just has a problem with monogamy." Her eyes returned to the food options. "That seems to be a pattern in my life."

"I never cheated on you," Ash said, wanting to make sure she wasn't lumping him in with the other men she'd dated.

"No, but in time you might have."

"Excuse me?"

Jesse closed the menu and dropped it to the table. "Don't take it personally. I'm just saying that every guy *eventually* cheats on me. Charmers like Frankie. Hipsters like Todd. More musicians than I'm willing to discuss—case in point, Ryan. The common denominator is me. I don't know if I come across as too needy or not needy enough, but I do something that makes them all jump into another woman's bed. Ingrid says I need to raise my standards and stop falling for the wrong guys. If that's the problem, then every woman has the same issue because these guys aren't cheating with Barbie dolls."

Ash blinked, struggling to process the load of crap she'd just uttered.

"There are men who cheat, and there are women who cheat. None of it is the fault of the ones being cheated *on*. But there are plenty of us who *don't cheat*, and the idea that I'd suddenly take up the practice if we were to date again is ridiculous." Returning to his menu, he added, "Ingrid is right. You're falling for the wrong guys."

"They don't seem wrong at first," she defended. "Or else I wouldn't go out with them to begin with."

"Call me crazy, but I'd bet my best Martin that Frankie there had a reputation *before* you met him. I know Dimitri did."

She crossed her arms and glared but held silent as Hailey returned with their drinks.

"Water here," the waitress said, setting a glass before Jesse. "Coke for you. And here's the flight from Frankie. Are we ready to order?"

"Margherita pizza, please," Jesse mumbled, handing over her menu.

"I'll have the veggie," Ash said.

"Great. I'll get the order right in."

As she walked away, Jesse picked up where they'd left off. "Do you expect me to run a background check on every guy before I date him?"

"A little research couldn't hurt."

"So you mean I should date someone I know more about. Like you?"

Not where he was going, but Ash wouldn't back down from the subject. "At least you'd know what you were getting."

"Yeah. Safe," she snapped.

"What?"

"You were *safe*. Steady. The opposite of every other guy I've been with since. You made me believe that you would always be there for me, but you *weren't*." Blue eyes dropped and her voice softened. "So you can criticize my choices, but don't forget that you were one of them."

Ash couldn't argue with that statement. He'd been her first choice, and he'd let her down. Using her parents as an excuse was a cop-out he'd clung to for far too long.

"You're right," he muttered. "I have no right to judge your life."

After a deep breath, Jesse nodded. "Okay, then."

He tensed, surprised by her use of their old phrase. "Okay, then?"

"Yeah." She reached for her water. "Okay, then."

TWENTY-TWO

THE LAST TWO WEEKS HAD BEEN A BLUR.

Things slowed down after that first day, for both the recording and between Jesse and Ash. They seemed to make an unspoken agreement over their respective pizzas, and neither uttered the *okay, then* thing after that night. The album became their only collaboration, at least for the moment. The truce, for lack of a better word, allowed Jesse to relax, enjoy the recording process, and abide by her decision to stay single for the foreseeable future.

Running into Frankie reminded her that she'd literally shifted from him to Ryan in a matter of days. After a seven-month relationship, and then learning that her boyfriend had gotten engaged two months before meeting her, Jesse had waltz from one philanderer to another. How heartbroken could she possibly have been to change boyfriends that quickly?

And she'd nearly done it again by going straight from Ryan to Ash. Granted, Ash would be a do-over, but that didn't make the situation any less predictable. Jesse had realized another truth over that pizza. She had yet to forgive Ash for leaving her after the accident.

Without even consulting her, he'd walked out of her life.

Forget her parents. Jesse and Ash weren't children back then. Not legally speaking. Maybe his belief that she'd agreed with her parents—that she also never wanted to see him again—was a fair assumption. But it had been an *assumption* none the less, and the least he could have done was confirm the situation by actually hearing the sentiment from her own lips.

Why hadn't he found a way in? Why hadn't he even tried to change her mind? If not while she was in the hospital, then in the weeks after. Or any time during the next ten years, for that matter.

Rationally speaking, Jesse knew that Ash wasn't responsible for the slew of bad candidates who had followed him into her life, *but* he'd been her first and only relationship experience until she'd left for college eight months later. With Ash, everything had been so easy. She'd naively thought that's how all relationships would be, which meant when things weren't easy, Jesse had bent over backwards to make them so for the other person. Basically, she'd become a doormat and convinced herself that being one was the way to be happy.

"This wig is itchy," Dana said, scratching beneath the trucker cap perched atop a jet-black wig.

"You can take it off in a couple of hours," Ingrid assured her. Because she was playing Garth to Dana's Wayne, the Scandinavian didn't need a wig. Though she would likely regret teasing her hair to such an extreme when the time came to brush it out.

Jesse's character wasn't supposed to have red hair, but she'd run with her own anyway, styled in a retro way that held the gold headband in place. She still wasn't sure how Ash had talked her into attending this party. Apparently, his ex-wife loved Halloween and threw this huge soiree every year. By the amount of cars parked up and down the street, the guest list was extensive, which meant no one would notice when they cut out early.

"Whose party is this again?" Ingrid asked as they trudged the block and a half from where they'd left Dana's SUV.

"Ash's ex-wife's. He says she throws it every year. I guess it's a thing." A thing Jesse wasn't about to crash without backup. Thankfully, Ingrid had been into cosplay years before. Not only had she helped talk Dana into coming, she'd also assisted with Jesse's costume. Most of it had come from Jesse's closet, the one exception being the little red number pulled from the photographers boudoir collection and required wearing a heavy coat to avoid freezing her tatas off.

The accessories had been ordered online and arrived at the house before Jesse had even agreed to wear the costume, thanks to Ingrid's enthusiasm.

The three women followed a smattering of stone pavers that led to a narrow two-story charmer with a double-decker porch, both floors of which were standing-room-only for costumed partiers. Jesse's gut tightened as they approached the home, and she hoped Ash would be easy to find. Otherwise, without knowing the hostess, let alone any of the attendees, they might be mistaken as party-crashers and sent packing.

"Holy smokes, is that you, Jesse?" came a voice from the upper porch. "Girl, I haven't seen you in forever."

Jesse looked up to find Kelsey Ellis waving down to her. The pair had worked the bar scene together for years, their paths crossing often enough that they'd once toyed with forming a duo of their own. But then Kelsey had landed a back-up gig she couldn't pass up, and the pair went their separate ways.

"Hey, Kelsey," she called, grateful for a familiar face. "How are you doing?"

"Not as good as you are, darling. How is that album coming along?"

Last Jesse heard, the lanky brunette was touring as a back-up singer for Reba. Not a bad gig if you could get it.

"I like what we have so far." Which was five songs that she

still wanted to tweak, but Ash had insisted she was being too picky. "Is there anyone else here I know?"

"Of course, girl. Everybody's here." Before Jesse could ask her to elaborate, Kelsey was pulled away by a man in a hockey mask. Only at a Halloween party would that not be a weird occurrence.

Did *everybody's here* include Taylor? Surely Ash wouldn't have invited Jesse if that was the case. Though now she wondered exactly what Ash's ex did that she knew so many industry people. She passed four more familiar faces on the lower porch.

"Do you think she's here?" Dana asked as if reading Jesse's mind.

"I don't know," she replied, hesitating at the bottom of the three steps that led to the porch. "Maybe we should skip it."

Ingrid pushed Jesse forward. "We are not wasting my work by going home now. Besides," she said, stepping around Jesse to take the lead, "you can't let Taylor dictate where you go or don't go. You were invited to this party, and you have every right to be here."

Jesse wasn't even sure if the hostess knew she was coming, but Ingrid had a point. They'd gotten the initial encounter over with that horrible day in The Gulch. This time, Jesse would keep her temper in check and avoid another confrontation.

Dragging her by the hand, the blonde stepped through the open door into a throng of costumed revelers, several made up to look like this or that horror movie character. There was a baseball player, a hockey goalie—likely the warmest person there—and the requisite sex-kitten numbers. The sexy witch, the sexy nurse, the sexy librarian, and what was a party without a sexy cop?

Considering her own costume, Jesse couldn't say much. She didn't have to sex up her character. The woman had just been drawn that way.

"Hello!" cooed a beautiful woman dressed as Morticia Addams—and looking the part to perfection. She descended the stairs in their direction with a warm smile. "I'm so glad you could make it."

This was their hostess? Jesse was too struck by how gorgeous she was to reply, and Ingrid blessedly stepped in.

"Hi there. I'm Ingrid Samuelson, and this is my partner Dana Mills. I hope it's okay that we tagged along with Jesse tonight."

The presumed hostess waved a hand in the air. "Of course. The more the merrier. Let me take your coats, and you ladies can wander off to the kitchen for some drinks. Jae-ho will make you anything you want, and we have plenty of non-alcoholic drinks for the designated drivers."

"That's me," Dana said, handing off her jacket.

Ingrid passed over her puffy vest, and Jesse faced the moment of truth. After sliding the long black coat down her arms, a chill from the open front door danced across her bare shoulders. When she handed the coat off to Ronnie, someone whistled and a male voice said, "Hey there, darling. If you want to test that lasso, you can tie me up and teach me a lesson. I promise I've been a bad boy."

Jesse wasn't in the mood for frat boy comments, but before she could inform Thor that he was barking up the wrong universe, a geeky-looking guy in glasses, a bow tie, and a blue lab coat stepped between them.

"This one is spoken for, Trevor."

Since when? Jesse almost asked.

"Sorry, Ash. I didn't know she was with you."

"Neither did I," Ronnie muttered behind Jesse.

She spun to catch a less-welcoming glare. Ash claimed that he and his ex-wife weren't in love with each other, but maybe he'd been only half right.

"Veronica Shepherd!" a voice yelled from across the crowd. "Calling Veronica Shepherd!"

Wait. *The* Veronica Shepherd? As in, the most successful female producer to ever grace Music City? Jesse's gut tightened as the revelation hit. Ash's ex wasn't just drop-dead gorgeous, she was an industry powerhouse, which explained all of the familiar faces in attendance.

The dark-clad hostess slipped past Jesse and gave Ash a kiss on the cheek as she went. "I'm here, Fran. What do you need?"

"She's gorgeous," Dana mumbled as Ronnie glided through the crowd.

"Close your mouth, baby," Ingrid purred. "You're drooling."

Remembering herself, the musician cleared her throat. "You know I prefer blonds."

"Ronnie's a blonde under the wig," the geek offered, no help at all.

Dana glared at him as Ingrid laughed. "Come on, Wayne," she said, taking her girlfriend by the hand. "I need a drink, and I think Jesse needs a word with her white-knight scientist."

As her companions walked off, she pulled Ash aside. "Your ex-wife is Veronica Shepherd?"

"I told you that."

"No," she corrected. "You told me your ex-wife's name was Ronnie."

"That's what I call her. Ronnie is short for Veronica."

"Yeah. Veronica Shepherd."

Leaning on the newel post, he crossed his arms. "I assumed you knew *my* last name, so the Shepherd part was a given." Without awaiting a reply, his eyes scanned the length of her, and Jesse felt as if he'd caressed her from head to toe. "You look amazing."

Instead of the stinging comeback she had for Thor, Jesse turned bashful. "Thanks. Ingrid put me together."

"God put you together. Ingrid just dressed you up." Taking her hand, he said, "You want a drink?"

"Sure." Ash tugged her through the crowd, clearing a path like Moses and the Red Sea. "Who are you supposed to be?"

He spun and held his baby-blue lab coat open. "I'm Bill Nye."

Jesse failed to withhold her laughter. "You are such a dork."

"Yep," he agreed with a grin before taking her hand and setting off again.

Science had been Ash's second love during their teen years. When he wasn't strumming a guitar, he'd been mixing some concoction that inevitably exploded in the Rheingold kitchen. To be fair, he'd had one of the worst assistants ever in Tommy.

Keeping her red cowboy boots moving, Jesse hustled to keep up while catching all the female attendees watching her escort with interest. A second later, their eyes landed on Jesse with a combination of disgust and judgment. Clearly, Ash wasn't single due to a lack of options. Ryan had received the same attention, and when Jesse would catch these same glares, she'd often grown insecure because she knew what they were thinking.

Why was Ryan with her?

To Jesse's surprise, that wasn't her current reaction. Instead, she felt annoyed and possessive, and flashed more than one woman an evil eye to let them know that Ash *wasn't* on the market. Not until they reached the kitchen did she realize what she was doing. While waiting for their turn at the bar, something shifted into place.

One statement rolled through her mind. *This is my man.* And for once in her life, no one was going to take him away.

* * *

"When were you going to tell me?" Ronnie said, cornering Ash on his way out of the bathroom.

"Tell you what?" he replied, eager to get back to Jesse. She looked good in anything, but the sexy costume drew more attention than he liked. Two brave souls had already received the same warning Trevor had.

Instead of answering, Ronnie pulled Ash into her bedroom—the one room in the house everyone knew was off-limits—and slammed the door.

"So you're back with her?" she asked.

"Back with Jesse?" Ash hedged, not exactly sure how to answer.

They'd been dancing around each other for a couple of weeks, but his patience was wearing thin. In the studio, there were days it felt as if they were back where they used to be. Friends, but more. And he definitely wanted the more. That Jesse hadn't argued when he'd claimed her the minute she arrived was a good sign they were on the same page.

Ronnie pinched his arm. "Stop stalling."

"Ow," he winced, rubbing his arm. "Fine. I don't know. That's the answer."

She tilted her head in disbelief. "What are you, nine? You either know or you don't."

And there was the crux. He'd driven her home several more nights from the studio when they'd worked late together, but there'd been no more meals and no dating talk of any kind— past, present, or future. Which was why he'd convinced her to come to this party. Ash needed to test the waters away from work. So far, the night had gone better than he'd hoped.

"It's complicated, Ronnie. Between our history and her recent breakup, we're taking it slow."

Ever astute, she pinned him with a look. "Does she know what you're up to?"

Ash hadn't shared his motives for the invite, if that's what she meant. "Why does any of this matter to you?"

"Because you matter to me, you big lug. The only thing I know about that woman is that she threw you out of her life, flits from one guy to the next, and no one wants to work with her. Forgive me if that makes me cautious on your behalf."

Temper hanging by a thread, Ash said, "She didn't throw me out of her life. Her parents did. And *I'm* working with her along with a studio full of others whom I can guaran-damn-tee you have no complaints."

Ronnie softened. "What about the guys, Ash? What about the

way she hops from one man to the next without even taking a breath?"

Jaw tight, he shook his head. "You don't know her, Ronnie."

"Do you? It's been *ten years*. You've been back in her life for, what? A few weeks. People change, and not always for the better." She took his hand in hers. "I don't want to see you get hurt."

Ash snatched his hand away. "I know what I'm doing. Jesse is the only one for me. She always was."

Ronnie flinched. Though the divorce had been mutual, it hadn't been easy for either of them.

"I'm sorry. I didn't mean—"

"Yes, you did. I get it." She took a step toward the door and turned back before opening it. "I always knew. I guess it just hurts more to hear you say the words."

As Ronnie whisked the door open, Ash moved to catch her. "Ronnie, wait."

She ignored him and stepped into the hall, only to come face to face with a wide-eyed Jesse. Ronnie cast her glance back to Ash before saying, "Sorry to have kept him. He's all yours."

Before Ash could speak, Jesse charged off in the opposite direction.

TWENTY-THREE

"I'm ready to go," Jesse told Dana as she returned to the far corner of the living room.

As the night went on, the size of the crowd had doubled. Jesse recognized many, but few she actually knew personally. Countless guests had approached Ash to exchange words with the popular songwriter, and he'd performed the requisite introductions each time. The men had admired what Jesse's costume failed to cover, and the woman had acknowledged her with friendly-enough smiles, but none showed much interest in having a conversation.

When Ash had excused himself, he'd joked that if he was gone for too long, she'd have to come save him. Jesse hadn't given the request much thought, but after he'd been gone for more than twenty minutes, she'd decided a rescue mission might actually be in order. After a thorough search—during which she'd encountered her engineer, session guitarist, and three other songwriting friends—she'd feared something might have actually happened to him. But then she heard a muffled argument coming from the other side of a closed door, and one of the voices sounded familiar.

Trying not to rouse suspicion, Jesse had lingered in the hall, but had only been able to make out short snippets of the conversation inside. Clear as day, she'd heard one particular declaration.

"The only one for me."

The door had opened moments later, with Ash begging Ronnie to come back. Jesse didn't have to be a genius to decipher the rest, but her hostess's words had confirmed her suspicions. She didn't know if Ash was a liar or just clueless, but the couple's relationship was far from over.

"What's the hurry?" Dana asked. "Ingrid just went to get another drink."

"We'll grab her on the way out."

"But we don't even know where our coats are."

Jesse yanked her out of her chair. "We'll find them."

Dana followed Jesse through the crowd. "What happened upstairs? Did you find Ash?"

She didn't want to talk about Ash. Earlier in the evening, Jesse had watched Ronnie carry an armload of coats down the hall that led to the back of the house. "I think I know where our coats are. Get Ingrid and I'll meet you out front."

Following the order, her bass player wound her way toward the kitchen, past hunters and jockeys and four guys dressed as the Beatles. Jesse went around the edge of the crowd and found a dark room at the end of the hall. The bed inside was covered by a mountain of coats. Thanks to the bright-red color of Ingrid's vest, she was able to locate their three quickly.

On her way to the front door, she spotted Ash leaning over the stair banister, scanning the room. Looking for an alternate route, she slipped out the back door and into a cloud of smoke. Holding her breath against the skunk-like scent, Jesse scurried around the side of the house and found Ingrid and Dana shivering at the edge of the sidewalk.

"Here," she said, tossing their respective coats. "Let's get out of here."

Jesse marched down the sidewalk, in too big a hurry to slip

on her cumbersome jacket, but she was too angry to feel the cold, so it didn't matter. How stupid she'd been to believe that Ash was different. He wasn't different at all.

"Slow down," Dana said, struggling to keep up. "My hat's going to fall off."

"You can take it off now," Ingrid said, having no trouble keeping pace thanks to her long legs.

"Oh, yeah. Thank God."

When they were three houses down, a voice called out behind them. "Jesse! Wait!"

Funny. He'd said the same thing to his wife not five minutes ago.

"Are you going to stop?" Dana asked.

"Nope," Jesse replied, head down and feet moving. When heavy footsteps sounded behind them, she sped up nearly to a run.

Ingrid put a hand on her arm. "You'll have to face him tomorrow. Running will buy you only so much time."

Panting, Jesse stopped and turned back to find Ash barreling toward her. "Just listen to me, please," he called.

Jesse met Ingrid's gaze. "You two go on and warm up the car. I'll be there in a minute."

"What am I missing here?" Dana asked as the couple continued down the sidewalk arm in arm.

"I don't know," the blonde said, "but running never solves anything."

The statement hit Jesse in the chest. Running is what she always did. Run away when things went bad. Run into the arms of the next guy up. And as Ingrid pointed out, the running never really got her anywhere. It was time to stand her ground and try a different tactic.

"Why did you take off like that?" Ash asked when he finally reached her, heavy breaths creating white puffs in the cold air.

"Go back to your wife, Ash," she said, too tired to fight. "She's the one you want."

"What? No. That isn't what I said."

"*The only one for you*," Jesse repeated. "I heard you through the door."

Ash shook his head. "I said *you* are the only one for me. That's why Ronnie was upset. Because even when we were married, she knew that I was still in love with you. I've never stopped *being* in love with you, Jesse. Ever."

With every fiber of her being, she wanted to believe him. To fall into his arms and never come up. But she'd been hurt so many times. Too many.

"We were apart for too long. We aren't the same people anymore." Stepping away, she added, "I'm not the girl you loved, Ash. I'm a train wreck on my best days, and I suck at relationships. You don't want to get involved with me."

"I'm already involved with you, Jesse. And that girl is still in there." Ash cupped her cheeks in his callused hands. "That tough, ambitious, brave girl is still in there somewhere. She has to be, or you never would have made it this far."

Jesse didn't feel any of those things. Fragile. Scared. Defeated. Those she knew well.

"What if we can't make this work?" she whispered. "I've screwed up so many times."

"Those just weren't the right guys." Ash pressed his lips to her forehead. "I've tried to be patient, Jesse, but I don't want to wait anymore. I know you need time to get used to the idea, and I'm good with that." He pulled her against his warm body. "But I'm not letting you go again."

She'd spent so many years hoping that this would happen, and then, somewhere along the last decade, she'd given up. The dream of holding him again. Of loving him again. Jesse had accepted the reality that Ash was out of her life forever. Now he was here, offering her everything she'd ever wanted, and Jesse couldn't let go of the fear.

"I need that time," she mumbled, stepping out of his arms. "I need to be sure I'm not making the same mistake again."

"What mistake?" Ash asked.

"I've only been single for a few weeks. If we do this, I want to make sure I'm doing it for the right reasons, and not because I can't be alone."

Nodding, he slid his hands into the lab coat pockets. "Okay. But I'm serious when I say I'm not walking away again."

The assurance helped. "Good. Because I don't want you to."

Dana's SUV pulled up to the curb.

"You'd better go before you freeze out here," Ash said.

Hugging her coat to her chest, she backed away. "I'll see you tomorrow."

"Yes, ma'am." He stepped back. "Good night, Jesse."

"Night, Ash." She opened the car door, and he lingered on the sidewalk, watching her. Instead of getting in, she tossed her coat inside and ran back to the only boy she'd ever really wanted.

"What's wrong?" he said.

"I forgot something." Rising onto her toes, Jesse pulled him down and pressed her lips to his. Ash engulfed her in his arms and lifted until her feet dangled high above the ground. The kiss lasted an hour or maybe only seconds, and though it was probably the hundredth between them, it felt like the first. Breaking the contact, she pressed her forehead to his. "Okay, then."

Ash squeezed her tight before setting her back on her feet. "Okay, then."

Jesse once again made the short walk to the truck, fingers pressed to her warmed lips and her eyes on Ash. Not trusting herself, she jumped inside and slammed the door. "Let's go."

"Are you sure?" Dana asked.

"Yeah," she said, her voice breathy. "I'm sure."

Her first love watched them drive away, and Jesse twisted in the seat to see him fade away through the back window.

"I assume all is well now?" Ingrid asked.

"Almost," Jesse answered. "Almost."

* * *

Other than a glance or two across a crowded room, Ash didn't
see Ronnie for the rest of the party. Things finally faded around
two in the morning—earlier than usual since many had to work
in the morning—and he found her cleaning up in the kitchen. A
duty he'd shared since the first year they'd met.

"Hey, there," he said, wading in slowly. "I did a thorough pass
and threw away all the cans and plastic I could find."

"Thanks," she replied, black sleeves rolled up high as she
rinsed another glass. The Morticia wig had been tossed on the
table, and she'd pulled her honey-blond waves into a
messy bun.

"Can we talk?" Ash asked, reluctant to leave things as they
were when she'd exited the bedroom earlier.

Ronnie wiped her forehead with the back of a soapy hand.
"It's late, Ash. You should go home."

He couldn't do that. Not until they talked.

"I'm sorry that I hurt you earlier."

"You didn't hurt me," she snapped, dunking a plate into the
water and splashing suds over the side.

Ash closed the space between them, grabbed a towel off the
counter, and turned her to face him, making sure she didn't drip
on the floor. "You know I love you, right?"

She kept her eyes down. "I love you, too."

With a finger on her chin, he tipped her face up. "Are you *in*
love with me?"

Her hesitation worried him. "I didn't think I was," she finally
admitted. "But the idea of you with her bothers me. A lot."

"You'll always be in my life. That's a given."

"Until you move on. I guess it's been so easy because even
after the divorce, we still had each other."

After drying off her hands, he pulled her to the table, urged
her into a chair, and pulled another close. "Moving on doesn't
change the fact that you're my best friend. You dated Nate

Lindham, and we were fine. And that Wilson guy. Nothing changed then."

"Do you know why those relationships didn't last?" Ronnie asked.

She'd claimed that both had run their course, and Ash had believed her. "I figured they just weren't the right guys."

"They weren't," she agreed. "Because I kept comparing them to you."

Ash sighed and sat back in his chair. "I don't know what to say to that."

Ronnie leaned forward and patted his cheek. "Neither do I, buddy." Rising, she returned to the sink. "My someone is out there, and I'm sure he'll make you look like the lemon that you are."

He didn't like the resigned tone. "I can't let her go again, Ronnie."

Nodding, she tossed a sad smile over her shoulder. "I know. I'm not asking you to."

No, she wouldn't. But that didn't change the fact that she was hurting, and there was nothing he could do about it. Ash crossed to the counter and kissed her temple. "You're a good woman, and another man is going to be lucky to have you."

"I hope so."

"I know so." Ash moved her over with a nudge of his hip. "Here's the towel. You dry, and I'll wash for a while."

She took the tea towel and pulled a bowl from the rinsing sink. After a long silence, Ronnie asked, "Are you and Jesse okay?"

Ash considered his answer while scrubbing a serving plate. "We're getting there. Like you said, we need to get to know each other again."

Laying her head on his shoulder, she said, "I really do want you to be happy."

"Right back at you," he replied. "At least now I won't fare so well in future comparisons."

Ronnie snorted. "You've got that right." Sliding the dried bowl into the cabinet to her right, she added, "Any guy who isn't still in love with his high school sweetheart is going to look like Prince Charming."

He passed over the plate. "And he'll sweep you off your feet. Or maybe fit you for a glass slipper."

A slow smile curved her lips, and Ash felt things click back into place. "You really are a sap, Shepherd."

"That I am."

* * *

Rain earlier in the day had moved on, taking the clouds with it and leaving behind clear skies and cooler temps. Dressed in her thickest pajamas and bundled in a soft blanket, Jesse sat on the back patio with her eyes on the heavens. Stargazing was something she and Ash once did together. Hand in hand, they'd pick out the dippers and Orion and talk about their future together.

She'd been so naive back then, assuming nothing would ever tear them apart. When he'd walked out of her life, he'd taken every dream with him, and Jesse had gone into mourning. For her brother. Her first love. Even her parents had seemed more distant after the accident. Maybe the losses and lack of connection were why, no matter how long her failed relationships had lasted, Jesse never really pictured any of them as husband material. Her heart had given up on the concept of happily ever after.

Carter Dunn, the boy she'd met in the middle of her freshman year at Georgia State, had become her boyfriend a couple weeks later. Though Jesse and Ash had grown up together, they'd been a couple only eighteen months before the accident, so that meant Carter held the record, having lasted three years. But not once in that time had they talked about marriage. In fact, it wasn't until *after* they'd broken up—because he'd slept with two of her sorority sisters during their last semester of school—that he'd even used the word in conversation.

To Jesse's amazement, Carter had assumed that they would get married after graduation, despite the meaningless encounters—*his words*—with other women. Which he'd blamed on panic. The realization that he'd never sleep with anyone other than Jesse for the rest of his life had driven him to the senseless acts. She'd nearly strained a muscle from the eye-roll at that one.

He'd never actually asked her, and Jesse had never hinted that she wanted to be asked. But that's just how life worked, or so Carter had believed. You marry your college sweetheart and move back to your hometown to raise babies and attend family barbecues and holiday gatherings. That they didn't share the same hometown hadn't been a hiccup because, of course, Jesse would willingly move back to his. To be fair, he'd known how she felt about her parents, who were unlikely to miss her if she never came home.

Few after that had lasted more than a year, with Ryan holding the second longest record at two. Ironic, now that she thought about it. He was probably the most prolific cheater in her history. It was as if Jesse had made a conscious effort to find guys who were worse than the ones who came before them.

She closed her eyes at the pain that revelation brought.

Not because she missed Ryan, who'd already appeared in the latest gossip magazine with a model on his arm, but because she'd done this to herself. As if she didn't deserve anything better. But now something better had come along. Returned, really. The dream of a life with Ash that she'd made every effort to stuff away, to forget and let go, could be hers again.

All Jesse had to do was have a little faith in herself. Believe that she wasn't defective, unlovable, or cursed to eternal heartbreak.

With a soft chuckle at her own melodramatic thoughts, she

rose from the chair and shuffled across the patio in her furry slippers with one clear thought in mind. What was done was done. She couldn't change her parents, bring back her brother, or undo the mistakes she'd made in the last decade. But by some miracle she would never be able to explain, Jesse had been given a second chance at a future with Ash. A future she'd be a fool to turn down.

Locking the sliding door behind her, she crossed silently to the stairs, feeling lighter than she had in years. Because a decision had been made. The best one she'd made in years.

TWENTY-FOUR

"Sorry we're late," Jesse said, breezing into the studio, hands full of instruments, as always, and cheeks pink from the cold. "Thanks to the rain, traffic was awful today." Hair in the usual ponytail, she slicked off her coat to reveal a navy Predators sweatshirt and tossed the heavy jacket onto the black leather sofa. "Today is 'Wild Horses,' right?"

No mention of the night before.

"Right," Ash said, keeping his disappointment to himself. "'Wild Horses.' Mason is also stuck in traffic, but we can start without him."

Jesse rubbed her hands together. "Good. I'm excited for this one."

"I'll go get set up," Dana said. "Morning, Ash."

The bass player was gone before he could respond.

"So," Jesse said once they were alone.

Expecting a more personal greeting, Ash rocked on his heels. "So?"

"We're working on the sixth song today. That means we have *half* an album. Halfway there in a month is good, right?"

Frustrated, he crossed his arms and dug deep for patience. "Yeah, we're actually ahead of schedule. About last night—"

"Nope." She held up a hand. "Not at work. At work, we work."

That left the obvious question. "And when we're not at work?"

She flashed a smile that stole his breath. "*Then* we can do non-work things." Ash took a step forward, and Jesse stepped back. "Cameras. They're always watching, remember?"

Why did he have to tell her about the damn cameras?

"No one ever really looks at those tapes."

Slipping away, she lifted her guitar case onto the couch and clicked open the locks. "Can't take that chance."

"Jesse—"

"Oh, I need a favor," she said, abruptly changing the subject. "I know you do the volunteer thing Saturday mornings, but how about the afternoon?"

Ash might have considered skipping one Saturday morning to do whatever Jesse wanted, but the kids were working hard on their Christmas song performances, and they only had two weeks until the show.

"I can't get free until after one. What do you need?"

Eyes bright, she said, "I got an apartment. It's a duplex, really, and small, but it's cute and not far from town." Practically floating, she whisked the guitar from its case and headed for the hall.

"Where?" he asked, following behind her. "Last week you hadn't found anything you liked."

"In Donelson. It's a cute little red brick house that's been split into two apartments." Pausing at the control room door, she called, "Hey, Aiden."

"Morning, beautiful," the engineer replied.

"It's nothing fancy," Jesse continued, "but it has new floors *and* paint, plenty of parking in the back, and a good-sized closet to hold all of my stuff." Sweeping into the booth where Reggie and Dana were setting up, she added, "I haven't had my own place without roommates in like four years, so I'm a little excited."

He couldn't blame her for that. "Do you want me to come see it?"

"Not exactly." Jesse cut a daunting glare Reggie's way. "Someone has a recital to attend for his twins, so I need you to help me move."

"I can't miss it," the drummer defended. "They've been working on these dances for months."

"I know," she said. "I'm just teasing." Jesse turned her attention back to Ash. "So can you help me?"

Not something he wanted to do on a blustery November day, but they both knew his answer. "Two questions. Are there stairs? And how much coffee have you had today?"

"No stairs and no coffee." She flashed the heart-stopping grin again. "I'm just happy."

And that made Ash happy. "Okay, I'll help." Recalling what they'd moved out of Dimitri's house, he asked, "Do you have furniture?"

"Yeah, it's been in storage forever." Jesse looked down to tune her guitar. "Thankfully, it won't take much to fill this little place so the few pieces I have will work."

Before he could ask what she considered a few pieces, Aiden's voice came over the intercom. "Mason is here."

Ash nodded in acknowledgment before bending to whisper in Jesse's ear. "You look beautiful today."

A blush rolled up her cheeks as she continued tuning. "Thank you."

Content with the progress made, he stood and headed for the door. "Everybody ready to work?"

"Yes, sir," the musicians said in unison.

"Count me in, too." Mason shuffled into the room. "I still say we should have taken today off," he grumbled, clearly hung over.

"No rest for the wicked," the producer reminded him.

"Yeah, yeah, yeah."

As the guitarist found his chair, Ash made his way out of the booth and around to the control room.

"You look more chipper than usual," Aiden said as Ash took a seat. "Anything to do with that little whisper session in there?"

Ash sobered. "What's that supposed to mean?"

The engineer shook his head. "You two were the talk of the party until the little superhero bailed. I expected things to be tense today, but I guess not."

Maintaining a tight grip on his temper, Ash said, "I thought you were above gossip, D'Angelo."

"People talk, man. You can't look at a woman the way you look at Jesse and think folks won't notice."

Shit. That was exactly what Jesse wanted to avoid. He'd need to be more careful going forward. "Those *folks* need to mind their own business. Jesse and I are old friends. Since when is that newsworthy?"

"To be honest, nobody cares about you, but Jesse has been giving them something to talk about for a while now." When Ash cut him a menacing look, Aiden raised his hands in surrender. "I'm just the messenger, bro. Thought you'd want to know that people are talking."

Jaw tight, Ash pressed the intercom button on the board. "Be ready to cut in five." He turned back to his engineer. "If I hear of any rumors about Jesse coming out of these sessions, I will make sure the ones responsible pay for their loose tongues."

Aiden sat up straighter and rolled up to the controls. "Message received, boss. Loud and clear."

Three hours into the day, the group broke for lunch, happy with the progress they'd made. Though "Save Yourself" was the front-runner for debut single, "Wild Horses" was one Jesse definitely wanted sent to radio. The up-tempo anthem for female empowerment could be a signature song, and she would be happy to perform the tune for as long as fans wanted to hear it. With any luck, that would be for the next three to four decades.

"So that's meatball on white with provolone for you," Dana said to Jesse while reading from her phone. "And a club with everything but onion for you?" she asked Mason.

"Yes, ma'am," he replied. "And extra mayo."

Dana typed in the note. "All right. Reggie and I will be back with the food shortly."

Ash had excused himself to make a phone call, and Aiden had gone out for his own food, so the bass player's exit left Jesse and Mason alone in the lounge. She hadn't spent much time with the studio musician, and though Jesse would love to hear stories about the amazing albums he'd played on, she'd never found a rapport with the man that made asking for details feel right. Since Mason had never sought her out for conversation either, Jesse assumed they'd pass the time staring at their respective phones.

Her assumption had been wrong.

"You've got some songwriting chops," Mason said, lounging in the corner of the leather sofa with an ankle draped across a knee. "I considered not taking this gig, but you aren't as bad as they say."

Dazed and a bit insulted by the remark, she replied, "Thanks, I guess?"

The affront in her tone didn't faze him. "So is Ash the reason you dumped Ryan Dimitri?"

Now he'd really stunned her. "Excuse me?"

"Not that I blame you," Mason continued, seemingly having a conversation by himself. "How long were you with Dimitri? A year?"

"Fourteen months," Jesse corrected, not sure why she'd even answered.

"Huh. That's longer than I thought."

She'd assumed that not only did Mason Dexter not know who she was before joining this project, but that he also didn't know or care anything about her life. Why would he? Jesse was a little-known artist who'd had moderate if short-lived success as one half of a female duo. Nothing she'd accomplished should have even registered with Mason.

"Do you know Ryan?" she asked, certain this was the only way he'd know anything about their relationship.

Mason nodded. "We used to run in the same circles back when he was first starting out. He's shit with women, but he knows music, and he knows how to schmooze. I'd have thought he'd have gotten you further than he did."

Jesse blinked, feeling as if she'd been caught in an ambush. Had this man really just given Ryan credit for her career? Or was it blame for her lack of one?

"Not that this is any of your business, but I wasn't with Ryan in order to *get somewhere*. And what I've accomplished, I've done on my own."

"Eh," he grunted, unmoved. "We all get a little help somewhere. There's no shame in it." Rubbing his chin, Mason pinned her with a narrowed gaze. "Shifting from Dimitri to Shepherd is a smart move. Go where the gettin's good, and all that. I don't blame you one bit."

How generous of him.

"I didn't *shift* from Ryan to Ash."

"I was trashed last night, and even I could see you two have more than a working relationship going on." Thin lips curled into a creepy grin. "By the way, that sexy getup was nice. I almost didn't recognize you."

Her control snapped, and Jesse bolted off the couch. "My personal life is none of your business."

"If you don't want folks to know you're sleeping with him, don't crawl all over him during a party in front of half the industry."

"I wasn't crawling all over anyone," she defended, growing more annoyed that she even bothered to argue with him. "Forget it. You know what? Why don't you take your snide remarks and sexist advice and call it a day. In fact, consider yourself off this project."

Mason shook his head. "You don't have that kind of power, little lady."

"The hell I don't. This is my album, and I want you gone. And don't worry. We'll re-cut your parts. I don't want a single note from you on anything I create."

The jackass had the nerve to laugh. Freaking *laugh*.

"You're cute when you're angry, but maybe you forgot who you're talking to. No matter how many players you get on your knees and blow, I'll still be a bigger name in this town than you'll ever be. And I sure as hell ain't stepping off a project because some upstart little girl tells me to."

"Wrong." Jesse spun to find Ash hovering in the doorway, hands fisted at his sides and jaw clenched. "Get your shit and get out."

Taking his time, Mason uncurled off the sofa. "You serious?"

"Do I sound like I'm joking?" Ash asked, his tone hard and level. As the guitarist stepped past Jesse, Ash said, "Apologize."

Mason stopped. "What?"

Crossing his arms, Ash leaned against the doorframe as if this were a casual conversation. As if he wasn't coiled and ready to rip the man apart.

"I said apologize to the lady."

"You can't be—"

"Don't make me repeat it again."

Looking as if he'd swallowed a lemon, Mason turned her way and with pinched lips mumbled, "I'm sorry."

He didn't mean the words, but Jesse didn't care. The jerk had probably never uttered an apology in his entitled life and watching him bow to Ash's demand was the best thing she'd seen in months. Maybe years. To show who truly had the power here, Jesse didn't offer a response, nor did she cower as he loomed a hair closer. It would be a cold day in hell before she gave this asshole the satisfaction.

In tense silence, Mason crossed to the doorway where Ash stepped aside to let him pass.

"Are you okay?" he asked once they were alone.

Jesse nodded. "I'm pretty good, actually. That was impressive."

"I could say the same for you."

Footsteps sounded in the hall as Mason returned from the studio where he'd left his guitar. "You'll be hearing from my manager."

"Tell him to call Shooting Stars. They'll settle on what you're owed."

Even concern for how Clay Benedict would react to this news couldn't lower Jesse's spirits. She'd stood up to a bully, and if that resulted in a conversation with her label head, so be it. The fact was, if she were a man, none of this would have happened. She wouldn't be the center of false rumors, and she sure as heck wouldn't be accused of blowing her way to the top.

"Did you hear what he said to me?"

Ash shook his head. "Nothing before the get-on-your-knees part." Running a hand through his hair, he added, "It's taking all I have not to go kick the shit out of him."

She'd prefer to do that for herself. "Apparently, he knows Ryan and thinks I *shifted*—his word—from him to you because Ryan hadn't done enough to advance my career. He assumes that sleeping with you will get me further."

"Does this have to do with the party last night?"

"I suppose so. He said that even drunk, he could tell there's something between us."

"Dammit," Ash muttered, smacking the wall. "I'm sorry. Aiden said something similar this morning. I should have been more discreet."

This wasn't their fault, and Jesse was tired of trying to win this game. People were going to say any dang thing they wanted, and what she did or didn't do played no part in it. Enough was enough.

"Screw that. All I've ever wanted to do was make music on my own terms, and I've never taken a shortcut through someone's bed to do it. If that makes me difficult or shallow or whatever they want to call me next, then that's just too bad."

Full lips curved into a smile as Ash pulled her into his arms. "That's the Jesse I know and love."

"Yes," she said, sliding a hand into his hair. "Yes, it is." Jesse rubbed her thumb over his lips. "I'm going to kiss you now and to hell with the cameras."

"To hell with the cameras."

Lifting her off her feet, Ash took her mouth with his, and the moment their lips touched, Jesse opened for him. Arms around his neck, she channeled the adrenaline rush into the kiss as warm hands slid beneath her sweatshirt to splay across the small of her back. Heat coursed through her limbs and turned her brain to mush. They were still kissing when Dana and Reggie returned with lunch.

"Whoa," said Dana. "Sorry to interrupt."

"Looks like we're interrupting just in time," added Reggie with a chuckle. "Y'all need to get a room but not this one. No telling what's already been done on those couches."

Dana groaned. "That's nasty."

It really was, and Jesse would be avoiding the sofas going forward.

"Thanks for the disturbing image," Ash said as he lowered Jesse to stand on her own. "I should have closed the door."

"Too late now." Dana held up the bag of food. "Sandwiches are here. Where's Mason?"

Jesse and Ash exchanged a look before he said, "Mason won't be working with us anymore. For now, I'll handle the lead guitar parts until we find a replacement."

Reggie withdrew his wallet and handed Dana some cash. "You nailed it."

"Nailed what?" Jesse said.

"We had a bet on how long Mason would last before he

pissed someone off enough to kick him out." Dana stuffed the money into her pants pocket. "I called this week, and Reggie took the end of the month."

Until today, Jesse had overlooked Mason's annoying habits—like talking over her, ignoring her input on the lead parts, and leaving before anyone else—because he was the prized professional she was so lucky to have on her album. Her friends had not been so blind, and she wished she'd grown a backbone sooner.

"Then we're all good with the change?" Ash asked, withholding comment on the bet.

"Yep," Dana said.

"I'm good," replied Reggie.

He looked to Jesse, and she said, "You know I'm happy."

"Good." She took the bag of food. "Then let's eat."

After a brief hesitation while they all glanced to the couches, Ash added, "Someplace else."

All agreed, and the group headed for cleaner surroundings.

TWENTY-FIVE

CLAY WASN'T A FAN OF DINNER MEETINGS, ESPECIALLY ONES HELD just off Broadway on a Friday night. While most tourist towns had an off-season, Nashville did not. Lower Broad, Printer's Alley, and 2nd Avenue stayed packed year-round, with music churning from every open door.

More than one of the original acts signed to Foxfire Records had come from scouting these clubs, and recalling those long nights put a smile on his face. Together, with luck, friendship, and unflinching determination, Clay and Tony created a business that was now one of the largest and most successful labels in town.

And it had all started right here.

Loosening his tie, Clay put off ordering a car to stroll down 2nd Avenue and see if anything good caught his ear. Nashville was loaded with undiscovered talent, and one never knew when the next gem might be playing around the next corner. From the first few doors came the standard covers, all trying to sound as close to the original as possible to please the tourists who came to Nashville to hear their radios come to life.

But then Clay reached the entrance to The Stillery and paused. The song was vaguely familiar, while at the same time wholly original. *Where had he heard that tune before?* Lingering out of the way, he found himself tapping along, and the answer finally came. This was the band Emily Garcia had signed to her previous label.

Clay tapped the bouncer on the shoulder "Who's playing tonight?"

"The Hard Way," the guy said. "They're a kickass band. Don't know how they aren't signed yet."

That made two of them because the music coming out of the club belonged inside the arena up the street.

"Is there room for one more?"

"Come on in," the doorman replied.

The room was warm, so Clay slipped off his suit jacket and loosened his tie even more. The venue resembled most others along this strip—industrial with an appealing mix of metal, brick, and polished wood. Though the music was louder, there was no stage in sight.

Catching a passing waitress, he asked, "Where's the band?"

She silently nodded to a set of stairs in the corner before moving on. Clay took the hint and headed to the second floor. The crowd was standing room only, but thanks to his height and width, he had no trouble cutting a path to the bar. An older man with a beard down to his belly button exited a stool on the corner, and Clay filled the empty seat, grateful for the direct view to the stage.

The lead singer, a tall, lanky man with dark, spiky hair and a goatee belted the rocking country tune with a steady baritone and an obvious passion for his art. He worked the stage like a pro, and the musicians behind him matched him for talent.

One of the reasons Clay focused more on solo acts was because finding a band in which all members possessed equal skill and commitment was near impossible. The second reason was the drama inherent in such acts. Competing egos. Jealousy. Unrealistic expectations.

These issues weren't unheard of with solo performers, but less likely.

Of course, there were always exceptions, or drama worth tolerating, if the music was good enough. From what Clay could see, The Hard Way landed squarely in that category. The talent and charisma were evident, and they had no trouble holding the crowd's attention. What surprised him the most was the number of people singing along. This wasn't a song getting hourly radio play. This was an original. And a damn good one.

The song came to a raucous end followed by thunderous applause. Even folks at the bar put down their drinks to show their appreciation. Clay took advantage of the brief lull to order one of his own. "I'll take a scotch on the rocks."

"You can put that on my tab, Phil," said a woman from behind him. Clay turned to find Samantha Walters, one brow arched high and a sexy glint in her dark eyes. "Fancy meeting you here, Mr. Benedict."

Considering himself off the clock, he replied, "It's about time you called me Clay, don't you think?"

Since receiving Silas's warning, he'd kept communication with the manager to a minimum. They'd spent the last week hashing out the terms of Dylan Monroe's contract renewal through a string of emails. Not once had a hint of anything unprofessional been included, but that hadn't stopped Clay from wishing he could negotiate with Samantha in a more intimate setting.

"I can do that," she said, sliding up beside him to rest her elbows on the bar. "So what's a label head doing in a 2nd Avenue bar on a Friday night? Are you meeting someone?"

The inquiry was casual, but Clay caught the underlying question. "No, ma'am. I'm here alone." He nodded toward the band. "I was passing by, and they caught my attention."

"You were passing by?" The brow arched higher.

"Obligatory dinner with my accountant went late, and I

decided to take a stroll. Being an executive doesn't make me too good for a Lower Broad club, Ms. Walters."

"Call me Samantha," she replied and accepted the drink the man she'd called Phil put down in front of her. Vodka tonic by the looks of it. "Do you like what you're hearing?"

Clay nodded "I do. What do *you* think?"

"They're the reason I'm here. Word is The Hard Way is looking for a manager."

The more their professional roles overlapped, the more difficult getting personal would be. Then again, thanks to Joanna, Clay wouldn't be getting personal with Samantha any time soon.

"Are you going to offer them representation?"

She gave a noncommittal shrug. "We had a chat during their break earlier. The dynamic is hard to read, but I'm considering it. Now that Wes has officially retired for good, I have a spot to fill."

Wes Tillman had been at the top of the genre for more than two decades but opted to slow down a few years ago. After toying with retirement, he went out on a farewell tour more than a year ago before finally calling it quits. Dylan had landed an opening spot, which had been fortuitous for him since that's when he'd crossed paths with Samantha. Dylan's manager at the time turned out to be skimming from the accounts, and the more trustworthy manager had stepped in to take his place.

"What do you mean about the dynamic?" Clay asked.

Samantha cut her eyes to the stage as the band rolled into the next song. To be heard, she had to lean close, and her breath against his temple made it difficult to concentrate on her words.

"The front man, Liam Bradshaw, is clearly the leader, and the others follow along. As a whole, they seem like a well-settled, cohesive unit, but I'm skeptical of anything that comes across that simple. Bands are never simple."

He couldn't argue that statement, but instead of warning him off, the assessment only piqued Clay's curiosity. Switching positions, he pressed close to her ear, ignoring the urge to taste the soft spot beneath her earlobe. "Do you know if they're talking to any other labels?"

This time he'd really surprised her, though the savvy businesswoman recovered quickly. "Not that I've heard. Are you considering adding them to the Shooting Stars roster?"

In case she stepped into the mix, he kept his intentions vague. "Maybe. I'd need to see more, of course. Do some research and hear where they want to go."

Falling into silence, Clay watched her lift the glass to her lips and noticed a slow blush advancing up her neck. Though the club was much warmer up here, the heat building between them had nothing to do with the temperature in the room. Treading into dangerous territory, Clay took a sip of his own libation and kept his focus on the band. Again, the spectators were singing along, and as the tempo soared, so did the tenor of the crowd.

Applause rang out again as the song ended with a crescendo, and the lead singer—Liam according to Samantha—announced they'd be taking a fifteen-minute break. Clay wasn't interested in hanging out until the end of the night, so he took this opportunity to have a quick chat with the band.

"Would you excuse me?" he said to Samantha.

"Of course. I should get back to my friends anyway."

An invitation to take their conversation someplace quieter danced on the tip of his tongue, but Clay swallowed the words. "Thanks for the drink."

The hesitant smile said she wanted that invitation, but Silas's warning echoed in his mind. *Sam doesn't deserve that.* And Clay didn't deserve *her.*

"You're welcome. I'd love to hear your take on the band after you talk to them."

Slipping into business mode, he replied, "I'll save that until after the negotiations."

Catching his meaning, she held up her glass in salute. "Very shrewd, Mr. Benedict."

"When I have to be, Ms. Walters."

As if nothing had changed between them, the beautiful woman walked away, black skirt hugging her slender curves and neon lights glinting off her jet-black hair. Clay watched her go with regret and the bitter certainty that he and Samantha would never be more than casual associates.

Downing the rest of his drink, he set the glass on the bar and made his way to the stage. The band descended the far side to gather around a cocktail table beside a window overlooking 2nd Avenue.

"Impressive set," he said, directing the statement at the band in general.

"The crowd seems to like it," the lead singer said before taking a swig from his longneck. The rest of the band held their tongues, confirming Samantha's read on who the true leader was.

Extending a hand, he said, "I'm Clay Benedict. I run a label in town, and I like your sound."

"Liam Bradshaw," the tall singer offered, accepting the greeting. "This is Bobby Mullins, Matt Keys, Olive Cindowski, and Eugene Pepper." Without missing a beat, he added, "You turned us down four years ago at Foxfire Records."

Clay had no memory of that, but he would never remember all of the hopefuls that came through their doors over the years. In this case, he hoped to have a second chance to get it right.

"My loss, obviously."

Either the singer had expected him to defend his decision or slither off in shame, but Bradshaw's demeanor changed after Clay's response.

"We think so, yeah. Good to know your taste in music has improved." Lifting a hand toward the bar, he asked, "You want a drink?"

"I'll pass, thanks. I hear you recently left Six String. Does that mean you're looking for a new label?"

"That depends. If you're talking about a development deal

where you use us to up your tax deductions and then leave us hanging in the wind, we'll catch the next bus."

Not many would have the guts to give such a bold—and in Clay's estimation, intelligent—answer. While some artists jumped at any chance that came along, The Hard Way had clearly made that mistake before. And learned from it.

"We don't do development deals at Shooting Stars. If we bring in an artist, we do so with our full support and belief that they deserve to make music and have that music heard."

He'd earned the attention of all members now, and the others tensely waited for their leader's response.

"You think our music deserves to be heard?"

"I do. At least what I've heard so far."

Ice-blue eyes narrowed as the man sized up the offer before him. A veteran well aware of the precarious nature of true artists, Clay waited silently for a reply.

"We don't have a manager right now," Liam confessed. "Does that matter?"

"Partially, but I have a feeling that situation might change soon." Pulling a business card from his wallet, Clay set it on the table. "I don't remember our original encounter, but my new A&R manager mentioned you in her interview. Emily Garcia?"

Liam's expression shifted from interest to open hostility. "Thanks, but no thanks. We'll take our chances elsewhere."

Bewildered by the abrupt change, he said, "You're saying no? Just like that?"

"We've worked with your Ms. Garcia before. We know how that ends up."

So they blamed Emily for their previous experience, not the label. Odd. And concerning.

"Seems shortsighted, but that's your prerogative. I'll leave the offer on the table for a couple of months, in case you reconsider." Keeping his tone casual, Clay added, "To be clear, Ms. Garcia will have the full weight and staff of Shooting Stars at her disposal. It's highly unlikely history will repeat itself."

Bradshaw snickered. "I can assure you, Mr. Benedict, that Emily Garcia doesn't want to work with us any more than we want to work with her. If that situation changes, we'll be happy to talk."

So it was The Hard Way or Emily Garcia. Clay didn't second-guess himself often, nor was he a fan of ultimatums, but in this case, he needed to determine which acquisition he'd been wrong about. Liam Bradshaw seemed to be under the misguided notion that an offer like the one just laid before him was easily dismissed. Whereas Ms. Garcia had recognized the opportunity Shooting Stars could provide and fought to join the team. That's the type of person Clay would willingly invest in.

"Thank you for your time, and good luck to all of you." Discussion over, he gave a nod to the entire band—disappointed in their willingness to follow a prima donna leader with an inflated sense of entitlement—and made his way through the buzzing crowd.

Once down the stairs and outside, he opened an app on his phone, ordered a car to the corner of 2nd Avenue and Commerce, and slid his suit jacket back into place. Sighing at the futility of his evening, Clay made his way up the block, vowing to leave the talent scouting to his new recruit, and cursing the blind stupidity that led him to ever get involved with Joanna Rossi.

TWENTY-SIX

"You said a *few* things." Ash grunted as he dropped the box of dishes atop the stack he'd already carried in. "Your definition and my definition of *a few* are very different."

"Not everyone is a minimalist, Shepherd." Jesse rinsed a glass and placed it on the towel with the others to dry. The apartment came with a dishwasher, but she hadn't gotten around to buying the soap for it yet. "This is just the basics."

"The basics for a small army." Pressing his hands to his lower back, he groaned with a stretch. "Thankfully, there are only two boxes left."

"One," Dana said as she lowered a box to the floor beside the stack. "I got the one full of blankets and left the pots and pans for you."

Jesse tried not to laugh as her friend flashed an innocent smile.

Ash cast them both an impatient glare. "I used to like you, Mills."

He lifted the hem of his Titans T-shirt to wipe the sweat from his brow, and Jesse nearly dropped the glass in her hand. Good Lord, the man was hot. Due to daily rehearsals with the academy kids, they hadn't seen each other outside of the studio until today. And though Ash didn't know it yet, she planned to make this an extended visit.

"She and I carried the couch," Jesse reminded him. It wasn't as if they'd left *all* the heavy lifting to him.

"And who do you think helped her get all this crap *into* the storage unit?" Dana said. "That was me. Who were you dating back then?" she asked Jesse. "All I remember is that he bailed on us at the last minute."

Sadly, Jesse had to scroll her memory banks to find the answer. "That was probably Ned. He was a master at avoiding manual labor."

"Ned who?" Ash asked.

"Ned Berman. Do you know him?"

He snorted. "Yeah. He's a roadie. His job is nothing *but* manual labor."

The irony still amazed her. "That might be the case, but when he was off the clock, he'd barely pick up the mail."

Dana grabbed her jacket off the arm of the sofa. "I hate to leave you with all of the unpacking, but I promised Ingrid I'd pick her up at six. She's got her master lights on the shoot with her today, and those don't fit in her car."

"I owe you," Jesse declared, wrapping her in a hug. "As soon as I get this place set up, y'all have to come over for dinner." When Dana cringed, she added, "Don't worry. I'll order out."

"Then count us in." To Ash, she said, "Thanks for helping out today. It's about time Jesse had a man in her life willing to step up."

Grimace easing, he nodded in recognition of the compliment. "Not a problem."

As Dana closed the door behind her, Ash pulled Jesse in close. "I thought she'd never leave."

His scent surrounded her as he nuzzled her neck, and Jesse held her breath. Pushing him away, she retrieved a few essentials from the box near the bathroom door. Handing over a towel, a wash cloth, and a bottle of body wash, she said, "You need to use these."

"I don't have a change of clothes," he said with a twinkle in his eye. "If you're goal is to get me naked, all you have to do is ask."

That was her *ultimate* goal for the evening, but there was one more thing Jesse had to do first. "Technically, you do, since I stole that outfit I wore the night I showed up at your house in the rain. But, the point here is that *I* will not be getting naked until *you* smell better."

Message received, Ash dropped a quick kiss on her cheek and darted into the bathroom. Knowing what condition he'd be in when the moving was done, Jesse had hung her new shower curtain an hour before. The black and white number had been on sale, and she'd even found matching rugs.

With a deep breath, she braced herself for what came next. Despite the fact that her parents rarely checked on her, Jesse had long felt an obligation to at least keep them informed on where to find her. After the breakup with Ryan, she'd called home to explain that she'd be staying at Dana's while searching for her own place.

In typical fashion, Enid Rheingold had been only half interested and hadn't even asked if Jesse was okay or needed to talk. Instead, she'd given a pat, "Thanks for letting us know," response before sharing the details of the memorial service they were planning for Tommy for the tenth anniversary of his death.

They held the same service every year, and every year it was like revisiting his funeral all over again. The condolences. The crying. Enid in head-to-toe black.

Jesse had loved her brother more than anything, but she wanted to celebrate his life, not his death. Tommy had possessed a smile that could light up a stadium, and he'd rather have a ball field or a scholarship named after him than a somber annual remembrance.

And still, she'd agreed to be there, as she did every year.

Because for better or worse, her parents were the only family Jesse had left. Though there would be one more face at the service this year, and that's what this phone call was about.

Pulling up her contacts, Jesse's thumb lingered over the phone number that had been connected to the Rheingolds since before she was born, but she didn't touch the screen. For this, she needed fortification. Part of Ash's official payment for the day included a six-pack of Music City Light. Jesse snagged one from the fridge, popped the top, and took a long swig for courage.

Now she made the call, and her father picked up on the third ring.

"Hello?" he said, louder than necessary, as if the lines of communication still involved a can and some string.

"Hey, Daddy."

"Oh. Hello, Jesse." The enthusiasm was overwhelming. "How are things in Nashville?"

"Good. I moved into my own place today."

"You moved? What was wrong with your old place?"

In other words, Enid hadn't bothered to share the change in Jesse's relationship status. "That was Ryan's place. Since we broke up, I had to find my own apartment."

"Ryan?"

Digging deep for patience, she said, "You met him last Christmas, Daddy."

A grunt came down the line. "I can't keep track of all the boys you see. Do you want to talk to your mama?"

The hand off happened every time. "Yes, please."

"All right." His voice became muffled as he yelled for his wife, and seconds later the phone changed hands.

"Hello?"

"Hi, Mama."

"Oh," she said in the same tone her husband had. "Vince, you could have told me who it was." Incoherent grumbling followed, and Jesse rolled her eyes. "Well? Are you all moved in?"

"I am. Did you not tell Daddy that Ryan and I broke up?"

"I'm sure I did, but you know your father. He never listens to a word I say." Jesse didn't blame him. "We had some rain today. Did your things get wet?"

Unwilling to explain to her mother how weather worked, she got to the point of her call. "Mama, I want to talk to you about Tommy's service this year."

"Of course, honey," Enid said with heightened interest. "We were thinking instead of you singing to that old recording that we'd get Lydia Sue Grenville to play the organ."

"That's fine, Mama. But I wanted to let you know that I'll be bringing someone with me this time."

"I'm not surprised you have another beau already. You rarely set one aside without having another already in the web."

She made it sound as if Jesse's love life worked like an assembly line with another coming down the belt right behind the last. If Jesse was being honest, that wasn't far off, but those days were behind her.

"This time it's someone you know."

Instantly suspicious, Enid said, "Who?"

Closing her eyes, Jesse answered, "Ash Shepherd."

The line went silent except for the sounds of Jeopardy playing loudly in the background.

"Mama?"

"No."

"Mama, you—"

"Jessica Marie Rheingold, you will not bring that boy anywhere near this family. Do you hear me?"

"Do you hear *yourself?*" she exclaimed. "Tommy loved Ash like a brother, and he'd be furious to know how you cut him out of our lives. He was hurting, too, and you turned him away. How could you have done that?"

Voice tight, she growled, "That boy killed *my son*."

"No, Mama. Tommy's death was an accident. We've been over this many times. There was a deer—"

"I said he isn't welcome, and that's the end of it."

Searching for a way to reach her, Jesse said, "What if it had been me? What if I'd been driving that night, Mama? Would you have tossed me away like you did Ash? Would you have refused to speak to me ever again?"

"It wasn't you."

"But it *could* have been. Or it could have been Tommy driving and Ash who'd died. Would you have called your son a killer because of an *accident*?" When no answer came, she said, "He loved him as much as we did, Mama. And he still hasn't forgiven himself. That's only going to happen if you forgive him first."

Still no response and the muted sounds from the television were the only way Jesse knew her mother hadn't hung up. Finally, Enid said, "I don't think I can do that."

"Try," Jesse pleaded. "Do it for Tommy. You know it's what he'd want."

After a brief hesitation, she said, "I need to go. The burgers are on the stove, and you know your father likes his rare."

Knowing she'd done all she could, Jesse sighed. "I'll text my new address to your cell phone."

"That's fine," came back in clipped tones before the call went dead.

Jesse shoved three boxes out of the way to reach the sofa, and then collapsed onto the faded blue cushions. She hadn't tried to reason with her mother in years. Not since the week after her college graduation when she'd insisted on moving to Nashville. That battle had been won only because Jesse had given them no choice. She was going with or without their support, and in the end, they'd conceded. Not enough to help her move or to visit more than once a year, but enough to send a small monthly stipend until she'd found her footing.

Where she'd gotten the idea that they might have mellowed on this particular subject, Jesse didn't know. Clearly, she'd suffered some delusional optimism brought on by temporary insanity. That was the only explanation.

* * *

Ash stepped out of the bathroom wearing nothing but a towel, expecting to find Jesse still unpacking, but the kitchen was empty. A few boxes had been moved, but there was no other sign of activity.

"Jesse?" he called.

"I'm in here," came a voice from the bedroom.

Stepping back into the bathroom, he crossed to the opposite door, which led into a large closet and eventually into the bedroom. It was an odd setup, but convenient for both Jesse and her guests.

He found her wrestling with the heavy box spring. "What are you doing?"

"What does it look like I'm doing?" she said with a grunt. "I'm trying to put the bed together."

Rushing into action, Ash caught the box spring seconds before it landed on top of her. "You should have waited for me."

"I'm not helpless," Jesse argued, pushing on the contraption with her shoulder and getting nowhere.

Ash grasped one end and said, "Grab that side and we'll lower it straight down onto the rails."

Rails she'd managed to assemble single-handedly while he showered, proving her previous statement. Once the box spring was in place, he reached for the mattress, but she held up a hand. "I need to put the bed skirt on first."

Waiting patiently, Ash watched her unzip clear plastic packaging and dump the contents onto the floor. Tossing stray pieces of cardboard aside, she came up with the dark purple skirt and tossed it over the flat surface of the box spring.

"Fix that corner, please."

He did as asked.

"Okay," she said. "Now the mattress."

They worked together to lower the bulky piece into place, and then Jesse went to work applying the sheets.

"Don't you need to wash those first?"

She froze. "I should, shouldn't I?"

When Jesse was thirteen, she'd slept with a brand-new, unwashed blanket and wound up with hives from her shoulders to her ankles. He'd never forget how miserable she was that day, and Ash had other activities in mind for this evening that did not include an emergency dose of Benadryl.

Remembering the box Dana had carried in before she left, Ash said, "Hold on."

A quick dash to the living room and he was back with the box. "How long did you say these have been in storage?"

"Those are fresh from Ingrid. She has so many blankets that she insisted I take some."

Then they were all set. Ash pulled a beige number off the top and tossed it over the bed before reaching in for the next one down, a comforter covered in penguins wearing raincoats.

"Why would penguins need raincoats?" he asked as he threw it over the other.

"I have no idea and don't care so long as they keep me warm." She rubbed her hands together. "The heater doesn't seem to be doing much."

Ash took that as his cue and closed the distance between them. "Guess we'll have to rely on body heat."

As if just noticing his limited attire, Jesse said, "You aren't wearing any clothes, Mr. Shepherd."

Sliding his hands over her hips, he muttered, "And you're wearing too many, Ms. Rheingold." Like a switch, her expression changed. "What's the matter?"

Jesse shook her head. "That name throws me off, that's all."

She may have taken on a stage name, but that didn't change the fact that she'd grown up as a Rheingold.

"I'm sorry, hon, but you're always going to be Jesse Rheingold to me." Ash brushed a loose lock off her forehead. "She's the girl I fell for."

"I know, but that name reminds me of my parents."

Not where he wanted her mind to go right now. "Point taken."

With a huff, she plopped onto her back on the bed and threw an arm over her eyes. "I called them."

Uncertain where this detour was leading, Ash sat down beside her. "Okay."

"I told them that I was bringing you to Tommy's memorial service next month."

And the fog cleared. "I doubt that went over well, but first, what memorial service?"

Jesse sat up. "Every year on the anniversary of the accident, Mama organizes this depressing service to remember him." Eyes on her hands, she added, "It's like attending the funeral all over again. I hate it, but I can't *not* go."

Ash cringed, certain that Tommy would despise such a ceremony. But if her parents needed an annual service to honor their lost son, then he didn't begrudge them the tradition.

"Just because I'm back in *your* life doesn't mean they're going to suddenly want me back in theirs."

"But they need to let this go," Jesse said. "What if we get married? Are they going to refuse to come?"

Ash would be happy to take that walk down the aisle with Jesse and doubted anything would change his mind—since nothing had in the last ten years—but they had a ways to go before she needed to start stressing about that particular issue.

"They might, but how about we focus on us right now?" Tugging on her shirt, he murmured, "I'm trying to warm you up, remember?"

Eyes dropping to his mouth, she whispered, "I don't want anything to mess this up."

Pressing a kiss to her forehead, Ash reached around and pulled her ponytail free. "I told you. I'm never leaving you again." He held her gaze, willing her to hear him. "I love you, Jesse."

Sliding her arms around his neck, she said, "I love you, too."

TWENTY-SEVEN

Jesse would curse the powers that had kept them apart for so long, but not tonight. Tonight she wanted to get lost in the man who'd never given up on her.

The moment their lips met, nothing else mattered. Dragging him down to the bed, she moaned as his thigh pressed between her own, and she couldn't resist exploring every bare inch of skin that she could reach.

"Hmmm . . ." she mumbled when his warm mouth trailed kisses along her jaw and down to the spot below her ear that drove her crazy. "Oh, yes."

Strong hands eased beneath her shirt, and Jesse arched as the pressure low in her core intensified. At the rate this was going, she would be begging in no time.

Desperate to feel his skin on hers, Jesse pushed on his shoulder until he backed away enough for her to sit up. In a rush, she yanked the shirt over her head and tossed it away, leaving nothing but black satin between them.

Before she could reach behind to unclasp the hooks, Ash leaned forward to lavish wet kisses along the swell of her breasts, dipping his tongue behind the thin material to tease her nipple. Her hands shot into his hair as a purr escaped her lips.

A subtle shift of his weight and Jesse found her back on the mattress with Ash working his way down her torso. With every brush of his lips, her heart rate doubled. She filled her hands with the colorful comforter as he tasted the skin just above her waistband.

"Time for these to come off." He freed the button and lowered the zipper slowly enough to drive her mad.

Impatient, she shoved them over her hips and let him drag them off the rest of the way. But instead of returning to her, Ash stood at the edge of the bed. Eyes dark. Hair damp and disheveled. Staring as if viewing a great wonder of the world.

"You're more beautiful than I remember."

A voice in Jesse's mind said she was rounder and less-toned, but that reality couldn't compete with the reverence in his eyes.

Jesse sat up and slowly reached for the swath of terry cloth hanging off his hips. Ash didn't flinch as the material fell away, and his arousal stood proud and ready to perform. Without a word, she kissed the tip, enjoying the power of nearly bringing this big, beautiful man to his knees.

"Baby," he moaned, jamming his hands into her hair.

Sliding him halfway in, she sucked and felt him jerk with pleasure. His grip tightened on the back of her head, and she took him to the hilt, the taste sweet and salty at the same time. Finding her rhythm, she cupped his back side, the muscles tight and firm beneath her touch, and with every suck and slide, Ash cried out a little louder.

His body was shaking, on the verge of release, when she pulled away and dragged him down to join her, cradling him between her legs.

"Condom," he growled through clenched teeth. "We need a condom."

Though she'd made a special trip to buy a box the night before, Jesse was annoyed with herself for not thinking to put them beside the bed while he showered.

Pointing toward the closet, she said, "They're in my bag. The red one."

Ash kissed her hard on the lips before leaving her with a whoosh of cold air across her bare skin. Jesse wiggled out of her underwear and was dragging her bra down her arms by the time he returned.

"I wanted to do that," he said before ripping the small square package open with his teeth.

"Next time," she promised, snagging the open foil from his fingers. With quick movements, she sheathed the condom into place and returned to her previous position.

Brow arched, he said, "We aren't kids anymore, you know. There's no need to rush before someone catches us."

Jesse leaned up on her elbows. "I've waited a decade for this."

"Good point." Ash crawled back into position, pausing long enough to kiss the inside of each thigh. Heat shot through her core, and she dug her heels into the bed. "The second time we'll go slow," he promised, hovering above her and taking her mouth with his at the same moment he drove one finger inside.

Something bordering on gibberish rolled off her tongue as her hips shot up to increase the contact. Another finger slid in with the first and curled just enough to send her teetering to the edge. He withdrew, leaving her slick and wet, and before she had time to recover, he rose with an arm on each side of her and caught her gaze.

Eyes locked, he thrust all the way in, and Jesse dug her nails into his biceps. Ash rocked his hips, and her breathing devolved into tiny pants and a series of mindless whimpers. Meeting every thrust with one of her own, she spiraled higher and higher, the pressure doubling when he nipped her taut nipple with his teeth.

"I can't... Oh, God... Oh, Ash..."

"Come for me, baby. I've got you."

Ash suckled her breast while his hips worked her hard and as the tremors lit through her, Jesse wrapped her arms around his neck, desperate to hold on lest she break apart. She was still quivering when he buried himself deeper still and with a growl, the orgasm ripped through him, turning every muscle to steel before he dropped down beside her.

Both panting and satisfied, they lingered there, catching their breath and holding on to each other as if they never wanted to let go. Ash placed a kiss on her breast before straightening and tucking her head beneath his chin.

"I love you, Jesse."

More content than she'd ever been, she rolled onto her side, clutching his arms around her and pressing her back to his chest. "I love you, too."

* * *

Ash never wanted to leave this bed. Or this woman. A decade was a long time to go without the one he knew was meant to be his. He believed that now more than ever. They'd parted long enough to find the pillows, and then came back together beneath the childish comforter.

"I'll never look at penguins the same way again," he muttered against her temple.

Jesse laughed. "Penguins in raincoats. Don't forget the raincoats."

He squeezed her tight. "Who could forget them? They're so practical."

She looked up and touched a finger to the tip of his nose. "I'm glad I remembered to buy the other kind of raincoat."

"When did you get those?"

"Last night."

Ironically, he'd also restocked and made sure to slide a couple into his wallet this morning, but that had been more a matter of wishful thinking on his part. Ash had begun this day with no expectations, happy to wait as long as she needed to reach this point again.

"So you already knew you were going to ravish me?" he asked, eager to hear her laugh again.

Sliding her leg between his, she rubbed his length. "You didn't seem to mind."

Ash lifted her onto his chest. "I didn't mind one bit. But I remember discussion of a second time."

Her knees dropped so she straddled his hips. "I was just waiting until you were up for it." When he flexed, her eyes went wide. "Impressive recovery."

He grinned. "At your service."

Jesse twitched her hips as her lips took his, her tongue sliding in invitation. Ash filled his hands with her bottom and kissed her back as his arousal grew more insistent.

"Where did you put the condoms?" she asked, as impatient as before.

Reaching up and around the pillow, he found the box where he'd tucked it for safe—and closer—keeping. "Right here."

"You're a smart man," Jesse said before sitting up and taking the box with her.

As if putting on a show, she slowly removed one package and tucked the box back under the pillow. Holding his gaze, she tore the foil and removed the condom, and then slowly eased down his legs. Before sliding it into place, she explored his length with curious fingers, sending bolts of electricity coursing through him.

Hands tight on her thighs, he said, "You're killing me."

"We said the second time would be slow, remember?"

Damn it, he did say that. "Slow is overrated."

With a sexy purr, she said, "I agree."

The condom was rolled into place, and Jesse lifted to position herself in just the right spot. Ash lifted his hands, and she placed hers in them seconds before her head dropped back and she took him full in.

He tried to say her name but only managed a guttural moan. Hands still in his, she began to move, making small circles first, then lifting and falling. He pulled her down for a kiss, his hips instinctually following her every move, and their tongues mimicked the action of their bodies. When Ash felt her getting close, he found her clit with his thumb and drove her over the edge.

Her gasp was muffled against his lips, and her whole body clenched. Holding her hips in place, he continued to drive up, and she arched back to brace her hands on his thighs.

Ash thumbed her clit once more, sending her into a second orgasm and the moment she screamed his name, his own release came, slamming into him like lightning through an ancient oak.

Chest heaving, she curled back against him to splay on his chest, her breath hot across his nipple.

"That one was even better," she mumbled as they remained connected and spent.

"Yeah, it was."

Once they caught their breath, Jesse lifted to rest her chin on his sternum. "The third time could be the winner."

A wicked smile curved her lips, and though Ash wasn't one to make promises he couldn't keep, there wasn't anything he wouldn't do for this woman.

Nodding, he twisted a dark-red curl around his finger. "Okay, then."

Blue eyes softened before she kissed the spot where her chin had rested. "Okay, then."

TWENTY-EIGHT

JESSE WASN'T QUITE A PESSIMIST, BUT THE LAST YEAR HAD TURNED her into a cautious optimist. For more than a week, she and Ash had been enjoying their time together, both in the studio and away from it. She was also enjoying decorating her new place.

Nearly all of the boxes were unpacked and several new items bought. The sheets were washed, on the bed, and thoroughly broken in thanks to Ash becoming a regular overnight guest. As for the album, recording had slowed down a bit due to having to replace Mason, but because they'd been ahead of schedule when the change came, the delay hadn't caused any problems.

Personally and professionally, life was good. Better than good. She was in love and making some of the best music of her career. Despite all the positives, she still felt nauseated while once again waiting in the Shooting Stars lobby. Silas occupied his usual seat beside her, and Ash filled the chair on her other side.

"He's going to love them," Ash whispered, giving her bouncing knee a squeeze.

Today was the official halfway point in the three-month recording schedule and that meant letting Clay hear what they had so far. To say Jesse was stressed would be an understatement. She felt as if she were taking a Monday morning exam and forgot to study.

"But what if he doesn't?" she whispered back.

This really was her best stuff. Between the arrangements Ash created for the songs she'd already written, and the three new ones they'd penned together, Jesse felt certain they'd found a winning formula. Yet, she couldn't help but worry.

"We've done what we set out to do," he replied. "These are great songs, and Clay will recognize that."

"He's right," Silas said. "Benedict knows the good stuff when he hears it. You've got nothing to worry about, child."

"Mr. Benedict asked me to bring you back," Belinda said.

The threesome rose together to follow the receptionist down the long hall and back to the conference room where their collaboration had begun. Back then, she'd never expected to see Ash again let alone have him back in her life in such a profound way. Amazing how much could change in such a short period of time.

"Good morning," Clay greeted them as they filed into the room.

"Morning," Silas said.

Jesse failed to speak around the lump in her throat and settled for a lame wave.

Once they were settled in their chairs, Clay got right to the point. "I listened to the files Ash sent me over the weekend. Are you thinking all of these will make the final cut?"

Jesse's heart plummeted. He hated them. Six songs and he hated every one of them.

"We're keeping that open this early in the process," Ash replied. "But I'm happy with what we have and believe that every song cut so far has the potential to be included."

Was he not paying attention? Clay didn't like the songs.

"I agree," Clay responded.

"What?" Jesse said, finally finding her voice. "You like them?"

Dark brows arched. "You don't?" he asked.

"N... no," she stuttered. "I mean, yes. I love them. This is the best music I've ever made."

Silas chuckled and patted the back of her hand. "He's agreeing with you, girl."

"Oh." Heart rate returning to normal, Jesse let out a breath. "Good. That's good."

Clay smiled, making him seem much less intimidating. "I'm impressed, Jesse. We clearly made the right choice pairing you and Ash together."

She glanced to the man on her left, who squeezed her hand beneath the table. "I agree."

"These songs are good enough to consider one for an early single. I'd like to send the first cut to radio in late December and aim for an album release date in early March. How does that sound?"

The sooner the better for Jesse. "We've talked about releasing 'Save Yourself' first, and also making that the name of the album."

Her boss's smile widened. "That would be my choice, as well."

This morning kept getting better. "Great. Then my debut album is called *Save Yourself*." As soon as the words crossed her lips, Jesse feared she might be dreaming.

"I'll let Naomi know right away so we can get more detailed on the promotions, and we'll need to get a photo shoot scheduled as soon as possible." Clay pushed back from the table. "Now I want to introduce you to the newest member of the Shooting Stars team."

As he exited his chair, Jesse wavered between excitement and apprehension at the mention of a photo shoot. Creating an image was part of the game, but the persona she'd cultivated in the Daisies didn't feel right anymore. Without a beauty queen to compete with, she wanted to put more of her own style forward.

Not that she knew exactly what that would mean, but big hair and glitter-covered outfits were off the list.

"Do you know who this is?" she asked Silas.

"No idea," he mumbled as Clay returned, a dark-haired woman in tow. All three of them stood as the pair entered.

"This is our new A&R Director, Emily Garcia," Clay said. "Emily, this is Jesse Gold, her producer, Ash Shepherd, and her manager, Silas Fillmore. I sent the song files to Emily this morning so she's up to speed on the sound we're working with."

"Nice to meet you all," Emily said, reaching across the table to shake each of their hands. "I love all of the songs, but I'm torn for a favorite between 'Save Yourself' and 'Wild Horses.'"

The response put Jesse at ease and made her like the woman immediately. "Thank you. We've agreed that 'Save Yourself' will be the first single *and* the title of the album, but I'm with you on 'Wild Horses.' I can't wait to play that one live."

"That reminds me," Clay cut in. "Dylan is doing a trial headlining tour next spring. We're sticking with moderate-sized venues that we're hoping to fill. He'll need an opening act and you're at the top of the list."

Knees weakening, she swayed to the left. Ash took a quick step to bolster her up. "Are you serious?" Jesse asked.

"I am. Mark your calendar now. The first show is April fourth."

Turning to Ash, she said, "I'm going on tour."

Heart in his eyes, he grinned like a loon. "I heard."

Unable to help herself, Jesse leaped into his arms with a whoop of joy. Ash caught her and hugged her tight before dropping her back to her feet. She immediately turned to Silas and repeated the action, though the older man wasn't as sturdy. Her enthusiasm nearly landed them both on the floor.

"You're on your way, my dear," her manager said without complaint. "I told you we could do it."

Eyes misting, she kissed him on the cheek. "Yes, you did."

Remembering where she was, Jesse swiped at her eyes and turned back to Clay. "Sorry about that. I guess I'm a little excited."

"No problem."

"I know you're busy in the studio," Emily said, "but I heard that you're participating in a Christmas taping later this week?"

Jesse had almost forgotten about the television show. "Yes, I am. Rehearsal is Wednesday, and the taping is Thursday night."

"Since this will essentially be your debut as a solo artist, I'd like to meet to discuss your look going forward. Would you have time for a quick visit tomorrow?"

"I guess I can get away," she said, looking to Ash. "At this rate, we won't get much done this week."

"We're in good shape," he replied. "Do whatever you need to do."

"Okay, then," she said, exchanging a covert message with the man who was so much more than her producer. In an effort to keep the world out of their business for as long as possible, they'd agreed to keep their relationship quiet until the album was finished. "I guess I'm available. What time should I be here?"

"How does ten o'clock sound?"

"Good to me." Testing the waters, she said, "I'm hoping to go with a more authentic look than I had with the Honkytonk Daisies."

The woman smiled. "I think that's an excellent idea."

Jesse breathed a sigh of relief. "Cool. Then I'll see you in the morning." To Clay, she said, "Thank you so much for giving me this opportunity. And for the chance to go on tour."

"It was Dylan's idea, actually. He was in the office early this morning for a quick visit and heard what I was listening to. By the time we got to the third song, he asked if you'd be ready to open his shows."

She made a mental note to send a sizable Christmas gift to the Monroe family. "That's nice to hear."

"Then we're set. I wish all meetings were this productive."

Clay motioned toward the door, and Silas took the hint, leading them out and toward the lobby. Goodbyes were exchanged and once out of the building, Jesse gave her manager another heartfelt hug before he shuffled off to his old Lincoln Continental.

She and Ash crossed the parking lot to his truck, then she pulled him around to the passenger side where they couldn't be seen from the street or the office.

"Thank you," she said, overwhelmed with gratitude. Jesse may not have a giant group of friends, but she'd somehow managed to surround herself with all the right people, the most important being the man in her arms. "Those songs are as much you as they are me, and I doubt any of them would be as good without your input. So thank you for helping make this dream a reality."

Ash held her close. "You make my job easy, Jesse. It's your talent in those songs. All I did was capture it on tape."

"You did more than that." So much more. "I'm so lucky you walked back into my life."

He kissed her softly on the lips before saying, "I'm the lucky one. Now let's get back to work before I drag you over to my place so we can both get lucky."

Laughter bubbled up as he whisked the truck door open. "To the studio we go." Jesse climbed in but clasped the front of his jacket before he could close her in. "If you show up at my door later this evening, that getting lucky thing can still happen."

Kissing her one more time, he said, "Deal."

* * *

"Emily, I need to see you in my office."

"Of course," she replied, and followed Clay down the hall.

He'd been waiting until she'd settled into the team and her workspace before presenting the new director with her first real task. After his conversation with Liam Bradshaw, Clay had debated how to proceed, deciding initially to forget about The Hard Way and move on to other acts.

And then he'd done a brief exploration of bands looking for a label and found few who could compare.

"I have your first assignment," he said, stepping behind his desk and motioning for her to take the chair opposite.

She took a seat. "Okay, but I thought my overall assignment was clear."

"It is, however, I have a specific act in mind to get you started."

Brown eyes narrowed. "No disrespect, but if you still intend to find the acts, why did you hire me?"

Clay didn't mind the question, as she did have a point. The entire reason he'd brought her on board was to take the burden off his shoulders.

"Technically," he replied, "you found this act first."

Hovering tensely on the edge of her seat, Emily said, "I don't understand."

"You signed The Hard Way to Six String Records, correct?"

"I did, but that isn't a mistake I would make twice."

"Why was it a mistake?"

"As I mentioned in my interview, the leader of that band is impossible to work with. Liam is arrogant, obstinate, and convinced that he and *only he* knows anything about this business. He responds poorly to the simplest of suggestions, and he refuses to even discuss potential opportunities that could enhance the band's reach and chance for future success."

His new hire was on her feet by the time she finished the last sentence, color high on her cheeks as she loomed over Clay's desk, looking as if she might heave the thing over. Mr. Bradshaw had clearly left an impression, and not a good one.

"Then you have your work cut out for you," he said, unmoved by the emotional rant. This was business, and if Ms. Garcia wanted to make her mark in the industry, she would need to set emotion aside and focus on the more profitable bigger picture.

Dropping back to the chair, she said, "Did you not hear a word I just said?"

He ignored the question. "I happened to be downtown last Friday and found The Hard Way playing at The Stillery. Liam Bradshaw and I had a brief conversation in which I mentioned that Shooting Stars might be interested in signing them. His interest waned when your name came up."

To his surprise, Emily snorted. "Of course, it did." More to herself than to Clay, she mumbled, "As if *I* was the problem."

"Then your task is clear. Convince Mr. Bradshaw to sign with Shooting Stars Records."

"Mr. Benedict—"

"I told you the day you started to call me Clay."

She sprouted upright again. "Liam won't work with me, Mr. . . Clay. He won't work with anyone. At least not reasonably."

"Change his mind."

"How?"

Leaning back in his chair, he said, "That's up to you, but I suggest keeping your personal feelings out of the conversation."

Expression cold, she crossed her arms. "Excuse me?"

"You clearly don't like the man, which is fine. You don't have to like him to work with him. But insulting him is unlikely to help your case."

"I don't—"

"You have your assignment." Clay reached for the pile of folders in his inbox. "I understand that they're between managers at the moment. Try to find out if or when that might change before contacting the band directly."

"Yes, sir," she replied in a clipped tone before marching toward the door.

"And Emily?"

She paused, shoulders rising and falling in a visual reach for patience. Turning, she said, "Sir?"

"Start your inquiries with Samantha Walters' office. I understand she's taken an interest in them as well."

"I'll do that," she said and made her exit.

Curious and slightly amused, Clay let the subtle slam of his door pass without mention and wondered what exactly had occurred between Liam Bradshaw and Emily Garcia. Based on her less-than-flattering opinion of the man, overcoming their differences might be more challenging than he'd first assumed.

She had fight, and that gave him confidence that she would make this happen. Clay certainly hoped so because he fully intended to sign The Hard Way as the next artist on the Shooting Stars roster. Whether that would mean choosing between the band or Emily Garcia was yet to be determined.

TWENTY-NINE

WHEN IT CAME TO BACKSTAGE AREAS, THE RYMAN OFFERED ONE of the most posh that Jesse had ever seen. Even though, as one of the lesser-known artists on the show, she'd been relegated to a tiny dressing room at the end of the long hall, the space was still nicer than any she'd had before.

This building that had begun as a tabernacle nearly one hundred and thirty years ago, carried so much history that Jesse was humbled just to be here. Everyone from presidents to era-defining performers had graced these halls, and now Jesse was making her own history, marking one more item off her bucket list in the process.

"Do you remember the first time you were here, Silas?" she asked the man struggling not to doze off in the only other seat in the room.

Shaking himself awake, he tilted his head in thought. "It was 1965. I was in the audience the night Johnny Cash stomped out all the stage lights."

Jesse spun from the mirror. "You're lying."

"Nope," he replied. "I was sixteen and here with my grandma. She was as scandalized as the rest of the crowd and insisted that I never attend the Opry again. Once they banned Johnny, she relaxed that rule, and I became a regular. As for getting backstage, that would be the CMA awards in 1972. My first artist, Buddy Lee Beauregard Jr., was up for Single of the Year."

"That's the year that Loretta won the Entertainer award."

Silas scratched his balding head. "Might have been."

As a longtime worshiper of the legend, Jesse knew the date well. "You've been present for so many amazing moments in this business. Why haven't you told me these stories before?"

Withdrawing a piece of hard candy from his pocket, he replied, "You never asked."

Had Jesse been so self-absorbed that she'd worked with this walking country music archive for two years and never asked about his past? What an awful revelation.

"Then consider yourself warned. I want to hear them all over Thanksgiving."

Ingrid and Dana were hosting, as they had the year before, and Jesse was looking forward to celebrating with Ash by her side. It had been two weeks since the Halloween party, and Jesse couldn't remember when she'd been so happy. Probably ten years ago, when her brother had still been alive, and she'd been expecting an engagement ring from Ash for Christmas.

"Some of the details might be a little sketchy, but I'll share what I can remember."

"That's all I ask."

A knock sounded at the door, and Jesse took the two steps required to answer it.

"Ms. Gold, we'll need you up front in five minutes," said a man who looked young enough to still be in high school. She assumed he was a college student possibly doing an internship. Before she could respond, he lifted the microphone of his headset back into place. "What do you mean you can't find him?" After a brief pause, he added, "I'll be right there."

With a huff, he was gone.

"Alrighty, then." Jesse checked herself in the mirror one more time.

Her meeting with Emily the day before had led to an afternoon hair appointment. The stylist had found a way to incorporate Jesse's casual style into something a bit more stage-ready. Instead of the basic ponytail, her thick, red hair was pulled to the side, gathered into a festive clip, and draped over her right shoulder.

She'd been worried about replicating the look for today, but she had pulled it off after only a couple tries.

"Are you going to wait in here, or come out front and watch the rehearsal?"

Silas shifted the candy to his other cheek. "I'll come out if you want me to."

Sensing the answer he wanted to hear, she patted him on the shoulder. "Stay here and relax. You'll see the show tomorrow."

Settling deeper into the chair, he nodded in agreement. "Yes, yes, that's true." Catching her hand to give it a quick squeeze, he said, "Go get 'em, girlie."

Jesse kissed the top of his head. "Yes, sir." With a smile on her face, she left the little dressing room, sending out a prayer of gratitude for whatever higher power had sent the old man into her life. He'd been her loyal companion through more downs than ups, and that unwavering belief was finally paying off for the both of them.

* * *

"Mr. Ash, I don't feel so well."

Butler was Ash's anchor guitarist. This was no time for the boy to get sick.

"Do you have a fever?"

He shook his head. "Not that kind of sick. I'm so nervous, I feel like I'm going to throw up."

Ash could relate. "This is only the rehearsal, big guy. Keep breathing and remember that this is nothing different than how we play at the center every weekend." Giving the teen a shoulder squeeze for support, he added, "Just have fun. That's all we have to do."

The words were as much for himself as for the youngster. The kids were ready, of that Ash had no doubt, but if their leader was this scared when the seats were empty, how were they going to handle the real thing?

"But the cameras. . ."

They'd discussed what this opportunity would entail back when the offer had come, and all of the kids had been given the option not to participate. A month ago, when being on television had sounded more exciting than daunting, everyone had jumped at the chance. Now that the day was here, the cameras were in place, and some of their idols were strolling the halls, Ash feared his musicians was starting to second-guess their decision.

"Remember when we played at the charity event earlier this year?" he asked.

"Out in front of the center?"

"That's right. There were cameras there, and you did great."

Butler's shoulders relaxed a bit. "That's true. But what if I play a wrong chord? The whole world will hear it."

He might be giving this little holiday show more credit than it deserved, but this was no time to debate the size of the television audience.

"There will be ten guitars all playing at once. No one will hear one wrong chord." Not the best pep talk Ash had ever given. "Besides, you haven't played a wrong chord since the week we started learning the song. And you won't play one today *or* tomorrow."

Butler swallowed hard. "When I told my mom I was nervous, she said it isn't as if I'm doing something important like performing brain surgery. I think I need to keep telling myself that."

Ash didn't appreciate the backhanded insult to his

profession, but if belittling an entire art form would get the boy through this, he'd let it slide.

"Mr. Ash," called Danny Little, barreling toward him at a full run and pulling a struggling Zoe Romero along behind. "We have a big problem."

Why did he volunteer with kids again?

"What is it?"

Danny paused to catch his breath and pointed to Zoe. "She can't sing."

"She can't what?" Zoe had the solo. She had to sing. The young girl was massaging her throat with a miserable look on her face. "Why can't you sing?"

"I don't know," she croaked. "I was fine yesterday."

Nerves. Ash should have spent as much time preparing them for the anxiety of performing as he had on hitting all the right notes.

He bent until his face was even with hers. "Listen to me, Zoe. You're an amazing singer who has been given a gift. The gift of a beautiful voice. All you have to do today is share that gift with your friends. I know you can do it."

"Yeah," Butler chimed in. "It's not like we're cutting someone's brain open."

Zoe turned confused eyes the boy's way, and Ash went with it.

"That's right. No one's life is on the line here. Sing like you do at the academy, and you'll be great."

"I'll hold your hand if that'll help," Danny offered. Contrary to his last name, there was nothing little about the boy who played nose tackle for his high school football team and loomed above the other kids by nearly a foot.

The young girl gave her outsized protector a wide-eyed look, as if seeing him for the first time. "You'd do that for me?"

Danny shrugged broad shoulders. "Sure."

The frog in Zoe's throat miraculous disappeared and with renewed courage, she said, "I'll be okay."

Ash breathed a sigh of relief. "That's our girl."

Hand in hand, Danny and Zoe headed back to the choir's dressing room while Butler stared after them. "You think he likes her?" he asked, as clueless as a teenage boy could be.

"I think he might. Are we good here?"

The boy nodded. "If Zoe can do it, so can I."

Ash gave his student a soft tap on the arm. "That's the spirit. Go join the others and make sure everyone is tuned and ready."

"Yes, sir," he said before rushing off.

These kids were going to be the death of him, and it didn't help that Ash was as nervous as they were. Performing in front of a bar full of tourists had never been fun, and in this situation, he couldn't rely on liquor lowering his audience's standards.

"Are you okay?" Jesse said.

Ash hadn't heard her come up behind him. "Yeah. Good. I'm fine."

With a soft chuckle, she said, "You don't look fine. What's the matter?"

Searching for a secluded corner, Ash settled on an opening behind a dark curtain to his left. "Hold on."

Taking her by the hand, he tucked them both into the small space and pulled her into his arms. She slid her fingers into his hair and kissed him back, easing his mind and making him forget the task ahead.

When the kiss ended, he pressed his forehead to hers. "I needed that."

A little breathless, Jesse said, "I'm not complaining, but where did this sudden need to kiss me come from?"

Reluctant to reveal his weakness, Ash said, "I always have a need to kiss you."

Jesse eased back and flattened her palms against his chest. "That's nice to hear. Now tell me the real reason."

"I need a reason to kiss you?"

"Ashland Shepherd, I've known you long enough to know when you're on edge about something. What is it?"

So much for keeping his dignity intact. "I hate performing live," he admitted. "That's why I write the songs and let other people sing them."

Instead of laughing, as he'd expected, Jesse cupped his face in her hands. "That's nothing to be ashamed of. I get nervous before every performance, but I love it once I'm out there and the music starts."

"I hate it the whole time." The confession wasn't as difficult with Jesse.

She touched her lips to his. "You create incredible music, and there's nothing wrong with letting others share it for you. But I don't think you can get out of this performance. Not without letting the kids down."

Ash would never do that. "I'll make it," he said. "And I'm looking forward to the day when we don't have to hide behind curtains like this."

"We won't have to sneak around much longer," she replied. "After all this time, we can wait another six weeks, right?"

"As long as I know you're mine, that's all that matters."

"I'm all yours. Now you'd better go check on the kids. We wouldn't be very good at sneaking if we both pop out from behind this curtain at the same time."

He reluctantly let her go, but he stole one more kiss before leaving. "By the way, you look beautiful."

Jesse patted the curls draped over her shoulder. "Do you really like it?"

"I do." Someone called Jesse's name in the distance. With one more quick kiss, he said, "I'm out of here."

Ash peeked around the edge of the curtain and found the coast was clear. Feeling better than he had before, he walked casually down the hall and heard the sounds of multiple guitars being tuned. The sound reminded Ash that this wasn't about him. This was about these students, who had very few positives going for them. That he could be the source of one made any suffering on his part more than worthwhile.

* * *

After what Jesse deemed a reasonable amount of time, she stepped out from behind the curtain to find Dennis Kohlman blocking her path. Damn it. *Why hadn't she checked first?*

"What are you doing here?" she asked, annoyed by his arrogant glare.

"I have an artist on the show," he replied, then tisked as if she were a misbehaving child. "You just can't stay out of trouble, can you?"

Jesse stepped to the left to go around him. "I don't know what you're talking about."

"Sleeping with your producer?" Dennis said, blocking her path. "That's a bit cliché, even for you."

"Let me by."

"I wondered how you finally managed to find one after I'd worked so hard to limit your options."

She knew it. "Then it *was* you who spread those rumors."

"I didn't say anything that wasn't true. You *are* a bitch to work with. Just ask Mason."

No matter what Jesse said to defend herself, Dennis would twist her words to serve his own demented purpose. "Screw you," she said, stepping in the opposite direction, but he cut her off again. "Knock it off, Dennis. I'm expected on stage."

"It's one thing to screw up your own career, but destroying someone else's is exceptionally selfish."

He would know. "You're the one who screws up careers, remember? Now let me by." Jesse was finally able to get around him, but his next statement stopped her cold.

"I'm sure Ash Shepherd might have found great success as a producer. Too bad we'll never know."

Hot rage surging through her, Jesse turned slowly. "What are you talking about?"

"Well," Dennis said, examining his fingernails, "when the

tabloids get wind of the affair, I doubt he'll have much credibility in this town."

"What affair?" she whispered, stepping closer and struggling to keep from strangling the evil jerk.

"The affair you and Shepherd had while you were still with Ryan Dimitri. After all the speculation that *he* had been the unfaithful one, I'm sure his fans will be happy to hear that the real cheater was you."

Hands clenched into fists, she growled, "I never cheated on Ryan. Whatever pointless vendetta you have against me, leave Ash out of it."

"Too late, darling. You brought him into this, not me."

"I didn't—" Choked with frustration, Jesse stopped wasting her breath. "What do you get out of this? Out of destroying innocent people's lives?"

"There's nothing innocent about you and Shepherd. I heard what you said behind the curtain about sneaking around and waiting to go public to make it look like a new romance."

The only reason they'd been sneaking around was to keep from giving the gossips more to talk about, but Jesse had never imagined anyone would assume she and Ash had gotten together before her breakup with Ryan. Her head spun as the truth dawned. Hiding their relationship—which they clearly hadn't done well enough—had provided more fodder than if they'd just been honest from the start.

"What do you want to leave Ash out of this?" she asked, certain that the man had a price.

"Fire him," Dennis replied without hesitation.

"What?"

"Fire Shepherd as your producer."

She couldn't do that. Not this far into the project. Even if she explained that she had to do it to keep Kohlman from going to the tabloids with his bogus story, Ash's career would take a hit without a complete album on his resume. And then there would be Clay Benedict to deal with, who wasn't likely to tolerate the lost recording time as they hunted down yet another producer.

As Jesse was about to argue, she realized that she'd be wasting her breath. Dennis already knew all of this. Why else would he make such a demand? His ultimate goal was for Taylor to come out on top over Jesse. He would make that happen at any cost.

"You want me to commit career suicide and endanger Ash's future in the process."

"You put Shepherd in the crosshairs, my dear. I just want you out of the way."

He wanted her alone, miserable, and defeated. All because she'd bruised his fragile ego.

"Do you really have so little faith in the artist you signed?" Jesse asked, feeling bad for Taylor for the first time since she'd altered both their lives.

"There's nothing wrong with stacking the deck," Dennis drawled. "Or handicapping the competition."

Jerks like Dennis were the ones who gave this business a bad name.

"You're asking me to throw away everything I've worked for."

"Ms. Gold?" said the same man who'd visited her dressing room minutes before. "I've been looking for you. We need you on stage."

With a victorious smile, Dennis said, "You can give me your answer tomorrow." He began to back away. "But I wouldn't put this off, or things will only get worse."

Yes, they would. He'd make sure of that.

Suppressing the panic rising in her chest, Jesse nodded to the young man in the headset. "I'm ready."

"Follow me." When they reached the front of the stage, he pointed to an X on the floor. "Stand there and wait for your cue."

Muttering under his breath, the harried young man left her alone behind the microphone stand, staring into a dark, empty auditorium. A spotlight clicked on loudly, blinding her as the musicians she hadn't noticed at the back of the stage started playing her song.

Shoving Dennis Kohlman as far out of her mind as possible, Jesse relied on all of her stage experience to get through her brother's favorite Christmas tune—I'll Be Home For Christmas—without bursting into tears. Though in that moment, she wanted to cry as much for what she was *about* to lose, as what had been taken from her all those years ago.

THIRTY

"You did it," Ash cheered as The Sunshine Academy Players filed into their dressing room. "Great job out there."

The rehearsal had gone off without a hitch. By the time Ash returned from his brief interlude with Jesse, Butler had shared his brain surgery antidote, and by some miracle, the perspective had calmed everyone's fears.

"I didn't even mess up," said Chadwick, the newest member of the ensemble who'd been with the group only four months. Playing must have been in his DNA because he'd picked up the instrument faster than any student Ash had ever had. Other than Jesse.

"Mrs. Hopewell is going to be blown away tomorrow night," Butler announced, brimming with pride.

Millie had checked in on several practice sessions but opted to wait until the big night to hear the performance in full.

"Yes, she is," Ash agreed.

He had to return to the stage to supervise the choir's rehearsal, but the singers had been nailing their song for the last two weeks, so he was much less nervous about their performance. It helped that he was a mere supporter in the wings for them and not required to be on stage.

"You guys get packed up and sit quietly while I see to the choir."

Sheila Worthing and Greg Etheridge, the two parent chaperones, gave him a nod of understanding, making it clear that they would keep the children contained in Ash's absence.

As he hustled from the room, Ash nearly ran Jesse over. "Hey," he said, steadying her. "Sorry about that. Are you okay?"

"I'm fine," she replied distantly. "I just wanted to let you know that I'm leaving."

"But we came together. I only have the choir left, and then I should be able to go." The kids were riding a bus back to the center where their parents would pick them up.

Jesse shook her head. "No, I need to go. Silas is going to drive me home."

Something was off. "Are you okay? Did something go wrong during your rehearsal?"

"I told you, I'm fine. I just want to go home." Eyes down, she mumbled, "I have to figure something out."

"Jesse, what's going on?"

The choir exited the room next door, and Zoe said, "Are you coming, Mr. Ash?"

"I'll be right there." He kept his focus on Jesse and lowered his voice. "Give me ten minutes and I'll go with you."

She finally met his gaze, her expression unreadable. "Not tonight. I'll see you during the taping tomorrow."

"What about the studio?"

"I'm taking tomorrow off to rest my voice for the show."

Was that the problem? They'd been working hard for weeks so he understood her voice needing a rest. But this didn't feel that simple.

Ash watched the last of the choir disappear down the hall. "I have to go. Are you sure you can't wait?"

Jaw tight, she crossed her arms. "I'm sure. We can talk this weekend."

This weekend? Today was only Wednesday. What the hell?

Confusion mounted. "There's something you aren't telling me."

"Come on, Mr. Ash," called Zoe. "We have to go on, and the risers aren't long enough."

Pulled in two directions, he squeezed Jesse's shoulders. "Wait for me. Please."

"I can't." She stepped out of his reach. "I have to go."

Without another word, she hurried down the hall toward the back door where Silas waited.

"Figure what out?" Ash muttered.

"Mr. Shepherd, we need you on stage," said a voice behind him.

As Jesse left the building, Ash fought the urge to go after her. What could have possibly happened in the twenty minutes since he'd kissed her behind that curtain? The question still ringing in his head, he followed the kid in the headset toward the stage, passing a dark-haired man in a suit on the way.

"Good luck," the guy said.

Ash glanced over to find one heavy brow arched high, and a smug smile on the man's thin lips.

"Who are you?" he asked, taking an immediate dislike to the stranger.

"Dennis Kohlman, at your service."

Ignoring the extended hand, Ash said, "Should I know you?"

"No," the reply came as the hand fell away. "And I doubt we'll meet again. Farewell, Mr. Shepherd."

Ash watched the Kohlman guy saunter away before he was hurried onto the stage to find half of his choir standing about in confusion. Zoe was right. The risers provided were never going to fit the entire group.

In the melee that followed, the stranger was completely forgotten.

* * *

What was she going to do?

Jesse had examined every option she could think of, but no solution came. Defeat weighed heavily on her chest as she lay in bed staring at the dingy popcorn ceiling.

There was no way she could avoid giving Dennis exactly what he wanted. She *might* survive the fallout. Clay *might* not drop her from the label. And another producer *might* be found to finish the album.

That was a lot of mights, and the truth was, the odds of any of that happening were not in her favor.

The more likely scenarios were that she'd lose her deal, her album would never be finished, and not only would Ash take a hit professionally, but their relationship would implode in the process. In fact, no matter what Jesse decided to do, there was no way to save her newfound happiness.

If she let Dennis do his worst, Ash would be dragged through a public flogging. Jesse wasn't famous enough to garner the kind of headlines that Miranda or Carrie might, but Flesh and Blood had a significant following that was highly active on social media.

Even a hint that she'd wronged their beloved lead singer would result in a Twitter storm that would leave Jesse in tatters and take Ash down in flames right along with her. He was a private person who didn't deserve that kind of embarrassment.

In a week, some other kerfuffle would steal the spotlight, but the damage would be done. Ash would forever be the guy who'd cheated with that no-name singer whether he deserved the title or not.

The alternative would be more painful for Jesse, but it would save Ash from the media spotlight. In fact, if she made sure to come through as the villain, her producer might get the benefit of the doubt. Ash would be the guy who'd given the difficult artist his best shot, but in the end, she'd been exactly as the rumors had claimed.

Impetuous. Impossible. Incapable of being professional.

Rolling onto her stomach, Jesse screamed into her pillow. A slew of expletives later, she curled into a ball on her side, desperately racking her brain for a third option. Her cell rang, and she closed her eyes. Ash had been calling for the last two hours. She'd sent every call to voice mail, but if she didn't answer soon, he'd show up at her door, and Jesse couldn't face him until she'd found some way out of this.

"Hello?" she said, pressing the phone to her ear.

"Why haven't you answered my calls? Are you all right?"

Hating herself for it, Jesse used the age-old excuse. "I don't feel good. It's that time of the month."

"Oh," Ash said, voice slightly less frantic. "Do you need me to bring you something? Pain pills? Chocolate?"

Jesse squeezed her eyes tight as a tear slid down her temple. "No, I just need to sleep. I'm sure I'll be better tomorrow."

"Are you sure? I don't mind."

"I know. Thanks for the offer, but I'm already in bed."

A heavy sigh came down the line. "Okay, then."

She did her best to smother the whimper. "Okay, then," Jesse replied, chest aching. "I'll see you tomorrow."

"Call if you need me to pick you up."

Voice shaking, she nodded before remembering he couldn't see her. "I'll be well enough to drive myself."

Silence loomed for several seconds before Ash said, "Then I guess I'll see you there."

"Good night," she said as another tear fell.

"Night, baby."

Before he hung up, there was one more thing Jesse had to say. "I love you, Ash. Please don't forget that."

"Never, hon. I hope you feel better."

"Me, too."

She ended the call and dropped the phone on the bed before rising to sit against the headboard. There had to be another way.

Dragging a pillow onto her lap, she hugged it tight against her chest, willing her brain to think.

The only way to avoid losing everything was to take away Dennis's power. But how? Start rumors of her own? Jesse wouldn't even have to lie. She could simply out him for the predator that he was, but there was no guarantee she'd be believed. He'd already smeared her name enough to stack the game in his favor.

If Jesse played this card and no one believed her, she'd go from being merely difficult to a liar who spread vicious rumors about her main rival's manager. If they *did* believe her, the one hurt the most would be Taylor. Despite how things had gone down, Jesse didn't hate her former partner enough to throw her under a bus in order to save herself.

Which led her right back to where she'd started.

Tossing the pillow aside, Jesse snagged her phone and fired off an email to Silas asking him to set up a meeting with Clay for Friday morning. Once the damage was done, she would be the one to tell Ash. She only hoped he'd find a way to forgive her.

Unable to sleep, Ash strolled into his studio to find something productive to do. For once, he didn't feel like writing a song, and he was too worried about Jesse to focus on anything else. Settling in front of the computer, he checked his email first, but there were no messages that needed his immediate attention.

Clicking over to YouTube, he typed a few familiar names into the search bar and found a new video by one of his co-writers. The performance was from the Songbird Cafe and featured a newly written tune meant to be a duet. The female artist performing with him, a woman Ash didn't know, had a nice voice, but she wasn't as strong of a singer as Jesse was.

They hadn't talked about adding a duet to the record, but it wasn't a bad idea. If they could convince Chance to join the effort, Jesse could have a ready-made hit on her hands that was sure to garner major attention.

Ash clicked back over to email to message the writer. With any luck, the song was still available.

Going back to the videos, he did a few more searches but found nothing he hadn't already heard. Failing to find a distraction, the events of the evening played back through his mind, and Ash couldn't shake the feeling that Jesse was hiding something.

Something happened between the time he left her behind the curtain and when she'd decided to leave without him. Maybe Dimitri had messaged her. Or she'd had another run-in with Taylor Roper. Had she been part of the show? Ash didn't remember seeing her, but there were a ton of performers involved, and he'd been too busy with the kids to check out the rest of the lineup.

Finding the info for the Christmas special online, he scanned the list, but Taylor's name wasn't on it. Curious, he typed her name into a search engine and scanned the info. Halfway down the page, a name caught Ash's eye.

Dennis Kohlman. That was the guy who'd been lurking backstage at rehearsal.

A few clicks more and Ash learned that Kohlman was Taylor's manager. He didn't have many other clients, but one name did match with an artist on the Christmas show list. There had to be a connection between Kohlman and Jesse's sudden change. Had he given her a message from Taylor? And if so, why wouldn't Jesse tell Ash about it?

Speculation was getting him nowhere, and there were no internet searches that would reveal what Jesse was thinking. Tomorrow he'd ask about Kohlman. If the man was responsible for whatever was bothering her, Ash would know from her reaction. And then he'd track down the snake and make sure he never bothered her again.

In fact, maybe he should call and make sure she was okay.

Glancing to the corner of the screen, he decided that after midnight was too late to bother her. If Kohlman was the problem, Ash could take care of that easily enough. If it was something else, they'd deal with it together.

Turning off the screen, he crossed to the door and flipped off the light on his way out.

THIRTY-ONE

THE BLARE OF A HORN SNAPPED JESSE OUT OF HER THOUGHTS. THE black Tahoe stopped mere feet from turning her into roadkill, and she hurried the rest of the way to reach the sidewalk. Keeping her head down, she hustled around to the back of the auditorium.

Jesse hadn't slept much, nodding off shortly before dawn, only to have a disturbing dream that involved a furious Ash damning her to hell before storming into the ether where she couldn't reach him. Dream Jesse had tried running after him but couldn't seem to move, as if her legs had been buried in thick mud.

She'd awoken calling his name and found herself alone on top of the penguin comforter. Two weeks was all she would get. Two weeks of being happier than she could have hoped, and by the weekend Jesse would be alone again.

There was a special place in hell for people like Dennis Kohlman, but his eternal damnation did little to ease the agony of letting Ash go.

Halfway up the historic curving staircase that led to the backstage entrance, Jesse heard a familiar voice call her name.

"Jesse, wait!" Of course he'd send *her* as his messenger.

Turning, she waited for Taylor without giving a single step. When the blonde ducked under the alcove, she said, "I need to talk to you."

"Dennis couldn't be bothered to come do this himself?" Jesse snarled.

"That's why I'm here. To let you know that Dennis won't be hurting you anymore."

The words didn't penetrate. "What did you say?"

"I'm so sorry," she said, shaking her head. "I had no idea what he was really like."

Knees failing, Jesse took a seat on the step behind her and spread the garment bag across her lap. "Don't mess with me, Taylor."

Her former duet partner sat down as well. "I'm not, I swear. A reporter called me this morning wanting me to corroborate a story that Dennis gave him. He said that you'd bullied me while we were together and had been abusive to everyone we worked with."

"I never bullied anyone!" Jesse defended.

"I know, and that's what I told him." Crossing her arms over her legs, Taylor stared at her boots. "I screwed up, Jesse. Bad. But I'm doing my best to make it up to you. That call made me suspicious, so I did some digging and found out that Dennis was the source of those horrible rumors about you."

"I could have told you that," she said, still annoyed with the former beauty queen. "I assumed it was the two of you together, and then Dennis admitted as much when he cornered me yesterday."

"He said I was in on it?"

Jesse thought back to the confession. "Not in so many words, but what else was I supposed to think? You ditched me over a text message and within days the rumors started."

Her Kentucky accent was thick as Taylor held a hand over her heart. "Jesse, I swear on my Jessamine County crown that I had nothing to do with any of this."

Reluctant to trust, she stared straight ahead. "None of this changes what he's done. Or what he plans to do next."

"That's not true. When I learned the truth, I confronted him and insisted that he take it all back."

Oh, to be as naive as this poor woman. "This isn't name-calling on the playground, Taylor. He can't *take it back*. Dennis has destroyed my reputation, and he's going to destroy Ash's if I don't do what he wants, which is basically kill my own career."

Another artist entered the alcove, and Jesse fell silent. The two women rose and parted to let the new arrivals pass. "Sorry," Taylor said. "We didn't mean to be in the way."

"Aren't you the Honkytonk Daisies?" the brunette asked. "Are y'all getting back together?"

"We *were*," Jesse replied. "And no, we aren't."

The woman and her companion looked to Taylor.

"We're just having a chat," she said with an innocent smile.

This was why Jesse couldn't hate her former partner. Taylor was like a newborn babe dropped into a pit of vipers when it came to this business. Which was why Dennis had so easily manipulated her. If Jesse had been honest with her former partner about that first meeting with sleazeball Dennis, this all might have been avoided. Which meant Jesse was at least *partially* to blame.

Still. Their friendship should have been strong enough to keep Taylor from wandering off, damn it.

The new arrivals continued into the building, and Jesse dragged Taylor out of the alcove and away from the entrance. "As I was saying, your manager is going to tell the tabloids that Ash and I were fooling around behind Ryan's back."

"Were you?" she asked, eyes wide.

"No," Jesse answered, stomping her foot. "But I can't risk Ash's name being dragged through the mud like that."

Taylor patted her arm with little concern. "I didn't think you were. And like I said, you don't have to worry about Dennis anymore. He's out of our hair for good."

"Our hair?" she repeated. "What does that mean?"

With a twinkle in her eye, the dumb-like-a-fox beauty queen revealed a wicked streak. "Let's just say, I have photographic evidence of a certain deficiency that Dennis Kohlman wouldn't want shared."

She had what?

"You know what I mean, right?" she said.

Jesse didn't at first, and then hope blossomed as the meaning became clear. "Are you saying he's . . ." Jesse wiggled her little finger.

"Could fit through a keyhole," Taylor confirmed. "I checked with his other three clients, and he sent them the same pictures."

"All of his clients are women?"

"Nope."

Jesse was a love-is-love person, but country music in general hadn't quite reached total enlightenment on that subject. "Did you threaten to share the pictures?"

Taylor snorted. "You best believe it. What he did to you was over the line, Jesse."

"What he did to us," she corrected. "Does this mean you're looking for a new manager?"

"I am. Do you think Silas might take me back?"

Spotting the sweet old man coming their way, Jesse nodded in his direction. "I don't know, but here's your chance to find out."

"Are my eyes deceiving me, or are my girls back together?" Silas asked, the thin wisps atop his head dancing in the breeze.

"Not in an official capacity," Jesse replied, "but Taylor has something she'd like to ask you."

The tall blonde looked ready to run, but she stood her ground. "I'm so sorry, Silas. I never should have left you like I did. Neither of you. Can ever forgive me?"

His round face grew serious as ice-blue eyes darted from Taylor to Jesse and back. "Do you have any idea what you put this poor girl through? What we had to do to make up the ground you yanked out from under her?"

Jesse hadn't expected Silas's response to be quite so harsh.

"I know," Taylor replied, standing up to her mistakes. "I was stupid and reckless, and I don't blame you one bit if you never want to speak to me again. But I really am sorry for the hurt I caused."

Softening, the old man relented. "All right, then. Come to my office on Monday and we'll talk." To Jesse, he said, "I got you that meeting with Clay for eleven tomorrow morning, but we need to make it quick because he can only give us fifteen minutes. What is this about anyway?"

Realizing that her life wasn't about to crash and burn, Jesse nearly whooped with joy. "Holy crap. This means I don't need that meeting after all."

"What meeting?" Taylor asked.

In response, Jesse threw her arms around her former partner, nearly dropping her garment bag in the process. "You're completely forgiven."

Taylor blushed, a bright smile revealing perfect pearly-whites. "Does this mean we can be friends again?"

"It sure does."

"What's going?" Ash asked as he joined them. "Someone said they saw the Honkytonk Daisies out here, and I assumed they were hallucinating."

Without offering a reply, Jesse bolted into his arms, not caring when the cargo she'd worked so hard to keep off her ground landed at his feet. The bag would protect the dress. Hopefully. She kissed him with all the relief running through her before pulling back to breathlessly say, "I love you, Ashland Shepherd. I love you more than anything in this world, and you're *never* getting rid of me."

Holding her nearly a foot off the ground, her soulmate flashed a sexy grin that rocked her to the core. "Is that a marriage proposal, Rheingold?"

"You bet your cute butt it is. What do you say?"

He lowered her to her feet as the grin faded into a look of wonder. "Yes, ma'am. The sooner the better."

* * *

"Why didn't you tell me?" Ash asked for the third time.

While changing into her performance dress, Jesse had rattled off the story of Dennis Kohlman and his evil threats from the day before.

"I told you. I was going to eventually."

"After you caved to the asshole. What were you thinking?"

"I was thinking of *you*."

Ash would have hated being dragged through a media frenzy, but he'd have done it if it meant keeping Jesse by his side. "I never would have let you go through with it."

"None of that matters now." There was a rustling sound before she said, "Okay, you can turn around."

Jesse had forced him to keep his back to her while she'd changed, insisting that she wanted the dress to be a surprise. Ash spun around, and the breath left his body. Before him stood a tiny cloud of emerald-green perfection, and the image triggered a memory.

"Is that . . ."

She nodded. "The dress I wore to homecoming two months before the accident." Glancing down, she twirled her hips, and the long skirt swayed around her legs. When she looked up, tears were in her eyes. "Tommy helped me pick it out, and it was the last dance we all attended together."

Grabbing a tissue from the box on the counter, Ash dabbed at her cheeks. "You look even more beautiful than you did that day."

Jesse took the tissue from his hand. "I had to have the waist expanded a little. I'm going carb-free after the holidays."

Ash swept her into his arms. "You're perfect just the way you are." After kissing the tip of her nose, he said, "Were you really going to leave me?"

Slender fingers toyed with the button on his dress shirt. "I didn't want to, but I would have to protect your privacy." With an earnest expression, Jesse wrapped her arms around his torso. "There isn't anything I wouldn't do for you, Ash."

"How about this. I walked away from you when I thought it was the right thing to do. And you *almost* walked away from me when you thought the same thing. Can we just agree here and now to never, *ever* walk away from each other again?"

"I can wholeheartedly agree to that."

Their lips met, and Ash had barely had enough before a knock sounded at the door.

"Who is it?" Jesse called, making no move to step out of his embrace.

"Kathleen Shepherd. I've been told my son is in there."

The pair stared at each other with a combination of shock and awe.

"Does she know we're together?" Jesse whispered.

That was a call Ash had forgotten to make. "I'm guessing she does now." Setting her away from him, he reached for the doorknob, but Jesse grabbed his arm and swiped at his mouth with her tissue.

"You have my lipstick all over you." Ash grabbed a clean tissue and finished the job, giving a quick check in the mirror before turning to Jesse. "Better?"

She giggled and used her thumb to clean one more spot along his bottom lip. "Now you're good."

"What's going on in there?" Mom called through the door.

"Nothing," Ash said as he whisked the door open and found two people instead of one looming outside. "Who is this?" he asked of the older man with the dark mustache standing beside his mother. He looked like a cross between Sam Elliot and Ernest Tubb, and he was standing entirely too close to Ash's mother.

"Neville O'Brien, meet my son, Ash Shepherd."

The stranger extended a hand, and Ash accepted out of habit.

"Nice to meet you, son. Your mom has told me a lot about you."

"Then you're one up on me." He turned to the statuesque woman who'd raised him. "You want to tell me something?"

Eyes that matched his own glared at the tiny woman behind him. "Do you want to tell *me* something? Why are you in here with the Rheingold girl?"

"You know her name, and you need to start using it since Jesse and I are getting married." His new fiancée choked, and Ash knew he wasn't handling this well, but the stranger in their midst was throwing him off. "Now who's the guy?"

"I guess we've both been keeping a secret," she replied. "Neville is my boyfriend. We've been together for a few months now, and I wanted him to see my boy at work."

Ash had made sure his mother had two tickets to the show, but he'd expected her to bring one of the workers from the daycare center, not a boyfriend.

"A few months? When were you going to tell me?"

"The show starts in five," called a stagehand down the hall. "All non-performers need to exit the backstage area now."

"We have to go," Mom said. "I'll expect an explanation after the show."

"That goes for both of us," he said as Jesse pulled him farther into the room. "Did you see that? My mother has a boyfriend. Women her age do not have boyfriends."

"Ash, she isn't even fifty years old."

"That's no excuse."

Sliding a loose lock off his forehead, Jesse said, "Maybe she's as happy as we are. You want her to be happy, don't you?"

Of course, he did. But that wasn't the point. "She's never needed a boyfriend before."

Tugging on his lapels, she pulled him down for a quick kiss. "I love you, but you're being unreasonable."

Maybe he was, but his mother had never introduced him to a boyfriend before. She'd dated when he was younger, but she never brought the guys home, at least not when Ash had been there. Then again, he'd spent a lot of nights over at the Rheingold house as a kid.

"What if it was your mom showing off a new guy?"

"That would be uncomfortable considering she's still married to my father, and they do everything together." With a hand on his back, Jesse pushed him toward the doorway. "Go check on the kids before they think you got lost, and when this shindig is over, you can help me get out of this dress. Again," she added with a grin.

Temporarily forgetting his mother's revelation, Ash leaned down for one more kiss. "I can do that. Have I mentioned that you look beautiful?"

"Thank you. Now off you go."

Ash ran a hand over her hip one last time before following the order. On his way to the kids, he muttered, "A boyfriend. That's going to take some getting used to."

THIRTY-TWO

A̲t̲ ̲t̲e̲n̲ ̲f̲i̲f̲t̲e̲e̲n̲ ̲o̲n̲ ̲a̲ ̲s̲u̲n̲n̲y̲ ̲S̲u̲n̲d̲a̲y̲ ̲m̲o̲r̲n̲i̲n̲g̲ ̲t̲w̲o̲ ̲d̲a̲y̲s̲ ̲b̲e̲f̲o̲r̲e̲
Christmas, Jesse stood before the Baptist church she'd attended
for the first eighteen years of her life and reminded herself to
breathe.

"Are you ready for this?" Ash asked, standing beside her in
the same suit he'd worn for the Christmas taping.

Jesse took a deep breath and nodded. "As ready as I can be."

Being forced to attend this service every year was by far the
cruelest thing her parents ever did to her. And that was saying
something, considering they'd actually forgotten her birthday.
Twice. She and Ash had talked during their drive to Eton, and
he'd supported Jesse's decision to make this the last memorial
she'd attend. At least the last depressing service planned by her
mother.

From now on, Jesse would find a more positive way to
celebrate her brother. To carry on his light and remember him
for the vibrant life that he led, not the tragic way that he died.

With Ash's hand in hers, they entered the church and found,
as it was every year, a full house. Jesse had no doubt that most in
attendance came out of obligation and likely dreaded the service
as much as she did. She would encourage her parents to join her

in planning a new, more uplifting event, but she held little hope that they'd actually do it.

As she and Ash made their way down the aisle, a buzz ignited in the congregation. They all knew the details of that night, and that the Rheingolds held Ash fully responsible for the death of their son. Though making a scene was not Jesse's intention, she was prepared for anything. Hopefully, her mother wouldn't disrespect her son by throwing an unholy tantrum in the front pew.

Jesse slid in first, taking her place beside her father, and Ash sat next to her on the aisle. Daddy turned and kissed her on the cheek before offering a silent nod to the young man he'd practically raised. Mama ignored them both, keeping her eyes on the altar.

That brief nod from her father had been more than Jesse expected, and if that was the only recognition they got today, she would consider it a breakthrough.

The service started as it always did, with the same readings, the same songs—including her rendition of Amazing Grace—and the same somber tone. By the time they reached the end, every muscle in Jesse's body vibrated with tension as the impending face-off grew closer. Though Enid Rheingold had maintained the sanctity of God's holy house, she was unlikely to continue the good behavior outside of its doors.

As the final notes of the closing hymn echoed into the distance, Ash squeezed Jesse's hand. "No matter what, we're good."

Yes, they were.

Jesse followed him from the pew and down the aisle as the attendees seemed to be holding their collective breath, waiting for the show that was sure to come. Once outside, sunlight warmed her skin, and she could feel Tommy hovering around her, giving her strength.

Turning back to the doors, Jesse expected to see her parents step through, but instead she watched every other person leave the church until only her parents remained inside. Was that how they were going to play this? Refuse to come out as long as she and Ash were there?

If that was the case, they were going to be inside for a long time, because this conversation was long past due, and Jesse had no plans to leave until they'd had it out.

"It's good to see you," said Pastor Beam, offering Jesse a caring hug. "And how are you, Ash? It's been far too long since we've seen your face in these parts."

The pastor was eighty if he was a day, and he'd presided over Tommy's original funeral. Either he'd forgotten the details of the accident, or he was playing dumb to keep the peace.

"Mama and I both live in Nashville now, Pastor, so there isn't much reason to come back."

"Well, we miss you." The older man turned to Jesse and leaned close to whisper, "She needs this. Good idea to give her a little push." The pastor winked and moved on to another group standing close by.

"What did he say?" Ash asked.

"I think he's suggesting that I shove my mother off her self-righteous cliff."

Speaking of the obstinate woman, Enid finally exited the church, holding tight to her husband's arm and giving a well-practiced performance as the grieving mother. Jesse wasn't heartless and would never suggest that her mother should somehow *get over* the loss of her son. But this never-ending mourning wasn't good for anyone, and a decade was long enough to wallow in her own misery.

"Hello, Mama," Jesse said as her parents drew near.

Predictably, the woman in black ignored the greeting and continued past them as if Jesse and Ash were invisible, dragging her husband along like the lap dog he'd become.

What she'd forgotten was that her daughter could be as obstinate as she was. Jesse dropped Ash's hand and stepped around him to cut off her mother's path. "I said hello."

"I'm not talking to you," Mama muttered, refusing to make eye contact.

"So you'll mourn the loss of one child, and then immediately toss the other away? You don't see anything wrong with that?"

Having the decency to look uncomfortable, Mama murmured, "You're making a scene."

"Someone needs to," Jesse replied. "Or we'll all be going through this depressing ritual for another forty years."

"Are you suggesting we forget that your brother ever existed?" she asked, literally clutching her pearls.

"I'm suggesting that you let him rest and stop forcing Pastor Beam to eulogize him year after year as if the accident just happened." Jesse reached for Ash, and he stepped up beside her. "Look at this man, Mama. This is the boy who ate at our table. Who slept in our house and who loved Tommy as much as we did." When her mother locked her eyes on the horizon, Jesse raised her voice. "Look at him. Because the longer you blame him for what happened, the longer you disrespect your son. Ash was Tommy's best friend, and he would *hate* you for cutting him off the way you did."

"I'm not going to listen to this."

"Yes, you are," her father said. "She's right, Enid. We never should have blamed Ash."

"He was driving!" she shrieked. "My Tommy is dead because of this boy, and I will not forgive him."

"Enid Rheingold," said Pastor Beam, "you've been coming to this church for more than fifty years, and now I know you haven't been listening that entire time. You couldn't possibly have heard God's message and say a thing like that."

Clinging to her bitterness, Mama shook her head, her gaze shifting from one onlooker to the next. "None of you know what it's like to lose a child. I lost my boy." She pointed to Ash. "He took him from me. He took my beautiful baby."

"I lost my daughter to cancer when she was nine," said a woman Jesse didn't recognize.

"And my son died in a construction accident three years ago," said Pete Dimwiddie. Jesse had been crushed when she'd heard that news. Jackson Dimwiddie had been sweet enough to take Jesse to their senior prom even though he'd known she was still pining for Ash. "Don't tell us that we don't know," he continued. "A lot of us know, and we ain't holding funerals every year."

Unleashing an angry mob on her mother had not been Jesse's plan, but there was no going back now.

"I don't want you to forget him, Mama," she said. "I just want to remember the good that he left behind. His smile. His laugh. The way he encouraged others to be better people." Jesse slid her hand into Ash's and pressed her cheek against his arm. "Tommy had a beautiful spirit, Mama. Let's keep that going. Let's turn on the light and pack the mourning clothes away for good."

On the verge of tears, Enid Rheingold began to soften. "He did have a lovely smile." Lip quivering, she whispered, "I miss him so much."

"So do I," Ash said, speaking for the first time. "I miss him every day, but I know he's with me, and that makes the missing a little easier to live with."

Tears falling freely now, Enid reached for Ash's hand. "I was so jealous that you were still here and he wasn't that I was relieved when you and your mother moved away. Then I didn't have to see what I was missing out on. That wasn't fair to you, but I couldn't change how I felt."

"It's never too late," the pastor said. "Why don't we call this a life celebration instead of a memorial? There's plenty of food waiting in the church hall, and I'm sure folks here have plenty of good stories they'd be willing to share about your young man."

Accepting a handkerchief from her husband, Mama managed a hesitant smile. "I'd like to hear those stories."

"Then we're all set."

Pastor Beam herded the crowd toward the hall entrance next door and to Jesse's surprise, her mother tucked a hand around

Ash's arm and let him escort her into the celebration. Her father offered his own arm, and she accepted with a relieved sigh.

"You did good, Jesse." He pressed a kiss against her temple. "Thank you for bringing her around."

"I had a little help," she said with a laugh.

Lowering his voice, he whispered, "I noticed a ring on your left hand there. Does that mean what I think it means?"

"Yes, it does. Do you think Mama noticed?"

"Not yet, but after today, I think she'll be ready to celebrate that, too."

Jesse sure hoped so.

The hall offered a completely different atmosphere than the melancholy one that had lingered in the church. People were smiling and laughing, and Enid Rheingold appeared to be at peace for the first time in far too long.

"That went better than we'd hoped," Ash said, finding Jesse just inside the doors. "I'm proud of you for standing up to her, and I think everyone here is grateful to have the cloud lifted."

"You know what I'm grateful for?" Jesse asked.

"What?"

"You."

Hazel eyes held hers as Ash said, "Okay, then."

Heart bursting, she repeated the vow. "Okay, then."

* * *

I hope you enjoyed this latest installment in my Shooting Stars Series. If you'd like to leave an honest review on Amazon, your feedback would be most appreciated. You can hop directly to the book page by clicking HERE.

OTHER BOOKS BY TERRI OSBURN:

All available in the Kindle Unlimited Program

Shooting Stars Series

Rising Star

Falling Star

Ardent Springs Series

His First And Last

Our Now And Forever

My One And Only

Her Hopes And Dreams

The Last In Love

Anchor Island Series

Meant To Be
Up To The Challenge
Home To Stay
More To Give

**Don't forget to preorder Terri's first stand-alone novel
coming March 5, 2019!**

Ask Me To Stay

*all links to Amazon.com site but books are available in all countries that Amazon covers.

Read on for a sneak peak at chapter 1 of Ask Me To Stay

ASK ME TO STAY CHAPTER 1

THERE MUST BE A HUNDRED PLACES TO HIDE A BODY ON THIS ISLAND.

This morbid thought exemplified a lesser-known problem of being blessed with a writer's mind—the overactive imagination that came with it. Standing beneath a weathered structure on the edge of remote Haven Island off the South Carolina coast, Liza Teller couldn't help but wonder whether she'd volunteered for a ghostwriting gig *or* to be the featured victim on one of those overly dramatic true-crime shows.

"No one would find me out here," she muttered, surveying the landscape.

Liza had seen beaches before, but Haven Island looked more like a forest with sandy edges. Rooftops peeked through the leaves in two or three places, but the rich green canopy dominated the view, seeming to float right up to the horizon line.

Even the salt-scented air smelled cleaner than any place she'd ever been. An entirely new experience for a city girl like Liza. A city girl with no survival skills to speak of and not a soul back home who would even notice she'd gone missing. Vanessa Dunsmore, her agent and only friend, would eventually miss her, but not before the dreaded deed was done and Liza's mutilated body lay buried in some dark corner of this junglelike island.

A morbid thought yet a promising premise. Maybe this crazy adventure would pay off in more ways than one. She could complete the memoir she'd come here to write and go home with a suspense plot or two that her agent could hopefully sell.

As Vanessa had reminded her several times over the last six months, she couldn't sell a product that didn't exist. But after Liza's debut work of fiction had leaped unexpectedly onto the bestseller lists nearly a year ago, her idea well had run dry, hence the no-product problem. Liza had never liked the term *writer's block*, nor had she really believed in the phenomenon itself, but as the cliché went, karma was a bitch, because she was definitely blocked.

One would think that living in New York City would be enough to fill a notebook full of plots, but Liza had tried everything from reading the papers to people-watching several days a week. Still nothing. If only being a bestselling author equated to being a highly paid one, then she wouldn't be putting her life in danger just to stay financially afloat.

"No one is going to kill me," she said, as if speaking the words aloud might convince her brain to nix the ridiculous notion. Though she had to admit, "Woman Lured to Remote Island"—and stupid enough to actually go alone—had "Destined to Be a Movie" written all over it. Liza withdrew her phone to make the note for later cogitation.

Since her phone was out, she double-checked the arrival instructions she'd received that morning. The original email said to locate the golf cart with her name on it and follow the enclosed map to her destination. Surveying the long line of carts parked down the narrow wooden walkway that extended from the covered landing, she considered the chance that one might actually have her name on it.

But the revised instructions said to wait for her escort at the landing dock. Since she hadn't received any new messages, Liza resolved to wait, resisting the urge to wave back the ferry that was quickly disappearing in the direction it had come. Not that they were likely to see her anyway.

Eyeing a fragile-looking bench, she left her suitcases where the boat captain had set them and settled in to wait. Though leery, she had to assume that if the bench could withstand a hurricane, as it surely had at some point in its life, it could sustain her 125 pounds.

Perching on the edge with a sigh, she mumbled, "Please, let this *not* be a mistake." And she didn't mean the bench or the murder fears. A journalism degree and one successful novel did not qualify Liza to write a memoir. The client, who Vanessa had assured her wanted his story told in narrative form, had insisted that Liza was the only person who could tell it.

Turning down the offer would have meant returning to her previous career as a reporter, and chasing down stories in the hope that some internet news site might carry them hadn't proved any more lucrative than writing fiction. If Liza's contrary writer's brain refused to cough up a workable idea, then writing someone else's story was better than not writing anything at all.

Bright-white Keds, bought days before departing for this trip, tapped out a rhythm of impatience as Liza waited. The sun would set soon, and there were no streetlights in sight. She doubted the flashlight on her phone would penetrate far and didn't want to think about the wildlife she might encounter. Birds were abundant in the distance, but what might be lurking in the brush was a mystery she had no desire to solve.

Maybe the first email had been the right one, after all, but the moment she considered checking the line of carts, the sound of a motor cut through the cacophony of chirps and caws echoing from the trees. A beige-and-green cart raced toward her, and through the cloud of dust, she could make out only the driver's shape.

His very large shape.

Like a grizzly bear riding a tricycle, the driver looked ridiculous. Shoulders filled the width of the cart, which she was certain would accommodate two normal-size individuals, and he was so tall that his dark mop of hair nearly brushed the covering above his head. One of the few facts Liza knew about her client was his age. The giant racing her way was nowhere near ninety-plus years old.

"So this is how I die," Liza mumbled, debating whether two years on her high school swim team had prepared her for a swim back to the mainland.

* * *

Great. His cargo had missed the boat.

Kendall James drove his cart to the end of the walkway and parked in front of the covered landing, hoping the guy hadn't just missed the boat, but that he wasn't coming at all. A memoir? What the hell was Ray thinking? After thirty years of making himself invisible, why would he want to put his life story on paper for all the world to read?

Stubborn old man.

He didn't know much about this L. R. Teller guy, but Kendall didn't plan to make him feel overly welcome. The writer was going to have Ray's life in his hands. Literally. And there was a good chance that after the book was released, he'd also have his subject's blood on his hands.

The ferry wouldn't return for nearly an hour, and Kendall had no contact information to call and check on Teller. He could hope for the best, return to the struggle of fixing the nonrunning cart that was giving him fits, and then come back again to see if the writer showed up.

A lot of back and forth, but better that than sitting here doing nothing. Kendall didn't like doing nothing.

Swinging the cart to the left to turn around, he spotted a beautiful woman perched on a bench under the covering. She was staring off across the water, curls dancing in the wind and the hem of her dress fluttering along the top of her knees. The image could have been from a magazine ad or a postcard beckoning visitors to a tranquil location.

When she shifted, swinging her gaze toward the island, he noticed the divot between her brows. Concern? Confusion? The stranger looked down at her phone, lips tight as if she were trying to solve a mystery. When her eyes cut again to the horizon, Kendall recognized the expression. Fear.

Whatever she was afraid of, he couldn't leave her there to fend for herself. After locking the brake and cutting the motor, Kendall spoke to the dog in the back seat. "Stay here, buddy." Exiting the vehicle, he pasted on what he hoped was a neighborly smile.

His heavy work boots thudded on the weathered planks, and he noticed the woman's grip tighten around her phone. Though she was smiling, she couldn't hide the suspicion in her intelligent blue eyes. Not wanting to spook her, Kendall stopped near the edge of the covering.

"Hi there," he said, keeping his body loose so as to appear less threatening. Not an easy task for a man his size. "Welcome to Haven Island."

Honey-blonde curls framed her slender face. "Thank you." Her eyes cut away as she exhaled, but her shoulders didn't relax.

Normally, Kendall didn't pry into other people's business, but this case clearly called for further investigation. Tourists weren't provided escorts from the landing, so she had to be a guest of one of the locals.

"Are you waiting for someone?"

Her nod was nearly imperceptible. "Yes."

To ease her tension, Kendall let her know why he was there. "I was expecting someone on the ferry, but I guess he must have missed it. Did you see anyone on the other side when you boarded?"

"There was no one else waiting when we left the dock." She

lifted a large purse from the seat beside her and hugged it to her chest. "How often does the ferry run?"

"Top of the hour on the other side. On the half hour over here. Unless there's no one waiting, and then they wait for a call."

"So there's a way to call them back?"

If he didn't know better, Kendall would think this visitor didn't want to stay. Odd, since someone must have been waiting for her.

"You can, yeah, but this time of day, they run pretty much on schedule."

Leaning his shoulder on a post, he considered who she might be visiting. On such a small island, everyone knew everyone else, and he hadn't heard mention of any impending company. The tourists came through regularly but always with plenty of provisions, since Haven lacked any sort of store or restaurant. A quick check of the area revealed two purple suitcases but no groceries or beach supplies.

If she was a tourist, she was going to starve.

Her eyes cut back to the distance, and Kendall dragged the phone from his pocket to appear distracted. From beneath his lashes, he assessed the stranger. She looked close to his age, which put her around thirty. A bit prim, based on the set of her lips and the way she held her shoulders. Feet flat on the floor, back stiff, and that tiny dimple still hovered between her brows.

"You been to the island before?" he asked, his voice casual.

She nearly jumped when he broke the silence. Kendall was big, but he wasn't *that* scary. This woman really needed to relax.

"No, this is my first time." Pulling the purse tighter against her chest, she looked ready to jump over the side of the landing to get away from him.

Taking the hint, Kendall shifted to his full height and slid the phone back in his pocket, planning to drive on up to the Welcome Center, where he could keep an eye on her without causing her any more stress.

"I hope you enjoy your visit." He spun to head back to the cart, but she stopped him with a question.

"You're certain the ferry will come back?"

"It'll be back," he replied, "but didn't you just get here?" No one boarded the ferry without their name showing up on the list, so she couldn't have made the crossing by mistake.

"I did, yes." Chewing the inside of her cheek, she scanned the distance. "But it's late, and the person picking me up doesn't seem to be coming. Maybe I should go back to the other side and try again tomorrow."

This was an easy enough problem to solve. "Who's supposed to pick you up? Do you have a number to call them?"

A white-tipped thumbnail slid between her teeth as she hesitated to answer. Surely she knew who would be looking for her.

"I'm not sure who is supposed to meet me, and I don't have a number."

This was not how the island worked. Tourists were sent pages of information before arriving, about everything from transportation to garbage disposal. And Kendall doubted any of the residents would bring someone in without providing at least a contact number.

"Do you have any name at all?" he asked.

The blonde glanced down to her phone. "I'm here to see Ray Wallis."

Kendall's jaw tightened as realization dawned. His cargo hadn't missed the boat. He was the wrong damn gender.

a As she contemplated her escape options, the inquisitive islander's expression changed. The casual demeanor vanished, and his hands landed on his hips.

"Are you L. R. Teller?"

He said her name as if it tasted rotten on his tongue.

"Yes," she replied, more anxious than before. "But I go by Liza."

The brute shoved a hand through his hair as an audible growl crossed his full lips. He was obviously her escort, yet she was not the person he'd expected. Seconds passed as he glanced from the inlet, to his cart, and back to her. Liza feared he might leave her there, but then he muttered a curse and pointed to her suitcases.

"Are those yours?"

"Yes, they are."

The stranger snatched the hard-shell cases and stormed back to his cart without inviting her to follow. How amazingly rude. Having lived in New York City for the last eight years, Liza was well acquainted with the most hostile of their species, but grumpy New Yorkers had nothing on this . . . Neanderthal.

Though he'd been nice enough before learning her name.

Loading up her purse and laptop bag, one on each shoulder, Liza strolled off after him, only to stop dead several feet from the cart.

"What is that?" she asked, feet frozen to the sandy path.

The man tossed her suitcases onto the back of the vehicle. "A golf cart."

He could shove the smart-ass reply where the sun didn't shine. "I mean the beast *in* the cart."

Deep-brown eyes looked her way. "That's Amos. He's a dog. Don't they have dogs where you come from?"

She didn't dignify that with a reply.

Liza had never lived with any dogs, nor did she seek them out. When she'd inherited her grandmother's tiny apartment in the Bronx, she'd been relieved to find herself in a no-pets building. It wasn't that she didn't like them, necessarily. She'd simply lacked the dog-loving gene that compelled normal human beings to canoodle with every canine that crossed their paths.

"He won't hurt you," the dog owner said as he squeezed his stocky frame into the cart. Muscles bunched, pulling the stained gray tee tighter across his shoulders. When Liza didn't move, he leaned his elbows on the steering wheel, his full lips flattening into a line. "What are you waiting for?"

"An animal-free option."

"You allergic?"

"No." Unless fear could be categorized as an allergy.

"Then what's the problem?"

Stalling, she said, "Where am I supposed to sit?" Even if the black-and-white pit bull hadn't been occupying the entire back seat, tongue hanging to the side like a slobbery pink noodle, the driver's broad shoulders and denim-clad tree-trunk thighs left little room in the front.

Moving his right leg one inch to the left, he nodded toward the minuscule patch of stained white vinyl beside him. "Right here."

Unconvinced, Liza crossed her arms. "I'd rather walk."

"It's too far to walk. Now get in. Ray is going to wonder where we are."

The dog barked as if to back up his owner, and a flock of birds burst from the trees at the same moment Liza nearly leaped out of her skin.

"Quiet, Amos." The words were said with kindness, the gentle tone calming woman and beast.

Telling herself the sooner she climbed into the cart, the sooner she could climb back out, Liza approached the vehicle anticipating a growl, though she couldn't say from which occupant. Pulling her shoulder bags in front of her, she edged one butt cheek onto the seat, careful to keep as much distance as possible between herself and the Goliath who still hadn't bothered to introduce himself. A woodsy scent carrying a hint of sweetness filled her senses as heat radiated from his big body. A quick glance to her left and the scent changed to dog breath, so Liza locked her eyes straight ahead.

"You in?" he asked.

Grasping the chrome pole with one hand, she locked the bags onto her lap with the other. "Yes."

Without another word, her driver hit the gas and made a hard right turn, sending Liza crashing against his side. She'd never been hit by a truck before but imagined the sensation would be similar. As the wind whipped through her hair and hot breath filled her left ear, she prayed whatever hut they'd put her name on wasn't far away.

Where did this writer get off being a woman?

Kendall was supposed to drive to the pier, find the writer guy, and take him back to Ray's. The last thing he'd expected to find was a woman—especially a beautiful one who looked as out of place sitting on that bench as a prairie dog would popping up through a manhole in Manhattan. In the weeks since Ray had shared this foolish idea, Kendall had toyed with a plan to intimidate the writer into backing out. A plan that was now dead in the water.

In the eight years since he'd returned from the service, Kendall had never given two thoughts to the size of the golf carts he drove every day. With Liza Teller pressed along his side, he might as well have been driving a little red wagon. The frilly blue dress fluttered in the wind, revealing enough skin above her knees to be more than a little distracting.

Maybe Francine was right. He'd been living like a hermit for far too long.

Not that women never showed up on Haven Island, but Kendall rarely paid them much attention. The majority were either newlyweds or moms hoping for some peace and quiet while their husbands entertained the kids in the sand. The locals were all married, and on the rare occasion single women stepped off the ferry, Kendall made a point to keep his distance.

No sense in starting something that was always guaranteed to end.

"You know, most people wouldn't do this," she said, raising her voice to be heard above the wind.

Kendall looked over, but her eyes remained on the path. "Do

what? Ride in a golf cart?" He'd had the misfortune of riding in a New York City cab. There was no way this cart was more dangerous than that.

She turned his way, one brow arched high. "Step onto a remote island and get into a cart with a stranger the size of an NFL linebacker. You could kill me, and I wouldn't even know the name of the man who'd turned me into fish food."

He considered listing the myriad ways he *could* kill her, but feared she'd leap out of the cart and run back to the pier. Then he'd have to explain to Ray why the ghostwriter had changed her mind before she'd even met her subject. A conversation that was bound to go poorly.

Instead, he shared his name, hoping the info would allay her fears and they could go back to riding in silence.

"Kendall James. And I haven't killed anybody in nearly a decade." A true statement, but one he had no intention of elaborating on.

With annoyance in her smoky voice, she said, "Is that a joke?"

He met her dark-blue eyes. "Nope."

"Right." She faced forward again. "I feel *much* better now."

As he'd hoped, the conversation died, though he continued to assess his passenger. A blush emphasized her high cheekbones, and she held her chin in a regal way, like a queen out for a ride to visit the peasants.

They cleared the trees, running headlong into the wind off the salt marsh. Loose curls whipped across her face, forcing his passenger to release her hold on the chrome post. And because Kendall was too busy looking at her to watch the road, he had to make a hard left turn at the last second.

Physics took over. In a matter of seconds, her scream cut through the air as her body was nearly flung from the cart. Kendall caught her in time, pulling her tight against his side and clamping his arm around her shoulders to keep her there.

"Hold on!" he yelled as he made a hairpin right before pulling the cart to a stop in a small patch of grass beside the trail.

Hair still covering her face, the writer's body remained rigid beneath his touch as they sat in silence for several seconds. As if to remind them that they weren't alone, Amos barked, snapping his owner back to reality.

Shrugging off Kendall's arm, his passenger cleared the hair from her eyes and stepped out of the cart.

"Who taught you how to drive this thing?"

Did she really think there was a golf-cart driving school?

"Get back in. It's getting dark and Ray is waiting."

Hugging her purse and what looked like some kind of briefcase to her chest, she shook her head. "I'm not going through that again. I'll wait here until you send someone else."

She'd been the one to let go. How was that his fault?

"There *is* no one else." Not technically true, but Kendall couldn't leave her standing out here while he hunted up Francine or Larimore. Bruce could show up at any minute, and then she'd *really* be running back to the ferry. "Get in."

The stubborn woman took a step back. "Give me directions and I'll walk."

Ray would kick his ass if Kendall obeyed that order. Instead, he turned to the back seat. "Come on, Amos. Up front."

The dog hopped over the seat, filling the vacant spot.

"Good boy," his owner said before returning his attention to the pain-in-the-ass writer. "Now you can sit in the back. Put the bags between your feet, and hold on to this bar." Kendall tapped the chrome handrail that ran along the top of the seat.

Accepting this new arrangement, she followed his suggestion, securing the bags between her ankles and locking a death grip on the bar. "Okay, I'm ready. But if you throw me out again, I'm not getting back in."

He hadn't thrown her out at all. "Fair enough."

Kendall stepped on the gas, grateful to have her out of his line of sight. Now he could concentrate on reaching their destination without thinking about pale thighs, honey-gold curls, and whether her skin would feel as soft as it looked.

ABOUT THE AUTHOR

Terri Osburn writes contemporary romance with heart, hope, and lots of humor. After landing on the bestseller lists with her Anchor Island Series, she moved on to the Ardent Springs series, which earned her a Book Buyers Best award in 2016. Her new Shooting Stars series is set against the glittering and gritty world of the Nashville country music scene. Terri's work has been translated into six languages, and has sold more than a million copies worldwide. She resides in middle Tennessee with her college-student daughter, four frisky felines, and two high-maintenance terrier mixes. Learn more about this author and her books at www.terriosburn.com. Or check out her Facebook page at www.facebook.com/TerriOsburnAuthor.

Printed in Great Britain
by Amazon

64757661R00189